HAMILTON

THE ALMOST TRUTH

Legend Press Ltd, 51 Gower Street, London, WC1E 6HJ
info@legendtimesgroup.co.uk | www.legendpress.co.uk

Print ISBN 9781915643704
Ebook ISBN 9781915643711
Set in Times.
Cover design by Sarah Whittaker | www.whittakerbookdesign.com

Anne Hamilton co-founded a UK based charity, Bhola's Children, supporting a home and school in Bangladesh for disabled children and remains a trustee today. She has been sharing her time between the UK and Bangladesh for the past 21 years, which inspired both her memoir and most recent novel, *The Almost Truth*.

The unpublished manuscript for *The Almost Truth* was the winner of the Irish Novel Fair, and a short story adaptation of it is included in an Edinburgh Charity anthology, *The People's City*, titled *The Finally Tree*.

Anne's first novel, a travel memoir titled *A Blonde Bengali Wife*, was published in 2010 and based on her experience in Bangladesh. All money earned from *A Blonde Bengali Wife* goes direct to the charity, Bhola's Children.

Follow Anne on Twitter
@AnneHamilton7

1

I've found him, Ali. But...

But.

There was always going to be a but, and it was always going to be a big one. Alina wondered which of the big three Ds it was: dead, disordered or dispossessed? They were an irreverent trinity that fitted most of life's 'buts'.

I've found him, Ali. But... Yes, that was all Fin's text had said, all it had needed to say. Alina wasn't sure when he'd sent it. Her phone had emitted a brief flurry of beeps, and then nothing. He wouldn't have expected her to call back. Maybe he'd even timed the message to fit her journey limbo, an attempt to let her get used to the notion – right. Eight years hadn't been long enough to do that, let alone eight hours.

A cry went up from the waterside, and Alina felt the cumbersome launch jolt hard against the harbour wall. With a choking waft of cheap fuel, the engines rumbled and shuddered, causing a flurry of last-minute passengers to race towards the deck, where willing arms were held out to haul aboard their varied baggage: babies and chickens, apples and cauliflowers, even a giant TV.

Alina adjusted her orna to sit neatly round her shoulders instead of sweeping the floor, and got up from the plastic garden chair plonked outside her so-called VIP cabin on the third deck. She leaned over the rusted rail and watched the commotion below her, scanning the crowd for the dozen or so children who had crammed themselves into the tractor and trailer. A wall of sad faces, jostling for a final cuddle or handshake; they were always insistent on coming with her and Mizan to say goodbye. There! She caught a flash of bright blue shirts: three of the boys, halfway up a cluster of palm trees, leaning over to wave enthusiastically, it being impossible to make themselves heard above the din. They gave toothy matching grins as Alina mock-admonished them with a waggling finger and pointed down to their less adventurous friends below. Alina blew some overly exuberant kisses that made the girls – Khalya, as ever, their ringleader – giggle behind their hennaed hands and dry their tears. *They* had worn their best red and gold party dresses for her send-off, and were a splash of sunshine against the grimy grey riverbank.

Half a year here in remote Bangladesh, half a year there, crossing from Scotland to Ireland. Alina had lived in all three camps for over five years now, and while she was no longer starry-eyed nor scared witless by her journeys into the Bay of Bengal, her arrivals remained exciting and her departures came with a pang. Now, watching her Great Uncle Takdir – who paused to look up and salute her – shepherd the boys and girls back to the orphanage that inside its doors was never referred to as an orphanage, Alina stifled a bigger sigh than usual. For the first time, her Irish grandparents, Miriam and Patrick, wouldn't be waiting at the other end of her convoluted journey. Instead, something else, something life-changing – *I've found him, Ali. But...* – was going to be there.

'Alina?'

She was using the end of her scarf to blot her tears when Mizan appeared at the top of the iron staircase, and his face stifled her sob to a grin. Mizan's horror of tears from females over the age of ten was well-documented and widely played upon.

'Don't bolt,' she said. 'It's just the engine fumes or something making my eyes water.' Which was true enough.

The scent of moist cooking oil, dirty water and gutted fish, horrible but somehow addictive, was, for Alina, evocative of rural Bangladesh. She turned her back on the river. 'You really didn't have to come with me, you know,' she told Mizan. The words were pointless, but it was a rite of passage to have the conversation. 'Especially when there are no children needing to come to Dhaka.'

'I know. I like to come. I enjoy this alone time we have.' Mizan was taking out a packet of cigarettes from his trouser pocket and feeling for a lighter.

'Right...'

He had the grace to look shamefaced. 'Okay. Also, I like to smoke, and where can I do this now you have banned it in the boundary and my wife has done the same in our rooms?' He held up the hand with the lighter in it in mock surrender. 'Yes, it is better for my health, and a good example for the children.' Then he looked at her, a hint of challenge. 'Still, I like our time alone more.'

'So do I, Mizan, but—' Alina wouldn't bother to disagree. Their exchange was nothing more than harmless flirting, a nod to the past. Her smile faded, as she remembered another, more distant, past: *I've found him, Ali. But...*

'Alina?'

'What? Sorry. I'm hot. I'm going to get changed.'

'Are you okay?'

'Fine.' She knew she sounded abrupt. She just wasn't sure she wanted to share the text message with Mizan. For all his machismo he had a perceptive streak – or maybe he simply knew her too well. Either way, was she ready to discuss it?

'I will bring us tea,' she heard him call as she disappeared into the small, stuffy cabin. Smoke wafted in through the open window on the other side, and she let it. A deterrent to mosquitoes, at least. This was one of the oldest, slowest launches: no air-conditioning, just a noisy fan with tangled, loose wires above each of the single beds; the obligatory, if old-fashioned, television set high on a shelf. There was a suspect blanket on a chair and a hairy cake of soap in the attached, unplumbed bathroom. Alina wasn't complaining. It was a square of private space. She only had to go down to the open deck, where whole families spread across the ground for the overnight sailing, to be grateful. And years back, on one of her earliest visits, she'd come face to face with the biggest homemade rat trap she'd ever imagined, and by morning it had been filled with the biggest, angriest rat she'd ever seen. *This* was luxury.

Darkness came suddenly over the Bay of Bengal. In the few minutes it took Alina to step out of her yellow and orange salwar kameez and into loose-fitting jeans and a muted long-sleeve top, the sun had become a mirror to the water. She left her long, dark hair loose and, winding her orna back around her shoulders, opened the door back on to the deck. Mizan was sitting on one of the battered plastic chairs, his bare feet up on the boat rail. His silhouette stood out against the lengthening shadows, and beyond him, across the water, Alina saw yet again the inspiration for the Bangladeshi flag – the red sun sinking below the green horizon.

Mizan was holding his phone aloft. 'Signal is gone. We are in no-man's-land for eight hours minimum.' He must have heard the creak of the door behind him.

Time suspended. A faint whiff of the forbidden – of possibility – hung in the air. Oh, nostalgia had a lot to answer for. But Alina felt some of her tension ease. Mizan was right: they were uncontactable for tonight. *You're the queen of compartmentalising*, she told herself. Enjoy the journey. *Worry about Fin and what he's found when you get home.*

'Do you know if Takdir got the children home alright?' A retired District Commissioner her great uncle might be, but he was first to point out that staff under him unquestioningly followed orders; twelve overexcited children, all but two of them deaf, were less biddable. Alina settled herself in the second chair and looked up to see Mizan nod.

'He is fine. They are fine. Safe home. He is staying tonight, to play Grandfather, while you and I both are gone.'

'He's always the perfect dadu.'

'Yes.'

There were forty residents, spanning the ages of five to late teens, living at Sonali Homestay, only made possible by Takdir and his family trust. They were ably cared for by houseparents, but Takdir brought stories and games, and sweets and treats for all. A night of being spoiled always helped them forget Alina would be gone for the next six months. *If* it was six months this time. Following the too-close deaths of her English grandparents, Takdir and his wife, Husna, were Alina's nearest relatives, and Takdir had asked Alina outright to consider a permanent move over.

'Will you come back and live with us now?' Mizan might have read her thoughts. 'Here is your home, Alina. Your uncle. Khalya. The other children. And, of course, me.' He paused and raised his eyebrows. Then added, 'Why not?'

Why not, indeed, with her own mother and father also long gone; did that make her an (albeit aged, well-aged, at forty-three) orphan, like the children she left behind? Takdir certainly thought so, but it was still a huge decision to make. Would relocating to Bangladesh mean going home or running away from it? Alina winced; she'd done that once too often, even if it had ultimately worked out well. Now, Fin's message had moved the goalposts again, but by how much she wasn't yet sure. Dead, disordered, dispossessed – maybe it all depended on which one.

'My Great Aunt Husna doesn't like me,' she said. Prevarication, but true.

'She doesn't like anyone. Nobody likes her.'

Also probably true. Alina sighed. 'There's Fin…'

'Your son, he is a man now. He can visit any time.'

It was all black and white to Mizan. All of it. He was still the only person in the world to refer to Fin as her son. Technically, he was correct, of course, and Alina knew from personal experience that families were more acceptably fluid, anyway, in South Asia.

She was still deciding how much to say when the rattle of crockery heralded teatime. The boy, he looked about ten, put the cups of milky, sweet tea carefully in front of them, glancing at Alina as he did so. 'Very boiling water, apa,' he said. 'You no get sick.' She smiled and played along, the foreigner commenting on his good English. The boy grinned and spoke Bengali to Mizan. 'Is she your wife?'

Mizan shook his head. 'She's my boss.'

Alina busied herself clattering a teaspoon. Mizan was stretching a point for effect. They shared the job running the Sonali Homestay, though Mizan lived there full-time. The boy looked disbelieving, as if he were being teased. 'Apa, speak in Bangla,' he challenged Alina, and when she did, he roared with laughter. When Mizan winked and tossed him a couple of taka notes, he skipped off and arrived back in seconds with a packet of cardamom-studded biscuits that he handed to Alina with a flourish.

'You look beautiful,' Mizan said once the boy had gone.

'I look foreign.' Alina indicated her clothes. 'Even after all this time.'

'This is what I like.'

They both knew that sometimes clothes *did* maketh the woman. Once in Western dress she was assumed a foreigner and people were fall-over surprised when she responded in – passable, mostly – Bangla. Changing dress was another travel ritual. Once on the launch, the first stage of her long journey back to Scotland, Alina began a metamorphosis from her Bangladeshi self to her Irish-honorary-Scottish self. More than that, for a few hours she reverted, outwardly at least, to the Alina who Mizan had first met, what, fourteen, fifteen years ago? It probably wasn't very sensible of them, she thought now, but it was harmless.

After a while, the whine of the engine distanced itself into white noise, and the night grew quiet. The boat's searchlight swept hypnotically over the river, highlighting an odd rowboat, duos of napping fishermen, or the startled eyes of cows under transportation. When deckhands, seeking any available space to stretch out their mats for the night, peeped over at Alina and Mizan, it was their cue to move to Alina's cabin, where they sat on a single bed each, the door carefully propped open, their innocence broadcast to prying eyes. Probably nobody aboard cared who slept where and with whom, but, as directors of a charity, they couldn't risk a whiff of rumour making its way back to Bhola.

'What is on your mind, Alina?' Mizan asked eventually. 'You are too quiet. You do not even abuse your sworn enemies, the mosquitoes.' When she remained silent, he went through a list of her favourite worries. Finances. Accommodation. Not being a 'real' Bangladeshi. The lack of enough signing interpreters. Whether Khalya was truly her niece or the daughter of the maid. How to keep rampant adolescent hormones under control in a mixed home...

'Do you keep a spreadsheet? Stop it!' Alina begged him, finally laughing.

'That's better,' Mizan approved. 'So, which?'

'It's none of those. Well, of course, it's all of them,' Alina admitted. 'Khalya, especially. She's of the age when her mother will decide marriage is a good idea, and whatever our actual relationship, I've no control—'

'But Takdir Sir has. These days, the law has. And that woman is crazy. No person will force Khalya into a child marriage, this I promise you.' Mizan frowned. 'Do you not trust me?'

'Of course I do. Idiot.' And she meant it. 'It's not that.' *I've found him, Ali. But...* The words might well have been superscript, hovering in the silence. 'It's home. Scotland,' she said eventually. 'It's, well, Fin has found his birth father.' Her voice seemed to ring out an announcement. It was a relief to blurt it out.

'Good,' Mizan said. 'Every man needs to know his father.'

'Even if it's not good news?' Alina shifted awkwardly.

'Is it not?'

'I don't know.'

'What do you know?'

'I… Oh, read it.' They could go round in riddles all night. Alina fumbled with her phone and passed it across to him.

'"*I've found him, Ali. But…*"' Mizan read the words, tried to scroll down the screen, then looked over at her. 'This is all?'

Alina nodded. 'It's the *but* I'm worrying about.'

'Of course you are.'

'I don't think he's being deliberately cryptic.' She went on as if Mizan hadn't spoken. 'He's giving me an early warning, time to prepare myself for – well, whatever it is. So it must be something big. You see?'

'Of course,' Mizan repeated. He fished for his cigarettes and put one, unlit, to his lip. '*But…* he is dead? *But…* he is a villain? *But…* he is uninterested to know his son?'

Alina, who had been nodding along, was startled at that most obvious one – why hadn't it occurred to her? *Because you're too concerned about what this news means for you rather than Fin*, an ugly but truthful inner voice spelled out. Was she? It was fifty-fifty if she was honest. Tears threatened and she blinked them away, impatient with herself.

Mizan swung his feet to the floor and sat facing her. 'My promise to you, Alina – that day, you still remember? Hmm?' He paused, needlessly. Cryptic to outsiders, it made perfect sense to her. 'My promise, those conditions, both of them still stand. Yes?'

'Yes.' Alina barely whispered it.

'Remember that, always.' He reached over and, unusually, touched her. He squeezed her shoulder and she held her breath. 'I would hug you, *but…*' She let it out. The smile Mizan gave her was rueful; she wondered if it was the hug or that he realised what he'd said.

'I am going to smoke,' he said. 'Right now, it is the littlest of all possible sins.'

2

'You've got friends in high places.' The airline rep tapped on his computer.

'Sorry?' Alina reached for her boarding card, distracted in the nowhere place where Mizan and Sonali Homestay jockeyed with thoughts of Fin and Scotland.

'An upgrade.'

'Really? Thank you.' Alina took back her documents and mustered a genuine smile. 'My neighbour is cabin crew. She must have arranged it.'

'Lucky you. Have a nice flight, Ms Farrell.'

Worrying in comfort was just about bearable, she thought. Good old Connie.

On board, Alina continued sloughing off one life in favour of the other. She put away her cotton orna for a cosy hoodie, ordered orange juice with lots of ice, and checked *The Sound of Music* hadn't been deleted from the film list. So far so good.

'Welcome home, my friend.' The familiar voice of the purser, handing out landing cards, stopped at Alina. 'For you, the best seat in the house, is it not?'

'Connie! You didn't say you'd be working. How are you? And thank you…' Alina glanced around in guilty satisfaction. 'This is luxury.'

Mindful of the seatbelt sign and taxiing aircraft, the two women shared an awkward hug.

'Don't you deserve it,' Connie said. 'Six months at the coal face of forty desperate orphans – I have no idea how you do it. Mind you…' She lowered her voice and inclined her head towards the economy cabin. '…another shift or two back there with two newbies and I'll be begging to swap with you.'

'They're not all orphans and they're not at all desperate.' Alina was laughing; nothing fazed Connie. She got things done with an unhurried grace that Alina wished she could bottle. Her own life spread across the skies as far apart as Scotland and Nigeria, Connie was the sole spectator of Alina's morphing half-Irish and half-Bangladeshi selves. 'Are you home today or—'

'I have no such luck. I'm on a quick turnaround and then it's back-to-back for two more days and a long layover in Dubai.' The dividing curtains rustled and a head poked through. Connie looked up to acknowledge it. 'I should go,' she carried on. 'All is well in Edinburgh. Your flat is fine. Morag has some kind of secret, but not even Elizabeth is privy.' Connie shrugged.

'I'll brace myself. And Elizabeth herself?'

'Well, she is our Elizabeth.' They both grinned at that. 'There is, I think, something on her mind, but it is a woman braver than I who would ask her before she is ready to tell.'

'Hear, hear.' Alina's response was heartfelt. It also hid a multitude. 'You know she's coming back to Bangladesh with me in September?'

'Girl, I'm pulling rank over the scheduling in real good time. That is a flight I do not want to miss.' Connie's laughter floated back over her shoulder as she moved off.

Elizabeth was their friend and landlady; Connie's flat was a stone's throw – literally, if you had a decent aim – from Alina's, although they met once in a blue moon. Morag, the third tenant, was a woman who approved of nothing and nobody.

On another trip she might have been predisposed to chat,

but this time Alina was relieved Connie was in a different section of the plane. Left to herself, she stared at Fin's message one more time, the hundredth time, before switching off her phone. She fiddled with the buttons on her armrest to make her seat into a bed, plugged in her earphones and prepared to doze away the air miles. None of it stopped her mind racing, and barring a spot of turbulence that she wouldn't wish on anyone, she had no further distractions.

Ever since Fin had begun searching for his birth father, Alina had prepared herself for... something. They both had. Someone who had been conspicuously absent for twenty-five years was hardly going to return unencumbered; if he returned at all, there would be The Story. She had hoped against the three Ds for Fin's sake, she really had, even if it being one of them would make her own life easier.

I've found him, Ali. But... As it had on the overnight launch, the comforting presence of Mizan snoozing a few feet away, Fin's message subtitled her half-dreams. She'd not expected an easy homecoming. With her stalwart and constant grandparents gone, Alina had anticipated feeling... not bereft – prior to their deaths she had promised both Miriam and Patrick she would not mourn them – but adrift. Well, Fin's news had certainly grounded that. In its place, anticipation – trepidation? – was killing her.

She'd get the gist from Fin, Alina decided, be strong and adult about it, and then blurt it all out to Elizabeth. Other than Mizan, only a handful of people knew Alina was Fin's birth mother, and Elizabeth alone knew the whole story. Or rather, Alina corrected herself unwillingly, the whole story as far as she'd ever told it.

Alina pictured Miriam soaring above her in some celestial nirvana, nodding in satisfaction. Somehow, that mingled with Julie Andrews twirling in the Austrian hills, and Alina dozed.

In London, she waved goodbye to Connie and her crew and made her short connection with ease. Constant travel schooled her to carry only hand luggage: 'No baggage carousel between me and coffee with a huge slice of cake,' she liked to say, and long gone were the days when she needed anyone waiting at arrivals. The one good thing – well, there were many good things, but this was an added bonus – about living in their slightly unorthodox housing co-op, was knowing Elizabeth had been in to ready the flat. Alina imagined Elizabeth talking to herself as she put the essentials – and a treat, always a treat – in the fridge. She'd frown at the digital heating control and leave a spider-scrawled note on the table, saying to call upstairs 'whenever'. This 'gently, gently' approach was the perfect culture-clash and jetlag-friendly return.

Edinburgh airport was quiet, and the sun was uncommonly shining as they disembarked. Alina shivered, as much from the benign sunlight as the March chill it did nothing to abate. There was something faintly unsettling about the unexpected Plasticine-blue sky and lack of gusting winds. Surreal.

Cruising through passport control, she resolutely set her mind to the immediate dilemma: Costa or Starbucks? She'd heard other travellers berate the lack of independent options, but Alina secretly liked the fleeting-greeting impersonality of the café chains. She could anonymously catch up on her messages and, sustained with caffeine and sugar, phone Fin. Now, Costa was nearest but Starbucks had—

'Ali. Ali. *Alina?*'

It took her a minute to register that the voice was calling her name, and another to work out where it was coming from. 'Fin?'

'Ali. I thought I was going to have to chase you all the way down the concourse.'

'Fin!'

'That's me. Come here. It's good to see you.' He grinned and folded her up in a big hug.

Alina blinked and stood back. 'Sorry, I wasn't expecting to see anyone. I was miles away. Is everything okay?' Text messages aside, the middle-aged, worry-wart words spewed out automatically.

'Everything's fine.'

And he did look fine, she thought, dressed casually for a rare day off, his laptop case slung over his shoulder. She was glad of the civvies. Fin didn't resemble her grandfather in looks, not at all, but there was something familiar about the way he wore his uniform that caught in her throat every time.

'I had a couple of meetings in Edinburgh yesterday,' Fin was saying, 'so I figured I'd stay over. Surprise you and drive you home. I thought it might be difficult – your first return trip without Miriam and Patrick.'

'And I really appreciate it…' She had to ask. 'Is that all?' Then she watched him feign innocence.

'All? Oh, you mean my text? Yes. So, er, did my "but" look big in that, Ali?' He raised one eyebrow – his party trick; Alina couldn't do it.

'Ha ha. Very funny.' Alina hugged him again. If Fin could joke about the cryptic text, then whatever it was about was going to be alright, too, and would serve her right for agonising. Except – he'd never come all the way from Carlisle to meet her before.

'Coffee?' He looked down at her empty hands. 'I take it your bags decided not to join you?'

'I don't bring bags home anymore. I'm getting to like it, travelling light.'

They wove in and out of the obstacle course of people reuniting to get to the nearest coffee shop. Alina headed for one of the worn brown sofas and sank down, letting out a deep breath. 'It's good to be home.'

'It's good to have you.' Fin dumped his bag down beside her. 'So, coffee. Don't tell me – double shot, extra hot, with chocolate fudge cake on the side.'

Alina nodded. 'One day I'm going to try tea and carrot cake, though, honestly.'

'Whoa. Don't rush things, Ali.'

With eyes half closed, she watched him queue at the counter, exchanging a few words with the customer ahead of him who carried a chubby baby in a pouch against her chest. He, or maybe she, it was impossible to tell, was squashed against their mother's shoulder like a cartoon character gone splat. Fin leaned over to stroke the baby's head, and the young woman's face lit up. No doubt he was telling her how he was on the brink of fatherhood.

That was something else Alina had yet to get her head around. Fin, a dad. What did that make her? Not a grandmother, thank goodness, that was Fin's adoptive parents' privilege, but a great aunt? A spinster godmother? Both filled her with dismay. She wasn't that old – people in their early forties gave birth all the time, not that she had any such intentions. No, for this baby, she'd settle again for being Alina, Ali, just as she had always been to Fin.

Alina had never regretted her decision to have Fin adopted, never. Not even in her 4 a.m. insomnia, that soul-searching time when the overnight launch ran aground en route to Bhola, or when she was wide awake here, unpacking her conscience in lieu of luggage. There were other adoptions she did question, ones she'd overseen in her own career as a social worker, but Fin's? Never. It wasn't a fashionable reaction. Alina knew some would be sceptical, or think it arrogant, but for her it was honest.

'You're away with the crows again, Ali. Jetlag?'

Fin was unloading the tray in front of her, and she had to blink half a dozen times to bring him into focus.

'Mmm.' She made a momentous effort to sit up straight. 'Actually…' She smoothed down her jeans. '…I was imagining myself in a tartan kilt and pince-nez. Don't ask.'

'You're nuts, Ali. You do know that?' He handed over her cup of coffee and pushed a plate towards her.

Alina took a gulp at the too-hot drink, then started on the cake. 'How's Kirsten?' she managed through a mouthful.

'The epitome of a yummy-mummy-to-be. Sailing through pregnancy like a how-to textbook.' Fin shook his head. 'I'm worried about the payback. I mean it can't be this easy, can it?

It's either going to be a gruesome birth or a baby who doesn't sleep for two years straight.'

'Do you share these highly optimistic thoughts with Kirsten?' Alina grinned.

'Yeah, right. She said hello and she'll see you soon.' Fin sipped his tea. 'How are the children? How is my little almost-sister?'

'All good. Except when they're extremely naughty, of course. Khalya is great…' She hesitated. 'She is. She got her national school diploma. Look…' Alina put down her fork and rummaged in her handbag. She switched on her phone and waited impatiently until she could swipe the screen. 'There she is. She's going to Barisal school on the mainland as a weekly boarder from now on.'

Fin took the phone and flicked through the pictures of the serious-looking little girl. Not so little, Alina reminded herself; Khalya, though tiny, was fourteen, which was why, according to her mother, she was ready for marriage – and why she was, as Mizan identified, firmly on Alina's worry list. She shook that thought aside and concentrated on the innocent photo. Neat in her blue and white school uniform, Khalya was also half obscured by a huge certificate.

'Did she like our present?'

'Do you need to ask? I've got pictures of that too. In fact, I've a tonne of photos to sort out for the blog and the sponsorship letters.' Alina took the phone back, and then ate her last bite of chocolate icing. 'She loves you calling her that, you know. Almost-sister.'

'Well, she's the nearest thing I've got,' Fin said. They'd once tried to work out Fin and Khalya's possible, hypothetical, relationship, but got lost at second cousin twice removed. *Little almost-sister* pleased them all. 'And I'll come with you and see her in person one day. We all will, Kirsten and the baby, too.'

There was a pause. Alina looked down at the table and rearranged her plate and cup so they were in perfect alignment. She knew Fin's eyes were on her. 'So,' she said, meeting them.

'So.'

They looked at one another for a long, long moment.

'You've found him, then?' Alina said. 'Jamie?'

'Ye-es.' Fin looked... not uncomfortable, but slightly bemused. Perplexed.

Then it was one of the big three Ds, just as she'd expected. No point in dragging it out.

'He's dead, isn't he?'

Fin folded his arms and sighed. 'No. Well, yes. In a way.'

Ah, thought Alina. *The Story.*

She waited. If there was one thing Fin had inherited from her, it was his ability to sit in silence for as long as it took. That it took him a good couple of minutes told her it was something significant. Not much upset Fin's equilibrium – he reminded Alina of Connie in that respect – but then again, it was above extraordinary to have traced the birth father he had never known – and about whom Alina herself, to be perfectly honest, had shared only selective information.

'The thing is...'

She watched him search for the words. Was he protecting himself, or her? Both of them, perhaps.

'Ali, Jamie doesn't exist anymore.'

It wasn't like Fin to be oblique either. 'I don't understand,' she said.

'Look. In a sense, he is alive and well, but...' Fin grinned faintly and so did Alina. '...*but*, there's no easy way to tell you this.'

For the first time in forever, she wanted to snap at him. He didn't need to coddle her. She bit it back, well aware it was Jamie she was irritated with. No, it wasn't, it was herself.

'Ali, for the last eight years, Jamie's been known as Sanna.'

'Sanna?' Alina's brow creased.

'Yes. Jamie, my birth father, is now Sanna. He's been living as, I mean he *is*, a woman.'

Alina picked up her empty cup and pretended to take a drink. Then another. 'Right,' she said, nodding slowly, mind whirling. 'Right.' She knew Fin wasn't remotely fooled.

After a few seconds, he went on. 'She's an academic, apparently. A professor.'

'Jamie? A *professor*? You're joking?' To laugh would be inappropriate, surely. Strange, though, that that should be the most unlikely fact. Maybe it was simply the easiest to comprehend.

'No, Ali.' Fin's voice was gentle. 'Sanna is.'

'Yes, of course. Right. Sanna.' Crockery rattled around them. The hiss of the coffee machine sounded like an exploding boiler. The world tilted for a second.

Whatever Alina had expected, it wasn't that. No way did being transgender – was that even the appropriate word? – fit into the three Ds. It was something to be celebrated, surely. It was… Alina stopped, stumped. She didn't know what it was. But, Jamie, really? 'I don't know what to say,' she admitted.

'I know you don't. Neither did I.' Fin shook his head. 'It's okay, Ali. You're not at work now, and neither am I, for that matter. We don't have to be poker-faced and unshockable. It is bloody weird.'

Alina gathered her wits. 'How do you feel? When did you find out?'

'A few weeks ago.' Fin picked up the teapot in front of him and swirled it round, pouring the cooling dregs into his cup. 'I'm fine now, I think.' He paused and looked up, as if assessing his feelings. 'Yeah, I am. In theory anyway. It's taken me a while to get my head around it, alright. I've prayed about it constantly. I mean, I'd considered all kinds of things, but not this. Who would? What are the odds?' Fin shrugged. 'It's not as if I was looking for my dad; you know that. I've got a great dad.' He spoke more fluently now, and Alina knew this was rehearsed, he'd been over it and over it, making sense of it – that was Fin; that was *her* too. 'And it's not horrible or terrible or anything like that. This is more … more *interesting* than anything else. I'm curious, mostly. Does that make me sound like a fucking cold bastard?' He acknowledged Alina's look of surprise – Fin never used bad language – and reddened slightly. 'Sorry. I suppose it really depends on what she, what *Sanna*, is like.'

'You haven't met her yet.' Alina knew the answer.

'No. And the agency hasn't said much more. I wanted to tell you before I did anything, and I'm supposed to arrange a few counselling sessions before… the next step. Kirsten knows, of course, and Mum and Dad. It even nudged the baby talk off the number one spot for a couple of days.'

'I'm sure,' Alina said. 'What do they think?'

'Mum and Dad?' Fin shrugged. 'Oh, you know—'

'"Live and let live, Fin."' Alina joined in the chorus, and they both laughed, breaking the thin thread of tension. That's what Jan and Hugh always said, though whether they always meant it was debatable.

'I don't know what to say.' Alina repeated herself. 'Of all the things… I mean, I never considered… *Jamie*.' Like an old-fashioned microfiche, her mind tried to settle on a page a quarter of a century back. It fluttered, out of focus.

'Me neither. There was no hint, was there, back in the day? You would have said.'

Alina shook her head, then nodded. That was totally true. But for the first time, she couldn't look Fin in the eye because of all the – albeit unrelated – things she hadn't actually said. His trust in her made her want to cry because she didn't deserve it.

3

They sat in silence for a few minutes. Alina felt weak. It was the jetlag, just the jetlag. Finally, Fin stood up and held out his hand. 'Come on, you look shattered. I'll drive you home.'

Alina slowly stood up, handed Fin his bag, and placed her own over her shoulder. 'I need to sleep,' she agreed, embracing the firmer ground. 'It seems like days since I left the homestay. The faster and newer boats were all booked out, so we came back on the overnight launch – like the good old days. I'll tell you all about it later.' She sighed and stifled a yawn.

'And then this.'

'And then this.'

'Are *you* okay, Ali? I mean, Jamie was your...' Fin hesitated. '...*is* your past.'

'My past. Exactly.' *If only you knew.* Alina mustered a proper smile. 'I'll be fine, Fin. I just need to take it in.' She was promising both of them; both of them were pretending she wasn't rattled. 'Thanks for coming to meet me and telling me.'

They strolled to the short-stay car park; the layout of the airport had changed again in her absence, and Alina, waiting at the pay and display machine, suddenly felt disorientated. Fin led her to his car and she buckled up, just wanting to get home.

'Do you want to send Elizabeth a message, let her know you're on your way?' he said.

'Good idea. I must send one to Mizan too.' Alina rooted out her phone again and squinted at the display. 'Oh, Elizabeth's sent me one. That's not like her.' Hadn't Connie warned she was out of sorts? 'It's clearly the day for random texts.'

Fin, reversing out of the space, glanced over at her. He looked vaguely alarmed to hear Alina's bark of laughter. 'Is she okay? Are you? Ali?'

'I think so.' Alina felt a rising bubble of hysteria. 'She says – I quote – *Others will have said this before, but not in quite this way. Alina: we need to talk.*'

'What does she mean?'

Alina made a face. 'I have absolutely no idea.' And right now, she didn't have the capacity to wonder.

Fin wound down the window and pushed his debit card into the machine before turning back to her. 'Ali? Welcome home.'

Forty minutes later, Alina shut the front door behind her, hung her jacket on the coat stand and paused, inhaling the atmosphere of her empty flat. For as long as she could remember there had been that moment of trepidation, of the need to break the stillness of being away so long and make the space her own again. She moved slowly from room to room, surveying all four of them as if they comprised a country estate. She'd been here three years, now, and she still revelled in living in such a pleasantly grand house on a beautiful street. Left to her own devices, Alina might have managed a tenement in Gorgie or off Leith Walk, the kind of perfectly reasonable places she'd grown up in – but this, *this*, was a bit of luck and a lot of Elizabeth. She ran her hand over one of the pale walls, reminding herself not to take either for granted.

In the kitchen, she unlocked the French doors and stuck her nose out onto a tiny stone terrace secluded from the rest of the lawned garden by an artful creeper and wooden trellis concoction. It might even be warm enough for a determined person to sit out – or at least one not just returned from sweltering thirty-plus temperatures. Alina shivered and closed the doors.

True to her word, Elizabeth had been in, leaving the flat warm and the coffee machine switched on; Alina might just have popped out for the Sunday papers. She opened the fridge, betting what she would find. Sure enough, there was bacon, butter, brioche rolls, cream, and bottles of elderflower tonic and fizzy water. In the fruit bowl lay a pile of Pink Lady apples, and Alina knew without looking she'd find a siege-worthy stash of Walkers crisps in the cupboard. Elizabeth had also left a copy of her latest novel, newly published, on the table. Her essentials defied any stereotyping of an eighty-year-old.

From the top of the neatly stacked post, Alina deciphered her note: *Have a good rest, lovey, and call up tomorrow. I'm in all day – 007 is cracking the whip.* She'd have written that before sending the text. But not long before; whatever Elizabeth needed to talk about couldn't be critical. Alina fetched her phone from her jacket pocket and found confirmation. Elizabeth had replied to her *I'm at the airport now. Are you okay?* with a flurry of, *Yes, of course. Ignore last. Senile moment. Interesting news best served lukewarm.* Alina grinned, reassured. This was Elizabeth at her novelist best.

First things first. Well aware, and equally unbothered, that her coming-home rituals bordered on the obsessive, Alina had her first truly comfortable pee of the year, stepped under the far-hotter-than-could-be-good-for-her rain shower, then changed into her favourite soft pyjamas. Over a cup of coffee pale with cream and a fried bacon roll, she fired off emails to Mizan and her Uncle Takdir – automatically offering a mental apology for the haram meat as she did so. There was a brief moment when her hand, also automatically, hovered over the phone to dial her grandmother, then she went to lay down on her bed with Elizabeth's book.

Now, Alina told herself, *time to get to grips with Jamie. With… Sanna. With Jamie and Sanna.*

She awoke with a start at midnight, reaching out for a non-existent mosquito net and puzzled that the ceiling fan had stopped. The disassociation of jetlag was always unsettling, depressing even, like trying to fight the fog of an anaesthetic; she couldn't quite place herself. Compartmentalising her six-month stints was not hard, but these few hours of transition were. Alina turned on the lamp beside her and lay still, letting her jumbled thoughts roam between the two countries, her two lives. It was a literal case of never the twain shall meet, well, until next time, as Elizabeth was all set to accompany her.

She'd left everything and everyone fine at Sonali Homestay; it would be arrogance to think anything else. Their missing her input was genuine but little more than superficial. Her presence or absence did not change their lives, which, until she made the decision – *if* she made it – to live with them permanently, was exactly how it should be. She missed them too, but it was surprising how quickly one place, one state of mind, could be superimposed on the other. And if things weren't ideal with Khalya, or rather Khalya's mother, there was little extra Alina could offer. Mizan and the other staff had seen off child marriage threats before, and Takdir was a powerful bottom line.

Tonight, Fin's news dominated Alina's initial homesickness. It had to. Fin had been looking for his birth father for nigh on ten years, so she'd assumed this moment would come one day. Still, as time rolled on without news, she'd learned to live with the risk. She'd think about Jamie now and again – who wouldn't? For a few months in Dublin, they had been close, very close. But life back then could have been another incarnation. Alina stretched, which did nothing to release her tense muscles, and sighed. Her hand had been well and truly forced, no more head in the sand. What to make of Jamie, let alone Sanna? Alina didn't know what she felt. Her brain was a machine; she pictured a dusty obsolete fax being fed a sheet of incongruous information which emerged the other side as a blank page. The facts were straightforward, so much so that Alina sat up and recited them for clarity: 'Jamie is Fin's father. Fin has traced Jamie. Jamie is now a woman called Sanna.'

And there, Alina hit a wall.

It didn't matter a bit who or what or how or when, even why, Fin's other birth parent had returned. That they *had* was the issue. It changed the past, present and, most likely, the future.

Alina pushed back the duvet and got up. She was thirsty and her mouth felt furry, a combination of the salty bacon and the central heating turned to constant. No point in trying to think straight on the brink of dehydration. She drank three glasses of water from the kitchen tap, leaving her insides sloshing around like a desultory washing machine. It was morning-time in Bangladesh, of course, and her body clock was haywire. Too restless to read, but too fuzzy to face the onslaught of social media. Alina sighed and thumbed through the pile of junk mail before dumping it en masse in the recycling.

In the small sitting room, she straightened the few ornaments – a Murano glass vase, a Lladro angel – and photos she had on display. Dusting Fin and Kirsten's wedding picture with her sleeve – she wasn't sufficiently bored or restless to get dusters and polish and do some real housework – she wondered if Kirsten were awake too, being kicked by the imminent baby they knew was a little girl. That was top secret, both of them confided individually. 'We aren't telling anyone,' Kirsten had said as she spilled the beans to Alina in a crackly, echoing and exorbitant phone call. 'Don't tell Fin I told you.' Five minutes later, Fin said the same thing.

Jamie had been Fin's father in name only; he would never be the baby's grandfather. Would Sanna want to stand beside Jan as her grandmother? Alina reverted to her thoughts of earlier, floored by the idea that either of them was old enough to be a grand-anything. A different person might pull out a drawer of treasured mementoes and do a bit of nostalgic wallowing. And why not? It wasn't that Alina wouldn't, rather that she couldn't. She hadn't exactly grown up living out of a suitcase, but her grandparents' vocation, as Salvation Army officers, had made for a lack of physical roots. That, and her subsequent adult choices, had left a legacy of suspicion over too many possessions. When they first met, she'd said as much to Elizabeth, joking that her ideal was to live in a hotel – all of the comfort but none of the responsibility for 'stuff' – and, ultimately, what Elizabeth had offered Alina here was so much better. What it all meant, however, was that she really hadn't any keepsakes: from her late parents, from Fin's birth, from her early visits to Bangladesh. There was Fin's formal adoption folder, but he'd kept that himself for years now… maybe she'd ask him if she could have a look through it again. It would be good to be prepared, if – no, when, it was definitely *when* – she met Sanna.

'Absolutely, Alina,' she mocked herself aloud. 'Being forearmed with a brown manila file full of officialese, a sanitised version of the truth and a couple of Polaroids, is going to make it all hunky-dory.' She wandered back into the kitchen, kicking herself that she'd never kept a diary. She wasn't sure if her memory was simply poor or highly selective. She'd always – mostly – answered Fin's questions as best she could, but Elizabeth still delighted in calling her the ultimate unreliable narrator, and while Alina knew nothing about writing stories other than what she'd picked up from *her*, she figured that was more or less correct. Oh, well. In lieu of Valentine's cards from Jamie, baby pictures of Fin, and total recall, she'd turn to fizzy drinks and crisps. Much, she suspected, as she'd done twenty-five years ago.

4

Mid-morning, a few hours later, she was a bit more in sync with the Edinburgh day. For one thing, the weather had reverted to dull and drizzly. Dreich, the Scots called it. Alina rolled the word pleasingly around her tongue. Give her a couple of weeks and of course she'd be sick of it, searching for blue skies like every other resident of the windy city. Still, as she walked up the short path to the gate, pulling the belt tighter on her raincoat, she figured there was no better weather to blow away the cobwebs of jetlag and – if she were honest – fear.

Edenfield Road was its usual genteel and deserted self. Parking spaces were only hotly contested after regular office hours because, such was the street's proximity to the Morningside shops and cafés, traffic wardens kept a close eye. Alina, awake enough to spy the straight back and poker face of Morag pulling her shopping trolley around the corner, sidestepped eye contact and set out briskly in the other direction. She just couldn't. Not yet. As Elizabeth put it, and Connie, too, Morag was a piece of work.

Trudging up the hill, Alina clicked through her mental to-do list: pick up a few things at Waitrose (just because she could), check in with Sonali Homestay's trustees (a formal report and a Skype for the gossip) and plan her next six months. It wasn't much. Thanks to a modest legacy from her grandparents, and the specific, now almost prescient instruction in Miriam's will that her granddaughter take time out to consider her future, Alina had no need to seek out the freelance work that usually funded life in Scotland. In theory it was wonderfully decadent, but in practice, she felt a bit loose-endish without a set routine. Plenty of time to think and nowhere to hide, she thought.

She was waiting at the pedestrian lights, slightly mesmerised by the accompanying zebra crossing, when she looked into a slowly passing car and thought she saw Jamie driving. No, not Jamie – she cursed her befuddled head – but someone else who looked familiar, someone from the more recent past. No. When she blinked and looked again, the car had passed, and of course it would be a stranger anyway. She made her way across the road, off-balance, wondering if she looked drunk, if this was what it was *like* to be drunk.

Shaking her head, she meandered through her errands as if through a cloud, pushing the boat out and buying some see-her-through groceries in Waitrose, and checked her bank balance, noting how she'd done all of her chores and exchanged no more than half a dozen words. Invisible once more. That, for Alina, summed up the fundamental difference between Scotland and Bangladesh.

Shopping unpacked, the washing machine spinning, her overnight bag stashed in the box room that was more glory-hole, Alina drank a pot of coffee and braced herself for a social media onslaught. *Mind-numbing in itself*, she thought, not sure if better or worse done with a jetlag hangover, but her sense of order was bothered by a messy email account. 'Get a life, Alina Farrell,' she muttered. She sent a round robin to the trustees, deleted the accumulated spam, and had a half-hearted click through the hundreds of inbox messages she hadn't bothered checking while away, dismayed by her illogical pleasure in getting it down to fifty or so addresses and headings she didn't recognise but figured she should read. *Be a devil*, she goaded herself, *delete them. What's the worst that could happen?* A huge legacy or grant for Sonali Homestay, that's what she could miss. Yes, it was a long shot, but it happened, and it left her resolute. There was, a small part of her mind couldn't help but notice, nothing marked Jamie or Sanna Drew. Well, what had she expected? She hovered over Google for a second... but no. Not now. Alina logged off. She looked at her watch and decided it was time to catch up with Elizabeth.

The conversion of the house into flats meant Alina had to go back outside – her own front door was tucked away to the side, the black 36B in the glass panel above it making her feel she was advertising her bra size – up the main path and knock on the far grander door of the main house. It was a beautiful old house of a soft reddish sandstone, Georgian, apparently, and from the front it was impossible to tell it was no longer the imposing family home of years gone by. Elizabeth maintained that when she was too doddery to haul herself up the stairs, she and Alina would swap flats, but Alina couldn't ever see herself in such grandeur. She stuck her finger on the brass bell and stabbed several times; Elizabeth would know it was her.

'I knew it was you. It's lovely to see you back.' Elizabeth herself, a baby blue pashmina thrown loosely on top of black jeans, flung open the front door with the flourish of one announcing the Duchess of Kent at a formal banquet. 'Come in, come in. Perfect timing, too. 007's just making coffee.'

'It's so good to see you.' Alina stepped over the threshold to hug Elizabeth and then drew back in alarm as, instead of soft cashmere and Elizabeth's narrow shoulders, she encountered something hard and cool.

'What—'

'Damn. I thought I could fool you until we'd at least caught up on all the good gossip.' Elizabeth used her right hand to tuck the pashmina more tightly about her, and then flapped it in the direction of the stairs. 'Go on up, madam. I'm explaining nothing without the aid of a double espresso.'

Alina, slipping off her shoes out of habit, did as she was

told, taking hold of the banister and looking backwards accusingly. 'Elizabeth, what have you done? Are you hurt?'

'Just a scratch.' She didn't meet Alina's eye.

'Hmm.'

Apart from this downstairs room – which would once have been half of the grand entrance hall and was now known as 'Christmas tree central', so seldom was it used for anything else – Elizabeth's apartment filled the centre of the house and made use of the two original first-floor drawing rooms. If the bedrooms and the kitchen were poky in comparison, Elizabeth didn't care. 'It's far from the fripperies and fancy parlours I was raised in,' she'd announce in her best Miss Jean Brodie; it had become something of a party piece, frequently quoted in the press. 'Ridiculously,' she'd add in private, 'given I actually own the whole house.'

Alina ran lightly up the stairs and paused, out of habit, keeping her eyes down. Directly on the wall in front, Elizabeth had a montage of family photos, in the centre of which was the one Alina could never look at without guilt. Therefore, she didn't look at all. It was the only incongruence in Elizabeth's welcoming apartment, and it would be churlish to ask her to remove it.

'Charles or Winston?' Alina asked.

'Winston, unfortunately. Double-0's being especially demanding today. Thank goodness you've arrived. I was about to fake a stroke.'

Obediently, Alina turned to the door on the left. Known as Winston, for its namesake, Churchill, it doubled as an office and dining room, and was where Elizabeth did what she called her grown-up work. Charles, on the right (after Charles Hawtrey; Elizabeth loved Carry On films and swore they were a constant source of inspiration – another oft-quoted media snippet) was set up for 'fun'. Elizabeth counted her writing – romantic fiction – in that, much to Alina's mystification; give her a report to write any day.

Sure enough, two laptops faced off over the mahogany

table, an open notebook beside one and a pile of print-outs next to the other. Alina hovered.

'Sit yourself down by the window, or we'll look as if we're having a board meeting.' Elizabeth's voice floated after her. 'I'm going to supervise the cutting of the cake.'

'She sounds like the mother of the bride. Alina, my dear, how nice to see you.'

'Hello... Claire.' Alina caught the '007' as it skimmed her lips and joined in a hearty handshake from the Yorkshire woman with the pudding-basin haircut who dumped a tea-tray on the table and barrelled across the room. 'Elizabeth said you would be here. I hope I'm not interrupting you.' She nodded over towards the table.

'Not so much interrupting as stopping me from poking out my eyes with my ballpoint.' The at-risk eyes twinkled. 'We've both been straining to hear the doorbell for nigh on half an hour.'

'Something we agree on.' Elizabeth reappeared with an oozing cream sponge. 'Alina, pet, take the sofa and feel free to lay down. Make up for all those months of rock-solid mattresses. I shall have to get in training.' She beamed at Claire. 'Did I mention I was going to Bangladesh with Alina next time?'

'You might have referred to it an odd hundred times or so.' Claire sighed. 'Aren't you singlehandedly building the centre a guesthouse, as well?' She winked at Alina.

'*Funding*, yes. Laying bricks, no.' Elizabeth intercepted the wink and added mock-grandly, 'One of my "charitable activities and good deeds", as I believe you may have tweeted.'

'Touché. I'll contribute mattresses and pillows,' Claire offered. 'Seriously.'

'Meantime, we'll sort something out for the Grand Dame.' Alina grinned. 'I don't mind hard beds actually. It must be my Bangladeshi genes. But I'll never say no to your sofa. Or to your offer, Claire. Thank you.' She sank down and sighed with pleasure.

Elizabeth and Claire, squabbling amicably over the pouring of the coffee, settled in the other two armchairs in front of the floor-to-ceiling windows.

'Now, I'd like to hear all about Bangladesh.' Elizabeth beamed between Alina and Claire. 'I must say, you do look very well. Doesn't she, Double-0?'

'You do at that, Alina – oh, don't worry…' She'd clearly caught the fleeting look of surprise. '…I thought if I told her to call me 007 to my face the joke would wear thin.' Claire paused. 'I was wrong.'

'Nice try, Elizabeth.' Alina pointed to the older woman's pashmina, still artfully hiding her left arm. 'I'm saying nothing until I hear what's happened to you.' Still, she relaxed. There, then, was the reason for yesterday's cryptic text.

'And so you shall. There's no secret, Alina, lovey, I just didn't want to worry you.' Struggling to unwrap herself, Elizabeth finally brandished a grubby-looking plaster cast, fraying at the edges.

'How did you break your arm?' Alina didn't know whether to laugh or cry. 'Are you hurt anywhere else? Are you ill?' Mind, she looked as well as ever. Her blue eyes were sparkling and her customary pale pink lipstick and dangly earrings were all in place. If her grey hair was in a more haphazard bun arrangement than usual, then that was to be expected with one arm out of action.

'Don't I look the picture of health?' Elizabeth might have read Alina's thoughts. 'Except for my hair—'

'Lookit, missus, next time call a stylist.' Claire tapped her own head. 'Do I look like a woman who can fix a decent up-do?'

'Anyway,' Elizabeth went on, 'I haven't broken anything. I've fractured two tiny bones in my wrist. The plaster cast is – and I quote – "a precaution at your age, sweetie-pie".'

'Oh, oh.'

'Precisely. That young lady won't be so patronising again.' Elizabeth nodded self-righteously, watching Alina and Claire share a grin. 'And neither should you two be. I'm old, not an idiot.'

Claire pointedly sipped her coffee. 'Ask her how she did it.'

'Yes. How did you?'

Elizabeth sat up straight. 'On that, I'm taking the Fifth Amendment.'

'You can't. We live in Scotland.'

'Taking the Fifth.'

'Elizabeth—'

'She won't tell anyone, Alina. Don't waste your breath.'

Alina gave a huge sigh and lay back on the sofa, her arms crossed behind her head. 'Oh, it's good to be home.' She squinted at them. 'Don't worry, I won't stay long. I can see you've work to do.'

'No.' Claire shook her head. 'Let me be the one to break up the party. I think we're sorted for today. Elizabeth?'

'Marvellous, Double-0. Stay to hear about Alina's trip though.'

'I'd love to hear more,' Claire said, after Alina had obliged with the edited highlights. 'Did you ever think of writing about it?'

'Dear God, no.' Alina shuddered. 'No offence, I know it's what you both do. But definitely no.'

'Authors would kill to have the interested ear of one of the best literary agents in the business.' Elizabeth was smiling. 'And here you are, sublimely unimpressed.'

'Oh I'm impressed, alright. By both of you.' Alina was sincere. 'I'm just not an author.'

'Fair enough.' Claire rose and started collecting her belongings. 'Right, I'm off. I know Elizabeth has lots to tell you, Alina...' Her meaningful look at the older woman, subtle as a neon flare, was politely ignored; *What next?* Alina wondered. 'See you soon. And Elizabeth...'

Alina tuned out, dozing, back in Bhola for a few more minutes; she could almost feel the sun, hear the call of the muezzin to afternoon prayers, see Khalya's face smiling down at her as the child's mother swathed her in the red and gold of a traditional wedding dress—

'Alina?'

'Huh?' Alina struggled back to the surface. Elizabeth was sitting opposite her, a book on her lap. 'Shit.' Her voice was croaky and she cleared her throat. 'Sorry. Did I fall asleep?'

'Not for long. But if you want to sleep tonight—'

'Good idea.' Alina pushed herself upright and rubbed her eyes. She glanced again at Elizabeth's arm, now resting openly across her middle, but she knew to leave well enough alone. Something was stopping her from launching into Fin's news. Elizabeth would be a great sounding board, but maybe Alina herself was too weary to go over it all again right now. Neither did she want to be all *me, me, me*.

Claire's *tell her* glance swam into view and Alina cast her thoughts over Elizabeth's life. 'What about all your news?' she asked. 'Have I missed anything other than the arm?' It wasn't her imagination – Elizabeth looked shifty again.

Trying to catch her out, Alina added, 'So, what else *have* I missed? Any secrets out of the woodwork? Bodies buried?'

'I... What? I...' Elizabeth rallied quickly. 'I think you mistake me for Ian Rankin.' She was at her most prim. 'There's not much room for criminals in my brand of middle-aged chick-lit. 007 would lose her mind.'

Alina gave in and went with her; when the lady Elizabeth was not for turning, waiting her out was the only solution. 'I expect she'd rather deal with that than have to do your hair again.' Despite herself Alina giggled at the thought of the forthright woman, who swore she only ever looked into a mirror to check her teeth for spinach, trying to pin up Elizabeth's locks into their usual smart chignon.

Elizabeth's laughter peeled out too. 'Oh, love, you'd have thought I'd asked her to be my birthing partner. But she rolled up her sleeves and got in there. Once a farmer's daughter 'n' all that.'

'I'm just glad you're alright.' Alina gathered her own shoulder-length hair in her hands and twisted it up behind her, enjoying the cool air on her neck. 'I read your text in the car with Fin – he came to pick me up. We both hadn't a clue what it meant. I was afraid something terrible had happened.'

'My—?' Elizabeth looked puzzled for a second, then guilty again. 'Oh, yes. That message. Error of judgement.' She rubbed at something on her jeans, plucked a stray hair off them. 'Anyway. Fin, yes. How is Fin?'

'In good form as ever. Looking forward to the baby.' *I've found him, Ali. But...* To tell or not to tell? Alina shifted in her seat.

'But?'

There it was again. 'But what?'

Elizabeth put on her reading glasses and looked over the top of her lenses for effect. 'Y'ar all edgy, like.' She looked supremely satisfied. 'I've been wanting to say that for ages.'

'Very down with the cool kids.'

'I'm working on it; forget eighty being the new fifty, why shouldn't it be the new fifteen? So, what has young Fin been up to in your absence? Lost his faith?'

'As if.' They both paused to acknowledge the quirk of fate, predestination, or whatever that had led Fin and Kirsten to follow in Alina's grandparents' footsteps and become Salvation Army officers. It always tickled Elizabeth, who trotted it out as her standard truth-is-stranger-than-fiction example. Alina had given up pointing out that the odds increased significantly because Fin had ended up being adopted by fellow Salvationists and had been submerged in that world all his life.

'And Kirsten hasn't had the baby, you'd have said. So?'

It was good news. It really was. Alina took a deep breath. 'Fin thinks he's found his birth father.'

'Oh, lovey, that *is* news.' Elizabeth leaned forward. 'Now, start at the beginning – the very beginning, mind – and tell me everything.'

5

Dublin 1994

'You did it, Alina. You got in to Trinity.' The warm and calm voice of Patrick, her grandfather, filled all the miles between Belfast and Israel.

'I did? What did I get?' In the kibbutz volunteers' office, Alina clenched the phone.

'An A, two Bs and a C. Congratulations, pet. We're very proud of you, but you know that already.'

With nobody watching, Alina did an awkward little happy dance. Her rapid mental calculations suggested that 'you scraped in' would be more accurate, but who cared. *One down, one to go*, she thought. All of their lives were changing. 'And you and Granny – what's your new posting?' She held her breath.

'Well, now,' Patrick sounded amused, 'I'll hand you over for that piece of news…'

'Alina? You clever girl! And clever us, too. You'll never believe where we're going.'

Her oh-so-practical grandmother sounded excited and just a bit smug, so that Alina heard the sound of wheels within wheels. 'Tell me.'

There was a ta-dah moment, then Miriam announced, 'We're being moved to Dublin Central. How about that?'

Alina laughed out loud. 'Of course you are. How did you work that one, Granny? Or is it pure good luck?'

'God's Work, young lady, and good management. Maybe a bit of luck,' her grandmother owned, a smile in her voice too.

'Hmm.' In hindsight, Alina would recognise her grandmother's formidable hand; Miriam hadn't been above engineering *God's Work* right up until the end. Yes, it was through the ranks of the Salvation Army she, and Alina's grandfather, the softer, amenable Patrick, had risen, but nobody doubted Miriam could have sorted the regular Army, too.

Alina was eighteen months old when her parents died and she'd gone to live with Miriam and Patrick, her grandparents on her mother's side. They'd moved around her whole life, and the routine of new bedroom, new school, new friends, always one step out of the fold, was something she'd taken in her stride. She endured her sixth-form years at a posh Protestant school in Belfast, where she'd kept her eyes closed to anything but study, before having them well and truly opened at this kibbutz at the foot of the Judean hills. It was, she'd said since, the perfect dual education.

Dublin, they decided as a trio, was the obvious place to regroup.

'It's home,' Patrick pointed out.

'Where we started out and where we want to retire,' Miriam agreed. 'Let's face it, another five years and they'll put us out to grass, so we're as well to get a head-start.'

'They'll be begging you to stay on until you're ancient, and you know it.' Her grandparents were 'one of a kind', 'exemplary officers', 'the Salvation Army poster couple' – growing up, Alina had heard every compliment, while they practised their faith and work, oblivious.

'Not if they've any sense,' Miriam said briskly. 'And God give us the grace and foresight to know ourselves when to go.'

Dublin wasn't home to Alina. She'd never lived there, but the mother she didn't remember had, and so the city held a certain fascination. A year ago she'd walked through the arch to Trinity College knowing it was where her parents had met, and was immediately determined she'd study there too.

Placing the phone receiver back in its cradle and thanking the volunteer leader for the use of his office, Alina felt the smugness she'd accused Miriam of displaying. Life was going to plan.

That September, it seemed the best of both worlds for Alina to live in university accommodation across the city from her grandparents, and all three had assumed Alina would settle into her first year with the consummate ease of practice. Somehow, though, it had all started to unravel.

'I'm not *enough* here,' she said to Jamie in those first few weeks of getting to know one another. 'Not clever enough, not experienced enough, not black enough but not white enough either.'

'Too slippery to get hold of?' he'd suggested. 'Too like those off-white paint colours – you know the ones, apple white or eggshell or champagne.'

'Exactly. Not the real thing.' She was impressed how he *got* her, how they got each other, so when he said, 'At least you're nuanced. Me? I'm bog-standard beige,' she told him, 'We're undercoats. Wait 'til we decide how we want colouring in. That'll show them.' Which, remarkably profound or pretentious codswallop, she ultimately came to see as prescient.

It was a point of honour that Alina didn't let on to Miriam and Patrick how unhappy she was, and true to form, they didn't press her. Instead they were there with the suggestion of a meal or a weekend with them, one of Miriam's inspirational books, or from Patrick, a slipped five pound note to take herself off to the cinema.

'Lose yourself in a big bit of nonsense for an hour or so,' he'd say. 'You'll come out into the bright lights with a spring in your step and the realisation you've survived another day.'

Whatever the logic, it worked. 'You're one hundred percent responsible for my addiction to *The Sound of Music*,' she told him over again. How fitting it would have been, she thought afterwards, if she'd bumped into Jamie during one of those Technicolour outings. Except that story would have had to have a different ending entirely.

The actual first time they'd met was at an initiative for Social Work and Policy students and their Computer Technology counterparts, the disciplines eyeing each other up like alien species. They were supposed to 'pair up and form buddies' in the name of advancing inter-departmental collaboration. Hard to imagine now, Alina thought, but publicly accessible IT was barely emerging from its infancy in the early nineties, and the college intention was driven by obscure EU funding, to dust down some of the academia in the name of community and computer literacy. It was, they were told, somewhat sniffily by the vice chancellor, 'the way forward'.

'It was,' Jamie was to mimic him later, 'the way to trouble.'

The assistant lecturer who had drawn the short straw as administrator couldn't have known the idiosyncrasies of Alina's dozen-strong intake. *Identity* was their buzzword, *freedom* and *self-expression* hot on its heels – fair enough, she thought, counterpoint to centuries of university tradition, except in the hands of zealots. All the tutor had done was perch on a table at the front of the room and read out a list of names, and at 'Sara Smyth' he must have been mystified by the collective intake of breath, rather than a half-raised hand. There was a second, another, one more, and then a pale, freckled young woman had stood up and said robotically, 'Your list is out of date. Sara Smyth was a capitalist and racist construct. She was reborn as Palesa X. It is a personal and political infringement on behalf of this university to systematically deny my human rights to my chosen name.' A slow smirk crossed the lecturer's face as he laboriously changed the detail. He ploughed on but after that, even triple EU funding and a trip to Brussels couldn't resurrect departmental bonding.

Jamie, randomly sitting beside Alina, scribbled a couple of lines, and angled the A4 pad towards her. *Can I be your partner*, it said, *I'm scared of everyone else.* She took her own pen and drew a smiley face. The day was looking up.

'Are they always that uptight, your lot?' he asked her as they out-waited the subsequent stampede from the room.

'Well, nobody cried today.' Alina was busy shoving her notebook into her bag. 'That's a bonus.'

Jamie laughed. 'Wait, you're serious? For fuck's sake.' He tried to purse his lips into a whistle but couldn't for laughing.

'Sadly not.' Alina found his grin infectious. 'What makes you think I'm not the chief crier? Or one of the scary ones?'

'Algorithms. I worked out the probability.' They walked outside, clicking off the lights, as instructed by a huge sign on the door. 'Joke. It was your shoes.' He pointed down at her feet, then his own. 'Same as mine. It was a sign.'

Alina followed his gaze. Well, they both wore trainers that fitted somewhere on a large spectrum of 'red'. It was a nice way of not saying they were both plain ordinary.

'I'm Jamie, as you heard,' he went on. 'Attempts to call me James, Jem, Jimmy and Jamesy will infringe on my human rights and as such result in a punch on the nose that will equally infringe on your human rights, and the world will slide into chaos theory.'

'I'll try to remember, then. I'm just Alina.'

'Well, just Alina, when do you want your first computing lesson?'

It was the start of a beautiful friendship, casual but close, teasing but respectful, united in a silliness that was an outlet for both of them. Like her, Jamie was an only child, and he had endured the boarding school he went to aged ten. Alina suspected that they had belatedly found in the other the sibling they'd never had.

'We just clicked in the indefinable way you do sometimes,' she was to say to Fin, years afterwards. What she *didn't* add was how the complete lack of any physical spark between them made it all so much easier. That, such as it was, came later. Ironic, that, thought Alina now, twenty-five years affording twenty-twenty vision.

Jamie wasn't her saviour. He wasn't her soulmate

either. He was the match to her odd one out. Most of the time they were overlooked: children at the adults' party. Alina was clueless about information technology, so had no yardstick for measuring Jamie's knowledge except that 'doing computers' meant he had to be clever. He arrived at their tutorials each Thursday afternoon with their joint homework done, a copy printed out for her. She feigned interest, collected her high marks, and as far as she could recall, managed the whole term without ever finding an 'on' switch in the sexy new computer lab.

'Best of all, he wasn't fighting the world,' was the other thing Alina went on to tell the teenage Fin. 'With Jamie, sharing a KitKat in the cafeteria didn't have to be a full-on tirade against Nestlé. Or saying my granny and grandad had done four weddings in one weekend wasn't an earnest discussion about religious institutional oppression. It was just conversation.'

In retrospect, Alina was relieved she'd grown somewhat more socially aware – as, presumably, had Jamie, given that he… no, not he, *Sanna*, was free to *be* Sanna – but she could forgive their nineteen-year-old selves a means of coping.

What Jamie had been, of course, was the foil to take home to her grandparents. To introduce them to her best friend who could easily have been playing second horn in their Salvation Army Corps band. To show them that their joint Dublin decision was the right one, that she was happy. Not, she thought in hindsight, that she'd really fooled either Miriam or Patrick for a second.

Jamie had always been different to the others. It wasn't a case of looking back and realising it; she'd always known it. Alina smiled to herself: no, she hadn't foreseen his transition, forced out a confession about how he was a man trapped in a woman's body or whatever the trite common parlance was. She meant that he always seemed to live far more in the moment than everyone else around them, herself included. Even at nineteen – at nine, if she went back far enough – she'd been a planner. She liked things neatly ordered and arranged, all bases covered and contingencies in place. She was a product of her upbringing and generally it served her well.

Jamie, though, made her appreciate the here and now – and if there was no appreciation to be had, they laughed at it all and the moment got better. It was his irreverence she cherished, she realised now. Her grandparents had always been the least judgemental people she knew and had never condoned the evil pleasures of sarcasm or innocently (enough) poking fun at people, even in private. At Trinity, her classmates purported to be the same but in Alina's mind, at least, it was rooted less in goodness than in striving for public display. They could be, and often were, vicious to each other in tutorials and lectures.

'They call it straight talking,' she said to Jamie.

'Bravado, more like,' was his take on it.

6

Alina stopped talking. For a moment, the only sound in the room was the ticking of the carriage clock on the mantelpiece. She struggled to bring herself back from her nineteen-year-old self; was this what being hypnotised was like? She blinked, and Elizabeth, sitting quietly opposite, came back into focus. She felt faintly embarrassed.

'God, sorry. When you said to tell you everything, you weren't expecting my thousand-words-a-minute life story in hectic and chaotic chapters, were you?'

'If I liked short stories, I wouldn't write novels,' was Elizabeth's ice-breaking response. She added, 'You've never spoken before about… about Fin's beginnings.'

'No. Not to anyone.' Elizabeth was her best friend; the *why not?* hung in the air. Alina took refuge in the obvious. 'It got complicated.'

'The past often does. Contrary to popular belief, hindsight often makes it difficult to accept why we did what we did.' Elizabeth's pause gave Alina time to mentally add *and how* before the older woman went on, 'I'm not derailing the conversation, but you only have to think back to how we met.'

Another whole set of complicated factors.

'Anyhow, that's not for now.' Elizabeth turned bright eyes

on Alina. 'I don't know whether I'm more curious about back then or about now. So, what does happen next?'

'I wish I knew. I think I need to clear my head. Would you be offended if I ran? I need to go for a walk or a swim or something.'

'Very sensible. I'd come with you if I could be bothered. I'll tell you what, come back later and we'll have something to eat. Or tomorrow, if you just need to collapse into bed.'

'You're a star, Elizabeth. I'll do that.' Alina dragged herself from the chair, and the warmth of the room, knowing how much better she'd feel for some air. 'See you later.'

Back behind her own front door, Alina glanced at her watch and wondered what best to do with her body to slow her mind down. She ran her hand through her hair and pulled at a knot tangling her fingers, wincing at the wiry grey roots that refused to lay down and die amid the black. She tugged at one or two more of them, emulating a mad Mrs Rochester, and made a mental note to phone the hairdresser. She needed an MOT. All of a sudden, her home clothes felt tight, which was probably due to the fact that anything remotely fitted pinched after the roominess of the salwar kameezes she wore in Bhola, but even so, she didn't do half enough exercise when away. Would she go for a walk, or a swim? Maybe she should take up jogging... That was a decision for another day.

Swim or walk? Walk or swim? That annoyed her too; she wasn't usually a ditherer. She banged her elbow on the doorframe, let out a furious 'Jesus Christ', which inevitably led to a vision of her grandmother drifting past, arching an eyebrow and murmuring, 'Exactly, dear.'

'Sorry, Granny,' Alina said to the ether, and managed a half-smile despite herself.

Miriam had been a proponent of mindfulness long before it became a thing – except she called it *being still in the presence of the Lord* – and Alina needed a hefty dose of that right now.

She shivered; she couldn't face total immersion in coldish water, so she'd go for a walk and hope the skies didn't release a deluge.

She'd walk along Princes Street, cut through to Holyrood and up Arthur's Seat. She'd only ever done it once before and that was years ago. It would take her ages.

She had a plan; she felt better, and outside she pounded the pavements. It was the small local surprises that Alina noticed after she'd been away: the Turkish tea shop that was now a smoothie bar, although the same servers and fittings were still in situ; the Bank of Scotland that was now a Greggs – presumably *with* staff changes; and the fact that, despite all her eight years of living in Edinburgh, she still confused Frederick Street and Hanover Street and ended up doubling back. Yet, over it all, Arthur's Seat and the castle stood unflinching. The city was in full weekend flow, but being part of it felt like taking a peaceful neighbourhood stroll after the frenzy of Bangladesh. That too, like Alina's appreciation of the continued grey skies and weak sunlight, would pass.

She tried to empty her mind as she walked, but she couldn't throw off the spectre of 1994. For a few minutes, in Elizabeth's sitting room, she'd been transported back. It was unheard of. She rarely let herself go back to the nuts and bolts of that whole time. Even in answering Fin's questions over the years, she'd collated a version that was, at least superficially, truthful. Was it going to be enough though, now with Jamie... Sanna... having come forward? Was it hell.

Jamie had known all about Fin before he disappeared. Well, not about Fin exactly, but about the arrival of a baby whose name they had already decided on together: Finlay for a boy and Rose for a girl. She remembered having one of those telephone-trolleys wheeled over to her in the maternity ward so she could phone him. Her grandmother had offered to do it, believing it would render Alina jelly-like and tearful. In fact, she felt invincible. She'd given birth to a perfect healthy baby and it had been hard, very hard, but not impossible; nothing else would ever be after that.

It hadn't been, either. Not the baby going to meet his parents. Not her first visit to Bangladesh. Not meeting Elizabeth. Not losing her grandparents. Not... Alina hesitated. No, not anything.

From where she stood now, ghostly reflections and muted, stationary traffic playing with her sense of time, something about that bit made Alina wince. Had she been smug? Self-righteous, even? Benevolently handing over her gift of a baby to two people, acquaintances of her grandparents whom she'd only just come to know as Jan and Hugh. It had been an odd situation. Newborn babies usually went to foster parents, a bit of a cooling-off period, and the professional in Alina had quickly learned since how very few of those already very, very few babies ultimately went anywhere other than home with their birth mother. But Alina had been adamant in her decisions, clear and logical, and Fin's was to be a truly open adoption. Uncommonly enlightened professional services and good matching, ultimately a 'private adoption order', meant that for everyone's sake, especially Fin's, theirs was a triangle made in heaven. Or that's how they'd made it. To the day her grandmother died, Alina was sure she alone remained unconvinced. She never said aloud, 'You're protesting a bit too much, pet,' but she'd lay bets on Miriam thinking it.

Once more deep in the past, Alina barely registered the rain starting as she passed the castle, towering and glowering above her. By the time she reached the galleries, however, it was like a glass sheet. She wouldn't duck inside; Philistine or not, there was no exhibition yet invented that would grab her attention today, but neither was she going to plough on up a muddy, obscured hill, however iconic, in wet trainers and a *shower*-proof raincoat. She turned heel, scrabbled in her pocket for change and amassed enough to grab the next 23 bus.

As the double decker struggled to life again and took the

corner, trundling down Princes Street, she leaned her head against the misted window and half-watched the straggling late-afternoon shoppers, all of them making more progress than the bus. Before Alina had gone off on her foray into the past, Elizabeth had taken her recounting of Fin's news very much in her stride; Alina had expected nothing else, and that was probably why she'd gone on about meeting Jamie way back when. It appealed, no doubt, to the storyteller in Elizabeth, but equally she didn't judge. Alina just hoped she and Fin had the open-mindedness to accept Fin's father – Jamie, Sanna – for whoever they turned out to be. Gender, the bit everyone focused on, was really the least of it, a smokescreen. But good, bad or immaterial, Alina didn't yet know.

She felt a rush of... of... discontent? Contrariness? Resentment, even. *Why now?* Why had he... she... chosen now to reappear? Not that any time would be easy, there was still so much at stake. So much to tell – or not tell – Fin. She'd loved Jamie, she had, and she knew he'd loved her in the same way. They'd worked as one on her pregnancy, friends rather than lovers, treating it like another college project, almost. They'd trusted each other. Trust. That was one of the (many) roots of her fears, Alina recognised. How much could you, should you, trust someone to keep the promises they made a lifetime ago? Because Jamie had made promises.

'I promise I will always be your baby's father,' he'd said. 'Whatever happens, that will never change. And when it's time for me to meet him, or when – if – he wants to meet me, I promise you're the person I'll come to first. Don't ever doubt that.'

And she hadn't, she realised. Which left her in something of a limbo now. Back then, Jamie had never, *never* broken a promise. Alina wondered now if Sanna would remember.

She leaned over and rang the bell, needing to walk the feeling off, rain or not. Again, Alina stepped out as fast as her feet would go, trying to out-do her thoughts. Back past the Gardens, past the castle, round the corner onto Lothian

Road she went. All of this was extraordinary: finding your child's father after years of invisibility; finding that man was a woman and – Alina's steps faltered – had made that change without you... *Ah.* She took a deep breath and continued more slightly. Something loosened inside her. Was that it, really? Despite everything else, was it that which irked her? That she'd been left out of Jamie's life-changing decision after she'd let him into the centre of hers?

And – she was on a roll now, thoughts all over the place, uncensored – this gender thing changed the goalposts: no longer, *wow, Fin found his dad*, but *wow, Fin found his dad and she's his 'mum'*; she could imagine the lurid headlines.

And there she had to stop, deflated. 'Because you have no bloody idea what Jamie has thought for twenty-five years or what Sanna thinks now,' she muttered to herself. 'Get a grip.'

But... Those three little letters again. But, but, but. *Get off your high-horse, Alina*, a little voice of conscience niggled, *you couldn't have asked for a better diversion*. A red herring. Or was it a straw man? Whatever best muddied the truth of Alina's past decisions. Elizabeth would know. *Shit. Shit. Shit.*

Temper-tantruming around the saturated streets of Edinburgh and thinking in riddles might not be quite the mindfulness experience her grandmother had advocated, but it had certainly needled out the sting.

Her feet were wet, cheap fabric trainers no match for the weather. She stopped at the next bus stop at the same time as the number 23 and waved her day ticket. It was the bus she'd got off twenty minutes before. The driver recognised her too. 'Are you sure?' the woman said, nodding at the jam ahead. 'You probably had the right idea.'

'But the wrong shoes.' Alina was cheered by the nonsense of it, her equilibrium on the way to being restored.

She got off again at Holy Corner, waving as the driver called 'Race you!' and squelched her way home. Turning the corner, Alina looked towards Elizabeth's lit windows. Should she, shouldn't she? An evening of easy company or... a thought rushed out, demanding credence: she could go home, google Sanna and see what came up; a pre-emptive strike. In idle moments over the years, she had typed in Jamie Drew, of course she had, usually around the time she ran a speculative eye over notes in the Trinity College alumni magazine. She hadn't tried very hard though, and nothing had ever come of it. She'd assured herself it would be time enough to face the complications when Fin or when Jamie made the first move.

How long should she wait for Sanna to keep Jamie's second promise? Her sudden, if thus far invisible, appearance had already started denting their lives in a way that wouldn't be smoothed over without a bit of chipping around the edges. It was a shame this conjured up the image of Alina wielding an ice pick rather than a dainty nail file. How long to wait, how frank to be?

Only now were the divided loyalties dawning on her. She owed Fin, and she owed Jamie then, and Sanna now. It was a lot of compatibility to ask for.

7

The next evening, the curtains were open directly above her and she could see a silhouette at the window. Alina was tempted to throw a handful of stones up, but that was hardly the done thing in Edenfield. Instead, she crossed the gravel and banged, flat-palmed, on the door, like a police officer issued with a warrant. Then she let herself in with the spare Yale attached to her keyring and ran lightly up the stairs.

In the comfort of Charles, Elizabeth was watching *Coronation Street* on an obscenely large television, wall-mounted between the two front windows. Her chair was reclined and on the table beside her was a pile of books, a packet of Ginger Nuts and a hefty amber glass.

'Come on in, lovey.' She fumbled down the cushion for the remote control and the screen went blank. 'Feeling better today?'

'Don't stop your programme—'

'Och. Don't mind me. I'm practising for the old folks' home I'm bound to end up in. So?'

'I'm much better.' It was almost true. 'But let's not talk about it this evening. I'm relying on you to distract me. We can talk about plans for the guesthouse at Sonali Homestay. It's about time we decided on our flight dates. And...' Alina sat down at right-angles and nodded at what appeared to be a triple whisky. '…hadn't you better swap *that* for a cup of tea if you're aiming for acceptance in your genteel nursing home?'

'It's mostly ginger ale, Matron.' Elizabeth took a ladylike sip. 'Help yourself.'

Alina shook her head in mock exasperation. She pulled one foot onto her lap and rubbed at the tender heel. 'Ouch. Blister,' she explained.

'Root in the kitchen drawer for plasters,' Elizabeth offered. 'And join me in my unorthodox supper? We can get something proper later on, if you like.' Elizabeth tapped the half-eaten packet of biscuits. 'Such a treat. I was just deciding whether it was worth getting some butter to spread on them. That's what we did when I was a little girl. Or maybe it was on Digestives. Same principle.'

'I'll get the butter and the plasters.' Alina put both feet on the floor and flexed them. 'Alright if I get a glass of water, too?'

'Anything you like, lovey.'

She was just outside the door when Elizabeth called after her. 'Oh, Alina? You might want to get something stronger…'

Alina paused. Elizabeth was well aware she rarely touched alcohol. She poked her head back into the room. 'Any reason why?'

Elizabeth flapped her good hand, Ginger Nut crumbs spraying. 'I've got something to tell you. To ask you, rather. And before you interrogate me again, I'm fine. Everyone's fine. The house is fine. The world in general, is… well, if not fine, no madder than usual. I want to run something by you, that's all. I was going to mention it earlier but you took the wind out of my sails with Fin's news.'

'Oh-kay.' Alina crossed to the kitchen. *See, I knew there was something, knew it*, she told herself. Something or nothing, you'd never know with Elizabeth. She could want her passport photo counter-signed or an opinion on same-sex romance in her next novel or whether it was worth seeing if veganism suited her. All three, and random others besides, had been run by Alina. It was also how she'd come to live in one of Elizabeth's flats, and despite their delicate first encounter and generational difference, how they'd become friends and equals. Alina dealt with her blister, collected the butter dish and a knife, and opened and shut cupboards to locate a glass and fill it with water, all the while recalling Elizabeth's original 'I've got an empty flat. If you'd like it?'

It was, what, four years ago now? Mentally totting it up, Alina realised it was gone five when they'd met again. Curiosity had originally led her to buy one of Elizabeth Maxin's books and then she'd gone on ordering each new one as some sort of private, idiotic payback. Miriam, visiting Edinburgh, enjoyed reading them, and on a whim – that her grandmother would call God's Work – Alina booked tickets for the both of them to go to Elizabeth's latest launch. She'd intended to loiter at the door of Waterstones for a quick getaway in the unlikely event she was recognised out of context, but Alina hadn't counted on Miriam's enthusiasm for a signed copy and a two-minute exchange with the author. Inevitably that led to a sharing of 'my son in New Zealand' countered with 'my granddaughter in Bangladesh', and Alina was summoned from her hiding place behind Scottish fiction. What a small world, they'd all agreed, each playing their part. Elizabeth not bearing any visible grudge that Alina had singlehandedly ruined her son's life, thus sending him to lick his wounds in New Zealand. Alina hiding guilt big enough to send her hot-footing it to Bangladesh for months at a time. Miriam sensing something important afoot that could – should – be fixed.

And slowly, fixed it had been: with a flat, a home, a good friend. Leaving only one elephant-sized hole in the room that neither of them could – or pretended not to – see anymore.

Staring out of the window at the darkening garden below, Alina gave herself a shake.

It was time she was over all that nonsense, and anyway, tantrums *and* melodrama in one day were too much for anyone. She decided to make a mug of tea instead of the water and set about boiling the kettle. It wasn't as if Elizabeth took that view about the ruined life, and Alina had no evidence anyone else did. Well, maybe *he* did, him and his wife. But they were entitled. And hadn't Alina just been 'doing her job', the ugly phrase that hid a multitude of sins?

'I'm rich by most people's standards,' Elizabeth confided over coffee, a couple of lunch dates after the Waterstones launch. 'But for most of my life I wasn't, and now people I barely know are obsessed with telling me how best to spend my ill-gotten gains.'

'Going on a world cruise?' Alina suggested, smiling. 'Investing in Bitcoin?'

'Exactly. Or, mystifyingly, buying a football club – yes, really.' She shook her head. 'To shut them up, I bought a huge old house, got it converted into proper flats, and I rent them out to women who deserve a helping hand. Pay-as-you-can.' Elizabeth tipped a sachet of sugar into her cappuccino and stirred it, saying, 'Would you like one?'

'No, thanks. Not in coffee—'

'I'm not talking about sugar, lovey. I'm talking about a flat.' Elizabeth had laughed out loud at Alina's gaping reaction.

Alina came to, staring at a kettle that had boiled and switched itself off a good couple of minutes ago. Hurriedly, she poured water and dunked a peppermint teabag in it. Picking that up in one hand, the butter in the other, she went back through to the sitting room, clicking the kitchen light off with her chin along the way.

'Sorry, I was in another dream.' She pushed the door open and then closed it with her foot and unloaded herself onto the little side table. 'I was thinking about how I came to live here.'

'Interesting you should say that… I thought you might be running down the back stairs.' Elizabeth arched her eyebrows.

Alina laughed. 'No. Like I said, anything you want to talk about is a welcome break from the Jamie/Sanna dilemma.' *Fingers crossed.*

'I'm always here when you do want to talk about

it.' Elizabeth looked concerned. 'What with losing your grandparents, you must feel a bit... burdened? Unsupported?'

'I'm okay.' Alina leaned forward and took a couple of biscuits, waving away the offer of the butter Elizabeth was lavishly spreading. 'Like Fin said, I just need time to get my head around it.' She wondered if that was true. 'And I've been going over it all afternoon. So, what did you want to talk about?'

Elizabeth laid down her untouched Ginger Nut. 'Maybe now isn't the best time, but—'

But.

Alina's heart sank.

'Oh, don't look like that.' Elizabeth leaned over and patted Alina's knee. 'I meant to tell you straight away, I promised Claire I would, that's why I sent the text, but you arrived already on information overload. Then I hid behind this...' She held up the plastered wrist.

'I'm not following you.' Then Alina suddenly cottoned on. 'Oh. The text at the airport. It wasn't about your accident?'

'No.'

'Go on then. Hit me with it.' Not as if it could be any more surprising than Fin's broadcast. Alina was uneasy though: *Interesting you were thinking that...* Shit. She might just have an inkling where this was going and... not that, please, not that. The timing would be the worst, a cosmic joke.

Elizabeth's features flickered between pleasure and pain. 'Rory's coming home. For good.'

Of course he bloody well was. Crap. Crap, crap, crap. Alina's eyes inadvertently flickered to the hall and the photograph there that always bothered her. His – Rory's – photograph. He'd only been about twenty-three, long before she'd met him. Carefree. She put on her best poker face.

'It seems it's been in the pipeline for a while but, honestly, he didn't say. It was a shock to me too. But a pleasant one, of course.'

Alina turned to her dignitary's politely interested face.

'It kind of makes sense that he'll come and stay here.' Elizabeth looked directly at Alina, and snapped, 'Enough of the vegetarian-queen-touring-the-abattoir look. Tell me what you think.'

Alina grinned faintly and took a bite of biscuit, her brain in immediate overdrive. 'I'm glad for you he's coming home.' That, at least, was true. Hope flared. 'Maybe I'll be back in Bangladesh by then.' Takdir's invitation was clearly a blessing in disguise. Moving to Bhola offered a smooth exit from having to face full-on Rory or Sanna or any of her past misdemeanours.

Decision made.

Or, looking at Elizabeth's face, not. Hope faded.

'That would be very convenient, but…' Elizabeth spoke in a rush, falsely cheerful now, like a character she'd created. '…but when I say he's *coming* home, I mean, he's *already* home. Just. He's staying in a hotel for a night or two and I had nightmares of you running into each other at the airport. He knows you live here, Alina. And he knows there's more than a fair chance you'll bump into each other regularly. He says he's fine with that. The question is – are you? I know how you clashed over… well, we don't need to spell it out.'

Clashed was one way of putting it. 'Don't be silly. Of course, he must come here.' Well, what else could she say? It was time to dig deep and man-up or woman-up, whatever the idiot in-phrase was. 'Of course he must come here.' Alina repeated it much more forcefully. 'It's daft for him to be in a hotel. *Please* tell me that wasn't because of me?'

'Paid for by the company. A perk of the job, he says.'

Plausible, Alina thought. 'You must really have missed each other. I wonder why he took so long a contract.' The words were out before she could stop them; stupid thing to say. Alina was well aware why Rory had stayed in New Zealand so long, and Elizabeth probably thought she knew too. The thing was, Elizabeth didn't have the full story. Thank God she had the more palatable half. *Oh shit.* Alina had another even more sinking feeling.

'What about his wife… I mean, um, Laura? Is she coming with him?'

'Oh no, definitely not.' Elizabeth was breezy now. 'Didn't I tell you about that?' They both knew she hadn't; they'd barely discussed Rory since Alina moved in downstairs. 'Rory and Laura got divorced. They separated not long after… after you last met them.'

'You mean not long after I oh-so-helpfully vetoed their adoption assessment,' Alina interpreted wearily. 'What? If this isn't the time to be upfront, when is?'

'Alright, yes. Something that should make you feel vindicated, actually.' Elizabeth all but jabbed her finger at Alina. 'You were right, weren't you? Their marriage didn't even last two more years. They weren't right to adopt.'

'What if the not-adopting caused the break-up?'

'What if? What if.' Elizabeth took a deep slug of her drink. 'Look, lovey, if we're putting our cards on the table, I might as well admit something that misguided loyalty prevented me from saying back then. Laura and I never really saw eye to eye.'

'Oh?' Alina was surprised. 'But she lived here, didn't she, in one of the flats. That's how… how they met. You introduced them.'

'Inadvertently. But I forgot you knew all that. Yes. It all burned brightly for a while.' Elizabeth shook her head. 'Then we realised we had nothing in common except Rory and we both wanted different things for him, for *them*. Mothers-in-law traditionally never think anyone is good enough for their darling little angel-boys, do they?' Elizabeth's lips twitched. 'All marriages are mysteries anyway. Mine certainly was.'

That was a topic for another time. Alina concentrated on counting her blessings that in this potential mess, she didn't have to factor in the arrival of the glacial Laura; tropical Queensland would have been hard-pressed to thaw her out.

'It's all a shame for him. For Rory.' She had to say his name at some point, might as well get used to it. 'He's a good guy.'

'Of course he is. Look at his mother.'

And his mother was currently looking hopeful, Alina thought, smiling faintly. True enough, Elizabeth went on:

'Maybe it's time the two of you finally work this out. Get over what happened. It's been nearly five years, Alina. Five. Prison sentences are shorter.'

Maybe. Maybe not. 'You have a point.' Alina sighed. It was a stupidly long time, given the circumstances. 'You're not to stick us in your next book and manufacture a happy ending,' she threatened.

'Scout's honour – if you give it a go in real life?'

'I will try.' In the moment, Alina meant it. Whatever anyone said, though, there was no doubt in her mind she had thwarted Rory's dreams in all manner of ways and if he still wanted revenge there was plenty of ammunition. The way her world was currently spinning, Alina was an easy target. 'It will be fine,' she lied, mostly to convince herself. 'Fine.'

'I wish I'd told you sooner. Claire told me I should have,' Elizabeth fussed. 'I didn't want to make it into a big thing and have you deciding to live permanently in Bangladesh on foot of it. And I didn't expect to have to pile it on top of your own big news.'

'Fin's news,' Alina said automatically. 'It's fine, Elizabeth, really. Just one thing…'

'Hmm?'

'Next time I ask you to distract me? Ignore me. Ignore me big-time.'

8

Sunday morning.

Alina lay in bed, thanking the last vestiges of jetlag for an unexpectedly decent sleep and the lateness of her wakening. Having nothing specific for which to get up had been a guilty pleasure all her adult life. The weekend had been her Salvationist grandparents' busiest time: one day, a coffee morning, lunch for the homeless and hospital visiting, the next, worship meetings, prayer meetings, youth meetings, with probably a Sunday School or two thrown in. Even now, she was exhausted thinking about it; did their faith give them energy or their energy faith? She knew what her grandmother would have said to that. The divisional commander, at their joint memorial service, had uttered the phrase, *If ever the mantle of Catherine and William Booth had fallen, it had fallen on Miriam and Patrick Farrell*, and for Alina, it summed them up perfectly. She reckoned her grandparents would have been quietly proud of that too.

Right now, Alina vaguely wished she had faith in their God, or in Takdir's Allah, or in any deity that could take responsibility for, and guide her through, her current... challenges. Maybe that was it, she thought. Maybe she was being punished. For breaking the rules of two major world religions so gloriously and then sitting on the spiritual fence for so long. Elizabeth's bombshell left Sanna and Rory jostling for front-page news.

Last night, she'd managed to sit through *Coronation Street*, *Emmerdale* and *Eastenders*, finding them slightly less unrealistic than usual and letting her thoughts slide around Elizabeth's news about Rory, with Fin's about Jamie on a sort-of B-side reel. Alina wasn't sure she'd convinced Elizabeth she was okay, but she awarded herself bonus points for not running away. Instead, she'd tensed through every noise from the street, sure Rory was about to appear, and planning how she'd act if – *when* – he did. If it wasn't farcical, it would be funny.

Alina got up and pulled her dressing gown on quickly before her thoughts could start churning again. She drank her coffee leaning on the kitchen doorframe, looking up at the sky and shivering. It was a cold and crisp spring morning, one of those rare days without wind. The clouds were a soft white rather than their scurrying grey, as if they were being backlit by a sun trapped high above them. Alina stayed there just a few more minutes than was physically comfortable, pushing herself. This, according to her grandmother, was something she'd done since she was a child: that bit too hot, too cold, too thirsty, too hungry. It made the consequent comfort all the sweeter. Mizan had commented on the habit too, telling her she was crazy.

Thinking of Mizan, Alina reached for her phone, charging silently on the kitchen counter. Swiping across the screen, she discovered he'd beaten her to it. Six missed WhatsApp calls. Alina frowned. Sundays were quiet in both worlds, a regular day to talk, but she always took the initiative.

Alina, why don't you WhatsApp. Quickly, the first message said. He'd sent it again, twice more. Shit. Maybe, she thought – a little ray of sunshine immediately quashed – there *was* a crisis of immense proportions and she'd have to rush back quick smart. Maybe Mizan was about to provide a hat-trick of blasts from the past... No, no, no, she retracted hastily, bad joke. 'Didn't mean, it, didn't mean it,' she muttered, crossing her fingers. *Don't let it be Khalya.* No, it would just be something she'd forgotten to do before she left, and Mr Impatient couldn't wait.

But still. *Come on, Mizan.*

It was his turn not to answer. One tick appeared in the corner of her text, the second remained elusive. Waiting for his response – Mizan adored his phone; it wouldn't be long – Alina turned to the photo that sat on her bedside table, one of her favourites of Khalya. The little girl had been eight then, still young enough to swim in the pond with the boys. Her dress was wet-through, and her hair dripping in her triumphant eyes, as she held up a wriggling silver fish. *I need to update that picture*, Alina thought. 'And let's just hope it's not one of you in your wedding sari,' she muttered. *The way things were going— Stop.* Khalya was safe with Mizan and Takdir; Alina would trust them with her own life *and* the little girl's.

Seventy-two hours ago, yes, that's all it was, her chief preoccupation had been the idea of a full-time move over there. Now that had slipped so far under the radar it felt simple enough to resolve on the toss of a coin. She'd never really been a bolter – well, only that once – in fact, quite the opposite, as Fin's birth attested. But now? If she shoved her toothbrush and passport into her pocket and ran directly for the Bangla Hill Tracts, could she blame it on middle-age-addled hormones? It wouldn't come out of the blue to Elizabeth or to Fin. Since her extended visit during a virulent outbreak of measles – a killer disease – they'd known it was what Takdir wanted, and known it was a decision Alina would make only when her grandparents were gone. Tempting, so tempting.

'Shame yielding to temptation is a sin.' She heard her grandmother's voice.

'Shame having to wait three weeks for a new visa scuppers spontaneity,' Alina said aloud, grinning in spite of herself. 'Sorry, Granny.'

Her phone beeped and she snatched it up. *Five minutes*, Mizan's message said.

Skype, she mused, had turned out to be a beautiful but tricky thing. Connecting with a predominantly deaf community in a land that used sign language to communicate, relied heavily on seizing the moment to practise extravagant gestures and manic smiling. Mizan's English was excellent, *chiefly thanks to me*, Alina thought smugly, and some of the staff spoke it passably – just as well, since Alina's Bengali honestly teetered between being able to decently get by and (apparently, judging by the reactions to her continued efforts) hilarious – but these bi-weekly sessions were for the children. Mostly, they took turns to cavort in front of the camera, demonstrate their dancing – Khalya earnest in the front row – and howl out a raucous chorus of *We Shall Overcome*; in Sonali Homestay, where all the residents were hard of hearing on some level, deafness was barely an inconvenience, let alone a disability.

It was usually a tonic to get lost in their exuberance but, things being what they were, she couldn't help worrying another brick of her carefully constructed world was about to crumble – *Let Khalya be okay*, she thought again, knowing she was hyper-sensitive. *Let them* all *be okay*.

'*Salaam walekum*, Mizan. At last! Hi. Is everything okay? What's wrong?' She couldn't help babbling, as first their office, then his outline, flickered into view.

'Alina, *walekum es-salaam*. How are you? Everything is fine here.'

The line was remarkably clear for once and Mizan sounded very chipper. Alina calmed slightly; Bangladeshi men – in her biased experience – weren't subtle. They always had a touch of bronchial pneumonia rather than the common cold, dysentery not diarrhoea. If there was even half a serious problem, he'd have launched into it immediately. Even so—

'But what's wrong?' she repeated. 'I missed all your

calls. Are you all okay? Is it Khalya? What…' Looking at his mystified face, she petered out. 'Sorry. Sorry. I miss you.'

'Of course. As we do you. This is why we tried to call you early,' he explained. 'The committee picnic – it is today, now. You have forgotten. The children wanted to see you before they left for the river.'

Alina put her hand to her forehead. Of course. What was that about overreacting? 'I did forget,' she admitted. 'I hope they weren't too disappointed. Apologise for me, will you?' The annual picnic was a treat next to none: meticulously planned, looked forward to, then chewed over for the whole year.

'They will get over it.' Mizan grinned. 'They already have done. They could not climb on the trailer fast enough.' His voice changed slightly. 'I am glad they are gone. I can ask in private: have you decided to come and live with us forever?'

'Give me a chance.' Alina was half amused, half exasperated. 'It's been… busy here.' If he asked about Fin's birth father, she'd wing it; debating gender issues would be challenging enough face to face with Mizan, and if he mentioned Rory… well, he wouldn't. She'd made sure he'd never even heard Rory's name before.

'Well, when you have taken rest and visited with your friends and got used to the cold…' Alina held in a hysterical giggle. *If only.* '…you must think very clearly. Takdir Sir is keen for your decision. Me, I don't mind one way or the other.' He winked at her, then became more serious. 'Your friend, Mrs Elizabeth, she is happy with the plans for our guesthouse, yes?' Shit. Another thing she hadn't done yet. 'I would like to confirm with the committee today. They are very interested to hear from our most generous donor.' Mizan grinned. 'Also, I would like to shame them into offering money themselves. They are rich men.'

'Elizabeth is delighted with the plans.' Alina gave him a slightly manic smile and held her crossed fingers away from the camera. 'You can tell the committee she'll be coming over with me for the whole month of September.' She crossed her toes, too, and tightened her pelvic floor muscles for extra luck. 'She could cut a ribbon and lay the first brick. The children would love it.' So would the committee and every dignitary in the district. Everyone in Bhola loved a ceremony.

'Yes. We could put up a stone with the date, a... how do you say it?'

'A plaque.'

'Yes. This is excellent news for the committee.'

She needed to talk to Elizabeth about this today, Alina told herself. She couldn't foresee any problems, but still. 'Okay, well, I'll say goodbye—'

Mizan cut her off. 'There is one more thing, more serious, to say to you.'

'Go on...' She braced herself.

'I am in control, but I wanted to give you some information. It is Khalya. Or really, I mean it is her mother. Khalya is a good girl. She is always a good girl. Only today, for the picnic—'

'Mizan?'

'Okay, okay. Alina, you must please remain calm, okay, I am in control—'

'Mizan!'

'Her mother has come to see me formally. She has found a husband for Khalya.'

'She has *what?*' Alina sat back heavily. 'I don't believe I'm hearing this.' She forbade herself to shout. Mizan and she, in fact the whole committee and board of trustees, were at one with the charity's position on child marriage. 'But you spoke to her, Takdir spoke to her.'

'Her mother says it is a good match, how not every man will take a deaf girl, and he can offer a lot of money. She says this. I say no.' Mizan sounded supremely calm.

Alina watched him lounging in his office, tapping his unlit cigarette on the desk.

'And?'

'We shout at each other for many long minutes. I bring

in Khalya – lucky it is the weekend so she is home – and I ask her.'

'Tell me she said no.'

'Of course she says no. Khalya is a clever girl. She will go to the deaf school in Dhaka next year. This, she wants. She is only going to get married – to a rich and handsome man, she says – when she is more than twenty and a teacher.'

'So?' Alina's pulse began to return to normal. The idea in Khalya's mother's head wasn't going away – and, divide and rule, the woman would make sure it took root in the minds of the mothers of other girls too. On the other hand... Alina paused. She knew Mizan well. Very well. She knew he loved telling a good story and showing off his own mastery of a situation. It wasn't a crisis. Yet.

'So, I send Khalya back to her playing. And I send her mother home to Dhaka, with many fishes from our pond and a tablecloth from our tailoring room.'

A bribe. What else? The 'gifts' would bring a good price at the ghat-side market. 'You think it was a bluff? She just wanted money?'

'Yes. And no. It will happen again. It has happened before. It is our culture. But Khalya is safe for now.' He paused. 'I reminded the mother that Mr Takdir is the chief of all of us and that he would not like to hear this plan.'

A bribe and a threat. Great. Alina sighed. 'And did you tell Takdir?'

Mizan had done exactly that, he said with complacency, and Takdir Sir would undertake a stern word with the mother. It was less ominous than it sounded; Alina's great uncle was a kind and mild-mannered man. If his authority came from his high-profile Civil Service career and his charitable foundation, it also helped that Khalya's mother was his household cook and had been since before Khalya was born. Takdir treated his employees, including the housemaids and drivers, very well, compensating, Alina thought privately, for his wife's less understanding nature – a wife who, nevertheless, was uniquely attached to Khalya's mother. Another long story. Alina resolved to phone Takdir directly later on.

'We'll need to do something practical.' She was thinking on her feet. 'Maybe Khalya can go to the deaf school in Dhaka this year? I know she's young but she's doing well in Barisal, isn't she? We could still spare Suna to chaperone her, and she'd be closer to Takdir's house. Mizan? What do you think?'

'Alina, we will deal with it. But you must not worry,' Mizan ordered. 'Do you hear? Do you trust me? Do you?'

There was a pause, in which they both heard things, things from the past that bound them together and that neither of them would say out loud. 'Yes, Mizan. I hear you and I do trust you.'

'Good,' he said. 'We all love Khalya and our other children. We will fight for them always. And Khalya is herself a zealous ambassador.'

Alina grinned. Otherwise, it appeared, life in Sonali Homestay was going 'supremely' well, mostly due, apparently, to the great skills of Mizan himself. Alina grinned again; some of Mizan's hyperbole was his pleasure in his English, some of it only a partially self-deprecating belief in himself. He had always been that way. She endorsed his spirit wholeheartedly. She just hoped that it never came literally to fisticuffs. She wasn't ever sure she could trust Mizan to keep calm in a confrontation that challenged his sense of male pride.

As soon as he hung up, Alina redialled, this time her Uncle Takdir. If ever there was a voice of reason in the chaos of Bangladesh, it was he. She missed her grandparents just a bit less because of Takdir and Elizabeth equally. It had been that way with her great uncle ever since he'd got in touch with her all those years ago. Theirs was a straightforward relationship borne of complexities beyond them both. *Same could be said of Elizabeth*, she mused.

Alina tapped her foot on the floor and waited for her great uncle to answer his phone.

When he did, he was at great pains to reassure her.

'Anxiety does not become you, my dear.' She could hear his smile across the miles. 'And Mizan should know better than to cause you drama. Yes, it is a problem with Khalya, but also a problem we have faced with our other young women. This is no different.'

Except it was *Khalya*, and that made all the difference. They both knew that, but neither wanted to play favourites. Circumstances also meant Alina couldn't easily voice what else was troubling her, but no matter; Takdir was ahead of her there, too.

'I have a keen eye on the situation,' Takdir went on. 'My wife – well, let us say her close relationship with Khalya's mother may not always be the asset you and I would hope for. I will speak honestly with both parties.'

'Thank you... I know it's hard.' Husna, Alina's great aunt, remained an enigma. Alina suspected the older woman did not like or trust her, still seeing her as an interloper, a cuckoo in the family's very feathered nest, even after so many visits. 'Oh, I wish I hadn't had to leave. I wish I was still there.' She couldn't help the outburst, slightly ashamed it was about much more than Khalya.

'Then come home, Alina.' Takdir's tone was measured. 'You know I wish this but still I suggest caution. My dear, think carefully. All I wish is that you come home for the best reasons, not for fear or worry.'

Or the sheer joy of running away. 'I am thinking about it,' was all she said. 'And I know if you need me specially, you'll tell me. Fin and Kirsten's baby is due in a couple of months and,' Alina tried to insert an upbeat note into her chatter, 'it seems that Fin's found his birth father, so I'm keeping busy with them while I'm thinking. I *will* have an answer one way or the other on the first of September, when I bring Elizabeth out to start building the guesthouse.'

'That I look forward to. We most certainly live in interesting times,' Takdir said. 'Never forget, Alina: things do not happen to us. We, ourselves, are the makers of the happenings. You know that.' For sure she did, but not in the way he meant. Alina's thoughts flew to 1994, to Jamie, to Fin, then to more recent times, and Rory. 'Help is always here, my dear, if you ask for it.'

She considered his words as she hung up. Alina knew that Takdir meant divine help, but there was something special about Takdir himself, a courtesy and empathy that soothed and encouraged.

It was Takdir alone who had paved her rocky foreign road to Bangladesh right from her very first step.

9

Dhaka 2004

A biblical rock concert. That's how Alina described Dhaka
airport to Miriam and Patrick after her very first visit. A mosh
pit of hot male bodies struggling to surge the barrier at the
arrivals gate, chanting, shouting, *grasping* to claim their loved
ones. The city itself assaulted her like a physical punch: the
noise, the smell, the heat – it was a heaving, clammy pressure-
cooker. She might look the part, but she felt less Bangladeshi
than she ever had in Belfast or Dublin or Edinburgh.

'Neither fish nor fowl, that's me,' she said to her Great
Uncle Takdir as he whisked her through the lines of rickshaws
and tuk-tuks into an air-conditioned, chauffeur-driven car,
thus applying a bonus layer of monied difference to her
considerable emotional baggage.

'You're family,' he replied simply.

But she wasn't, not yet. Shell-shocked and searching, she
was a stranger. And all this was strange.

Takdir's apartment block was in the well-off district of
Gulshan-1, at the end of a side road leading to a large, greenish
and stagnant pool of water – river? Lake? Flood? A security
guard waved them into an underground car park that petered
out into a makeshift stable on one side and adjoined a full
basketball court on the other.

'There they are fattening cows for the Eid celebrations.'

Her great uncle saw her confusion. 'And the other side is the sports ground of the American embassy.'

Inside the third-floor apartment the windows were barred behind tightly closed curtains, a whirring ceiling fan cooling the main room. Carved ornate furniture sweated on the tiled floors, the sofas were covered in plastic wrapping and the wide, undressed beds were rock hard. Afterwards, all Alina could really remember of that day was drinking endless cups of sweet and milky tea with the cacophony of visitors – cousins, neighbours, the local police superintendent and his curious family – all come to see Takdir Sir's foreign great niece and wish her well.

When the last of them melted away, Takdir invited Alina to sit at a long dining room table, groaning under food left by invisible hands, and to eat.

'Chicken, fish, rice, vegetables, roti...' He served her a spoonful of each in turn, and then when she didn't immediately start eating, pointed to a covered plate on the dresser. 'They have made you sandwiches, too, if you prefer. Cucumber. Chicken. Sliced cheese.'

'No – no, this is delicious,' Alina said hurriedly, because it was – she'd just been waiting for an army of other people to join them. She wanted to ask about her great aunt, Husna, conspicuous by her absence, except Alina wasn't sure the woman *was* absent; she could have been introduced already and overlooked in the throng. She settled on, 'Is Aunt Husna eating with us?'

Takdir finished his mouthful and broke a disc of bread in half before he answered. 'My wife is resting at this hour. She's not a strong woman. Tomorrow is another day.'

With no idea what to make of that, Alina simply nodded. And ate. 'That's one thing I did learn quickly,' she told her grandparents later on. 'If in doubt, eat. Everyone wanted to feed me and the more I ate the more they liked it.'

In the evening uncle and niece sat on the roof terrace, a tiled expanse of dust and dripping plants, watered in a lacklustre way by a little boy gardener. Takdir was kindness itself, a gentleman in the true sense of the word.

'I must make amends,' he said, and when she opened her mouth to contradict him, he held up his hand. 'Hear me out, my dear. I have written this speech many times in my mind, but it takes some while to express myself well in English.'

Alina sipped her lassi – steeling herself, faintly ashamed, not to question the purity of the water or the refrigeration of the yoghurt – and listened. It was odd hearing him refer to her forgotten father and unknown grandfather as real, live people who had sat right where she rested now. Takdir gazed over the rooftops, over the grainy smog-filled Dhaka skyline, dark from a power cut, before he spoke again.

'My brother, your grandfather,' he said, 'was hot-headed and proud. He had such grand plans for himself, and then for his only son. But he was a greedy man, made lazy by being the oldest child of five in a wealthy family – waited on, treated as a king. Big ideas need hard work and there he failed. And so he turned to Nozmul. But Nozmul had his own path to follow.' Takdir turned to smile at Alina. 'Nozmul was more like me: honest, studious, and interested in administering the family trust for maximum good rather than for himself. Everyone said it.'

Alina held her breath and then let it out, as if she could breathe life into the laughing young man whose black and white photo she held on her knee. For a second, he felt close by.

'There was much rejoicing when your father was accepted to study medicine in London,' Takdir went on. 'In the nineteen-seventies it was almost unheard of for a rural boy to get a scholarship and a visa for the UK. There was even a street party, a festival in his honour. Your grandfather presided over events like a king. His son, a doctor! In five years, Nozmul would come home to a good job in the city, his pick of wives…'

'But he married an Irish nurse and never came back,' Alina finished softly.

'It was like a Bollywood story of love and tragedy.' Takdir sighed. 'Your grandfather was horrified when he learned of Nozmul's intention to marry your mother. He condemned their differences in religion, culture, education. It shames me still to say my oldest brother was a racist and bigoted man who felt dishonoured. Who knows if or when he would have relinquished his disownment.'

The stark truth was that an IRA bomb in London at the height of the Troubles had killed Nozmul and Helen. This, Alina's Bangladeshi grandfather had announced to the world, was *qisas*, divine retribution.

'You don't have to tell me all of this, Uncle Takdir.' She put a tentative hand on his shoulder, and he clasped it with one of his own.

'Yes, I do, my dear. For us to move forward, I need to be absolved of the sins of my brother.' *No, you don't*, Alina bit back, only because it clearly mattered to him so much. Painfully, Takdir spoke of his brother touting himself publicly as a devout Muslim who piously prayed for his son's soul. At home he railed and roared and wept over her father's old school reports and the faded sepia photograph of his coming out parade at Cadet Class.

'And he did it all under a veil of alcohol. My brother, your grandfather, died after an undeserved long life, a drunken bully, abusive to his family and his staff.' Tears clouded Takdir's eyes. 'It was cirrhosis of the liver relabelled cancer – a cover-up because he had the family standing to do so. I am ashamed.'

A long silence was interrupted only by the evening muezzin, the hum of traffic and whine of mosquitoes. Alina knew Takdir was asking for her forgiveness, but she didn't feel it was hers to give. Her grandfather had had an attitude, uncalled for and reprehensible, but all too common, probably even more so back then. He hadn't killed her mum and dad, but it seemed like he ended up killing himself. None of it was personal to her.

She stumbled over saying as much to Takdir, afraid of hurting him but wanting to match his honesty. 'It's more a Rabindranath Tagore tale than a Bollywood movie,' she chanced, to lighten the mood. 'Families for good and evil but less of the music and happy-ever-after finale.'

'You've read our national poet?' It *did* cheer him up. 'In our family place on Bhola Island we kept all of Nozmul's books and study aids. His copies of Tagore are there. They are old and worthless but priceless as a connection between father and daughter.'

'I'd love them—'

A dark movement in the corner of her eye distracted her. Two figures – women – were hovering in the shadow of the stairwell, one with glasses and a severe hair braid muttered behind her orna to a slight, much darker-skinned woman. Both were glowering at Alina. Takdir saw them too, said something in a quick, heated exchange, and they faded further back. Her uncle didn't explain or apologise, and Alina didn't ask. She suddenly felt stupid with jetlag, but she would lay bets she'd caught a fleeting glimpse of a very suspicious and unwelcoming Great Aunt Husna.

Takdir intercepted Alina's stifled yawn and stood up. 'Remember, my dear,' were his parting words as they said goodnight, 'you do not need to have a Bangla past to have a Bangla future.'

10

Alina rolled her shoulders backwards and grimaced, contorting her facial muscles in an effort to relax them. She had an awful habit of tensing up when she was talking. Scrolling through her computer files she located the most up-to-date electronic version of the plans for Sonali Homestay's proposed guesthouse – Elizabeth's baby – and forwarded them to her with a note, a) promising to bring the 'real' ones round sooner rather than later – Elizabeth liked pen and ink; and b) paraphrasing the words Alina had already put in her friend's mouth when speaking to Mizan. She wasn't unduly bothered about having done that: Elizabeth wanted to fund the bulk of the ambitious project, but deciding exactly how best her money was used she delegated to the experts. Elizabeth's only stipulation, at first something of a joke, but now within plain sight, was that she'd like to visit Sonali Homestay herself. Mizan and the committee were charmed with the suggestion; Alina still wasn't sure if this was the novelty of value of a visitor of Elizabeth's age and (minor) celebrity, or if they wanted to reassure themselves that the fabled 'wise old lady donor' wasn't simply a figment of Alina's imagination.

Just sending this now so I don't forget, she wrote in her email, *as long as you're still happy in principle your money is being used appropriately, we have until September to talk about it all.*

Alina clicked on the attachment before she pressed 'send' and spent a few happy minutes distracted by the trustees' vision. The proposed guesthouse – called a rest-house locally – had been on the charity's something-for-the-future wishlist for years. Its purpose was two-fold: accommodation for visitors and a place of training, work, and refuge. Girls throughout the district remained at risk of child marriage, forced marriage and, if they weren't amenable – sometimes even if they were – abuse and, on occasion, acid attacks. It wasn't just Khalya, Alina reminded herself now, though she admitted it was Khalya she had in mind when she and Mizan had needed the impetus to push the proposal. Elizabeth had been captivated from the start. She was, she confided to a surprised Alina, the patron of a women's refuge in Midlothian, and it was something she felt very personally about. She hadn't elaborated then or since; she'd simply written a cheque big enough to get the basic house in Bangladesh built, and told Alina to refuse it at her peril.

'I've taken financial advice,' she'd said, 'and there is no conflict of interests. I am not a dotty old woman. Anyway, it's my money and I'll do what I like with it. Please let me. There were years when I never dreamed I could be so helpful.'

Helpful was the understatement of the year, Alina thought as she sent Elizabeth the email. The foundation stone would be laid in September and this time next year, the guesthouse doors would be open. Try as she might, though, Alina couldn't summon her usual little thrill of excitement. *Rory will probably think I'm a do-gooding gold-digger who coerced his mother into it*, she thought gloomily. Maybe that's why he'd come home now, to row and kick her out of the flat so he could move in. Alina groaned and put her head in her hands. Utter nonsense. Rory was returning because his contract was up. End of. She had to stop getting in a sweat over someone she'd known for a few months five years ago.

There should be a time limit on holding grudges, candles and what-ifs, she decided, and half a decade (*Not to mention a quarter of a century*, a voice niggled in her ear) was way too long. Like Elizabeth had implied last night, Alina needed to get a little perspective.

Her usual recourse was to lists – Alina had a list for everything – but that only worked for practical matters, not emotional ones. She had to find another way to get her full-to-exploding brain straight. She recalled a psychology experiment of her Trinity days: the class being asked to describe the insides of their heads. Others had struggled to produce messy mind maps, spider diagrams and philosophical excuses. Not so for Alina. Her thoughts were brown paper packages tied up with string, neatly shelved in the appropriate pigeon-hole. Boxes that could be taken out and examined, checked approvingly, and put tidily away. Her life, she knew, validated rather than disturbed the arrangement.

Until now.

The string around Fin and Jamie's boxes was unravelling and the oblong parcels nudged off the shelf by the one labelled Sanna. Rory's was wobbling dangerously. And by default Mizan's, Khalya at heart, was in jeopardy. Alina could feel them all about to rain down on her and she didn't know which to lean out and catch first.

She needed another pair of capable hands, but the ones she wanted were gone. 'Oh, Granny,' Alina said aloud. 'What should I do? What would you do? Except not be in this mess in the first place.' To the forefront of her mind came a memory of Miriam, sitting in her office, quietly planning her day, only to be accosted by a triumvirate of despair: the junior-band leader unaccountably in floods of tears in the hall; a GP's request to administer to a lonely rough sleeper; a malfunction in the kitchen ovens meaning thirty vulnerable pensioners were at risk of missing their hot dinner.

Alina had looked up from her maths homework and asked, 'How do you choose who to help first?'

Miriam had put her pen down and considered the question seriously. 'Officially, you fill in a thing called a risk assessment.' Anyone else, Alina thought now, would have rolled their eyes at that point. 'Now, none of these problems are life or death, are they? So, I'll start with the nearest and take them one at a time with my full attention. With Lesley out there.' She looked over her glasses and indicated the weeping woman outside. 'The important thing, Alina, is to start somewhere, and to give it your full attention. Then move on.'

Sage advice, if easier said than done. Alina imagined herself spreading all her current cards out in front of her, as if she could shuffle them and play the game properly. After five minutes, she squared her shoulders – literally – and put Khalya and Mizan in a holding pattern beside Rory and faced the conundrum of Jamie, Sanna and Fin.

The ringing doorbell made her jump. Two staccato bursts generally indicated an impatient delivery driver who was really hoping to dump and run, but she wasn't expecting anything, and unlike in Bhola, nobody in Edinburgh called without arranging it first. Half the time visitors couldn't find 36B, anyway, and ended up with Morag and a flea in their ear. Pushing her chair back, she automatically flicked a glance at the video entry phone Elizabeth had installed 'just in case' – and it came into its own.

Two things happened. Alina froze, simultaneously remembering the addendum to Miriam's advice. 'Mind you,' she'd added, as they both watched the main door open and two grim-looking policemen appear, 'sometimes the problem will choose you and scupper any best-laid plans.'

The buzzer went again, an angry wasp, and because she didn't know what to do, she did nothing. Alina stood motionless in her kitchen watching Elizabeth's son, Rory – the man she dramatically considered her nemesis – standing on her front doorstep. *He looks furious*, she thought, *or very, very cold.* Unless the bird's-eye-view camera made everyone look out of sorts. He didn't ring again. He shrugged his hands into his coat pockets and turned away down the path, and Alina watched him disappear round the corner.

She sagged against the wall, relieved and ashamed in equal measure. She had to face him sometime but not, she looked down, on the backfoot in a tatty dressing gown and bare feet, with an unmade bed behind her. Why hadn't Elizabeth warned her he was coming? Girl code and all that. But she couldn't, could she? Elizabeth was piggy-in-the-middle. Right. Well, if he'd tried once, he'd try again, and this time she'd be more ready to receive him than a nineteen-fifties housewife.

With another quick glance at the video phone, Alina grabbed some clothes and shot into the bathroom – deriding herself for locking the door. What? Did she think he'd filch Elizabeth's spare key and scope out her flat before making himself at home? It was in the shower that another jigsaw piece clicked into place: it was Rory she'd seen at the pedestrian crossing on Morningside Road. She'd had Jamie in a fuzzy mind that was playing jetlagged tricks, but the figure in the silver car was Rory… no, she couldn't be sure of it, but it made a certain sense. She was pummelling her hair dry when she heard her mobile ringing and cursed that she'd left it in the kitchen. What if he was calling from the doorstep, a double whammy?

'What're you going to do, hide in the bathroom 'til nightfall?' Alina asked her tousled reflection. 'Face the music, wimp.' She took her time drying off, dressing and combing her hair with her fingers – the only tool to hand – before tip-toeing to rescue her phone and, with a sliver of déjà vu, checking the call log.

Fin. 'Just passing,' his voicemail said. 'I've got to pick Kirsten up later from the city centre and thought I'd drop in if you're home. No worries if not.'

I'm home, she texted back quickly. It was the adult thing to do, putting paid to going pointlessly out to avoid Rory. Less adult was obsessively checking the entry camera as she dried her hair – the cord pulled to its extreme – and put on some lipstick and mascara. Fin wouldn't care about her appearance and neither, she supposed, would Rory, but she wasn't going to be outdone. As well as looking furious and cold, he'd looked good. Tanned and well-dressed. Not like a man who had been brooding over his life choices for five years. In fact, he'd looked the same this morning as at that last awful meeting. Their head-to-head, the session Laura was never going to attend.

Exactly the same, she thought. *Right down to that grim determination on his face as we shook hands and he walked away from me.*

11

Edinburgh 2014

There were no harsh words, but the tension was palpable. Neither of them sat down. They stood by the window looking down into the bleak Midlothian car park. Despite the prevalence of empty spaces – it was mid-afternoon on a Friday, only the unlucky duty social worker and one bored student still roamed the offices – Rory's car was parked as far away from the building as possible; a quick getaway, Alina guessed.

She'd faced her fair share of confrontation. Social workers always had, always would. Anger was manageable. Being sworn at, spat at, and on one occasion, slapped, was generally a gut reaction, forgivable. Disappointment was harder to bear. Adoption, frequently seen as the softer end of the job, was still an emotive business – people cared very strongly, and rightly so; Alina did herself – in which the outcomes could be as disappointing as they were joyous.

This was something else though. Rory was hurt. He was *hurting*. And, professional or not, so was Alina. She was also quaking in her metaphorical boots as they stood apart, not speaking. The meeting room felt far too small to contain the atmosphere between them.

She wished he'd brought Laura with him. It was easy to dislike Laura, blame her for all this. Cold... no, dig deep and she was *glacial*, Laura, outwardly perfect in every way, except, it finally transpired, in the ones that counted. Alina's then-team leader had been there when Alina had quietly explained to Rory and Laura in detail why she felt unable to recommend them to the Adoption Panel. Actually, she explained to Laura; she could barely look Rory in the eye, whereas Laura had stared at Alina. She must have blinked, *must* have sometime in that excruciating half an hour, but even now Alina couldn't recall it. Her stare was without question, without menace, without, apparently, interest. Alina, usually not averse to prolonged silence, was goaded into saying far more than she had set out to say; her team leader finally jumped in to wind things up. *She* did an official summing-up, talked about paperwork and appeals, which Laura had waved away, rising stiffly to say only: 'There are other ways to make a life,' and leaving the room without waiting for the ashen-faced Rory. *There are other ways to make a life.* Statement, threat, promise? The words preyed on Alina's mind.

She didn't expect to see either of them again, and alarm bells rang when Rory had written to her directly to ask for one more meeting: *The assessment and its outcome threw up issues I'd never considered,* his letter said. *I'm not sure my voice was heard. I'd like to rectify that and move on without unfinished business.* She'd dithered. The department had dithered. Ultimately, though, it was a reasonable request, rationally put. A client had the right to a voice.

And that's how they'd ended up in this anonymous little room that stank of despair, on an ironic Friday thirteenth. Earlier in the day Alina's team leader had gone home sick, and by rights she should have postponed. She was tempted to see him alone – whatever about Laura, Rory was no threat – but given the formal warning not to do exactly that, Alina asked the duty social worker's student to sit in. The girl perched by the door with an iPad, ostensibly catching up on her notes but more likely watching YouTube with subtitles.

Taking charge, Alina cleared her throat, starting with – to

her – his most pointed remark. 'You said your voice wasn't heard,' she said. 'I think… I *hope* you know that was never my intention.'

Rory nodded slowly. 'I realise now it's more that I can't have what I want. I'm not even sure I know what I want anymore,' he added with an attempt at a smile. Before Alina could respond – if she had any response to give – he went on, 'Anyway. I want to thank you, Alina, for your commitment and your honesty. I appreciate all your time. We gave you a lot of challenges.'

The words were genuine, if stiff, and not what she'd expected. 'I'm sorry it didn't work out. I really wish things were different,' was all she could say.

'I apologise too for Laura's behaviour—'

'No need.' Alina could easily brush that aside. 'Feelings are hurt. Tempers fray. You're not responsible.'

'Well, I feel it.'

Alina had no more pithy comments in her repertoire, so she said nothing. Rory didn't either and the silence went on so long that even the social work student momentarily took her eyes off her screen.

'I expected it,' Rory said suddenly. 'You'd already told us as much – and even if you hadn't, it was becoming more and more obvious we'd never be approved as adopters. It was that final session, hearing all our failings read aloud like that. Do you know what? I'm glad we avoided the Adoption Panel.' He folded his arms across his chest, a gesture of personal comfort rather than antagonism. *Literally holding himself together*, Alina thought. She had a fleeting urge to gather him up in her arms and give him the hug he craved. Damn and blast the *boundaries* to hell. Of course, she resisted.

It took all her reserves not to blurt out – truthfully – how all her professional misgivings were about Laura. He was maintaining a united front, sort of, but Rory already knew it.

'I have to be sure you really want the warts and all of a child,' she'd said to Laura one day, meaning *I'm fairly sure you don't.* Laura's textbook reply hadn't been reassuring. Rory, on the other hand, had dad material written all over him. But it didn't work like that, it was never that black and white, and the couple had come as a package.

'I wish the exit interview hadn't come across like that.' Alina traced a hairline crack in the glass as she spoke, almost a perfect circle, as if someone had thrown a well-targeted stone. Maybe they had. She tried to think of something else, something positive, to add, but all the stock phrases were trite, if not downright insulting. 'Is there anything else I can say now?' she asked instead. 'Anything you want to go over? Anything you want to say to me?'

Rory was watching her finger on the window. She had the strange feeling he wanted to reach out and grab it, still her movement. Self-consciously, she made a fist and put her hands down by her sides.

'No,' he said. 'Nothing. I wanted to say my piece rationally. This is me being rational. You know how I deal with conflict just like you know everything else.'

Ouch. There was no malice in the words, just resignation, but it stung.

'Rory—'

'Don't, please, Alina. It's too late now. And…' He looked directly at her. 'I haven't finished.' He sighed, from his boots it seemed. 'Look, I wanted to see you again. *You.* Not the frigging Adoption Panel. I didn't want to leave it as it was. As if there was bad feeling.' He held up his hand. 'We got on well, you and I, and that makes this bloody mess all the harder. No, please don't say anything. There's nothing more to say.'

And she knew there wasn't.

'What will you do now?' she asked instead.

'Oh, you know. Pick myself up, dust myself down, and start all over again.' He shrugged, trying, probably, to introduce some levity. 'After all, I'm the optimistic one, aren't I?'

Another dig? She didn't know. He'd already started crossing the room towards the door, causing the student to swipe smoothly at her screen and practise her professional smile. Then he hesitated and came back to Alina, holding out his hand across a long divide. She'd taken it, felt his firm, warm grasp.

'Good luck, Alina,' he said. 'For what it's worth, I wish it could have been different.'

'Good luck, Rory. And... me, too.' She tightened her grip on his fingers, for just a second, knowing they wouldn't see each other again. She wracked her brains for something useful, hopeful, to say. It didn't come. He was at the door when she called him back. 'Rory?'

'Yes?' He waited.

But Alina breathed out and tried a smile. What could she possibly say to a man whose life she had ruined. Social workers didn't just take children away, sometimes they took away the dream too. 'Nothing,' she said. 'Just, goodbye.' She stood there, hearing his footsteps disappear down the hall, an outside door bang, a car engine. When she did speak it was an undertone, into the ether. 'You'll make a great dad, Rory.'

The social work student followed Rory's progress, too. Then she turned back to Alina and offered her professional opinion. 'Well, that was freakin' weird,' she announced.

12

'I've got cold feet.' Fin hunched inside his coat like a teenager.

At first, Alina wasn't sure if he meant it literally. The afternoon had grown chill, more autumn than spring, and with a threatening spit of rain in the air. She shivered in sympathy and opened the front door wide.

'Which one?' She said it lightly, no big deal, and it worked. The agitated look in his eyes made space for the quizzical.

'The baby, your birth father, the weather, or none of the above?' Alina elaborated. She watched Fin relax slightly.

'I knew you'd be the best person to talk to,' he said, adding with a sheepish grin, 'and I was practically at the end of the road. Have I interrupted your day?'

'Don't be daft. You're welcome anytime. Let's go and sit down in the comfy seats.' Alina indicated the sitting room and aimed his jacket haphazardly at the coat stand. She flicked a switch and the cosy glow of the mock coals in the gas fire looked satisfyingly real.

'I had to take Kirsten to the hospital last night,' he said. 'Oh, don't worry. It was nothing. Wind, probably, or NFP – nervous first parents. The midwife didn't even pretend to write anything clinical in the file.'

'Is Kirsten alright now?' she asked. 'I mean it's Sunday, you're usually both hard at it. I got a fright.'

'She's fine.' Fin shook his head. 'More than fine. I've got cadets covering for me, and she's officially on maternity leave. Today her sisters have taken her on a mother-to-be spa day at the Sheraton on Lothian Road. It was that or a baby shower.'

Alina laughed. 'Good for her.'

'Yeah.' Fin stretched out his legs and inspected his trainers.

It didn't happen often because very little fazed the calm and grounded Fin. He'd always been that way, but Alina wanted to gather him in her arms and give him the type of hug suited to a six-year-old who had just been somehow cheated by the big bad world. No, she amended, he looked older than that, uncertain. The way he had as a teenager, when they'd met in the Botanics and he'd first broached the subject of finding Jamie.

It looked like they'd come full circle. That gave her an idea.

'So. It's the Jamie/Sanna thing, then?' Alina gave a far larger sigh than necessary. 'Thank *goodness* for that.'

'What?' Fin's eyes flew up to hers. 'What do you mean, Ali?'

'Exactly what I say.' Alina held Fin's gaze. 'No, I'm not humouring you. I had a bit of a strop yesterday. Seriously.' Fin's eyes widened and Alina laughed as she settled on an approximation of the truth. 'I was cursing the day you found Jamie. Sick of being polite and politically correct and agreeing it's a *good thing*.'

'You? You thought that?' Fin looked incredulous, and sat up straighter, his faux apathy gone.

'Yes.' Alina said it as emphatically as if she was undergoing a lie-detector test. 'And you know why it's all so stupid?'

Fin shook his head.

'Because Jamie was the least politically correct person I've ever known.' Alina glared – at the world, the past, whatever, but not Fin. 'In fact, the two of us made a career of it.' Before Fin could respond she made up her mind. 'I've an idea,' she said. 'You came in the car, didn't you? Good. We're going out.' Better than lounging around, dreading another knock at the door. She'd only drink too much coffee, soften it with biscuits and subsequently feel queasy all day.

Rory, Mizan in Bangladesh, the lot of them, were pushed out of her mind – like one of those old-fashioned weathervanes where the figures came out to show rain or shine – and Fin and Jamie came out. Alina was on a mission. Fin obviously recognised it because he simply grabbed the coat she threw back at him before picking up her bag and shrugging on her own, and followed in her wake. Three minutes later they were in the car that was, miraculously, only a few parking meters away, and the engine was running.

When Fin didn't pull away, Alina twisted her head around to look through the back window. 'It's all clear. Go.'

'Er, fine. Ali?'

'Yes?' He looked slightly nervous, Alina thought.

'I need to know where we're going to.'

'Oh. Where do you think we're going?' she boomed, and the twitch of his lips suggested she sounded like one of his Sunday School teachers. She moderated her tone. 'To the Finally Tree, of course.'

Fin's face cleared. 'Where else?'

They were more or less silent in the car, parking and walking through the Botanic Gardens, searching for the secret place they'd so long ago made their own. Alina, mentally retracing that first journey like an old-fashioned video film on fast forward, was sure Fin was doing the same. She wondered how their versions would compare. Ever grateful for her memories, she hoped Fin's were as rose-coloured as her own.

'Do you remember—?' and 'I was just remembering—' emerged from their mouths at the same time, and they smiled and said no more, until:

'There it is,' Fin said. 'Through there.'

The Finally Tree had taken root when Fin turned eleven. It was the first of their one, then two, then three meetings a year – regular as the seasons, solid as the earth from which the magnificent gardens grew – in the Edinburgh Botanics. Jan and Hugh had waited in the café by the East Gate, overpriced cups of tea and the Sunday supplements in front of them, while Alina and Fin walked over the bridge, followed the winding path, only later diverting through the trees. She was horribly nervous – had a new respect for the prospective adopters of older children on her caseload – and worried he'd be bored, mooching with his hands in his pockets and scuffing his feet through the grass. It was one thing to know you had a birth mother who was in touch on the fringes but another to give up a precious afternoon to the stranger that she was.

In hindsight, she'd underestimated Fin: he was the one who initiated meeting her 'properly' and he took charge on the day.

'I've written a list of questions to ask you,' he said gravely, nodding like an old man when she confessed so had she. Unfolding their pieces of paper broke the ice and they swapped answers, pacing like Victorian gentlefolk, polite and moderated, around the lawns. They hadn't been the big questions, but things like their favourite colours, TV programmes, the things that made them happy and sad… maybe the biggest questions after all.

Afterwards, Hugh had taken their photograph; it wasn't a good one; forced smiles and miles apart, but it didn't matter. Alina knew others would come. When it was time to say goodbye, Fin asked Alina what he should call her.

'Alina?' she'd asked, feeling stupid for not having given it any prior consideration.

'That's what Mum and Dad think.' Fin nodded. 'It's a nice name. We looked it up. It's Greek. Why is it Greek?' He was side-tracked. 'If your mum was Irish and your dad from Bangladesh, why'd they give you a Greek name?'

Alina had occasionally wondered the same but not even her grandparents had an explanation. 'I expect they just liked the sound of it.'

Fin accepted that as quickly as he'd questioned it. 'Okay. But I think I'd like to call you something different. Does anyone call you Ali?'

'No,' she said. 'But I'd like it if you would.'

Alina smiled now, as she traced that first journey, ever grateful it had all worked out. The Gardens had been bright with summer flowers that day. Now, as she looked for the first signs of spring in the snowdrops and leafy buds, she realised she'd probably only been back in the Botanics half a dozen times since she and Fin stopped meeting there. She must make more of an effort.

'Come on, Ali.' The grown-up Fin interrupted her trip down memory lane. 'Keep up. It's this way, isn't it? What if it's been cut down? What if someone else has claimed it?' Asking the questions was a lucky charm against that happening.

'I was just remembering the day we discovered it.' Alina hurried after him.

That autumn, gone was Fin's fascination with pinecones and horse chestnuts. He was immersed in the fantasy world of elementals and root spirits, gnomies – 'not *gnomes* like you think, Ali' – leading them to stray deep into the woodland garden, damp and deep in shadow. In a tangle of ancient rhizomes and stems (his words) they came upon a tree resembling a teapot, a long spout-like branch up high and on the other side, another curling back on itself to create a huge circle against the trunk.

'Ali, look, it's a window into another world,' he said, and she'd felt it too, for a second, the illusion of a curious mirror-land just beyond them. She shivered, but Fin shattered the momentary melancholy with a delighted battle cry. He hoisted himself up, climbed through the hole and taunted her from the other side.

'I'm too big,' she protested, but she wasn't, not quite.

On a dry-enough bed of leaves, cushioned by jackets and hoods, they picked through the ritual jelly beans – she'd brought him a present of them on their first meeting and it stuck – all the green ones for him, the purple ones for her.

'This is our tree,' Fin announced, mid-chew. 'Finder's keepers. The Fin and Ali Tree.'

Soon it became the Fin–Ali Tree, and ultimately, the Finally Tree. It was there, a couple of years later, when they'd fought through the scarlet flowers of a flame creeper to find the place that now symbolised their core, that Fin had spoken about his birth father.

As he had grown, Fin's forthcoming nature had ebbed and flowed but he'd always kept in contact. It was inevitable he'd ask about the past and she braced herself for recriminations and incredulity, but they never came.

'Ali, I think I'd like to search for Jamie one day,' was all he said. 'Mum and Dad are cool with that. How about you?'

What could she say? Jamie had been absent, a mystery for more than twelve years at that point, but she still believed, if she thought of it at all, it was the minutiae of lives on parallel lines that maintained their separation, nothing sinister. Her tongue-in-cheek theory of the three Ds came later. She crossed her fingers and gave her blessing.

'I'll look when I'm sixteen,' Fin decided, giving them much-needed leeway.

He was as good as his word, but while Fin and Alina's relationship blossomed, it seemed that Jamie had vanished – and Alina had begun to relax again.

Had.

'Shall we walk the long way round?' Alina said now, as they stood and stared, daring to add, 'It's too cold for anyone over eight to want to sit down under a tree today. And you don't want literal cold feet to add to the metaphorical ones.'

'I'm not sure why I've got such a... wobble on.' Fin pulled the collar of his jacket up. 'I mean, nothing's happened.'

'You had to tell me. You didn't know how I'd react. Maybe that hit a nerve. The mind's a funny thing.' Alina shrugged. 'If we rein ourselves in too tightly we're bound to blow up sometime. Or something like that. I'm not a psychologist.'

'You're an adoption social worker though, or you were. Haven't you come across anything like this before?'

'No. No I haven't.' Alina spoke slowly, looking around at the trees and shrubs as she did. There was little colour. Everything still looked blanched and sodden from the ravages of a winter not yet yielding to spring. It had to come soon though; Easter was around the corner. Sometimes Alina longed for the regularity of the seasons in this half of her life as well as the other, even though it wasn't guaranteed there either. Look at all her weather-aborted attempts to speak to Mizan. That was the lesson, wasn't it? Nothing was guaranteed, nothing ever certain. She reverted to Fin's question. 'That's part of *my* problem with all of this – a bit of pride coming before a fall. I was complacent. I thought I'd seen everything, dealt with it all and then – bam.'

'Bam, as in bring on the transgender birth father as a test case?' Fin stopped. 'Or do I mean birth mother? Sanna's a woman so… Aargh.' He looked towards the sky and took a deep breath. 'See? I can't get the right language even.'

'I've always thought it would make a great piece of research – how often do adopted people get the birth parents they want?' She spoke lightly, hoping to give him chance to collect his thoughts and, whatever they were, know they were okay.

'Wouldn't work,' Fin said. 'When I was six, Mum said I kept telling people mine were dinosaurs, and at ten, I'd've wanted them to be Jedi. Now, I just want…'

'A man?' Alina said it quietly.

Fin rubbed the side of his head. 'You'd think it wouldn't be too much to ask.'

In step, they carried on walking. Alina was silent because she simply had no idea what to say. Objectively, would it be easier if Jamie were Jamie and not Sanna? Not necessarily. There would probably be something else about him that unsettled Fin – the chances of perfection, as she'd just implied, were low. They circled the woodland walk and then went off-road slightly, no need to push through bare branches or delve deep into the trees. The Finally Tree was easily accessible when you knew where to look, and when you weren't seeing the secret adventure through the eyes of a child.

'Still here.' Fin put his hand on the curved branch he'd first called a window. 'Unclaimed and undamaged,' Alina noted.

Nobody else would ever find a Finally Tree, of course, in those or any other gardens, and that was the point. It was theirs. Their secret. And probably the only one they had ever shared because their lives, well, Fin's life in particular, was so well-documented. Adoption files lasted a lifetime, or seventy years of one anyway.

'I could still climb through.' Fin considered it.

'*You* could. I'm not trying.'

'Spoilsport.' Then: 'I'm curious about Sanna for all the wrong reasons, Ali,' he said at length, then lowered his voice. 'All I can think about is the trans bit, not the birth dad bit.'

'Don't give yourself too hard a time. If he were a famous actor or sportsperson or, I don't know, even a serial killer, you'd be just as curious.' Alina paused. 'Fin, all I can say is, the whole gender thing might be a bit of a red herring.' She looked up at his face and laughed. 'Truly. Probably every single one of the people – adults and children – I've worked with was as nervous as you about what – who – they might find. We went through it ourselves, for goodness sake! Remember that old saying about being careful what you wish for? And you know what? In some ways, it's easier for you...' She held her breath for a second, conscious she was walking a fine line. She didn't want to be too parental or too professional, but what the hell? She was, in theory, both.

Fin looked vaguely amused if anything. 'Go on.'

'Alright. Well, first you're not looking for a dad-sized hole to fill. You've said yourself, many times, you've got Hugh. Agreed?'

'Hundred percent.'

'Okay. And second, whoever you find, they're not going to be perfect. But if they're "ordinary", rather than "special" or "different", people are often disappointed or confused.

But they can't say that so they're even more disappointed or confused.' She stopped, wondering if she was digging a hole with a spade made out of convoluted logic that ended up being illogical.

But Fin was nodding slowly. 'So, by Sanna wearing her gender on her sleeve, I've got something obvious to be concerned about?'

'Exactly.'

'There's a strange logic in there somewhere, Ali.' Fin tucked his arm through hers and they resumed walking. 'Basically, the wobbles are normal and it's all about me, not Jamie or Sanna. I'd be feeling something like this even if my birth dad was what Jan would call a real man's man.'

'I think so.' She meant it, she wasn't just trying to make him feel better. 'I don't mean her gender isn't important. You can't ignore the statement she's made to you or to the world.'

'It's doubly brave, isn't it, Ali?' Fin suddenly sounded like the little boy she'd first met here, all those years ago. Trusting. Wondering. 'Coming out to the world. Then coming out to your son, and his mother.'

'Jamie was always brave,' Alina said, without thinking. *Always.*

'Ali? What do you mean?'

She must have said it with more emphasis than she'd meant to, because a whole undisturbed memory suddenly woke up. 'The Harvest Festival,' she said slowly.

13

Dublin 1994

'I've never been in the Salvation Army before,' Jamie said on the DART into town. 'My lot are those wishy-washy C of E types who invite the vicar round for tea when they want his cutesy church for a wedding but do their damnedest to make sure God stays on the porch.'

'You're not going to be in it now, you clot.' Alina nudged him, thinking how Miriam would love the analogy. 'You're just coming to a meeting.'

'But what will I have to do? It won't infringe on my human rights, will it?' They smirked together; the joke hadn't yet worn thin.

'Mostly put up with everyone, seriously, *everyone*, welcoming you like the prodigal son. Just smile, shake hands and agree it's a great turnout.' He looked slightly underwhelmed, so she added, 'Or I can get you a uniform, a tambourine, and suggest you do the sermon?'

'And there's me thinking it would be the Catholic majority who'd capture me. Bring it on, Alina X.'

'You really don't mind me dragging you home?' It was the twentieth time she'd checked.

'Sure an' isn't it a day out?' His Dublin accent was atrocious. 'I'll be the best little friend you've ever brought home, promise.'

That was a big part of it, Alina owned, a big, 'See, look – I'm okay' to reassure Miriam and Patrick she had made friends. Jamie had agreed so readily she knew he was on to her. But it was more than that.

'My family's a bit crap,' he confessed. 'So don't blame me if I steal yours.'

'They're enough for both of us,' she replied happily.

They were going to the Dublin Central Harvest Festival, hardly painting the town red, but an outing nonetheless. It was the end of October already, late for harvest, but Miriam explained a certain poetic licence was in play for the festival to coincide with the Salvation Army corps centenary.

'We'd love to see you, pet, if you've nothing better on.' Patrick invited her. 'A double bash to lure the crowds in. And,' – knowing she was listening in on the phone extension – 'your granny is hard to argue with.'

'The Lord doesn't carry a diary. The hungry and homeless don't carry diaries,' Miriam had been challenged by a stickler in the congregation. 'The food hampers will be welcome whenever we can deliver them. Especially if a bigger event means a bigger box.'

'Do we get a food hamper?' Jamie wondered as they got off the train.

'Are you needy?' Alina gave him a sideways glance. 'It's more tinned soup and beans than caviar and fancy cheese. But my grandparents will feed us and I'll buy you chips on the way back tomorrow.'

'Deal.'

Jamie played his part perfectly that afternoon. As had she. They'd sung along cheerfully, closed their eyes politely, drifted off when the sermon ran on. 'You should have let me do it,' Jamie murmured. 'It's just like being in a lecture.' Tacitly they ignored the knowing glances. Nobody actually asked Alina if Jamie was her boyfriend because they clearly assumed it a foregone conclusion. Had they been heading that way? No. It was never really on the cards.

Most of the harvest produce was borne away by willing volunteers, who would drop it off with whatever charity could use it. Patrick and a few of the bandsmen were sharing out the rest to deliver to a dozen local families whom Miriam said would usually have attended the lunch club on Saturdays. Jamie offered to help, join the gang, he said, and laughed when someone stuck a band cap on his head, lopsided, as he picked up a box and followed Patrick out of the hall door.

When they hadn't returned two hours later, neither Alina nor her grandmother – used to the unreliable nature of the ministry – gave it a second thought. A week didn't go by without Miriam or Patrick being waylaid by someone in need of counsel or practical help: a coat from the closed charity shop, a lift to the hospital, a shoulder to cry on – none were refused.

It was from the Mater hospital the call came. Alina and Miriam were watching *The Late Late Show*. Miriam always watched it; since moving to Dublin she'd cheerfully joined Gay Byrne's band of loyal fans. They both stifled a groan when the phone rang.

'I'll get it,' Alina said. 'And put the kettle on.'

'Thanks, pet. It's been a long day and I suspect it's not over yet.'

'Grandad!' Alina gave Miriam a thumbs up. 'When will you be home? The kettle's on.'

'Ah. I'm afraid the tea will have to wait.' Patrick sounded resigned. 'I'm coming home with Jamie but tell your granny to get to the Mater as quick as she can, will you? I'll meet her outside. Tell her it's Mrs O'Herhily.'

Briskly, Miriam pulled her uniform back on. 'Gives me access all areas,' she said. 'Now call me a taxi, good girl. I can't rely on the buses this time of night. It might be a long one,' she warned from the door. 'Your grandad will look after you and Jamie if you help him. The beds are made up for you to stay tonight.'

She left Alina smiling – *your grandad will look after you if you help him* was one of Miriam's stock phrases from her childhood – and knowing better than to ask what the problem was. She'd find out soon enough.

When she heard the key in the lock, Jamie came in, alone.

'Your grandad dropped me off. He's gone back to the house… What?'

'Whose house? Why are you wearing one of Grandad's shirts?' Alina stifled a grin. The white uniform shirt had blue and gold epaulettes on the shoulders, making Jamie look exactly like a brand-new Salvation Army officer fresh out of training college.

'It's a looong story.'

'Are you alright? What's happened?' Alina beckoned him into the kitchen and began to refill the kettle.

'I'm fine. Just got a bit more than I bargained for.' Jamie grinned at her, but his eyes were strained. 'Though not quite as much as Mrs O'Herhily lying in her kitchen in a pool of blood with bits of a gin bottle embedded in her hand.'

'*What?*' Alina whirled around, the lid of the kettle clattering to the floor. She saw Jamie wince as she bent to retrieve it. 'Jamie?'

He looked around appreciatively. 'It's so calm and clean here… Oh. She's going to be fine – Mrs O'Herhily, I mean. The hospital is patching her up. Her kids are with her sister. Her kind and loving husband is in the local nick.'

'Jesus Christ – sorry.' Alina, leaning against the countertop and staring at him, had been automatically apologising to her absent grandparents, not Jamie, whom she presumed had said, or at least thought, much worse. 'He hit her?'

'So he says. With the gin bottle she was clutching as she climbed into a boiling hot bath to, I quote, "murder their unborn baby".' Jamie gave a hiccup that might have started life as a wry laugh. '*She* says she'd had a miscarriage and was drowning her sorrows. They were, um, discussing it frankly and physically, when I arrived with the tins of fucking beans.'

'Hell.' Swiftly, Alina reached over and pulled him into a hug. His arms tightened around her.

'It was that alright,' he muffled into her hair. 'The front door was wide open, so I went in and it was all kicking off.' He straightened up and looked at her, confusion all over him. 'Except that it seemed fairly normal to them. I called an ambulance – the blood, Alina, honestly – and I thought they were both going to lynch me. But the Mrs sort of passed out, and he gave me a beer and started to cry. The Guards came with the ambulance and it turned into a big party. First name terms, the lot of them.'

'Just another Saturday night.' Alina released herself and made tea, strong and milky, heaping in the sugar – *the panacea*, she thought; she'd watched Miriam do it a thousand times. 'Sit down and drink that,' she told Jamie. 'It's the best I can do in a teetotal household.'

'You can't spring the Communion wine?' Jamie sipped, screwing up his face.

'They don't do Communion,' Alina said automatically. 'It's historical rather than theological—' Alina stopped herself. 'I'm really sorry, Jamie. When I asked you to come with me I thought the biggest drama would be who was doing the flowers.'

'Not your fault.' He downed the tea. 'Ouch. That was hot. I'm fine. I got a fright, for sure, but all's well and all that. The swarm of O'Herhily kids didn't even wake up. Her sister was round in minutes and had the mop out before we left. She tried to haggle over the harvest box too. She told your grandad that none of them liked the frigging kidney beans, tinned mushrooms were muck and why didn't anyone send in Spaghetti Hoops. Good point, I thought.'

At breakfast, Miriam and Patrick were their usual selves in their usual seats. The medical records would show that Mrs O'Herhily had had a miscarriage and passed out, and that Mr O'Herhily had panicked when he found her.

'No lasting harm, the doctors say.' Miriam shook her head, her lips tightening. 'Until the next time. That poor woman. I can't condone what she did... what she may have done,'

Miriam corrected herself, 'but she should never have been in that position in the first place.'

'Jamie, here, was the hero of the hour.' Patrick clapped him on the back. 'Did he tell you that, Alina?'

'No?' She stared at Jamie, who was studiously buttering his toast. 'You said you called the Guards.'

'I did,' he protested.

'And checked the children, stemmed the bleeding, calmed the husband and waited 'til Mrs O'Herhily's sister arrived.'

'God certainly sent you to us this weekend,' Miriam said cheerfully. 'The Gardai said that without your quick thinking they could have been dealing with... well, a lot worse.'

14

'You've never told me much about what you and Jamie did,' Fin said as they meandered back to the car. 'Not down to brass tacks like that.'

'I suppose not.' Alina thought about it. She'd passed on the getting-to-know-you details from the start, the superficial layer that was the birth father, but Fin was right: the real stories had somehow got lost in translation. Now they were knocking each other over like dominoes, clamouring to land face up.

'I like the sound of you both.' Fin sounded wistful, and Alina heard alarm bells. She had no business tinting anything rose at this late stage.

She raised her eyebrows. 'I'm not sure we were actually very nice to know. We bonded over being affectedly superior because...' She had a flash of insight. '...because we both felt so inferior.' Poor Sara Smyth, Alina thought, another story Fin didn't know. Alina felt a twinge of guilt for not remembering Sara's reborn name; she might have been extreme, but she had been sincere, made a stand. *So did you*, a little voice spoke in her ear, *so did you*.

'There's nothing unusual in that,' Fin said, with a world-weary twenty-five-year-old sigh that was only half put on. 'You sound so in-tune back then too when you tell stories like that.'

'We were. We really were.'

The 'so what went wrong?' hung between them. Life. Youth. Unexpected pregnancy. Expectations. Take your clichéd pick. All were good enough. None were good. If she dug deep there were so many things she'd hidden a long time ago, but they were not for Fin's ears, not until she'd spoken to Ja— Sanna. And the truth was: nothing *had* gone 'wrong'. Everything had gone to plan, even if it was Alina and Jamie's specific, convoluted and, from where she stood now, frankly bizarre plan.

On a whim, she ducked into the pop-up florist inside the East Gate and bought early daffodils and gerbera, pleased by the mismatched colours.

'A little blast of sunshine,' the florist said, wrapping them.

'For Kirsten.' Alina thrust them at Fin. An unspoken apology; she was suddenly kicking herself for recounting a bloody, do-it-yourself abortion to a father-to-be. She hoped Fin wouldn't join the dots.

'She's not a very visible individual, Sanna.' Skirting the city, Fin kept his eyes firmly on the road, hands at ten-to-two on the wheel.

'Meaning?'

'Is it wrong to admit I've googled her, Ali? Looked on LinkedIn and Facebook.'

'The obvious thing to do, isn't it?' But Alina's heart sped up slightly. 'And?'

'Nothing. I don't know whether to be relieved or disappointed.' Fin pulled into Edenfield Road and double-parked outside the house; cars filled all the kerb-space. 'Kirsten figures that when Jamie became Sanna he, *she*, changed her surname too. Makes sense, doesn't it? But it does mean needle and haystack. All I can do is wait for her to respond to my message on the agency books.'

The opportunity was there with bells and whistles. 'I think it's possible that Sanna might contact me first,' Alina said slowly. 'Jamie always said he'd get in touch with me before asking to meet you.' They were idling beside a silver hire car, another part of her brain noted; Rory was home. 'I don't know if that still stands, it's been so long.' She turned back to Fin, preparing herself for the 'Why?'

'That makes sense.' His eyes were bright.

'It does?'

'He knows – knew – you. You're both my parents. I'm sure it's easier to meet your ex-partner after twenty-five years than a random bloke who says he's your son.'

'Put like that…' Alina and Fin smiled at each other.

'So, we wait?' he said.

'I suppose so, at least give hi— Sanna chance to contact me. If neither of us have heard anything in, say, a month, you can go back to the agency and ask what they suggest.'

Fin considered that and nodded. 'Fair enough. It's not like I haven't plenty of other distractions. And you don't mind? Being thrown into the deep end?'

'I'm glad to be part of it.' There was a toot from a driver behind, wanting to pass. 'You could get a double decker through there,' Alina muttered, but obligingly she opened the car door and got out. 'Love to Kirsten,' she said. 'And Fin? I don't think you'll have to wait that long. Jamie always kept his promises.'

'But are they Sanna's promises?' Unknowingly mirroring Alina's yesterday thoughts, he gave her a crooked smile. 'It will take as long as it takes. Don't worry, Ali. God bless!' With a wave to Alina and another to the driver waiting patiently behind him, Fin drove off, indicating right onto the main road.

Deep in thought, Alina made her way onto the drive of number 36. Kirsten was right, wasn't she? Jamie Drew didn't exist anymore; of course Sanna would have a brand new surname. Any one of her recently discarded emails: junk, unknown senders, corporate round robins, could actually be the golden ticket. Suddenly certain that Sanna's message was already in her computer's recycle bin, Alina stopped dead – forgetting to worry that Rory would be lying in wait to accost her – and shook her head. 'You've been a fool,' she muttered. 'It's obvious. Stupid.'

A movement in a window to her left caught her eye and galvanised her. *Not* Rory. Not Elizabeth. It was Morag, ostensibly adjusting the fall of her curtains, but watching Alina with gimlet eyes. Alina gave her a cheery wave, which may or may not have been reciprocated with a brief nod, and hurried round to her flat.

Rummaging in her bag for her keys and intent on her mission, she was almost on top of Rory before she saw him. He had his back to her, shaking a pen, and apparently trying to write on a piece of paper he was holding against her front door. Either she let out a loud gasp or he heard the crunch of her feet on the gravel because he whirled round to face her, dropping the pen and the paper and scrabbling to pick both up. The pen bounced to Alina's feet and she bent automatically to pick it up.

'I was just leaving you a note—'

'I was just out with—'

Their words crossed and it was impossible to say which of them was the most awkward, she thought later. Both of them looked as if they'd been caught with their hands in the biscuit tin.

Alina strode forward, he stepped back, and they did that little dance of getting out of each other's way. With the key in the lock, Alina looked over her shoulder and summoned a smile. 'Come in,' she said.

'Are you sure?' His face said he'd rather do a tracheotomy with the pen she was holding out to him.

'Of course. I was expecting you… I mean, Elizabeth, your mum, said…'

'Hallo, Alina,' he said formally, as he stepped over the threshold.

'Hello, Rory.'

He followed her through to the small sitting room where Alina watched as he hesitated, then took up a stance, arms folded like a policeman on an official call, in front of the fire place. He ran a hand through dark hair that was greying slightly at the temples, she noticed, and he wore glasses, which he hadn't when she'd known him before. In jeans and a rugby top, he might have been the any-man advert for life in New Zealand. Not maniacal or broken-hearted.

Rory cleared his throat. 'I thought we should get this over with. See how the land lies. Make a truce. Whatever. There's no point in pretending this is anything but awkward.'

'No.' Alina's wits had temporarily deserted her; she couldn't think of anything better. 'Sit down,' she managed.

'I'm okay, thanks.'

'Right.' Alina perched herself on the edge of the sofa, her legs suddenly shaky. She wasn't afraid of him, just of what the hell he was going to say.

'It doesn't feel like five years have passed,' is what he did say.

It didn't – in the same way a mostly healed cut felt when it was suddenly ripped open again.

'My mother said you were recently back from India.'

'Bangladesh. But yes, I am. A few days ago.' *Days.* She'd lived a lifetime.

'Bangladesh. I meant to say Bangladesh. I *knew* it was Bangladesh.' He rolled his eyes, a parody of someone wanting to slap his own head. 'Bangladesh, as used to be part of Pakistan...' Rory frowned. 'The only good thing about digging a hole this deep means I can crawl into it.'

'It was East Pakistan before the 1971 War of Liberation.' Now Alina wanted to laugh, a cloak of surrealism fluttering over her shoulders. So far on this ordinary Sunday morning, she had had a virtual chat about the child-marriage risk of a little girl who might or might not actually be related to Alina. Then she had gone with her long-adopted son to find a mythical tree and discuss the woman who had once been the man they called the baby's father. Why not add into the mix a stilted exchange about the history of South Asian politics with the man whose life she had turned upside down, despite being best friends with his mother?

Her lips twitched at the absurdity, and she heard Elizabeth's voice: 'Everything makes a great story – afterwards.'

Alina pondered whether asking Rory about his life in *Australia* would break the ice or cause them to drown, when she realised he was pre-empting her.

'People do that all the time. Muddle up New Zealand and Australia,' he said. 'It drives me mad.'

'I'm sure.' Alina agreed. 'In Bangladesh, they do the same with England and Ireland, and England and Scotland.'

There was another moment – literally a minute, Alina counted the seconds – of silence, as their eyes caught one another's before they respectively let them drop. Rory glared around the room, but she was sure he wasn't taking much in. She scratched a non-existent itch on her wrist.

'Would you like some coffee?' she asked eventually. 'Or tea?' Maybe his tastes had changed.

'Um. I don't… Yes, please. That would be nice.'

'Mostly black with a splash of milk?' *How the hell had she forgotten the Harvest Festival carnage but remembered how an ex-client took his coffee?*

'What? Oh, yes. Please. Thank you.'

As she escaped to the kitchen and pushed the pods into the coffee-maker, letting it grind away, the penny dropped. His face might say angry, but his actions said nerves. *Great people skills, Alina.* But there was nervous – *she* was nervous – and then there was *Nervous*, which Rory seemed beyond.

Well, it was never going to be a hearts and flowers reunion, was it? And an hour of discomfort never killed anyone. Now their encounter was happening, Alina was calmer. You did nothing wrong, she reminded herself, as she heated milk she didn't want. Nothing wrong.

She realised she'd said the words aloud and was thankful for the final rumblings of the coffee machine.

'So, how was *Bangladesh?*' Rory's voice came out of

nowhere and made her jump, splashing the warm milk over the counter and catching her sleeve. Shit. How long had he been in the doorway? Had he heard her muttering?

'Fine. Good.' She shoved her wet sleeve up her arm.

He hesitated, then crossed the room, tore some kitchen towel from the roll on the windowsill, handed half to her and wiped up the spill with the other. 'Sorry. I didn't mean to make you jump. So much for small talk.'

'You can't hear anything over the sound of that.' Alina nodded at the Nespresso machine. 'Behind the door,' she added as he held the wet tissue aloft, clearly looking for the bin. She put two full mugs on the table and gestured towards his.

He picked it up and took a sip. 'It's good coffee.'

'Yes. I drink too much of it.' Alina pulled out a chair and slowly sat down, motioning Rory to copy her. This time he did. Maybe the table between them would help, more business-like. Props always helped awkward encounters, too, and she had chocolate biscuits. They were in the fridge though and somehow showing him the inside of her fridge and announcing she kept biscuits in there seemed far too… intimate.

'Was it a holiday with your family, or were you visiting the… er… orphanage?'

Now it felt like a job interview. Stilted or not, Rory was trying hard. She should too.

'Both.' She fell back on the short, easy, answer, but it sounded rude in the circumstances. 'They're kind of one and the same these days.' She was taken aback he remembered as much. The nitty-gritty of an adoption assessment meant that Alina once could probably have recited everything from whether Rory chopped his carrots into circles or batons to his thoughts on ten-year-olds walking to school alone. In return she always shared something of her own life, but most clients were too tied up with their own experiences to care. Rory – not so much Laura – had always listened. 'Inside, we call it a homestay rather than an orphanage,' she said. 'It's to differentiate from the bigger, more formal government institutions.'

Alina got up and opened the fridge wide, pulling out the Chocolate Digestives and shaking them onto a plate. 'I've been spending six months living at Sonali Homestay and six months here, doing international adoptions. Maybe Elizabeth said.' She was fishing; had they talked about her? But she could see Rory already forming his next question – or carefully *not* forming it – and she saved him the trouble. 'This is my ninth year of the half and half. It's worked well.'

'Nine years.' This time he nodded. 'Ever since—'

'Yes.'

'Shit, Alina. I hope I didn't—'

'No. Well, not really.' She wanted to be honest. 'There was a lot of upheaval… there, I mean. Building work, NGO registration, my co-director was getting married. So when Takdir, my great uncle, asked if I'd take more responsibility, it seemed like a good time.'

'A big step. Though, I suppose it wasn't as far as New Zealand.'

They both smiled faintly at that.

'And how was, *is*, New Zealand?'

'Very like here but a long way away. I suppose I went there because I knew nobody – did the opposite to you.'

'Umm.' Alina hesitated; somebody had to mention her.

'Laura isn't here.' Rory pre-empted her again.

'No. How is she?' *Idiot.*

'I've no idea. Fine, I expect.' Rory shrugged. 'We're divorced.'

Silence filled the room again like smoke. They sat there and breathed it in.

'Sorry—' The best choreographer couldn't have better timed the way they spoke at the same time.

'Stop.' Alina sat up straight. 'We need a ground rule, Rory, and that's that neither of us should keep saying sorry.' She put her hands flat on the tabletop, the wood grainy to her touch. 'What happened, back then, happened. And what didn't happen didn't happen.' She wasn't going to elaborate. 'We can't change the past, but we can find a way to make the future work. If we're both going to be here...' Were they? She didn't know her own plans, let alone Rory's. 'I mean, we've got Elizabeth in common— What's funny?'

To her surprise, Rory burst out laughing. It was his first natural action since she'd opened the door. The pinched look left his face and his eyes crinkled in humour. It made Alina laugh too, a sudden lift in which she remembered how much she had liked him.

'I'm not sure why we're laughing,' she admitted. 'But I'm glad we are.'

'The years rolled away,' he explained, still grinning. 'You suddenly sounded exactly like the Alina who used to visit once a week with question after question and a lot of good sense.'

'Rather than the quivering, speechless wreck you see before you now?'

'You're hardly that – well, maybe a bit. Not as much as me though. I'm sorry—' He held up his hand. 'You need to allow me that one.' Alina wrinkled her nose. 'I'm sorry for calling unannounced and putting you on the spot. I convinced myself it was a good idea to get it over with without any angst of anticipation or, or sense of occasion.' He paused. 'Mum will probably kill me.'

'I think she wants to bang our heads together and send us to play nicely in the sandpit, actually.' He smiled again at that. 'But you're probably right – doing it this way, I mean. Getting it over with.'

Rory looked at her directly, probably for the first time. 'Where do we go from here?'

'It's a good place to start, I suppose.' Rory sounded dubious and she couldn't blame him.

'We try and make friends again?' Alina took the baton of hesitation. 'We were friendly before. We had a lot in common.

Then it just all got too...' Complicated? Messy? Official? '...
big,' she settled on.

'Big.' Rory repeated. Then, 'Friends? Friends sounds good
to me.' Deliberately, he stuck his arm out and stretched it
across the table. 'Nice to meet you, Alina.'

She took his hand, briefly, and was shocked at the muscle-
memory of recognition. 'You too, Rory. Want to seal it with
another coffee? Or, I don't know, orange juice? A bottle of
prosecco?' she added, slightly desperately.

'You don't drink. I mean, you didn't.'

He knew *way* too much about her. How she must have
wittered on about herself while filling in those endless forms.
She raised her eyebrows. 'I don't, much. But I am Elizabeth's
friend first, you know.'

'My mother, the bad influence. Tempting, but maybe
we should quit while we're ahead. And I need to return
my hire car.'

'A silver one?'

'Yes. Why do you ask?'

'Idle curiosity. I saw it parked outside.'

He got up and Alina followed him to the door, handing him
his coat on the way. 'Thanks for coming.' she said, wondering
if she meant it.

'Thanks for letting me in. I'll see you at Mum's, then?'
Rory blurted it out like a teenager suggesting the prom. It hung
there for a few seconds. 'You don't mind me staying there
for a bit? It won't affect you and her. I wouldn't dare let it.'

'Neighbours *and* friends.' Alina smiled, even though it
would affect her and Elizabeth. Running spontaneously up the
stairs with a bag of Greggs' sausage rolls and lolling around
in Charles would be Rory's prerogative now, not hers. Alina
blinked. He was looking at her hopefully, maybe less prom-
date than canvasser; she half expected him to ask if he could
count on her vote.

'I'll let you tell Elizabeth we've met,' she told him. 'She
can bombard *you* with her questions.'

15

Alina threw herself down on her bed, glanced at the time, and closed her eyes. How could it only be ten to three? *Stands the church clock at ten to three? And is there honey still for tea?* she recited to herself. Mizan said it without fail every afternoon when they downed tools and went out into the dusty street to have chai and cardamom-studded biscuits at the tea stall. He'd learned the poem at school, he told her, but they were the only two lines that stuck. He was going to be very disappointed if he visited the UK, she thought. She'd have to scope out Grantchester-esque villages and buy a three-tier cake-stand for afternoon tea.

In any case, she'd done it. She'd met Rory MacLeod and she'd survived. He didn't hate her – unless he was a very good actor – and it appeared they were starting again with a clean slate. She lay back and considered her feelings – analysing them, as recommended by the latest edition of *Psychologies* magazine – relief; surprise; a slight reservation that he was next door; but most mostly relief. Oh, and a hefty dose of anti-climax.

'Well, what did you expect?' she asked the ceiling. It was a classic response: dreading something and putting it off – then doing it in last-minute desperation and finding it wasn't so bad after all. Speaking of which… No time like the present and all that jazz. 'One down, one to go,' she said aloud. 'Prayers, please, Granny. I'm going in!'

Alina hauled herself up and clicked the keyboard on her computer, watching her Gmail spring to life. She still had the fifty or so unread messages to check. If there was nothing there, she'd scroll through the deleted items – thank goodness she hadn't binned them entirely – and she knew, with a certainty she couldn't explain, that she'd find something from Sanna. She went down the page forensically, checking each address and subject bar carefully and deleting ruthlessly. She'd know what she was looking for when she saw it, she thought: something beginning with S; an academic email address; anything in the header mentioning Fin or adoption or Trinity or 1994. It was a long list of possibles, but finite.

Connie was on her way home, she learned: *I'll call when I've slept for a week.* A couple of monographs she might be interested in from Oxford University Press. Junk. Junk. Ah…

Alina paused, mid-click, staring at an unknown sender's address.

It had to be. Didn't it? The subject header simply said 'Jamie'. She frowned, conscious of her heart pounding. 'Well, open it, you idiot,' she muttered to herself. She didn't though. Methodically, she carried on until she'd emptied the inbox, sure that there were no other possibilities.

The email *was* from Sanna. Of course it was. Alina ran her eye over it quickly, needing to know the worst. Then, reassured there absolutely was no 'worst', she went back to the beginning and started again. By the third time her heart rate was normal and she'd taken the words in:

Dear Alina,

A promise is a promise even after twenty-five years, but I'm still not much good with words so I'll plunge straight in. Shall we meet up? You'll know I'm Sanna now but what you'll find it harder to accept is that I'm a – wait for it – university professor of – wait for it again – Peace Studies. Yes, you read that right. You can laugh, but better if we laugh together?

Clerys' clock? I'm free for a week from next Sunday.

Love, Sanna née Jamie x

How long, how many drafts, had that taken to write? To get it so right? It was like hearing Jamie's voice. Shockingly so. Alina put her hand to her mouth to suppress an involuntary sob, but just as quickly she was laughing through her tears. Jamie and Sanna, two distinct entities in her mind, merged just a little closer.

The sun had long set by the time Alina was happy – happy-ish – with her reply. *They wrote the* Book of Kells *faster*, she mocked herself. Then she sat there for twenty more minutes before pressing 'send'. And a further twenty agonising over her two sparkling lines:

Hi Sanna,

This Tuesday? Lunch time? But Clerys' gives me palpitations – I wonder if the university café is still there? Or somewhere new for a new start.

Love Alina x

When a response pinged back almost immediately, she thought it must be a bounce-back, an undeliverable notice, but it wasn't. *You're on.* The message said. *Tuesday week at noon. I'll find a place. Details to follow x.* Jamie's techie streak clearly lived on through Sanna and a generation of iPhones.

With no further reply to Alina's expansive *Great x* by bedtime, she resolutely switched off the computer and muted email notifications on her phone. She'd be checking every hour otherwise.

So much for Sunday being a day of rest, was her last waking thought.

Sanna's email the next day confirmed a lunch reservation at somewhere called the Oleander Rooms on Nassau Street.

She'd added her mobile phone number, prompting Alina to do likewise, and that was that. It seemed they were both content to wait out the week before sharing any more about their lives. A date and a telephone number was a flimsy enough framework to rekindle – build? – a relationship, the social worker in Alina worried, as she navigated the Ryanair website. Then again, people successfully manoeuvred the minefield of Internet dating with less – so what did she want, three months' counselling and supervised contact?

It was only when she was booking her flights that it dawned on her she was going to Dublin. The city hadn't been home to her since she left Trinity, but her grandparents, true to their word, had retired to a flat just outside, in Bray. The last time Alina had been in Dublin was to arrange and attend Miriam's funeral, and – Sanna aside – she didn't know how she felt about going back. A day trip would do her, she decided. An early morning arrival to visit her grandparents' final resting place (God, she hated that phrase. If Miriam's afterlife was her heaven, Alina seriously doubted it would include resting) in Glasnevin, lunch with Sanna, and a late-afternoon flight back. She'd plan a proper visit another time – then blankly wondered why. With Miriam and Patrick gone, her ties were gone. Alina allowed herself a few tears, then sent a Skype link to Mizan demanding (with smiley emojis) that he amass a posse of the little girls to cheer her up. School would have finished, afternoon chores not yet begun, and it would make up for missing them yesterday. Khalya she'd save for another day.

Mizan was on within minutes. 'They don't deserve to see you,' he grumbled. 'Naughty girls. I have sent them to their room to do sewing.'

'Uh oh. What nonsense are they up to this time?' They had a particularly feisty bunch of eight-year-olds who managed to get into mischief that nobody had thought to ban.

'Hair cutting. They can tell you themselves.' Mizan cheered up. 'You can be stern, okay? No fun chatting, Alina.'

'Okay,' she agreed meekly. She had to bite her lip when

she was faced with a jostling row of six, who couldn't decide if they were penitent, petulant or proud to have an extra audience with Alina apa. The sound became animated in telling how Asma had taken all their hairbands, so in payback, Sofi had cut off her braid when she was sleeping and tried to sell it. 'To buy new hairbands,' she signed rapidly. Asma, sporting a ragged bob, wanted a share of the non-existent money, 'To make up for no hair and no need for hairbands.'

Once Alina had told them, so sorrowfully, how *very disappointed* in them she was, metaphorically dried their dramatic tears and regally bestowed her forgiveness, all was well in their world and hers.

Still chuckling, Alina recounted these events to the stylist doing her own hair a couple of hours later. She left the salon with blacker, bouncy locks, a spring in her step, and pink Shellac nails. *What the heck, why not?* she thought, admiring them. It was a modest enough treat from Miriam and Patrick's money, and neither of them would be averse to a mild frittering. It made her think of Patrick slipping her the odd fiver to go the pictures on O'Connell Street, and on a whim she diverted to the Dominion and spent a nostalgic hour or so watching a screen adaptation of Nancy Drew.

She'd practically reached the gate on Edenfield Road before she registered her impromptu welcome party. Elizabeth, Rory and, judging by her overnight case and flight attendant garb, a newly returned Connie were congregated in the front garden of number 36. Their huddle reminded Alina of Open-Air meetings when she was a child, the Army band playing. If Morag appeared to join their merry throng, they'd have a full house, but the closed curtains at her converted coach house confirmed she was away. They were spared.

'Alina, lovey, just the person. Come and join the plotting.' Elizabeth's energetic gesture suggested she thought Alina might slip past.

'Plotting? That sounds interesting.' Alina mustered up a general smile. 'Hello, everyone. What's happening? Connie, you're back!'

'In body, for sure.' Connie rolled her tired eyes. 'You look beautiful, Alina. Rest and recuperation, hmm?'

'More like hair colour and nail polish.' She held her hands out, feeling vaguely uncomfortable; Rory altered the interaction.

'A get-together. A catch up.' Elizabeth reverted to the original conversation. 'I thought we might go posh and get some food delivered. My treat. We're not often all together.'

'Sounds good,' Alina agreed. She hesitated then said, 'When? I'm going to Dublin a week tomorrow but only for the day. To… my grandparents' memorial.' *Granny and Grandad, forgive me the white lie.* 'Otherwise I'm free.'

'Oh, lovey. By yourself?'

'I'd rather be alone,' Alina said a bit too quickly, in case any of them offered to go with her. 'I'm used to it and it's a flying visit.'

'Well, you know where we are.' Elizabeth's voice said that. Her eyes said, *There's more to it, Missy, but I'll leave it be for now.* 'What about Wednesday the second in the evening, then?'

They all nodded, and Connie added before Alina could ask, 'Morag is away this week visiting her brother in Berwick. I met her as I was arriving. She will be back in good time.'

'Sounds great. I'm happy to chip in,' Alina said. 'What "posh" are you thinking of?'

'Chinese or Indian. You get the casting vote.' Elizabeth saw Alina's face. 'You can suggest Beluga caviar if you like, but I did mean posh compared with sausage rolls and crisps.'

'Thank goodness. Um, okay, Chinese? Are you sure Morag will agree?'

'Dear Morag.' Elizabeth's tone was neutral. 'You'll remember Morag,' she said to Rory. It sounded like a warning rather than a question.

'Yes.' His face suggested, momentarily, that a less polite person would have added 'unfortunately'.

'She doesn't like *foreign* food.' The slight inflection in Connie's voice made Alina's lips twitch; it was a perfect copy of the absent Morag's.

'Morag doesn't much like foreign anything,' Alina said cheerfully and met Connie's twinkling eyes.

'Now I must go and sleep away the miles,' she said. 'And you, Elizabeth, must go to the hospital.' Connie turned to Rory. 'It was a pleasure to meet my friend's first-born.'

'What a lovely voice that young woman has.' Elizabeth stared after Connie, filling the silence. 'Lovely all round, in fact.'

'Isn't she.' Alina was conscious that Rory hadn't yet spoken – she didn't blame him, what was there to say? – and now the four were three, she didn't want Elizabeth to get into a 'So, I hear the two of you have met and are burying the hatchet' kind of discussion. She picked up Connie's remark. 'Did she say hospital?'

Elizabeth raised her arm as if asking permission to leave. 'Getting the cast off. Hallelujah. Rory's coming for moral support.'

'Good idea.' Alina smiled at Rory, striving for natural. 'I'll see you later, then.'

'See you.' Rory nodded.

'Yes, we'd better go before the Edenfield Neighbourhood Watch decide we constitute an unruly crowd. Bye, Alina, love.' Elizabeth was nodding towards the house opposite, and as she walked away, Alina heard her summarising for Rory its notoriety. Twice the residents had called the police on an intruder in Elizabeth's garden. Twice it had been her, wandering up and down, plotting – her latest novel rather than a mid-week take-away.

'I'm a harmless old lady getting some fresh air and exercise in my own garden,' she told the apologetic PC sent – twice – to apprehend her. Tactfully, he mentioned that *Mrs Maxin was in her dressing gown, one time carrying a pineapple, and bare-footed.* 'Research, not Alzheimer's,' Elizabeth insisted and invited Alina to vouch for her. Reassuringly, her next novel confirmed it.

'Alina?'

She was getting her key out, in a hurry for a pee, when Rory's voice called her back.

'Yes? I'm here.'

He appeared round the corner. 'I wondered…'

She waited patiently, just managing not to shift from one foot to another to ease her bladder. Latchkey incontinence, it was called apparently. So near yet so far. *I'm so bloody middle-aged*, she thought.

'…Shall we go out for a drink afterwards?' he said in a rush. 'Next week, I mean. I'm going to Aberdeen tomorrow, work stuff.'

'Well…' Would she be all companied out after one of Elizabeth's sessions *and* meeting Sanna? Would she want *Rory's* company? For that matter, would he really want hers?

'The ulterior motive is showing Mum we're… er… okay? She's fishing,' he went on.

They shared a faint grin at that.

'Alright, then,' Alina said. *Live a little.* 'I'd like that.'

'So would I. Great.' He looked both pleased and surprised, but mostly surprised.

That made two of them.

There was a saying, wasn't there, about having all your ducks in a row? It was about order, a nice neat line, all present and correct.

Sitting – blessedly – on the loo, a few minutes later, Alina considered her ducks. Fin, Jamie, Sanna, Rory, Mizan, Takdir. She might even add Elizabeth to the list. For someone who had so farled a largely blameless enough life (she did a rapid calculation: three secrets over what, thirty years? Yep, still verging on blameless, even if they were humdingers) all her ducks were coming home to roost. So far they were behaving well, but, well, a row also meant a firing line, didn't it?

What if her ducks, her in the middle, were going to be shot at? Picked off one by one in a dodgy Russian Roulette. And Alina herself hadn't an inkling as to the final outcome.

16

April the first, April Fools' Day. How fitting was that? Alina hoped it wasn't an omen.

It was like walking the gangplank, going back. A Y-shaped gangplank, at that, with Miriam and Patrick at one tip, and Jamie and Sanna at the other. She boarded the half-empty Ryanair plane, uncomfortably wondering if she'd bitten off more than she could chew.

Just over two hours later, having arrived at Connolly Station, she kept her head down and focused on finding the right bus and the right fare. Glasnevin was barely another half an hour away – back the way she'd come, in fact – but it was early still, and she welcomed the extra journey to sort herself out. As the bus trundled down Parnell Street, Alina distracted herself watching the other passengers, idly wondering if the ones with the Moore Street flowers peeping from the top of their carrier bags were heading to the cemetery. They were just as likely shoppers, tempted by a splash of colour to brighten their suburban hallways, or visitors to the Ben Secours hospital.

Alina had no flowers, and she wasn't visiting the cemetery or the neighbouring crematorium grounds. She left the bus at the Botanic Gardens to wind her way slowly through the arboretum to the glasshouses, letting her mind flit this way and that. Her grandparents had always been matter-of-fact about death, treating it as others might retirement: a bittersweet change of direction after a long and busy career. *Going to Glory*, they called it, preparing as if Glory were an all-inclusive holiday resort in the sun, and the manager a lifelong friend. In the same way, Muslim Takdir was looking forward to Jannah. To Alina, it was clearly the sister hotel of Glory, and he was taking a different route there.

Alina had been far too young to remember her own parents' deaths. She didn't even remember *them*, and if she missed their presence it was as a concept; her grandparents were her mum and dad. As a little girl, she'd imagined *their* Glory as a giant Butlins, all swimming pools, playparks and ice cream, without ever having to count the days until home-time. Teenage Alina decided Miriam and Patrick were bonkers: dead was dead. The End. Except... was it? Her upbringing left a little spark of faith – unignited, but there all the same – and she couldn't totally un-believe.

Miriam frequently lamented that her body couldn't be vaporised, puff and gone – Alina had a lot of sympathy with that – but in lieu of that, Miriam and Patrick had both stipulated a brief cremation, and that's what they'd got, nine months apart.

'And don't put us in one of those lost-luggage lockers...' Miriam warned.

'A niche in the columbarium wall,' Patrick translated, doing nothing to demystify Alina.

'...nor go and talk to a stone. Or leave flowers at it.'

'Grow the flowers in Sonali Homestay and think of us in the sunshine,' was Patrick's way of softening that.

'Better still, make it vegetables and let us be useful.' Miriam was laughing, though, as she spoke.

The reality of death was still five or six years away, but Alina had taken the thought to heart. That's why she had put Khalya in charge of a changing band of children responsible for a little garden plot – next to what would now be the new guesthouse. It was a celebration of life rather than a memorial of death, and something her grandparents had seen flourish. They were eternally part of the whole endeavour.

Then Patrick died; a mild stroke followed by another from which there was, the consultant explained, no viable return. Miriam and Alina sat either side of Patrick in his hospital bed, Miriam chatting as naturally as she did over breakfast at home, Alina striving to copy. In the late afternoon, as the machines bleeped disharmoniously and the rain spattered the windows, they'd fallen silent. Her grandmother's eyes were closed and Alina assumed she was praying. She herself was trying to suppress the unbidden thought *how much longer*; her grandfather had never been one for long drawn-out goodbyes.

Slowly Miriam leant forward and stroked Patrick's sparse hair, speaking softly, as if responding to a silent cue. 'I'm ready when you are,' she said. 'I'll see you later.'

It was, for all the world, as if Patrick was popping down to the shops for the daily paper.

When they were sure he'd gone, Alina went to find a nurse, while Miriam cried like a child; the first and last time she did so.

Three days after the funeral, her grandmother sat Alina down, explained that she had ovarian cancer, time was short and that taking it up with treatment was not part of God's plan.

'Not part of God's or not part of yours?' was Alina's tart, reeling reply.

'One and the same.' Miriam's spirit wasn't broken. In fact, she radiated satisfaction that God had managed it so well: she hadn't needed to 'mention' the 'cancer thing' to Patrick and she wouldn't have to talk Alina out of hanging around, indefinitely, to care for her.

Breathless at the sheer audacity, the news itself hadn't surprised Alina. The disease was present, but the real cancer eating away at Miriam was the loss of her soulmate. It was her grandmother's certainty that led Alina to dig deep. She wasn't being brave when she said 'I'll miss you, Granny, I'll miss you both more than I can say. But I'll miss you less knowing you're together.'

The spark in Miriam's eyes told Alina she'd got it right.

'That's my girl. I knew you'd understand.' Her grandmother squeezed Alina's hands tight.

There was only one thing she couldn't ignore. 'You promised Grandad you wouldn't be long…'

'…And I won't betray that.' Her grandmother finished the sentence when Alina couldn't.

That was their real goodbye, Alina thought now, that perfect moment of shared understanding. The months following were little more than marking time, like waiting on a delayed flight. Afterwards, Alina sorted out the very little Miriam had left outstanding and headed off to Bangladesh as usual. Of course, Miriam had arranged her journey to her Maker to hit bang in the middle of Alina's six months in the West.

How lucky was she, Alina reminded herself again, to have had her grandparents into her forties. How many people could claim that? And right now, among the glasshouse palms, Miriam and Patrick didn't feel far away at all.

Alina checked her watch. Time to harness some of her grandmother's crazy confidence. 'Make your time count.' She heard her grandmother's voice from the ether.

'Granny and Grandad,' she said out loud, 'let's go and meet Sanna. You must be curious.' *I know I am*, she added under her breath, looking around hurriedly to see if anyone could hear her. As she walked with renewed purpose back to the bus stop, she realised she was humming a long-forgotten hymn's tune: *Count Your Blessings*. Miriam's influence if ever there was one.

Alina counted.

Counting her blessings lasted until she got back to The Quays. With Trinity College on the horizon, they did a swift about-turn and her inclination was to run for the hills – or the airport – as fast as she could.

It was an increasingly grey, drizzly day that was, like

her, too indecisive for an umbrella. The blacker the sky, perversely, the more Alina was pleased. She expected a deluge of memories at every corner, a saturation of emotions, and she wanted the weather to match. With the next step, she'd remember something significant. Or the next. Or the next.

As she'd suspected, it was Clerys' clock that did it. Famous for making and breaking assignations, she and Jamie took to meeting there in parody. Alina was devouring Maeve Binchy novels at the time and was starry-eyed in the long-gone romance of the nineteen-sixties. In present-day O'Connell Street, she stopped suddenly, as if the clock itself struck her, not any bongs or chimes that marked the hour.

Behind her a stooped and tiny woman ran her shopping trolley into Alina's ankle. A slew of apologies burst from her despite being blameless. Alina gathered her wits and pretended she was window-shopping – not reliving one of the defining moments of her past. She had a vision of herself, another twenty-five years on, ready meals for one in a similar trolley, encounters with odd strangers her only interaction. Was it so unlikely? She'd certainly never imagined *this* day in her heady youth in 1994.

'Have you seen a ghost, my dear?' the old lady was asking. 'Sure, an' there's many a ghost in the reflection of *that* window.'

Alina shivered. 'Do you know, I think I might have.'

The woman took a neatly folded handkerchief from her pocket and dabbed her nose. Then she nodded. 'Lay it to rest, pet.'

'I'm on my way to do just that,' Alina confided, surprising herself. She added, 'There was a Bewley's near here—'

'Gone. You'll have to go to Grafton Street.' She snorted under her head-scarfed perm. 'Celtic Tiger, my arse. You take yourself over into Temple Bar now and have a couple of cocktails instead. Sit yourself in a fancy bar and let the world go by. Sure, I'd join ye, if I wasn't meeting my sister in Ranelagh. She's very pass-remarkable about the drink.'

Alina laughed for real; it was barely eleven o'clock. The woman winked and touched her lightly on the arm. 'I'm away to catch my bus. Safe home.'

'Wait...' Alina watched her trundle off. The woman turned. 'What's your name?'

'Nora,' she called over her shoulder.

'Thank you, Nora,' Alina said, then more quietly to herself, 'Thank you.' Guardian angels came in all shapes and sizes.

Bewley's was gone. She wasn't sorry. The two of them – her and Jamie – had made it their HQ. It would be terrible if it had changed beyond all recognition. Even worse if it hadn't changed at all. Why, oh why, couldn't the ghosts stay in the past where they belonged? Nora's buoyancy faded. Alina wasn't ready for this; she wasn't bloody ready for any of it. Alina looked up again at Clerys' clock, the precise spot where her nineteen-year-old self had broken the news to Jamie.

17

Dublin 1994

She was late.

Late, late, late. Late on all counts. How could she have been so stupid?

'Alina.' She heard Jamie's voice before she saw him, dwarfed by the rush-hour crowd. 'Save me! Old ladies keep stopping to talk to me and promising me my wee girleen will turn up. What have you been doing?'

'Getting pregnant,' she blurted out. 'Oh, Jamie.' She hadn't meant to reveal it like that, in the middle of the street on a wet Wednesday evening. They were supposed to be going to the cinema and getting chips on the way home. Jamie had already got the tickets. She could see them flopping out of the top of his waterproof coat as he leant against Clerys' wall, his hands in his pockets. She'd spoiled everything.

'I'm so sorry.' She sobbed, throwing herself into the safety of his arms, and immediately felt better. He'd know what to do.

Jamie held her like that for a minute, until she calmed down enough to pull back and look at his face. He knew straight away she was serious, she could see that, but he didn't look shocked or outraged. He didn't even say, 'Are you sure?' which were the only two reactions Alina had been contemplating.

Instead, he said 'Oh, you poor thing, come here,' and had gathered her back into his arms, nearly suffocating her in the crinkly waterproof. More big blotchy tears fell and he let her cry, patting her gently on the back and whispering that it would be okay.

Standing right there. Under Clerys' clock while the world went on around them.

After a few minutes she calmed down enough to realise the movie tickets were digging into her left eye. She fished them out of his inside pocket and squinted at him. 'We've missed the start of the film.'

'Alina, I don't think *The Silence of the Lambs* can compete on any level,' he said. 'Come on. Let's go to Bewley's and talk about it.'

The drizzle gained momentum as they ran to the café and squeezed on to the tiny end table furthest away from the counter. The windows behind them steamed up and Alina felt cocooned in dampness, drinking hot chocolate that was not hot enough, sticky and cloying.

'Do you *want* to talk about it now?' Jamie asked, watching her over his mug. 'Or was telling me enough for today?'

His niceness made her cry again, but not for long. She was reaching the point of being all cried out. 'I can't think straight,' she admitted. 'I tried to make a list – that's why I was late. I wanted to be calm and grown up and sensible.' Jamie's lips twitched, Alina's too. 'I *know*. I thought we'd watch the film and eat our chips and I'd tell you on the bus.'

After a moment, he pushed back his chair, and Alina had a momentary sickening, lurching feeling that he was leaving her. 'Right. First, I'm going to ask them to remake our warmish chocolate hot and I'm going to buy some buns. Everything will look better with a bun inside us— *Shite*.' Jamie's eyes widened and he put his hand to his mouth as he realised what he was saying.

But Alina, who had spent the day thinking she would never smile again, was already laughing out loud. 'Bring on the buns,' she gasped. 'If I've already got one in the oven, I might as well have another to eat.'

18

The Oleander Rooms was a dystopian-posh filmset of a place, so far off Alina's radar that she was nonplussed. If this was Sanna's thing, then the person Alina once knew had changed in far more fundamental ways.

I'm not ready for this, Alina thought again, and given Sanna's non-appearance, it seemed she wasn't either.

It was dark, angular and monochrome with a surfeit of glass in the wrong places, muted colour only arising from self-conscious accessories on the tables: blue napkins and yellow-white flowers. Alina didn't open the menu, just asked for coffee while she waited, and she still couldn't fathom the silver-plated flask it came in. Instead, she focused on the silk and crystal daisies, but however many times she counted off their petals: *love her, love her not, love her, love her not, love her...* the result was the same. Alina was going to love Sanna. And why not? She'd loved Jamie, a lot.

Alina itched to take out her phone. Usually astute at guessing the time – she had to be, spending so much of the year in a place where days were still governed by the position of the sun – she found her instincts had deserted her. Two minutes could have passed, or ten. Whatever, Sanna was not just late, she was *late* – later than Alina had been under Clerys' clock.

She would check the time again when the waiter with the pink socks passed by. She wondered whether their colours – orange, green and red so far, as well as the pink – were a slick marketing ploy or a staff in-joke. It had to be calculated; the trousers were just the length to highlight them. Maybe the restaurant was a joke? Another parody of what the student-them had mocked.

Pink socks passing. Alina slipped her hand into her bag and her phone lit up. Sanna was nearly thirty minutes late. Alina had been stood up, hadn't she? There had to be good reason, a sensible reason. She refused to dwell on the remote possibility of accident or injury. Fin's cold feet were probably contagious.

She'd give her until quarter to exactly, Alina thought, then she'd... well, then she'd decide what to do next. After all, what was a few more minutes after twenty-five years?

Alina had placed herself diagonally opposite the entrance desk, all the better to look up casually at the bare trickle of diners, and she watched them, male and female, cursing her stupidity. Along with their phone numbers, she and Sanna should have swapped photos. Alina tried to work out how much she'd changed in the intervening years: older but not, thanks to her hairdresser, greyer; fatter but not significantly overweight; even her dress sense hadn't altered much. Jamie presumably had grown into Sanna and must look different enough for the both of them, but Alina couldn't imagine how. Perhaps, in solidarity, *she* should have attempted to look different, donned her favourite salwar kameez – green and blue, embroidered with silver threaded stars. Much loved in Bhola, here – as anywhere that people knew the Western Alina – she would have felt she was playing dress-up.

She recalled her primary school carnival when she was seven or eight – though she was unsure of the location: somewhere in England? – being dressed up in some kind of sequinned belly-dancing-cum-sari number that the cheerful teacher, congratulating herself on having a ready-made brown face among the white, called 'Indian Princess'. Alina sat on the float, feeling pretty and very exotic, until a crowd of older girls – dressed as fat and rosy Russian dolls – yelled, 'Oi, Alina, we didn't know you were a Paki.' She'd been surprised; she didn't know she was a Paki either. As far as Alina knew, the Pakis were the family who ran the open-all-hours corner shop on Raglan Street. Alina only usually got stick about the Sally-Army.

The girls were smiling, sort of, so maybe it was a joke – except that something not nice twisted in her tummy. She didn't tell anyone about it and now she couldn't remember how she'd found out it was an insult and, far worse, that it meant she'd been insulting Mr and Mrs Paki at the shop, when they weren't called that at all. She never ventured into the newsagent's again. Neither did she veer again from being a perfect not-actually-white-but-near-enough-to-pass little girl. And the next time she'd worn a salwar kameez was on her first visit to Bangladesh.

She'd just wanted to pass muster, she scorned herself now. Presumably Sanna did too. *And if she doesn't, am I embarrassed for her – or myself?* Alina wanted to put her head in her hands. She was scared, she admitted. Scared of seeing a vision of Jamie and even more scared of being judgemental. 'You're a coward, Alina Farrell,' she muttered under her breath, 'a bloody coward,' and with conviction she raised a mental glass: *Good for Jamie. Good for Sanna. Good for Sara Smyth, wherever and whoever she was now.*

Defiantly, Alina put her phone on the table. She'd give Sanna five more minutes.

Four more.

Three… Two…

'Can I bring you anything else, Madam?'

Pink socks made her jump, wondering if she looked as deranged as she felt. *Get a grip*, she thought. 'Could you pour me some more coffee?' She looked up at him and smiled. 'The mechanism's lost on me, I'm afraid.'

'Of course.' He dealt with it expertly, leaning over her to pour. 'Style over substance,' he whispered, making her feel immediately better. She decided to be frank.

'It doesn't seem like my friend can make it, but I'm going to nip to the ladies. If she arrives, I don't want her to think she's missed me, so—'

'I'll watch out for her,' he promised. 'What does she look like?'

'Oh. Um... I don't actually know. It's a long time since we saw each other... Her name's Sanna Ellis, if that helps.'

'Don't worry. I'm unlikely to miss her in the crowds, aren't I?' He arched an eyebrow, then pulled out her chair, fussing as if both of them were twice their ages. 'Downstairs, on your right.'

'Thank you.' Alina fairly bolted for the spiral staircase. In the privacy of the ladies' loo, she put her hands either side of a marble wash basin, and stared into the mirror. 'You're just meeting an old friend,' she said aloud. 'So what if it happens to be the long-lost female father of your child. What's the big deal?' The absurdity of it made her grin. With new resolve she washed her hands, brushed her hair, stuck out her chest – great for confidence, Elizabeth had told her more than once – and marched back upstairs.

One missed call. Sod's Law. Alina glanced down at the phone she'd left on the table and, heart thumping, listened to the voicemail. There was a beep, a pause, then: *Alina? I'm sorry, I found the place and I couldn't do it. I've been walking up and down outside. Could we...* The voice faded to static as if the phone was being held out or waved around... *Look, what about the old uni café, like you said originally. It's called something else now but it's still the same greasy spoon. I'll go there now. I'll see you. I hope I'll see you.*

Alina clicked off the phone and sat for a moment. Then she replayed the message. It had sounded like Jamie but distant and tinny, as if he were time-travelling, forever a ghostly nineteen. The years rolled away easily. Problem was, she thought, signalling the waiter, there was nowhere for them to roll to.

19

She'd been early for the restaurant deliberately, wanting to be calmly – *yeah, right* – in situ to greet Sanna, and now, heading out, she felt on the back foot. Alina could recite a litany of disasters about accosting the wrong person – the downside of meeting a new client or colleague in a public place – but she wasn't sure this would be as easy to laugh off. She forced herself into her tourist walk, leisurely checking out the This Is Dublin gift shops.

The café was called Cook of Belle's now – Alina stifled a *ha* – not gentrified at all, but cleaner. Alina gritted her teeth and went straight in. Empty.

'What can I get you, love?'

Alina looked blankly at the comfortably overalled woman whose bosom was resting atop a glass dome of brack. 'Oh. Tea, please. White.' She carried the brimming mug to a seat at the window where she could watch all comers and have plenty of time to settle the right look on her face. Passers-by were sparse: a briefcased figure leaning heavily on a walking stick and a cluster of Japanese students taking photographs. Not in the most hectic of imaginations could they be Sanna.

Alina counted her heartbeats with the seconds. One… Two… Three… Two women hesitated at the corner across the street, one gesticulating with what looked like a Keogh's paper bag waving through the air. The other was listening, holding on far more carefully to a square box. Forty-six... Forty-seven... Forty-eight... Alina's expectant shoulders drooped; colleagues collecting carry-out for their lunch breaks.

But wait. Alina tensed again. The Keogh's woman, suited and booted, was vanishing back the way she came, leaving the other, more casual one in red Converse trainers and a cream raincoat looking around as if lost. She crossed on the diagonal, passed the window of the café and paused, her hand on the metal-grilled door.

Is it? Alina squinted, then stood up and took a step forward, just as the other woman looked directly at her and did the same. They walked towards each other, pace for pace, and part of Alina wanted to laugh; all that was missing was the Glienicke Bridge. And to think she'd seen documentaries where long-lost families reunited in front of TV cameras... *Well, is it or isn't it?* And then something clicked.

It was. It was Sanna.

The familiarity in her gait, the way her right hand was in the pocket of her mac, and the angle at which a satchel was slung over the same shoulder. Jamie once walked like that. The flash of déjà vu was infinitesimal but sufficient: this *was* Sanna coming towards her, and coming towards her looking as uncertain as Alina felt.

They stopped a couple of formal feet apart. Alina swallowed.

'Sanna?'

'Alina.'

Slowly, Alina put out a hand across the no man's land between them, and Sanna reached out to take it. The firm grip held for a second, then one of them – Alina was never sure afterwards who – gave a strangulated giggle, and somehow they were enveloped in a hug. An awkward hug, Alina thought, but nowhere near as awkward as a quarter of a century, an adopted child, a gender transition – and a cardboard box – might have been.

Then they just looked at each other. Sanna's frame was

as slight as it had ever been, her hair shoulder-length and darker, highlighted, and those perfect American teeth that nobody else had even seen outside the movies in nineties Dublin were still perfect. The glasses with dark, angular frames were new; Jamie hadn't worn glasses, but they suited Sanna's high cheekbones, the cheekbones Alina might once have coveted.

'So, what do you think?' It was Sanna who spoke first. She held her arms out wide, then gestured head to toe. 'Would you have recognised me?' She smiled, a shadow of Jamie's smile, but it didn't hide the anxiety in her voice.

'You... you...' It was on the tip of Alina's tongue to say, truthfully, *you haven't changed a bit*, but would that be the ultimate insult? 'I recognised your walk.' Alina tempered it. 'And your smile. Oh, and the satchel, except you've upgraded cotton for leather.'

They smiled, the bubble of relief almost palpable.

Then Sanna pointed down, first at her trainers, then at Alina's pumps, and grinned. 'Some things don't change. Red shoes?'

Another silence before Sanna gestured to the table. 'Now we've established neither of us is going to bolt straightaway, shall we sit down?'

They did. The woman behind the counter called, 'What'll you have, love? I'll bring it over.'

'Coffee, black. Thanks.' Sanna smiled over at her.

Good as her word, she padded over with a mug and a dinner plate full of buttered brack. 'I can't give this away today, so help yourselves.'

'Thanks, that's kind of you—'

'Thank you—'

There was a pause. Alina racked her brains. 'Did you see the name of the café now?'

'I did. Hmm, Cook of Belle's, *Book of Kells*...' Sanna pulled a face. 'It wouldn't make our best-ever puns list, would it?'

'Not like Chipadora.'

'Or Cycle-Ogical. My all-time favourite.'

The conversation lapsed again, but it wasn't blind-date awkward. More, Alina thought, like the few minutes familiarisation when you settle into a different model of car to drive. After a solicitous few minutes offering each other the brack, the sugar, teaspoons, a napkin... there was nothing else left to share out, and Sanna finally said, 'Oh, you remember Sara Smyth? I met her a couple of years afterwards.'

'You did? How was she?' Alina pounced on another neutral snippet of their past. 'I've felt bad, over the years, the way we laughed at her. I can't even remember her new name.'

'Me too, in fact I was going to apologise for the both of us, until I realised we'd never actually ridiculed her to her face, horrors that we were. And she didn't recognise me. Anyway, it turns out we've both wasted time crying over that particular bit of split milk.'

'Really? How?'

Sanna poked at an escaped raisin. 'Palesa X was, I quote, "a phase". She only lasted a few months past graduation. Basically 'til Sara met a man called Mike and went to work as an education welfare officer in Wolverhampton.'

Alina laughed. 'Fantastic! So we're vindicated?'

'For our opinions, maybe—'

'But not the scornful way we expressed them?' Alina held up her cup. 'Well, here's to Palesa-slash-Sara. For being true to herself. Cheers.' She hesitated. 'And to you.'

'And you.'

'Maybe...' *It's going to be alright*, Alina told herself, exactly the way she had when Fin had dropped his news on her in Edinburgh airport. *It's going to be alright.* But it was the past that was alright, really. The rest was so big that she actually had no idea where to start. Twenty-five unknown years hung like a yawning fathomless canyon between them. Trembling, she pushed the crumbled barmbrack away. The sudden urge to run was almost overwhelming.

'Don't.' Sanna reached over and put her hand over Alina's

as it gripped the edge of the table. 'You're not the one who runs away, Alina. I am. I did. But not anymore.'

Alina was silent. Fighting. She closed her eyes. Every six months she was still running, but Sanna didn't know that or the reason why.

'We've done the hardest bit,' Sanna persisted, in Jamie's voice. 'We're here. If that's all we manage today, it's enough.'

She was right, of course she was right. Alina had to hold this together for Fin's sake, if nothing else. For Fin, whom she hadn't told she was meeting Sanna today. Alina breathed deeply and exhaled. She picked up her discarded slice of brack and took a big bite, even though it might have been sawdust.

'So... what do you really think? Be truthful.' Sanna indicated the length of her body. 'Come on. Spit it out.'

Alina smiled faintly. 'You're sure you want to know? Warts and all?'

'Yep. The two decades of heartache. Wondering, hoping, hiding. Of hormones and outrageous surgical procedures. The specially made shoes.' Her voice was droll; nervous eye tic invisible if you didn't know her. 'Ally-Bally, was it worth it?'

Ally-Bally. Alina had to get this right. She had to. A memory flashed – more déjà vu? – and she saw the two of them, 1994-style, across another table in another café, Jamie grasping her hand so hard she could almost feel it still. 'I'll never change,' he'd said. 'Do you hear me, Alina? *Never.* I promise you.' He'd been talking about something quite different, of course, but even so...

'Sanna Ellis,' she dared finally, careful to get the name right. 'You haven't changed a bit.'

Five seconds and about a hundred years passed. Alina, unable to tell whether Sanna remembered that long ago pact or not, could have ruined everything. Then:

'Fabulous.' Sanna's rapidly blinking eyes twinkled. 'Er, you don't notice *any* difference?'

'New wrapping, old contents?'

'Unoriginal, Ally-Bally.'

'That's because it's true. It's a compliment,' Alina assured her, the absurdity – their trademark – of the conversation loosening her tongue. 'I know hindsight blah blah blah… but you were always like, I don't know, an Easter gift wrapped in Christmas paper; what was on the outside didn't quite match the inside. Which didn't matter and wasn't even very noticeable until you changed it for the right thing.'

'Thanks. I think.' Sanna screwed up her eyes, but she was smiling. Then, quietly, 'I remember what I promised,' she added.

Alina sighed. 'Did I ever thank you for saving me?'

'Once or twice.' Sanna followed her train of thought without effort. 'I think we saved each other.' It was Sanna's turn to hesitate. She took a napkin and wiped her fingers, one by one. 'Seriously, Alina, if it wasn't for you, I don't think I… I mean, *I Sanna*, would be here today.' She looked up and caught Alina's eye. 'But hey, we can spend the *next* twenty-five years musing on all that. Right now, tell me about Fin.'

'He's great.' Alina was strangely relieved Sanna had mentioned him first. 'Happy, kind, married to Kirsten, about to become a dad. Imagine.' She was unsure how much the adoption-tracing agency had already passed on.

'I can't imagine. But I'm really glad. I would like to meet him.'

Sanna cleared her throat, and Alina braced herself for what was coming. 'He doesn't know I'm here today,' she said quickly. 'To be honest, he doesn't know we've had any contact at all yet. Well, we hadn't 'til a couple of days ago. I will tell him, of course…'

Sanna nodded. 'You wanted to see how this…' She swept her hand around the still-deserted café. '…went first?'

Alina nodded. 'And I thought I might have a better idea about… well… you know. What I, we, should tell him…'

'Ah, yes. The real elephant in the room.' Sanna said it as Alina thought it. That had always been their way. 'I'll do the honours, shall I? I'm assuming nothing's changed, then?' She

lowered her voice slightly. 'That you still don't know for sure
– whether Fin *is* my son?'

The café door opened and an old man, with an even older
dog, lumbered in. Alina was surprised animals were allowed.
Surely there was a sign somewhere forbidding it.

'Alina?'

She winced. Sanna's words sounded so stark. Then she felt
Sanna's hand on hers again, gentle, reassuring. Alina turned
to look at her.

'No. I don't know if Fin's your son,' she said, her breath
hitched. 'Sanna, I don't know.'

20

Late in the afternoon the next day, Alina was still looking at the unopened cardboard box that had lain on the café table. Sanna thrust it on her when they parted.

'I thought you'd like it.' She shrugged. 'Or you'll think I'm a fool. No – don't open it now. Save it 'til you get home.'

Alina wasn't sure what stopped her ripping off the lid and having a good look inside. Something to do with Sanna's face as she'd handed it over said it was special... And Alina didn't want to disappoint either of them by not appreciating the mystery contents.

She'd travelled back to Edinburgh with a sense of affection at her core. While her reunion with Rory had been civil, cordial even, the meeting with Sanna had warmth. Neither of them could have hoped for more. They'd etched an outline of their lives, ready to fill in later with the shapes, colours and twirly bits of the years.

Alina's grandparents were a point of reminiscence, Sanna genuinely saddened by their deaths. Alina's Bangladesh family, too, was an easy topic, and Sanna's scholarship move to Cal Tech. Fin, of course, was the common denominator, a Sara Smyth-like buffer with far more substance. Alina had a ready store of recent photos on her phone, the perfect prop. Their conversation was,

Alina knew, identical to any separated parents of a long-lost family.

It was as if they'd both ring-fenced a specific timeframe for the day. *Next time* had been the tacit agreement. That there would be a next time, and imminently, was all they needed to know.

'Come to Bradford,' Sanna said. 'Come for the weekend. Come next weekend. Or overnight, if you're cautious. There's a good train service from Edinburgh, just one change...' Sanna flushed. 'I've some cheek to push, after keeping you waiting for twenty-five years.'

'No. Not at all. It's not like there's an etiquette. I'd love to,' Alina decided. 'If you've room?'

'Plenty. It's just me and a daft dog.'

Alina had already phoned Fin to tell him what she'd done ('Wow! Way to go, Ali!'), what she'd said, what Sanna had said, what it was like – and what they were going to do next weekend. Alina half-expected Fin to demur at that. After all, what was more natural than his impatience to be involved?

Instead, he was content to let her take the lead. 'It's a lot to take in,' he acknowledged. 'Are you sure you don't mind?'

'It suits me,' she said. *In more ways than one.* 'It feels like the right thing to do for all of us.' That was absolutely sincere.

So it was all very happy-for-now, if too soon to call it happy-ever-after. Confessing – or not – how Sanna might not, as she'd always led him to believe, actually be his other birth parent was going to be another story altogether.

Alina jumped off the sofa with such force the springs twanged under her and snatched at Sanna's box. Kneeling on the floor, she eased off the lid – and was met with a puzzle.

Letters, anyone else would have guessed; handwritten letters tied up in a red ribbon, perhaps. Except there'd never been an ounce of romance between them and they'd certainly never written to one another beyond surreptitious lecture-room scribbles and vulgar post-it notes. This, though, was a sheaf of paper, old-style printer paper with perforated-hole edges, closely typed and interspersed with tables and diagrams. A smile spread slowly across Alina's face. She couldn't believe he'd... she'd... kept it. Their joint term project, November 1994. What the heck was it called? Alina read the title: *(In)Human Interaction: A Study of the Relationship between Social Policy and Information Technology.* 'Gosh,' she murmured. 'I wonder what our study found?' She had no recollection of the contents of the document. Though she did remember waiting three days for the original to be laser-printed and laminated.

'I'll pay,' Jamie had said. 'If I have to listen to those dot matrix printers one more time... TCCHHKK TCCHHKK BAHHHH BAH BAH.' It was a remarkably good impression; Alina could hear it now.

She set the project aside and reached for the second item, a stiff A5 envelope. *Photographs*, she thought. Settling her back against the lukewarm radiator, Alina peeled back the seal and extracted a single print from between two pieces of cardboard, one of which was the inset of a pair of 'American tan' tights – Alina grinned; did anyone even wear that colour anymore? – and was confronted by the past.

She and Jamie had been photographed in the midst of what looked like an entire grocery store, incongruous with a Salvation Army crest on the wall behind them. The infamous Harvest Festival booty, of course. It looked like the kind of staged action shot that made the community pages of a local newspaper – Jamie was even holding up a can of soup in each hand. It was clichéd, obvious, to say they looked so young, but there was no getting away from it. Alina still had her eighties flicked-back hair – a dark Farrah Fawcett, she'd fancied – and a Denim shirt over leggings. Jamie's navy sweater and jeans were neat; he'd always looked neat – they'd call him preppy now – and nondescript (*pot and kettle, Alina*) until you got to his shoes.

'Your personality is all in the shoes,' she'd told him one day when he'd dragged her along to browse in Brown Thomas.

'Yep. People judge me way before they get that far, then write the shoes off as an anomaly.'

'Which might be very profound if I had a clue what you mean,' Alina complained. 'What about those grey ones?'

The Harvest Festival ones were cowboy boots; she remembered noisy heels and dirty-yellow suede. 'The hue of baby poo,' she'd called them. He'd thrown them away after that weekend when it turned out that a spattering of Mrs O'Herhily's blood had stained them beyond repair.

Jamie wasn't quite as thin as the image she'd held, and his hair wasn't as fair – though that might have been the print fading – and it was shorter, curling at the edges as it touched his collar. Lengthen that, add twenty-five years, glasses and a bit of make-up, and Alina stood by her words to Sanna: she hadn't changed a bit.

Alina rose from the floor and stretched. She didn't want to turn back the clock, but it had been a mostly happy time. Even the advent of Fin, once her plan was up and running, was nowhere near as stressful as her forty-three-year-old self figured it should have been. Before she put the lid back on the box she reached for her phone and took a photo of the old photo and sent it to Fin with the caption, *Look what Sanna gave me. Serendipity x*

As she went to put the phone down, it buzzed a text message from Elizabeth. *Come over as soon as your ready*, it said. *Tell me about Dublin. E. x.* It was followed by a second with one word: **you're**.

Alina grinned, feeling the exasperation oozing out. Elizabeth had taken to texting like a pro but remained old-school about language. She refused to use emojis, and wouldn't let Claire Bond, who had an intern always updating the Elizabeth Maxin social media brand, countenance them either.

'Words are my living,' she declared. 'It would be looking a gift horse in the mouth to replace them with short-hand cartoons.'

'It would be looking a gift horse in the mouth to use clichés, too,' Claire countered, and the two bickered happily.

Alina often wished she had a Claire. The two women couldn't be more different but were united in Elizabeth's writing. *A business marriage*, she thought. Anyway. She ought to get a wriggle on and get over there. She hadn't exactly been avoiding Elizabeth's flat since Rory arrived, but she equally hadn't dropped in without a second thought. Elizabeth wouldn't have missed the hesitation. Sure enough, the thought had barely formed before a third text beeped; the woman was a witch: *Rory's not home, so it's a nice safe girly chat.*

Alina quickly changed her clothes and brushed her hair, pinning it up into a knot and letting it down because however hard she tried, it looked messy rather than casual. If she was going out for a drink with Rory, she didn't want to either dress up or dress down, but she was buggered if she knew which was which. It's not like it was a date. She couldn't even imagine going on a date. Alina's heart thumped, and she felt a frisson that might have been adrenaline, but was probably, she thought ruefully, just her age and the beginnings of a hot flush.

Elizabeth's front door was on the latch, so Alina gave the bell a couple of warning dings, before going in and running lightly up the stairs. Out of habit, she still avoided Rory's photograph in the cluster at the top. *Idiot.* 'It's me,' she called.

'Come in, lovey. It's all clear,' she heard in return.

In the bright warmth of Charles, Elizabeth appeared to be engaged in dragging an Eames recliner across the floor. At that exact moment, she was leaning on its back and eating roasted nuts from a packet. 'Have some?' She proffered the packet. 'They won't fit in the bowls I've put out and there's not enough left to put back in the cupboard.' She glanced around the room and added, 'I've nearly finished rearranging. Just that little couch to move.'

Alina rushed forward to prevent Elizabeth singlehandedly hefting the heavily cushioned sofa. 'You'll do yourself an injury!'

'That's what Rory said. But I'm showing this off.' She waved her cast-free wrist in the air. 'Liberated.'

'Didn't the hospital tell you to treat it gently?' Alina scolded, as they stood back and admired their furniture removals.

'Rory said *that* too. Are you in cahoots? Is this a get-at-the-old-folk conspiracy? The physio said not to try typing for a couple of days, nothing about light housework.'

'Light housework? What dictionary do you use these days?' But Alina was laughing. 'I'm glad it's better.'

'Me too.' Elizabeth adjusted her newly replaced watch on the newly mended arm, supported her elbow with the other hand and flexed her joints, watching them proudly. She looked like a puppeteer who hadn't noticed the puppet was gone. 'Healing bones of a woman half my age, I've got,' she said.

'Tell me…'

Elizabeth raised her eyebrows.

'How *did* you break it?'

'Oh, no, you don't side-track me like that.' She sank down on to the sofa and patted the cushion beside her. 'Come and sit down and tell me about your adventures. Rory can get us a drink when he comes back. It'll break the ice. I mean, you are alright with—'

'Perfectly.' Alina sat down firmly, burrowing for space among the cushions and chucking a couple of the more uncomfortable brocade efforts onto the floor.

'Good. We'll talk about all that another time,' she threatened. 'How was your trip to Dublin, lovey? I worried about you there all alone.'

'I know you did. I worried about myself a bit,' Alina confessed. 'But honestly, Elizabeth, when I got there it was fine. Really. The Gardens…' As she described the morning in Dublin, Elizabeth nodded, shrewd of eye and sympathetic.

'And what else?' she asked, after a decent pause.

'What else? What do you mean?'

'What I say. I know you too well, missy.' She held up her hands. 'You did something else. Was it about the elusive Jamie–Sanna? It was, wasn't it? Any cats out of any bags?'

Any more, you mean. Alina was caught off-guard. 'Sort

of. Yes. I...' She tried to change tack. 'Sanna's a university lecturer. Did I tell you that already?'

'Maybe.' Elizabeth almost imperceptibly flicked her head to one side, reminding Alina of the gesture she saw all the time in Bangladesh. 'Did they tell you what university or does that come under the Official Secrets Act?'

Alina grinned. 'An adoption agency hardly warrants that level of secrecy.' She gave in, enjoying the anticipation of a bombshell. 'And there's no "they".' She paused for dramatic effect. 'I've met her. I've met Sanna.'

'You little madam! I'm agog. Tell me all.'

'Have we time? I'm not sure... Alright. I'm only joking. I met her in Dublin,' she admitted. 'Her idea. Back at the scene of the crime, you might say.'

'Well. That's the way to do it.' Elizabeth looked as impressed as Fin had sounded on the phone. 'What happened? What is she like? Did it rekindle old memories?'

'You could say that.' She gave Elizabeth the highlights, ending with, 'She's like I remember. It was all different, but it was all the same.' Alina cocked an ear. Had the door banged or was she on edge? 'Is that someone coming in?'

'No. We've a good half hour before anyone comes knocking.' Elizabeth wasn't to be put off. 'It's sounds like the kind of relationship that picks up as if you've never been apart. That's lucky.'

'God, yes. And I definitely don't deserve to be that lucky,' Alina said without thinking.

'Why not?' Elizabeth looked puzzled. 'What's deserving got to do with it?'

'Oh, nothing really.' Alina backpedalled. 'I suppose it's just that in hindsight, some of the decisions we – well, I, to be honest – made weren't that responsible.'

'You were teenagers, lovey. That's the definition. Throw a baby into the mix and its dynamite.' Elizabeth shrugged. 'This is nosiness, but, back then, how did you and Jamie... Maybe I shouldn't ask.'

'How did Jamie and I "get together"?' Alina guessed. 'And the answer is, we didn't. That is, not until later. It got complicated.'

'What relationship doesn't? My own marriage...' Elizabeth shook her head. 'Ask me about that another time. You can't leave me hanging here on a Facebook status.'

'Brace yourself, then.' Was she going to tell the truth or stick to the party line? Alina dithered. Either way, it was far from the type of youthful, heedless romance she knew Elizabeth was imagining.

'It was the professor, in the library, with a reference book,' she said recklessly. 'Alina Farrell's own private Cluedo.'

21

Dublin 1994

'Star of my sociology class, the very person I'm seeking!'

The voice boomed behind Alina, breaking through the Enya track playing on her illicit Walkman and making her jump in fright. She dropped the reference book she'd just rescued from the back of the dimly illuminated stacks.

'My fault entirely. Please, let me.' He bent to pick it up at the same time as she did, ignoring her squeaky 'No, it's okay, really' as she snapped the headphones from her ears and shoved them in her pocket. One white wire trailed down, accusingly.

A roguish look entered his eyes as he clocked Durkheim's *Suicide*. 'Librarians just aren't what they used to be,' he commented, brandishing the hardback at Alina. 'Mis-shelved again. Lucky you found it.'

'Yes.' *Least said soonest ended*, her grandmother would say, not that she'd condone Alina's actions. It wasn't the worst of sins, but it was worthy of a fine Alina didn't want to pay. The same went for using a Walkman, which would also be confiscated. She sighed. She'd hidden the book behind about a hundred years' worth of dusty economics journals because it was impossible to borrow one of the university's endlessly reserved lending copies.

The lecturer winked at her. Not in a lascivious way, but complicit. It was his 'thing'. 'Steven King, PhD. Senior

Lecturer in Sociology,' he had introduced himself at the beginning of term. 'Like the horror writer but spelt differently, and ever hopeful there will be no horror stories in anyone's essays.' He waited for the appreciative titter before adding, 'Call me Ste. We're all equals here.'

'Other than the fact you mark our papers and grade our exams,' someone in the group shouted. That got a louder titter. 'Ste' showed his *we're-all-in-this-together* stance by laughing heartily along.

Alina, waiting, wondered if that ran to breaking library rules. It wasn't as if she'd raided the hallowed, tourist-centric fancy library that was home to the *Book of Kells*. She'd just holed up at the remotest point of the modern block where nobody ever came, especially lecturers. Alina and Jamie had a theory that there was a palatial staff room hidden somewhere, all half-eaten packets of Mikado and boxes of Milk Tray, a sort-of academic business-class lounge, where they slept between lectures and, in Alina's opinion of the social studies faculty, worked out what small group discussions they could contrive to avoid actual lecturing.

So, why is he down here now? popped into her mind. He couldn't have been looking for her. Despite recognising her from his sociology lectures, she bet he hadn't a clue of her name.

'Were you looking for me?' She called his bluff.

'Actually, yes.' He beamed at her. 'Yes, I was... er...'

Alina wished Jamie were there to egg her on before supplying guilelessly, 'Alice.'

'Alice, yes, of course! Well, Alice, I'm glad you're getting ahead with your sociology essay.' His eyes slid back to the Durkheim. 'Do you know, I think I've a spare copy in my office. Why not grab it? Keep it as long as you like.'

'Oh. Well, thank you—'

'I know! You could do me a favour at the same time,' he hurried on as if he'd just thought of it.

'Ye-es?'

'I've got a...' He made quotation marks in the air. '..."graduate student" with me for the term. American, but keen on finding his...' The air quotes again. '..."Irish roots". From Dartmouth College, or Drake, one of those places. Just off the boat, so to speak.'

He leaned in to her, his cheese and onion Tayto breath conspiratorial, and Alina's heart sank. The request for a 'buddy' had gone unread on the departmental noticeboard for weeks now. Clearly, Ste was on a last-ditch mission to volunteer someone and she, with the book and music misdemeanours, had walked herself into it.

'To be honest, Alice, I've inherited him from our own lofty Professor Meyers, and I'm pushed for time. Would you take him around for a day or so? He's an interesting lad. Confident. I'm sure you'll still do well on your essay.'

And so, Alina made her deal with the devil, by agreeing that she'd stop by Ste's office in the morning and babysit, indefinitely, Damien Blake III.

'You're a lifesaver, Alice.' Business done, patsy found, he was in a rush to be off. 'If you leave the Durkheim on a trolley upstairs, they'll see to it. Oh, and maybe stick the Walkman in your bag before you go, yeah?' He indicated the trailing headphone wire. 'What are you listening to, by the way?'

'Enya,' Alina said. 'And Chris Rea.' In fact, Jamie was the greater Chris Rea fan but, they'd agreed, anything to knock the interminable and sickly Bryan Adams, '(Everything I Do) I Do It For You', off the chart.

'Hmm. Eclectic taste. Very good.' Ste nodded. He hummed a few off-key notes. 'Recognise that? That's my kind of music. Bryan Adams.'

When Alina recounted the scene to Jamie, he howled with laughter. They nearly got kicked out of the newly fashioned computer centre where they were waiting for a copy of their inter-departmental project notes to be printed off.

'He got you good, Ally-Bally,' he chortled. 'Damien Blake *the third*, just off the boat, listening to Bryan Adams and reading some book called *Suicide is Painless*...'

'Idiot,' Alina swatted at him good-naturedly with the first print-off. 'How bad can it be? I get a free book loan out of it and Call-Me-Ste will feel obliged to look kindly on my sociology essays.'

'Except that he'll be looking kindly on the mythical Alice. That'll teach you to rechristen yourself.' That set Jamie off again. 'Off you go and get your *buddy*. I'll man the printing barricades.'

It had seemed a strange thing to remark on, the American student's confidence, Alina thought. That was until, a few minutes later, she met Damien Blake himself. He manifested the American Dream; it shone out of him, alongside his orthodontically perfect and gleaming teeth.

'The real thing, even better than yours,' she teased Jamie later: payback.

Jamie was unimpressed. 'He looks like an Osmond who fell off the path to righteousness.'

Damien was charming too. He called Alina 'Ma'am' as if they were in an episode of *The Waltons* or *Little House on the Prairie*, brought her a rose every morning and hung on her every word. It took precisely two days of ferrying him round for Alina to realise it was all a front. There wasn't that much to Damien beyond his studied all-American-ness. He was on a vague sabbatical from a community college in Des Moines, 'finding himself' in the country his great uncle's mother's aunt – or some such tenuous link – had sung about.

'Damien's out to have himself a Guinness in a claddagh-themed pub, murdering a bodhran session with a red-headed colleen on his knee,' Alina complained to Jamie. 'He's murdering American *and* Irish culture with his pea-brained ideas. He asked me if I was Black Irish today. *Please* will you help me out with him?'

'He's got under your skin, alright,' Jamie said. 'Is there

anything redeeming about him? Come on, there must be something you can latch on to?'

Alina considered the question. 'That's the thing,' she said eventually. 'He should be horrible, but somehow he's not. He's really sincere about all this crap. He believes in it all. He's like a big fluffy gorgeous Labrador that wags its tail at everything and hasn't a brain cell in its head.'

'I'll take him for a walk tomorrow, then, shall I?' Jamie grinned. 'Convince him he's "done" Dublin, and Galway or Cork is the place to be?'

Whether Jamie did put the idea in his head or whether Damien would have floated off anyway in search of newer and brighter and shinier things, Alina didn't know. But a few days later, Ste did seek her out and say she could step down from buddy duties and that Damien was moving on.

He didn't even tell her himself. That irked Alina a little bit, but maybe less than it should have, given that she'd slept with him the night before he left. In fact, she was more concerned with the eighty-five percent she'd managed in her essay, and how exactly she'd earned it. Damien Blake III was a glitch.

Until Alina worked out she must be pregnant.

22

'*What?*' Elizabeth was on the edge of her seat. Literally. 'Alina, lovey, you're telling me that this Damien the whatever is actually Fin's father?'

Alina shook her head slowly. She glanced at the clock on the wall: three minutes to spare before the stickler Morag rapped on the door. 'No, I'm not telling you that,' she said. 'Jamie is, was, Fin's father.' He *was*. 'That's the thing, you see.'

'I don't see.' Elizabeth sat back with a frustrated thump. 'I've never seen less in my life—'

There was a shrill burst from the front doorbell, followed by rapid footsteps running up the stairs and a light tap on Charles's door.

'We've got high drama in Bangladesh, too.' Alina said the first thing that came into her head.

'It's all happening, isn't it?' Elizabeth played along. 'Don't tell me – your Uncle Takdir has left that shrew of a wife for Mizan and they're living in sin on a houseboat on the River Megna?'

'Elizabeth! Where do you get such notions?' Laughing, Alina threw a cushion at her. 'First, I never, ever said Takdir's wife was a shrew, and second, it would be far more than a sin if they did. Can you imagine?' Actually, Alina couldn't.

'I just wanted to see you laugh.'

'I think you succeeded, Mum. Hello, Alina. Am I interrupting?'

Alina froze only momentarily at Rory's voice behind her. 'Hi, Rory. Your mother has the most outlandish notions about Bangladesh.' Her tone was light and friendly, and her shoulders dropped slightly. 'She's going to be very disappointed when she gets there.' *Shit!* He did know she was going, didn't he?

'In September, right?' Rory inadvertently answered. 'Sorry, I couldn't help overhearing…' He paused and Alina gulped. 'About Bangladesh. Is everything okay?'

They seized on the neutral topic. Alina breathed deeply. She *could* do this, but it didn't make it any less odd seeing Rory, her disappointed ex-client, here, remembering that Elizabeth was his mother and that his ex-wife, her daughter-in-law, had once lived in Connie's flat.

'I was exaggerating a bit,' Alina assured him. 'At least I thought I was until I heard your mother's suggestion.'

'Hello? I was being funny.' Elizabeth shook her head. 'It's called imagination. It's what I do, remember. Make things up for a living. To entertain people.'

'So you say.' Rory looked at her. 'I think you called it telling fibs when I made up things as a kid.'

'Well, you really were the most incredible wee storyteller, lovey.' Elizabeth's eyes lit up. 'He really was, Alina. You'll never guess what he said about throwing stones at the greenhouse and breaking a window?'

'Mu-um…' Rory threw a glance at Alina as he spoke.

She was laughing again. Rory sounded like the little boy he must have been, and Elizabeth the indignant 'I thought I'd heard it all before' parent.

'Go on, Alina, guess!' Elizabeth said.

Alina looked at Rory. 'I don't need to guess, I know,' she said smugly, and they chorused, 'It only broke cos the cat moved.'

'The adoption assessment, Mum,' Rory added lightly. 'I think it came under "pets". Or maybe "punishment".'

'Whatever – he was a little monster! That poor long-suffering cat. I forgot you knew all my son's darkest secrets, Alina.' Elizabeth was still smiling at the joke; only Alina caught the fleeting look of anguish crossing Rory's face.

Saved by the bell had never been so apt.

'Party time.' Elizabeth stood up. 'That'll be Morag. Mind and ask her about Berwick. Maybe one day she'll give notice here and move in with her brother.'

'Morag the one to watch.' Rory pulled a face. 'Shall I go down, get it over with?'

'No, you get the booze, and plenty of it. You'll be less big bad wolf if she's tipsy, although she won't set on you in public. She's a tartar for etiquette.' Elizabeth made for the door.

'What do you mean?' Alina looked from one to the other.

Elizabeth glanced back over her shoulder – she would have flung her cloak over her shoulder and flounced had she been wearing one – and in her best am-dram tones, proclaimed, 'Didn't you know? Darling, she absolutely *adored* Rebecca. Ha!' And she closed the door with a flourish, leaving Alina none the wiser.

'For Rebecca, read "Laura",' Rory explained glumly.

'I don't—'

'The novel, *Rebecca*, remember? Daphne du Maurier. It was your favourite, you said… you know, back then.' Rory looked embarrassed. 'Strange, the useless things we remember,' he mumbled.

'Ah! So that leaves you as Max de Winter and me as the new wife?' Alina could have bitten out her tongue as soon as she'd said the words. She even felt a blush washing her face, for goodness' sake.

Rory politely ignored any sign of it. 'Something like that. You know,' he went on thoughtfully, 'I always preferred the other bloke – Frank Crawley. Hidden depths, still waters and all that. Respectability stopping him seducing his best friend's wife.'

'Respectability? Nothing to do with the fact they *were* best friends?'

'Nope. *And* she felt exactly the same way.'

'You think?'

'Yup.'

'Hmm. I'll dig it out and reread it.'

They stared at each other for a second. Alina could tell he felt the shock she did; five years wiped away, chatting almost as easily as they had before things turned tricky.

'Yes, well, I'd better see about those drinks,' Rory said hastily. 'Er... what would you like? Elderflower cordial? Mum said she keeps some in for you.'

'I'll have a beer, actually,' Alina said. 'A Lite one. If there is one.'

'This is my mother's house. There's everything,' he said before turning towards the kitchen.

Alina busied herself setting out a couple of side tables and putting Elizabeth's lined-up bowls of nuts in easy reach.

'I'll write about it.' Rory appeared back with a bottle and glass. '*Rebecca*. On my blog.' There was a question, maybe a hint of challenge in his voice.

Easy, Alina thought. 'The Literary Electrician.'

'You remembered.' Rory looked surprised. 'I hadn't until just now.'

'Me neither,' she admitted. 'Did you really start one?'

'One what?'

'A blog.'

'Not bloody likely. Anyway, wouldn't it have to be a vlog now? Or TikTok?' Rory shook his head. 'I learned today that my mother has an Instagram account and something called BookTok. I feel old.'

'You should hear the arguments she and Claire have over it – you know Claire Bond, her literary agent.'

'The one she calls 007? Now I see.' Rory raised his eyebrows. 'I should have guessed, what with "Charles" and "Winston". I'm glad she took up writing, not stand-up comedy.'

'The secret joke is that Claire's name is officially Claire James Bond. Her parents were huge fans, apparently, and she's mortified. I don't know how Elizabeth found out, but she thinks she's hilarious. Don't say I told you.'

'Some people just shouldn't be parents.'

The temperature dropped a couple of degrees and arrested the tentative camaraderie. Alina lowered her head and poured beer into her glass.

'And we were doing so well.' Rory ran his hand through his hair and cursed. 'More drinks,' he said abruptly.

'Story of our lives, Rory,' she whispered once he was out of earshot. Then she rearranged her bleak face into a welcoming smile to greet Connie and Morag as Elizabeth ushered them in.

'Oh,' said Morag. 'Are we the last? I'm late. I apologise.'

'Morag and I met on the doorstep.' Connie stepped forward to give Alina a warm hug. Morag stood where she was with a thin-lipped smile and a stiff nod, as if having to share the doorstep was vexing. Connie gave Alina a barely perceptible flick of the eyes to the gifts they were carrying: identical boxes of M&S biscuits. Ah, poor Morag did like to be a cut above. When Rory came in with the drinks, her lips grew even thinner.

'Rory,' she said. 'It's been a long time.'

'Hello, Morag. Hasn't it? You're looking well.'

She inclined her head, which could have meant anything, and gingerly took the glass he was offering her.

'Sherry for you, my mother says. White wine for Connie, and Mum, your whisky.' He handed Elizabeth a shot, rather than the casual doubles and triples of her self-poured measures. 'Another beer, Alina?' he asked politely.

She shook her head and held up her glass. 'Still full, thanks.'

'Beer?' Morag sniffed as if he'd said 'meth'. 'I didn't know you were a closet beer drinker. I understood you were teetotal.'

'I let loose occasionally,' Alina said, smiling, the devil in her wishing she was drinking from the can.

'Sit down, for goodness' sake.' Elizabeth gestured at the various soft seats. 'Morag, sit here. It's the most comfortable. I'm longing to hear about your trip to Berwick. Beautiful town. How's your brother? Do have some nuts.' She pushed one of the bowls in the direction of Morag, another at Connie. 'The food is on its way. I'm following it on the app.'

Nobody, Morag included, seemed to notice she hadn't answered – hadn't been given the opportunity to answer. 'You just have to *manage* her,' Elizabeth had declared to Alina more than once. 'Once her position is recognised, she's a lamb. Thirty-odd years in the middle-ranks of the Civil Service would do that to anyone.'

Drinks, snacks, conversation… the evening still didn't gel somehow. There was a curious formality of a polite reception as opposed to the cosy, chatty sessions Alina had grown to look forward to. Usually, it was a communal effort to jolly Morag along, not allowing her curious mix of puritanism and veiled gossip-mongering get them down. It wasn't *all* Morag – Alina tried to be objective, though the woman did seem to be struggling more than usual. Was Rory still such a thorn in her flesh too? Alina felt a pang of sympathy for him. Connie's serene neutrality could always be relied on, but even she was subdued, on standby, her phone glued to her side. Maybe none of them were at their best. Even Elizabeth was manipulating her wrist and using it very carefully, clearly in discomfort if not pain.

They fell into reminiscence, a 'best of the Edenfield get-togethers' session, filling Rory in on the highlights.

'…then there was the time 007 was here.' Elizabeth brightened. 'Why *did* she have that karaoke machine in her car boot, I wonder? She never said. You must remember that, Morag?'

'Yes,' said Morag, clearly wanting to add, *unfortunately*.

'Claire was persuaded to perform her party piece.' Connie turned to Rory.

'Ah. Should I ask what that was?'

'Have a guess, go on,' Elizabeth said. 'You can refill my drink at the same time.'

Obligingly Rory got up. 'Guess? I can't even... Alright. ABBA – "Dancing Queen"? Or, Bonnie Tyler? Adele?' He valiantly entered into the spirit. 'No idea. I give up. Who? What?'

'*Goldfinger*,' Elizabeth declared. 'Does that farmer's daughter give Shirley Bassey a run for her money.'

Morag, accepting another sherry, said, 'We had much more intellectual fun when Laura lived here. Don't forget that.'

There was all but a stampede when the food delivery arrived.

Alina slipped out of Charles and bypassed the cloakroom to take the liberty of peace in Elizabeth's en suite. She set the alarm on her watch; she probably had ten minutes before she'd either be missed or someone else's bladder would unearth her hiding place as precisely that. Alina closed the toilet and plonked herself down, hooking her curtains of hair behind her ears and pushing them back over her shoulders. She rubbed her palms along her jeans and scratched her head, and in doing so caught the handle and caused the toilet to flush. *Stop fidgeting*, she told herself. Maybe she should find an app for yoga, Connie swore by hers.

Alina couldn't put a finger on why she felt so unsettled. Rattled. In the great scale of bombshells that had dropped recently, the fallout was remarkably little. Her apprehension over meeting Sanna and Rory had – so far – proved to be far worse than the actuality. There was so much good in the place she was now compared to where she'd been a week, two weeks ago. She was anticipating the weekend with Sanna, not dreading it. Fin was on board, and the looming situation around his parentage was really no better or worse than it had ever been. Yet here she was, holed up in the bathroom like a dumped teenager at a party.

She let her mind rove over the closed circle of characters in her life, as if they were suspects in a murder mystery. Who was the culprit, who was making her feel this way?

She made herself face the conclusion it was Rory. It wasn't

the tension between them, or the inevitable awkwardness, not even the guilt. It was, she recognised, those snatched moments of *normal* this evening. They reminded her of how naturally they'd taken to each other during the early weeks of the ill-fated adoption assessment. She had liked Rory and he her. She still liked him. She wanted more than moments of normal between them; she wanted to rekindle what they'd had before… before… Laura had spoiled everything.

Alina knew that was childish, petulant. Laura had just been Laura. Nothing she'd done was unreasonable. Like Rory had said tonight, some people weren't made to be parents. And some people weren't meant to be together—

The alarm on her watch beeped, her time-out was over, and if her mind was unsettled, her stomach wasn't. Alina was ravenous. *Hangry*, she thought. *Stop overthinking the rest.*

She stood up awkwardly, stumbled over the edge of the bathmat, and managed to hit her elbow off the flush once again.

Alina had left Elizabeth's bedroom door ajar and, attuned to spending half of the year sleeping with one ear open, listening for any calamity in the girls' dormitory below her room, she was quick to compute heavy footsteps and the squeak of a stair outside. She stood up and flushed again – if she wasn't careful, someone would have Rory marching up the stairs with a plunger to do manly but unnecessary repairs – immediately wishing she'd paused for the pee she realised she needed, and turned on the cold tap so the water gushed out noisily. It would be a bit much to hum as she dried her hands, so she settled for pulling back the lock on the door and opening it with gusto.

Morag was hovering in the doorway, the Brocken spectre of Maggie Smith minus the dry humour. She was clearly torn between reluctance to enter another woman's boudoir and curious to get a good look at it via innocent means. Alina wanted to giggle; it was a toss-up which of them was more fazed.

'Great minds?' she offered up to Morag's pursed lips. 'The bathroom, I mean. Sorry if I held you up.'

'You didn't.'

It's you, Alina thought suddenly, *you pious old goat*. Morag made her Great Aunt Husna seem all Pollyanna. Locking eyes, if not horns, she bit back saying, 'If you weren't suppressing your weird need to mention bloody Laura at every turn, then I wouldn't feel this way.' Instead, she smiled brightly and said, 'Oh, good. I'll see you back downstairs, then,' and they performed an awkward little two-step to decide who was coming or going first.

'After you,' Alina murmured, trying to marshal charitable thoughts as she ran down the stairs.

'It's loneliness that makes her bitter,' Elizabeth always insisted to Alina and Connie. 'There's no excuse for her racism, but the fact that you two are "always off gallivanting" and "failing to settle down" is what needles her. Has she ever asked about your set-up in Bhola, Alina? Connie, does she even know that you have two teenage children in Kano, let alone why you've left them to work? No and no. She doesn't like me much either,' Elizabeth went on cheerfully, 'because I was her age when I got this whole new life.'

Chanting 'be nice, be nice,' Alina noticed the door to the downstairs cloakroom was ajar and she disappeared inside for her much-needed pee. Three minutes later she emerged directly into the path of the returning Morag, whose surprised and accusing eyes suggested Alina was up to something. Stealing loo rolls or snorting a line or two of cocaine, probably – Alina was fairly sure all sins were equal in Morag's book.

Back in Charles, Alina cleared the sideboard of its bits and pieces to make a space for the Chinese take-away that Connie and Elizabeth were unpacking in the kitchen. Behind her, Morag cornered Rory, commiserating that he was back living with his mother, jobless and alone.

'It's a lovely place to have your holiday, Rory.' Connie returned from the kitchen. 'Take your time to decide the next step in your life.'

'Thanks for having me.' Rory turned to Connie, then

looked around the room. 'Cheers, one and all.' He held up his glass in a mock toast. 'I'll do my best as the token man. I can contribute a twenty-four-hour electrician service – no call-out charge – and... what else? I know. I can chase spiders out of the bath.'

'Man, we chase our own spiders, okay? You never hear of girl power?' Connie was laughing.

'Do you need Rory to chase your spiders, Alina?' Morag asked loudly.

She made it sound like a dodgy euphemism for sexual favours, Alina thought. What was she up to? 'Me? I'm not bothered one way or the other. There are some fairly hefty, leggy examples in Bhola. It's the cockroaches that make me shiver. They're indestructible. If you step on one, they crunch—'

'Then maybe he's servicing your electrics.' Morag blundered on.

'You've lost me.' Alina, Connie and Rory were all staring at Morag now.

'Oh, it's just with Rory in and out of your flat, I thought he must be doing some work.' Morag gave a little hiccup of a laugh. 'Or maybe you're just catching up. After all, you knew each other before, too, didn't you?'

Was the woman stationed at her window? Alina was fuming. Once. Rory had been at her flat once. Twice, if you counted the time she'd pretended not to be at home. But by the time she opened her mouth to set the record straight, Morag had made her point and moved on.

'I admire you, Rory, coming back here. You are very sanguine about the whole *affair*.' Her tone heaved with meaning. 'It's beneficial that you have business in Alina's flat. You won't want to face the ghosts of Connie's.'

Connie, innocent, said, 'You think my flat is haunted, Morag—'

'Oh, the only ghosts in it are Rory's own.' Morag announced triumphantly. 'Haunted by the error of his ways – if I may be candid.'

It was the closest Morag had come to outright rudeness. From the satisfied look in her eyes, she had been practising that statement all evening.

'I think what Morag is reminding us, Connie...' Rory smiled an oh-so-polite smile. '...is that my ex-wife, Laura, used to rent your flat.'

'It's how they met.' Morag had a little pink patch of heightened colour on each cheek. 'He lived there too. I remember it well. I'm the only one still here now who does remember, of course.'

'I remember.' Elizabeth's voice came quietly from the door. 'You were such friends with Laura, weren't you, Morag? For a while,' she added, pointedly.

Morag drew herself up, as if a game known only to her had played directly into her hands. 'I still am,' she announced. She left a grand pause, then, not looking at Rory. 'I wonder what she'll think when she hears you're back?'

'I wonder indeed.' Elizabeth crossed to the sideboard, murmuring, 'Forks, serving spoons, napkins. Good.' Then she raised her voice again and added lightly, 'And before you rush home to tell her, my dear, do have something to eat.' Elizabeth looked warmly at each of them and then raised her glass:

'To friends and family, to past and present, to peace and harmony. In short, to each of us. Cheers! Now get stuck in like there's no tomorrow.'

23

'That was awkward.' Elizabeth sat down in one of the armchairs by the window and fanned herself dramatically.

'Brutal.' Alina was making a desultory attempt to clear the leftovers. Rory was in the kitchen filling the dishwasher and Connie and Morag had gone home.

'Leave that for a minute, lovey,' Elizabeth said. 'Come and talk me down.'

Alina did as bidden, bringing a plate of cold dumplings with her. She could feel the tension in her neck and shoulders and decided feeding it was the best, if ineffective, option. Elizabeth took one and nibbled at it.

'I should have guessed Morag would be hot on her Laura agenda.' She sighed. 'She was spectacularly strange though, even for Morag. Rory should be grateful he got off so lightly. I'm sorry she dragged you into it.'

'Were they really so friendly?' Alina couldn't imagine it.

'Gal pals of the first order. I couldn't fathom it either, still can't for that matter.' She motioned for Alina to pass the dwindling plate of food. 'Something in Laura captivated Morag. She couldn't do enough for her, oohing and aahing and cooing and cawing. And it suited Laura to have Morag running after her like an overzealous PA.'

Alina considered the two unlikely women. 'I bet Laura

didn't pander to Morag like the rest of us do. Maybe she – Morag, I mean – admired someone standing up to her.'

'Possibly. Maybe she just replaced Laura's late mum.' Elizabeth smiled suddenly. 'She took all the credit for introducing Laura to Rory. When they got married, she went all mother-of-the-brideish, but Laura hired a wedding planner and Morag had to make do with a few crumbs of wedding cake.'

Alina frowned, trying to remember something. 'Morag's name never came up in the adoption assessment. Close friends and family were, present company excepted...' She flashed a grin at Elizabeth. '...fairly thin on the ground, especially from Laura's side.'

'It blew hot and cold once Laura no longer lived here. I do know that Morag was Laura's shoulder to cry on when they separated and divorced. Morag was livid with Rory. It was, according to her, entirely his fault.'

'Of course.' Alina murmured before enquiring, 'So, they're still friends now, then? Or is Morag just supremely loyal, out to get anyone who hurt her precious Laura? Does Laura even care anymore?' The potential power of a combined grudge made Alina weak.

'Your guess is as good as mine, lovey.' Elizabeth sounded tired suddenly. 'You can see why I don't want you and Rory hating each other for ever more, can't you? It was all a disaster waiting to happen before you went in to do a job. To be honest, I've no idea why they got married in the first place. I don't think Rory was—'

'Was what?' Alina's heart thumped.

But Elizabeth shook her head and grinned faintly. 'I should shut up. Nobody likes an interfering mother-in-law.'

They sat in silence for a few minutes, before Alina said slowly, 'Rory and I don't hate each other. We never hated each other, just the situation we were in. We'll get through it, Elizabeth, just give us time.'

'Time! How much more time do you need to get over

something that happened five years ago?' But Elizabeth was laughing now. 'I should bang your heads together. Where is that boy of mine, anyhow?' She cocked an ear but clearly didn't hear anything, so leaned forward towards Alina and tapped her knee. 'I'm fed up with Laura and Morag. Tell me all the gory details about your Jamie and Damien menage a trois.'

'No, I will not,' Alina said firmly, but her eyes twinkled. 'It definitely wasn't a menage a trois and my ancient and ill-fated love life is not some lurid entertainment channel. I *might* tell you the rest another day.'

'Hoity-toity. Alright, then, let's talk about the plans for the Bhola guesthouse. If madam has no objection?'

'None,' Alina said. 'You know very well I can talk non-stop about that.'

They spent a few happy minutes hunched over Elizabeth's tablet, squinting at the plans while Alina tried to bring alive the vision. She was conscious of Rory in and out of the room but when she half rose to resume helping him, he waved her back. Finally, he returned and stood looking over their shoulders at the drawings on screen.

'Can I get either of you anything,' he asked.

'Not for me, lovey.' Elizabeth twisted round and ran a weary hand across her brow. 'I've got a bit of a headache. I think I'll go to bed. I'm too old for parties.'

It wasn't a half bad performance, Alina granted her, until the overkill shudder at the end.

'You're a terrific author and a terrible actor, Mother,' Rory said. 'It so happens that Alina and I were planning to go for a drink, so no need to play the old lady to get us talking.'

'You're only embarrassing yourself,' Alina added.

'You've both spent too long in Morag's company.' Elizabeth held her own, but she was very obviously pleased with Rory's words, and her quiet 'I just want my favourite people to get along,' was sincere enough to bring a lump to Alina's throat, which was quickly cleared when Elizabeth fairly skipped out the door.

'My mother is transparent and shameless at the same time,' Rory said into the silence that came between them.

'She's absolutely my role model— Oh. That's my phone, sorry. Where did I put it?' It had to be Alina's unless one of the other guests had taken a liking to Bangla music and left their phone behind.

'Here.' Rory rescued it from the sideboard and handed it over, by which time it had stopped, of course.

Alina stared at the screen. Fin. 'I'll just…' She indicated her phone and Rory made 'I'll go and… something' signs, leaving the room. Her 'You don't have to leave,' was lost.

Hi Ali, it's me, Fin's voicemail said. *Bit of excitement here that came to nothing – er, again! Kirsten was having pains and we went to the hospital, but turns out it was a false alarm. We'll be getting a bit of a name for ourselves, but the main thing is all's well.*

Alina deleted the message then dialled him back. When he answered she was immediately reassured.

'Turns out it was probably wind and indigestion and we're home and having a chicken tikka masala. Yep, I'm aware those two statements don't work together but you don't argue with a pregnant woman, do you?' he said.

Alina could hear Kirsten's thoughts on that in the background, followed by a shouted, 'Hi Alina, I'm fine, just feeling fat, farty and foolish,' which made her laugh.

'Tell her I'm glad she's okay,' Alina said to Fin. 'I'm at Elizabeth's just now so…'

'Say hello from us. I'd better go anyway while there's still some food – ouch, Kirst, don't kick; it was not the baby – and talk to you tomorrow. G'bless.'

'Bye.' Slowly, Alina clicked off the phone. The baby was still two months away, and a scare was a scare.

'There's nothing like imminent life or death to put things in perspective,' Miriam would have said.

Alina tried to put herself in Fin and Kirsten's shoes. She didn't think she'd had a day's discomfort until the very end of her pregnancy, when she felt she was carrying a space hopper in her belly. But her experience was hardly typical, and she wasn't likely to remember tiny twinges of twenty-five years back. She did remember the baby, Fin, kicking, though. Tiny flutterings that she hadn't understood at first, and later on a powerful left heel that winded her under the ribs...

The momentary daydream had caught her unawares, and by the time she put the phone in her pocket and refocused, Rory was sitting on the armchair Elizabeth had vacated, staring into the dark night. She wondered how long he'd carefully not been looking at her, and cringed.

'Sorry,' she said.

He turned to her now. 'Is everything okay?'

'Yes, fine. Thanks.' She tapped her pocket. 'Just Fin... my son... his wife...' Alina attempted to gather her wits. 'She, Kirsten, is pregnant and had a bit of a scare. All's well though.'

'Good. That's good.'

'Yes.'

'Do they know if it's a boy or a girl?' he asked politely.

'A girl. No names divulged though. I think Fin's mum is hopeful of the middle one – Janine.' *Stop babbling, Alina*, she scolded herself.

'Nice name.'

In the ensuing silence, when Alina was desperately clicking through subjects that kept *away* from babies, adoption, parents, Laura, Morag, the past, the present... Rory suddenly said, 'Doesn't that bother you? Saying "Fin's mum" about somebody else?'

At least it was a question she could answer truthfully. 'No. It never has. I gave birth to Fin, I'm not his mum. I generally describe Fin as my "godson without the god – his odd-mother". I feel like an aunt or cousin, maybe, and the older Fin's got the more I feel like a bigger sister. He's so sensible and smart.'

'So are you,' Rory said.

'Not at twenty-five – Fin's age.'

Another pause.

Rory let out a sigh. 'So, here we are again, discussing babies.'

A discussion that would never go anywhere. Suddenly Alina was weary of it all. 'That drink—' she began, at the same time as he said, 'Do you still—'

'What about just going for a walk?' Alina suggested.

'Suits me.' Rory put his hands together and clicked his joints. 'I thought I was ready for Morag, but I feel mentally battered. I know she hates me, but it would be so much easier to be told that to my face instead of the mind games and innuendo.'

'She was particularly bad tonight.'

'Well, she would be, wouldn't she?' Rory stood up. For a second, Alina thought he was going to reach over and take her hand to pull her up, but of course he didn't. He said, 'Have you got a coat?'

'I'll squeeze into the waterproof Elizabeth keeps under the stairs. Let's head to Bruntsfield Links,' she said as she pulled the front door shut behind them. 'If it's not far enough to out-run the spectre of Morag and clear our heads, we can go on and do a lap of The Meadows.'

Both turned their heads to look at the coach house, but the curtains were closed, no light behind them.

'Surveillance in the dark?' Rory commented. 'Alina, I swear I didn't go into your flat at any other time when you were out.'

'I never thought you did. She was stirring.' She paused before they turned right out of the gate. 'Pact? No talk of Morag... or... babies or Laura,' she added awkwardly.

'"Don't mention the war"?' Rory quoted dryly.

But walking meant they didn't have to talk and conversely it made conversation, when it did come, easier. Well, marginally easier.

'There must be good walking in New Zealand.' He'd once

said he liked walking, hadn't he? Hill walking or hiking, she dimly remembered.

'I lived in downtown Auckland, but I believe so. I drove from north to south islands, though, saw most of the country in holiday-sized chunks. I'm not much of a hiker. Not a Munro bagged to my name.'

'Oh. I thought…' Suddenly she realised her mistake. One of those long-gone Monday mornings, they'd talked about how he visualised spending time with a child. Reading came high on the list; he had happy memories with his mum in the library and at bedtime. They'd diverted slightly into their favourite books – that's where *Rebecca* came in – and Alina joked he got nine out of ten for being the ideal man: a practical job and a literary hobby – throw in a penchant for hill-walking and he'd have women lining up. Except, of course, he hadn't been looking for a line of women. He had Laura and they were hoping to adopt a child.

Rory didn't say anything, and she wasn't going to catch his eye to see if he understood, so she hurried on. 'I miss it when I'm in Bangladesh, walking. I'd have a huge gang of children begging to come, and Bhola town is just a heaving crowd of people. It's too easy to jump on a rickshaw.'

At the edge of the Links, they paused and by tacit agreement went on the diagonal, the park growing darker as the sparse streetlamps replaced the brighter lights of the restaurants and shop fronts they'd passed by. It was quieter, too, shielded from the cars on the main road.

'Alina?' Rory stopped momentarily. 'About when you were talking earlier to Mum, when I came home, before the others arrived. I wanted to tell you… that I know.'

'Know what?' She tensed up.

'I wasn't listening in. I already knew.' He started walking again. 'Well, it was more putting two and two together from something you said back in those Monday meetings and then when Mum—'

'Just tell me.' She didn't mean to snap, but why couldn't

either of them finish a bloody sentence? Alina was going to scream. She wracked her brains while he stumbled over his words. She was first to put her hands up to oversharing back then – adoption assessments were intrusive; it was only fair she gave something back. Had she named Jamie? She *couldn't* have mentioned Sanna, and she never revealed Damien – nobody other than Jamie knew he existed – until Elizabeth, tonight. *Crap.* 'What do you know?' she repeated.

'About your father's—'

'You mean Fin's father.' Alina corrected him so sharply that Rory flinched.

'No.' He shook his head quickly. 'No. I was going to say your father's father. Your grandfather, I meant, but I don't know if you called him that. The Bangladeshi one.'

'My...?' Alina put her hands to her face. 'You need to spell it out, I'm lost.'

'Him being a shit,' Rory said succinctly.

'Oh.' Her shoulders went down. 'Oh.' As the wholly unexpected confession sunk in, Rory went on:

'And how the little girl, Khalya, might be his daughter, which makes her your...' His brow furrowed. '...cousin? Step-sister? Aunt? Fuck. That doesn't matter. What I'm trying to say is that Mum told me. She doesn't make a habit of it. I mean we don't, didn't, talk about you, but she told me about Khalya and your grandfather because of the hostel – the guesthouse, you call it.'

'Right. *Now* I see.' Alina felt as if she'd been let off a giant hook. 'I call Khalya my niece. Even if she's not family she is family, if that makes sense. And my Uncle Takdir, well, he makes up for my sad, misguided, utter dickhead of a grandfather.'

'I got that.' There was a smile in Rory's voice. 'The guesthouse, you see, is something I wanted to talk to you about. To make sure you understand.'

Was this where he raised his objections to Elizabeth spending his inheritance on a mythical guesthouse in a land far, far away? No more Mr Nice Guy? 'I was afraid you didn't know about it,' she said carefully. 'That Elizabeth hadn't talked to you about it all.'

'She didn't at first. You know my mother: she's both very good and very bad at keeping secrets.' They shared a brief smile. 'It was only recently she told me the truth. Claire knows, I'm sure. But well, I didn't like to ask about you.'

'Of course I knew. How could I not?' Alina had the beginnings of a headache. 'I was worried *you* would think I'd coerced her.'

'You? What could you have to do with it?' He looked as confused as she felt. 'I'd suspected something was up for years, but I couldn't force her to talk about it. She always clammed up. Then your guesthouse popped up on the website wish list. I guess it's a really practical way for Mum to make sure nobody else need go through what she did.'

Now Alina was sure they were at cross purposes. It must have shown on her face.

'You didn't know,' he said flatly. 'The years of domestic abuse. My dear old dad being as big a shit as your Bangladeshi grandpa.'

Slowly, Alina shook her head. 'I suspected things weren't great, that she and your dad didn't get on that well, but nothing like that. Oh, Rory. Poor Elizabeth. Poor you.'

'He died when I was two, so don't feel sorry for me. And...' There was a flash of anger, or maybe hurt, in his eyes. '...in case you're wondering, I didn't know any of it when we were trying to adopt, so I didn't withhold it to avoid any talk of "genetic predisposition" that would have been another nail in the coffin.'

'Another time your voice wouldn't have been heard?' Alina flared back. 'Don't be so stupid.'

'I'm sorry. I didn't mean that,' Rory said immediately.

'Neither did I.'

They looked at each other miserably, still walking. They were at the top of Jawbone Walk on The Meadows, the old hospital, now new apartments, looming solidly behind them. Alina had no recollection of passing the playpark, crossing the road and coming this far. It was cold, too, she noticed, cloudy and spitting for rain. No other figures emerged from the shadows; they might have been the last two people in the city, save for the traffic that never ceased.

'We should head back,' Alina said. 'Unless you want to climb Arthur's Seat for a sunrise breakfast.'

'I'm more inclined to hail a late-night taxi. Come on.' In step, they upped their speed, and Rory turned to her, looking puzzled. 'If you didn't know what had happened to Mum, what were *you* talking about?'

Shamefaced, she said 'I thought you might be going to tell me I'd coerced Elizabeth into giving me her money and to put a stop to it. It wouldn't be unreasonable for you to worry,' she added. 'It is thousands of pounds. But I underestimated both of you. I wasn't thinking straight. But I'm glad I know why it's so important to her.'

'It's important to me, too,' Rory said shortly.

He might have been going to say more, but in unison they spied a black cab with its light still on and ran to flag it down at the traffic lights. The driver was chatty, glad to get a final fare and curious as to why anyone would be out for a walk, sober, in the wee small hours.

Back on Edenfield Road, Rory waited until Alina had unlocked the front door and was safely over the threshold.

'One last thing,' he said. 'Somewhere in that muddle, you said, "Fin's father", and you looked very stressed.' He hesitated. 'You thought I was going to talk about your ex.'

'My *very* ex.'

'Well, to reassure you, the only thing I know about him is what you told me before.'

Alina was exhausted. 'Tell your mum what you told me tonight – and ask her to explain who Sanna is. Quid pro quo.'

Preparing for bed, Alina vowed that Elizabeth would have the time of her life in Bangladesh, and more importantly that the guesthouse – Elizabeth House; what better name? she thought – would make a real difference. Her last waking thought, though, was of Rory. Or rather that when she and Rory stopped obsessing over themselves and what had and hadn't happened to them in the past, they still got on. And that made her happy.

'You two need to stop being up your own arses,' she murmured.

Somebody had said that to her once. Annoyingly, they'd been right.

24

Edinburgh 2014

Like a game of reverse pass the parcel, a brown folder was passed round the circle until it stopped at Alina. Everyone else in the allocation meeting breathed a sigh of relief.

'Holmes/MacLeod. First-time assessment,' the team leader explained. 'I want you to take this one, Alina, because it needs a senior worker. On paper they look good, very strong.' He flicked through his notes. 'But the initial interview flagged up a couple of issues. Hang around for a few minutes afterwards and we'll have a chat.'

When the room cleared, Alina perched on the edge of the team leader's desk and turned the pages of the abnormally thick file. 'I can safely say I've never worked with anyone who filled in all their forms in such detail before the assessment even starts,' she said.

'Me neither. Enjoy.' He sat back in his chair and tapped his pen on the edge of the desk. 'Off the record, they come across as the most mismatched couple I've ever met. He's too warm, she's too cold. Think Gina Ford in bed with Attachment Parenting.'

'Opposites attract? Best of both worlds? Cold plus hot equals warm?' Alina grinned.

He shrugged. 'Could well be. I don't know. Give it your best shot. If anyone can get them to the panel it's you, but don't flog a dead horse.'

Alina read their application over a cup of coffee. Rory and Laura. They certainly were textbook. He was early thirties, she a couple of years older, two good jobs – his as an electrician and hers in marketing, whatever that meant – and a house with plenty of space. Slightly unusual was their reason for adopting. Laura had severe emetophobia and was adamant she couldn't be pregnant, and while Alina was an advocate of 'each to their own', it did beg the question how she'd cope with a sick child. Oh, well, she'd broach that in the assessment. The first move was to arrange her first visit. Alina picked up the phone and got through to Rory, who seemed very pleasant and was keen to get going.

'I'm flexible,' he said, 'but Laura isn't – her work isn't, I mean. If you give me some dates and times, I'll ask her to call you to confirm.'

And confirm she did. Alina arrived at the office the next morning to find a voicemail telling her Laura and Rory would be at home waiting for her on Thursday afternoon.

'I have an hour free,' the clipped voice said. 'I expect that's enough to get the measure of each other.'

'Certainly is,' Alina agreed to the room at large. 'Can't wait.'

Their house was on a newish estate in Bonnyrigg, just outside the city. By virtue of idling the car round the corner, Alina was exactly on time. The couple met her at the door, opening it as she was about to ring. Both greeted her perfectly pleasantly. She was led to the dining room where they all took a separate side of the table, and the session started exactly as a hundred others had before it.

'I'm happy to share my own experience of adoption,' Alina said, as she always did. 'People often appreciate that—'

'Why?'

Laura went from polite to intent so quickly that it took Alina a minute to catch up. 'I'm sorry?' she said.

'Why do people want to know about you?' Alina opened her mouth to speak but Laura raised her hand. 'Hear me out. I go to Sainsbury's for a tin of beans. I want to be served quickly and efficiently by a shop assistant. I don't care if they've eaten those same beans or if they've never had beans in their life. I just want to take my beans home and eat them. You see?'

Alina did see. She was quite impressed with the novel analogy and saved it up to share back at the office. 'Then we'll move on—'

'I'm interested,' Rory said quietly. 'I'm interested in all the stories. Can we talk about it another time?'

Laura countered each of Alina's questions with another, often rhetorical, question. Rory then gave his own answer to Alina. It was a game of mental tag, quite unlike anything she'd experienced since the group work sessions at Trinity. At fifty minutes of the appointed hour, Alina was fairly sure that not once had Rory or Laura either agreed or disagreed on any single point. 'They're like trains on parallel tracks,' she summed up to the team leader later. 'Same destination, no common ground. Neither is overshadowed nor embarrassed by the other, but they're by no means a team.'

'The pet test?' The team leader grinned.

'Oh, he's a dog, any kind of dog. She's a cat – but not a moggy, a rare breed or one of those hairless things.'

'Good luck.'

With ten minutes left – it was no accident that Laura's watch beeped, Alina thought – she asked them if they had any specific questions.

'How long will this take?' Laura asked. 'I'd like to book the appointments in a block. Is there a pass mark, or a quota of couples that gets to the Adoption Panel? I've already filled in all the forms, done all the tasks you want done, discussed all the talking points set out. Have you read all that?'

'You're asking if you can be fast-tracked?'

'Exactly. I've read the legislation and guidelines with forensic concentration,' (Alina didn't doubt it) 'and we are certainly within the top ten percent who meet the criteria. Surely it's a waste of limited resources to draw out this procedure unnecessarily. We were on your waiting list fourteen weeks to reach this point,' she added. 'We've had plenty of time to think it all through. And we have a five-year plan, and a child is part of it.'

Alina had plenty of responses, but it was Rory who replied. 'A pregnancy would take nine months – plus the time it took to get pregnant,' he told his wife. 'And babies disrupt the best-laid plans. You're going to have to be a bit more flexible, Laura. We know the theory, not the practicalities of having one.'

'Nobody knows what having a baby is like, but normal women who are pregnant don't get grilled for months, do they?' She turned to Alina. 'Did you? Until you decided to have it adopted?'

It was a valid point, not original. Alina was well aware nobody would have batted an eyelid if nineteen-year-old her had taken Fin home from Holles Street. She'd have had the obligatory social-work visit, provided for – or foist upon – all unmarried mothers, but like Laura, Alina had all her answers ready.

And that was another thing they'd have to address another day. If Laura and Rory got that far, it was hardly likely to *be* a baby. They had to be aware that these days it was older children who were the most in need of homes.

Laura stood up. 'We can follow this up in your next session. My free time is up now.' She reached across the table, hand out, and shook Alina's. 'Goodbye. Rory will make you tea or coffee before you leave.'

She left the room, leaving Alina trying not to let her shell-shock show.

'It's alright.' Rory caught her eye. 'Laura has that effect on a lot of people. She certainly did on me – before I knew it, I was married to her.' His friendly smile faltered and he added hastily, 'That was a joke.'

'I know.' Alina gathered her diary and notebook up. 'Well, I'll be off—'

'Please do stay for a cup of coffee or tea,' he said. 'I really am interested in what Laura calls the touchy-feely side of adoption stories.'

'Then, coffee would be great, thanks.'

He led her to the kitchen, which was as smart as the dining room but warm, and far friendlier.

'Do you do most of the cooking?' Alina couldn't help asking.

'Is it that obvious?' He grinned. 'Yes. I'm not a chef, but Laura would live on cereal and salad. There's nothing wrong with her, she just isn't interested in food.'

'I've heard there are people like that,' Alina said cheerfully, relaxing for the first time that morning as she settled at the pine kitchen table and watched Rory make a cafetiere of coffee and put milk and sugar on the table.

'I expect you're used to people like us being either defensive or trying to impress,' he said as he stirred his black coffee. Alina copied him, surprised at the insight. 'Laura is doing both. I'm doing neither – I don't think. I'm sure you'll tell me.' The dry humour made her laugh, and he went on:

'I think of you as an Olympic coach who can help me push on to get a really, really prized bronze medal, but Laura wants to achieve a whole host of golds through sheer genius alone. Not,' he added quickly, 'that I think a child is third best or that I should be awarded one for hard work.' He looked at her and shook his head. 'This is a bloody minefield. I'm afraid to open my mouth, let alone offer you a Chocolate Digestive in case you think it's a bribe.'

'This *isn't* a test, Rory,' Alina said, not adding, 'Even if Laura would like it to be,' but she was certain he got the message. 'And – I'd love a biscuit.'

It set the tone for the next few weeks: they had a formal session in the dining room, then Laura inevitably went off on an appointment and Rory made Alina coffee and they talked about what Laura did indeed call the touchy-feely stuff of adoption stories. Once or twice, Laura had an extra fifteen minutes and joined them, but outside of the more formal interview, it was very much 'three's a crowd'.

Laura was the closest Alina saw to being pleased when she suggested it was time to interview the couple separately.

'We'll get so much more done,' Laura approved. 'To be frank, you two are so up your own arses with this *in my experience* and *here's another example of how to make the child paramount* stuff that this assessment will never be done. I don't disagree with anything you say, I just don't see the need to keep going over and over it.'

'It's interesting,' Rory told her simply.

'But is it necessary?' Laura looked between Rory and Alina and said matter-of-factly, 'If anyone came in here now, they'd think you were the couple and I was the interviewer. It's the fundamental difference in the way you and I think, Rory. Alina is more like you. We need to rationalise to achieve our outcomes.'

25

On the train south, midway between York and Bradford, Alina got out her notebook and mulled over her six-month plan that was not at all going to plan. Leaning her head back against the seat and watching the scenery rush by, she reminded herself that these six months were always going to be different – but then again, there was different and then there was *different*. Even Miriam's uncanny prescience couldn't have foreseen Sanna and Rory turning up, even though – Alina grinned in spite of herself – her grandmother always presented the matter-of-fact impression she had the Lord on speed-dial, and that their conversations were frequent and two-way.

When Alina first decided to devote half of each year to Sonali Homestay, the Edinburgh months still felt like the real-life option. She earned enough processing international-adoption assessments to pay the rent, already on the low side, and have enough left over to subsidise charity fundraising and her trips to Dublin to see her grandparents. When a measles epidemic hit Bhola Town only a few miles away, she was heading towards the end of her six months in Bhola, so she just stayed on. They closed the doors, increased self-sufficiency almost to isolation, and ultimately nobody caught the infection. It was a turning point: Takdir and Mizan had seriously broached the question of her staying full-time, and Alina seriously believed it was an option.

'Not immediately and not forever – unless that becomes the way of it,' her great uncle said, referring to her commitment to her grandparents and to her less conventional 'family' in Elizabeth and Fin.

Whether he had spoken to Miriam and Patrick directly, or whether their minds were naturally in tune, her grandparents, too, had debated her options for the future. The modest insurance policy bequeathed to her was without obligation, their joint will stated, but they hoped it cushioned a period of decision-making. And that's what her current time in Edinburgh was supposed to be about. 'Instead,' Alina said to her reflection in the window, 'here I am, having to address the *what-ifs* of my past decisions.' But she could do both. In Miriam's words, 'It wasn't life or death.' In a push-pull scenario, Sanna was a reason to stay and Rory should be a reason to go, but he wasn't, she acknowledged, not anymore. Not since the spectre of Rory-past, Laura's husband, had become Rory-real-and-present, Elizabeth's son.

'And isn't that a turn-up,' she told the raindrops now spitting at the glass. The sky was darkening as the train pulled into Bradford Interchange. It was just the day to cosy up by the fire and chew over a mishmash of memories. She hoped… She didn't know what she hoped.

Sanna's house was part of a short-terraced row in a village once surrounded by green fields and meandering rural roads, but now a suburb of Bradford at one end and attached to the M-something at the other. 'The bypass still gives the illusion of countryside,' Sanna said as they parked on the road right outside her front door. Alina, marvelling at the novelty, realised she'd lived in a city too long.

'Come on in.' Sanna put the key in the lock and looked backwards before turning it. 'Unless you want me to go ahead and shut the dog in the garden for a bit? He's a bit out of proportion to the house.'

'I like dogs.' Alina could hear an enthusiastic whine and a series of thumps that lead her to question the neat little Scottish terrier she'd randomly attributed to a small, mid-terrace house.

As Sanna shouted, 'Get down, Sid!' a furry fireball launched itself straight at them and Sid revealed himself as an all-purpose collie crossed with something shiny and conker-coloured. He had a tail resembling a feather that whipped like bamboo.

'Just give him a shove if you want to get past.' Sanna demonstrated, creating a game to the dog, who ducked and dived, did the same to Alina, then just as quickly lolloped away and flopped down in a donut bed that dominated the kitchen. 'He doesn't go upstairs,' Sanna said. 'He was like a Dalek when he was a puppy and has never bothered since, but down here he's the master of the house.' Sanna opened a cupboard and took out a handful of bone-shaped biscuits, throwing them in Sid's direction.

'I know a small dog would be sensible, but he was the sad-looking one at the rescue place. And anyway…' Sanna tapped a burgundy leather ballet pump on the tiles. '…these clod-hoppers would crush it like a cartoon.'

They both looked down. It felt like a challenge, and Alina rose to it, carefully. 'You've very neat feet. You always did have.' Then she added, 'Feet must be one of the hardest things to transition.'

Sanna looked at Alina with respect and… relief? 'You said it, hun,' she drawled, then paused. 'Seriously, it's the silly things… I get my shoes handmade. It's my one extravagance. Lucky I was never a beefy six-footer, hey?' She busied herself with the kettle, then, 'Right, I'll show you the palace. Come on.'

The open-plan kitchen, with its doors out to the narrow, fenced garden, was the biggest room in the small house. As she peeked into the sitting room and made the two strides between bedrooms and bathroom on the landing, Alina wanted to laugh. She let her overnight bag fall onto the bed in the spare room. Sanna must have seen her face in the mirror.

'What?'

'Apart from having an upstairs and a dog, it's all just like my flat.'

'Really? Except for the computer stuff, I bet,' Sanna said. 'I'm still a geek. I love the logic of it all. You know exactly where you are with codes and cables and machines.'

'You might.' Alina grinned, adding, 'I wouldn't have thought there'd be much call for computer scientists in Peace Studies.'

'Don't underestimate us. We'll be the ones leading a quiet revolution via vacuum wires. Now, I'm going to drive into Pudsey and pick up a take-away,' she went on. 'You have to try it. I swear you'll think you're back in Bangladesh. Why don't you stay here, make yourself at home?'

'I could take Sid for a walk, if he'd like it?' Alina offered, and the dog's ears pricked up.

'If you don't mind him taking you, he'd love it. Go out the back gate, along the grassy bit and then just follow him. He's like a homing pigeon. Oh, and if a feisty six-year-old accuses you of dog-nap, that's Ashley from next door but one. Tell her you're minding him while I bring her dinner home. She lives with her mum and her aunt, but they haven't got a car and the restaurant doesn't deliver here. I owe them,' Sanna explained. 'Naisha's sister never goes out, but she cooks. She feeds me and Sid often.'

'You've never taken to cooking, then?' They'd eaten a lot of jacket potatoes in Jamie's digs, Alina remembered. And cheese mixed with boil-in-the-bag rice – or was she making that up?

'Sadly not.' Sanna turned back when Alina checked. 'If it was a special occasion, we crumbled cheese and onion Tayto over the top, too. Shit. I'd forgotten that. Don't worry,

I have more decorum these days. I've upgraded to tipping crisps into a bowl.'

So far, so good, Alina thought, slowly edging the field that backed on to Sanna's house. Sure enough, Sid ambled ahead, sniffing here and there, then at some invisible point, turned and trotted back.

'Hey Sid! Siddy!'

Alina heard the voice just as Sid cocked his ears, wagged his tail and took a running jump over the hedge into a garden she was pretty sure was not Sanna's. She hurried to catch him, peering over the wooden fences as she went. The dog was in a yard cluttered with a rusty swing, a small slide and a full paddling pool, and was being petted by a small child clad in top-to-toe waterproofs and boots.

'Hello,' Alina called over. 'I see you know Sid.'

The child looked up and frowned. 'Yes, I do. He's Sanna's dog. We look after him sometimes. Who are you?'

'I'm Alina. I'm friends with Sanna. I was just taking Sid for a walk,' Alina leant on top of some unruly cotoneaster and explained. 'Are you Ashley?'

'Yes, I am and I'm a girl. I'm telling you that because everyone asks.' She got up and pulled Sid towards the back gate, pointing at her outfit. 'I have to dress up like this or I'm not allowed in the water pool. My mummy's a fusser.'

'Well, that's a mummy's job,' Alina said.

Ashley nodded. 'She brings us sweets when we do. She's good at sweets. She's gone to get our dinner tonight. I expect she'll bring you some too. Did you know her when she was a boy?' she shouted, launching herself at the ecstatic, wriggling Sid.

'Um, yes. Yes, I did,' Alina said. 'A very long time ago.'

'So did my mummy. When she said Sanna was a boy who decided to grow up into a lady, I thought she was joking. But it's true.'

'That's good.' Alina felt slightly weak. 'It's only fair that everyone grows up to be their real self, isn't it?'

'Ye-es.' Ashley hesitated. 'But what if your real self is a murderer?'

Alina was never more grateful to see a young woman emerge from the kitchen. She was tucking a headscarf over her hair and rolling her eyes. 'Ashley, send Sid back to the lady, and come here.'

'But Mu-um…'

'No buts.' The woman turned to Alina. 'I apologise. My daughter has no filter.'

'Ashley and I were having a great chat,' she said. 'I'm not sure I can answer her questions though.'

'Nobody in this world can.' Ashley's mother opened the back gate and shunted the reluctant Sid through. She took the equally reluctant Ashley by the hand and said, 'I'm Naisha. Sanna's just pulled up. We'll go round the front way and collect our tea.'

Alina hurried two doors down to find Sid already chomping down his kibble, and Sanna pulling paper boxes out of a paper sack.

'You met Ashley? She's a great kid,' she said, looking up. 'I was going to come and rescue you, but then I saw Naisha had beaten me to it.'

'She's very smart. She likes you and Sid a lot.'

'She likes Sid and the sweets I give her a lot.' Sanna grinned. 'Ah – that's her at the front door. Can you grab the dog and I'll hand over their food.'

'Do they usually eat with you? I wouldn't mind,' Alina said when Sanna returned.

'Occasionally. Sometimes Ashley comes by herself. Naisha spends her free time with Tanzima, her sister. She's widowed and I think agoraphobic. I've only seen her a handful of times in two years.'

'That's tough.'

'Very. I've known Naisha a lot longer. She's a biochemist

at the opposition – Leeds Uni,' Sanna explained. 'She told me about this house. Right. That's the food all out. Sit down and help yourself.'

Alina's stomach was growling at the familiar aromas of biriyani and khichuri. 'This really is Bangla food,' she said in surprise. 'Even in Edinburgh it's mostly Indian by any other name.'

'Told you,' Sanna said smugly. She helped herself liberally then added, 'Alright. I admit I only know which is which because of Naisha. The paratha is as near to homemade as you'll get, according to her sister.'

They concentrated on the food, drawing out the meal long into the evening, picking at the bread and rice long after they were full. Then Alina fetched a box of chocolates from her bag, a gift. 'Lily O'Brien's,' she said. 'Both sides of my heritage.'

Sanna opened them immediately. 'No Mikado? 'tis a long way from fancy chocolates you were raised, Alina Farrell,' she mocked.

'And your Dublin accent would still get you lynched on the north side.'

'It's a lifetime ago, isn't it?' Sanna studied the flavour card as she spoke. 'Yum, orange bergamot. I often wondered what you'd do after Trinity, but I never actually saw you joining the enemy. I thought you might work for something like DFID or whatever it's called now.'

'FCDO,' Alina said. 'Foreign, Commonwealth and Development Office. Maybe I would have if it hadn't been for Fin.' She considered it as she bit into a second chocolate. 'I didn't go into adoption because of him, more like it was the only type of social work I could visualise. Then along came my Uncle Takdir and his plans... best of both worlds.' She added, 'And there's you in Peace Studies – which is what exactly?'

'Peace Studies and International Development, *if* you please. The two departments merged in 2015 and were recruiting. I was already teaching, and I had an obscure and shiny PhD that fitted right in. My field is conflict resolution – there's a prospectus or ten in the bedroom if you need some light bedtime reading.'

'How ever did you get time to do a PhD as well as everything else?'

Sanna looked amused. '"Everything else?" Being trans isn't a career choice, you know. It's not something I do. It's what I am. Admittedly, it probably takes me longer to shave my legs than it does you; hormones can only do so much. But that still leaves me a lot of hours in the day.'

'Sorry.' Alina cracked a leftover poppadum into pieces. 'I just meant that, well, PhDs are complicated, aren't they? Hugely time-consuming. I can't even imagine where you'd start. It takes me all my time to write end-of-year reports.'

'Good recovery.' Sanna offered her the box of chocolates. 'We should go to the next Trinity reunion,' she said. 'I'd fit right in with you and the social-work crowd now.'

'Except we'd find they're all middle class, middle-aged, mid-life crisis yoga instructors now. Or out on long-term sick leave with stress,' Alina said. 'It'd be complete role reversal. Case study, Sara Smyth.'

'Surely the law of averages puts one of the class of '94 dead and one more in prison?' Sanna chucked a piece of paratha at a loudly snoring Sid, who jumped up and snapped his jaw as if catching flies.

'I had a theory that everyone who goes missing has a story: dead, disordered or dispossessed. I thought it about you,' Alina admitted. 'But you've kind of disproved it. What's funny?'

Sanna grinned. 'I think you've got the perfect PhD thesis right there, Ms Farrell. I'll be a case study.'

'Don't.' Alina shuddered in the way she did whenever Elizabeth or Claire got into the fundamentals of writing novels.

Sanna changed tack. 'That reminds me. Did you open the cardboard box, by the way?'

'The…? Oh! Yes. I can't believe you kept our project. And the post-its.'

'I didn't know that I had.' She waved her fork. 'It was all tucked into the box of books I took to Cal Tech. I found it a few years ago when I was choosing the bits of my life I wanted to keep.'

'I'm glad you kept a bit of me, a bit of the old us,' Alina said, after a pause. 'Even if we were insufferable.'

26

The light-hearted, flippant mood on which they'd always thrived lasted until they said goodnight. Her room was quiet, the bed comfortable, but Alina couldn't sleep. Ghost stories, she thought, that's what they were telling each other: ghost stories from a shared past both experienced so differently. When Alina remembered 1994, it was like viewing a film of two people she'd known but no longer quite understood. *They had done what they'd done, but here we are, picking up the pieces*, she thought.

She was wondering whether to brave going downstairs for a glass of water, or whether Sid would go mental, when she heard another door open, feet cross the landing and go lightly down the stairs. Alina waited another few minutes, then threw on her jumper over her pyjamas and followed Sanna down.

'You couldn't sleep either?' Sanna looked up from the teabag she was dunking in a big mug. 'Want one? It's camomile.' Alina nodded. 'Tastes like grassy nothingness so we might fall asleep out of boredom.'

They took their tea to the cosy sitting room where Sanna pulled the curtains across and switched on the standard lamp. 'There's a light on the gas fire that makes it look homely, too. Unless you're cold? I *can* actually put it on.'

'I'm not cold at all,' Alina said. 'I'm not sure why I couldn't sleep.'

Sanna sipped her tea and pulled a face. 'I was thinking about that night.'

Alina didn't need to ask which one. 'I must have been crazy,' she said. 'When I look back…'

'It's amazing what we took in our stride. Especially when we were striding off in crazy, unknown directions.'

'There's so many little things coming back,' Alina confessed. 'Things I haven't thought of in years. It was all in a little room in my mind, and I'd open the door periodically and let something out for Fin, then clang it shut again.'

'Before the monsters could escape.'

'And they never did.' Alina shrugged. 'Until now.'

'Until I yanked the door as wide as I could and jammed it open.' Sanna's hand tightened around her mug of tea.

'It was always going to come to this, Sanna. I knew it the day Fin started looking for Jamie… I mean, for you.' Alina sighed. 'As far as Fin's concerned, he's found his other birth parent.'

'He doesn't know there may be a "get out of jail free" card if he doesn't fancy this one.' Sanna tapped her own head. 'What *does* he think about me turning out to be me?' Her tone was light and self-deprecating, but it fooled neither of them, and neither did the unspoken *what do* you *really think about it, Alina?*

'Fin is sanguine about everything.' No need, she decided, to mention his one perfectly reasonable little wobble. 'Really. He's the most together twenty-five-year-old you can imagine. I don't mean he's old before his time, but he is wise.' Alina gave a sudden giggle. 'He doesn't get that from me. Jan and Hugh, his adoptive parents, treat me like his slightly wacky elder sister. Sometimes I wish some of his faith would rub off on me, but if I'm not a convert to something by now, I never will be.' Alina's eyes were drawn to the dancing flames in the fireplace as she thought about the words Sanna was waiting to hear. 'He's curious – that's the word he used – curious about you. He wants to meet you, he's *excited* to meet you, but he's not looking for a dad. Any more than he's ever looked for a mum in me.'

'Does he know—'

'That I'm here. Yes, he does.'

'Progress.' Sanna nodded. 'So, Ally-Bally, it's down to one single elephant in the room.'

'I'd forgotten you called me that.' Alina ceased on an easier topic. 'Ally-Bally. Fin calls me Ali – as in A-L-I – but nobody else does— Hey! You used to call me doll-face too. Doll-face! How could I have forgotten that?'

'That was ironic,' Sanna protested. 'Do I mean ironic? It was meant as a joke anyway. Funny in the face of the extreme PC nonsense your lot spouted.'

'I know that. I'm just constantly amazed at what the human mind decides to recall or forget. Mine, anyway. Like the O'Haras after the Harvest Festival. Do you remember? I didn't until I was talking to Fin on Sunday, and then I blurted out the whole story.'

'You mean the O'Herhilys.'

'See?' Alina flopped back in her seat. 'Point proven.'

'You didn't see the blood,' Sanna said. 'It was the most gruesome real-life thing I'd ever seen in my sedate little middle-class life. And the fact that neither Mr nor Mrs was freaked out by it bothered me most of all. Huh.' She shivered. 'Anyway, I was going to say what *is* ironic is how I've turned into the person who everyone ties themselves in knots over with political correctness.'

'I suppose people… I suppose *we*, are just trying to get it right,' Alina said, wondering if that was just a cop-out.

'They could just ask, Alina. Just ask.' Sanna sighed.

Alina took it as an invitation and bit the bullet. 'Does everyone know about you being Sanna – I mean, you being… Oh, shit.'

Sanna laughed. 'Exactly. 'nother point proven. It's alright,

Alina, you can say it. Me being a trans woman.' She paused, then: 'Go on, say it. Seriously. It's like saying "I love you": a bit awkward the first time, but once you've said it out loud, it gets easier. Try it.' Sanna raised her eyebrow.

Alina wasn't sure if she was being mocked or challenged. She deserved it either way, and she rose to it. 'Sanna, you are a trans woman. A trans woman,' she repeated loudly. She looked around the room, an exaggerated, pantomime look. 'Ooh, you're right. The world hasn't ended.'

'I told you so.' Sanna's smug face changed. 'And, hey, maybe one day, the world will drop the trans and I can just be a plain, ordinary, simple woman.'

Alina stared at her. 'Oh, God, I'm sorry. I'm as bad as anyone, aren't I? I just—'

'I'm teasing, Alina.'

Alina sat up too fast, and swayed slightly. 'No, you're not. And if you are, you shouldn't be.'

'Well, no. Not in general,' Sanna agreed. 'But I am teasing *you*. You and me, of all people, shouldn't need to censor anything we say, or ask, or think. We crossed that line a long time ago.'

'I suppose so.' Alina slumped back. Once you've asked your best friend to... to do what I asked of you – see? I still don't want to say *that* out loud – well, a bit of gender-identity banter doesn't even feature.' She glared at Sanna. 'What was I thinking of? What on earth *were you* thinking of, agreeing to it?'

Sanna got up, went to the kitchen and refilled their mugs before she answered. 'There was a sort of convoluted, youthfully arrogant logic to it as a solution. I believed you. I believed *in* you.'

'You asked me if I was insane back then,' Alina said. 'But then you agreed to do it anyway. And you know what? I still don't really understand why. Explain that to me, Jamie Drew.' She took a large gulp of her tea, forgetting it was hot, and spluttered, wiping the corner of her mouth with her hand.

Sanna's voice sounded like a whisper after Alina's outburst. 'I loved you, Alina. I loved you. I would have done anything for you.' She smiled a wry smile at Alina's face. 'I might even have gone after Damien Blake if you'd asked me. Thank Christ you didn't.' Sanna got up again, pushed the curtain to one side and turned to stare out of the dark window, her hands in her pockets. Alina watched her reflection as she spoke, and it was Jamie she heard.

'I told you I couldn't sleep because I was thinking about that night. I haven't forgotten anything about it. I'd never seen you look lost before; you always seemed so in control, so sure of yourself. I admired that more than anything. When you told me under Clerys' clock, when *you* asked *me* for help, all I wanted to do was make it better.' Sanna sighed. 'I didn't spend all those missing hours looking for an open pharmacy that night. I spent them wandering up and down O'Connell Street, and I was halfway down Gardiner Street before I noticed the dealers and the sex workers in the shadows. When a Gardai car stopped and asked me if I was alright, I came to my senses.'

'And?' Alina asked.

'And… I asked the guard where the nearest open chemist was, got a lift there – yep, your pregnancy test had a police escort; I didn't dare tell you back then – and came back to the history you were rewriting.'

27

'How could I have been so stupid?' Alina wailed at Jamie. 'How am I going to tell people?'

'What the fuck do we care, Ally-Bally?' He was sitting beside her, tucking a blanket around her and stroking her forehead as if she had a fever. His voice sounded loud suddenly, and purposeful. 'We'll stand up to the lot of them.'

The *we* made her cry all over again. Jamie hadn't wavered since that evening under Clerys' clock. Whatever she wanted to do, he said, Jamie was with her. He said it holding her hand over the table in Bewley's, and he was saying it now, with her curled up in his bed wearing his spare pyjamas, awash with repeat fear – whether the greater fear was of pregnancy or the humiliation, she couldn't say.

'Are you sure you'll be alright if I go out?' he asked her. 'I don't need to, I can go in the morning, although if you keep crying I'll have to go and get tissues anyway.' He squeezed her shoulder. 'It's not the end of the world, Alina. It's the beginning of a new one.'

That made her laugh, hiccupping through her tears. 'Did you get that off the back of a cereal packet?'

'It was the blurb on a video game, I think. But don't knock it – crisis and opportunity are all the same thing, right? Alright, stop groaning.' He jumped up, pulled his jacket on and lifted his satchel from the hook on the back of the door. 'I'll stick to the practical and leave the self-help to your social-worky friends, who, by the way, are going to love this. Brown and pregnant: you'll be a superstar.'

He was all too right. She'd become their little mascot, the latest one with a cause they could jump on. They'd *support* her. Her grandparents would, too, though their support would come from a place of love and understanding, pouring out from them and the whole of their congregation. She would be smothered. Jamie's tone she understood; just as there was humour in tragedy, so was there levity in gravity.

She flapped him out of the door.

'Back soon,' he promised. 'One pregnancy test in a brown paper bag coming up.'

The late-night shopping trip was Jamie's idea, the only practical thing he could think of, she realised, in the wake of her sudden onset hysteria. Alina the sensible had stopped thinking straight; her head was a panicked 'if only'. *If only I could reverse the one stupid action of my life and wipe the slate clean.*

Jamie was gone ages. She shivered under the blanket, got up and paced his tiny room, sat at his desk and nudged the Newton's cradle pendulum until half-hypnotised by the swing of the silver balls. There had to be a way to right the wrong. There was always a way, she thought, she just had to find it. Alina rummaged in her bag for paper and a pen and returned to Jamie's bed, leaning the notepad on her knees. The familiar action was soothing, and she doodled. PREGNANCY she wrote in capital letters in the middle: bleak but a fact. Then on the left side she listed all the bad things about it, scribbling 'Damien' with a groaning *Oh God*, and on the right, the good things. There was only one good thing in this situation: Jamie.

Damien and Jamie. Jamie and Damien. Slowly, the worm of an incredulous idea burrowing through her brain, down her arm and into the pen on the page, Alina crossed out everything until she was left with one line: Damien – PREGNANCY

– Jamie. She looked at that for a minute then underneath changed it to Jamie – PREGNANCY – Damien. And like a mathematical equation in the midst of being solved, she first put brackets around Damien and then a line through his name.

Maybe, just maybe there was a way to reverse time.

Alina looked at her watch. *Where was he?* She used the rest of the time alternately to fret and to work out exactly how to sell her idea to him. It all hinged on him. 'Whatever you want to do, I'm here for you,' he'd said. His very words, and she believed him absolutely. But it all depended whether Jamie's idea of support went as far as holding her hand on the boat to England, or even in the delivery room, because what she was asking went way beyond.

When he did get back a good hour later, Alina was wrapped in his dressing gown – she was impressed he had such a thing – and staring at the screen of the black and white portable TV, which was very unimpressive for someone who knew so much about computers.

'I had to go halfway around the world,' he complained. 'Who would have thought it so bloody hard to find a late-night chemist?'

'Did you get it?' Alina had sat up and hugged her knees, wondering when to tell him he needn't have bothered.

'Yep.' He opened the satchel and brandished a paper bag. 'One pregnancy test as recommended by the pharmacist himself, and a big box of tissues, just in case.'

'You're very brave.' Alina meant it. 'I'd have skulked and snatched.'

'Which is why you sent me.' Jamie handed over the bag. 'Although I don't believe you for a second. All joking aside, Alina, you're the most together person I know. Look at you – already a zillion times better than when I left.'

'My head's clearer now.' Alina hesitated, still holding the pharmacy bag, and Jamie misread it. 'Do you want me to read the instructions to you? I know what you do, I read them on the bus—'

Alina shook her head and got up slowly, placing the unopened bag on his desk. 'I know, too.' She wasn't going to tell him she'd done her skulking earlier, just before meeting him, a guilty speed-read in the big pharmacy on Dame Street. 'It says it's best to do the test in the morning, but Jamie... I've got an idea. A big idea.' She leant against the desk and looked at him. She watched him take off his jacket and hang it up on the back of the door. He kicked off his trainers and pushed them with the side of his foot to jumble with hers at a spot near the door. Then he sat down on the bed and looked up at her.

'Go on, then,' he said.

But she stood there, dumb, not realising she was twirling at a thread on the dressing gown until it bit into her finger and cut off the circulation. 'Ouch.' She unwound it and sucked her finger. 'I don't know how to ask you,' she said at last.

'Oh-kay.' Jamie's glance didn't falter. 'Well, I can't think of anything you can't ask me. I'm tougher than I look, you know. Although,' he added, and she wasn't sure if he was being serious, 'I'm not sure I'm tough enough to go and give Damien Blake III a good thumping if that's what's on your mind?'

'No, of course it's not. He doesn't want to know. I mean I don't want him to know, he made it clear...' Alina was distracted, flustered. 'Damien was a dick. I should have seen that.'

'Isn't the problem that you *did* see it?'

'What?'

'Damien's dick.'

'*What?*'

Had Jamie blushed? Actually blushed? 'Was that a joke too far? Sorry.' He didn't look that repentant.

'It's actually very funny.' Alina sighed. 'Or at least it would be if it wasn't bloody true.' She sat down beside him, heavily.

'So, what's the big idea. Do you want me to tell your grandparents? Book you the boat to England? Marry you? What is it, Ally-Bally? Tell me.'

When she didn't answer, just looked down at her lap, he put his hand on her cheek and turned her to face him. 'Alina, whatever it is, I'll do it. I love you. You're the best friend I've ever had.' He swallowed. 'You've made such a difference to me.'

'I have? How?' She was surprised, adding a slightly belated, 'I love you, too, Jamie.'

He shook his head. 'Not now, Alina Farrell. This is your crisis time. Come on, what's your solution?'

'I thought, well, I thought... Look, I'm pregnant, Jamie, I'm sure of it. I don't need the test. But, alright, maybe there's a tiny chance I might not be, but it's not real.' *Contradict yourself in the same breath, Alina, why don't you?* She searched Jamie's face but it didn't change – he actually looked as if he might understand. 'I couldn't have an abortion, I just couldn't. And anyway, how would I even do that in Dublin? And I can't keep a baby, it's just not the right time.' She stopped, making sure Jamie was with her.

'Then you're talking about having a baby and having it adopted?'

'Yes. Exactly.' She looked at him hopefully.

'But?' Jamie took her hand. 'Don't look at me like that, Ally-Bally. There's a huge screaming "but" at the end of that sentence.'

Slowly, she saw realisation dawn across his face. She was quaking, but he didn't let go of her hand so that had to be a good sign.

'You want me to pretend to be the baby's father, don't you?' he said.

Alina blinked, fitting in a momentary prayer to Miriam's all-understanding, all-forgiving God. 'Yes. But...' She plunged on, now or never. '...but we could make it so it wasn't really a lie. I mean, if we slept together a few times, had sex...' *Jesus, Alina, he knows what sex is.* '...the baby could be yours. Technically.' She stopped. Did it sound as plausible out loud?

'Technically,' Jamie repeated. 'Like the Lotto? Or a game of Russian roulette?'

She listened for sarcasm, but his tone was neutral. Even in the moment she admired his self-control. He'd been eighteen, had a pregnancy dumped on him, gone out and made small talk with a pharmacist over a pregnancy test, and then was hit with Alina's idea of the century. *He really does love me*, she thought.

The next minute, though, it all crashed around her.

He still didn't let go of her hand. In fact, he tightened his grasp.

'Alina Farrell,' he said, 'are you *completely* insane?'

28

'I've asked myself over and over again why I didn't just do the bloody pregnancy test,' Alina said. 'The Clearblue box was right there, you'd gone out and bought it – out of your own money, too; I never did pay you back. I felt pregnant; I had all the early symptoms. I would have sworn my life on it being positive. Three minutes and we'd have known for sure.' Alina wanted to shake her younger self. 'It took me years to accept that there might have been absolutely no need for our god-almighty charade.'

'Hindsight is as useless as regret.' Sanna still stood at the window, but she turned to face Alina. 'We did what we did. If it changed our lives, then let's just decide it was for the better. Think of Fin? Imagine him not being here.'

Alina sighed. 'You always were the voice of reason.'

'Oh? Other than that one time I didn't insist you pee on a stick, you mean?'

'The exception that proves the rule.' She smiled faintly. 'Remember when we told my grandparents? We all agreed that baby deserved to be born and deserved a proper family, but I knew they thought that, all together, we could be that family. Then you said…'

'…I said, 'With the best will in the world, Mr and Mrs

Farrell, we're too young and you're too old.' Sanna winced. 'They took it in good spirit.'

'It was true.'

Sanna sighed. 'You have to let it go, Alina. We did what we did,' she repeated. 'Nothing, *nothing* bad came out of it. Let's put our energies into where we go from here.'

'Telling Fin. Or not telling Fin.'

There was a pause as the two women looked at each other before Sanna said, 'We are going to tell him, aren't we.' It wasn't a question.

'Of course we are. I think I was always just waiting for you.'

Sanna put out her arms and Alina crossed the room, folding herself into the hug. Twenty-five years on, their bodies moulded into a familiar position, head against shoulder, arms tightening... Despite herself, Alina stiffened suddenly, and managed to resist the impulse – based on shock, not distaste – to pull away. Sanna's voice, muffled in her hair, sounded amused.

'You've just noticed the difference, haven't you?' she said. She pulled back slightly at glanced down at the modest swell of breasts under her loose dressing gown. 'Don't worry, it still surprises me sometimes.'

They looked at each other and began to giggle, far more than was warranted. Outside, the moon came and went between the clouds, and they talked on until another day dawned.

The sun was palely breaking through by midday and Sanna suggested they take Sid out. 'There's a dog park just down the road in Pudsey where we're booked into a social session on Saturday afternoons. Don't judge me,' she added in fake shame. 'Sid's not my fur baby and I don't dress him up or arrange actual playdates. This is a chasing, wrestling and sniffing free for all. The social bit's for Sid – we can lurk at the field perimeter. I just wade in if he's actually suffocating any other dog he's pinned down to lick.'

'Sounds like the picnics we have with the children in Bhola,' Alina commented. 'I'm game.'

It was only when they'd driven the few miles, parked up, and Sanna checked them in as 'Sanna Ellis and Sid, plus one guest human' that something hit her like a tonne of bricks. *Shit.* Alina waited until they were in the acre field – Sid had slipped his lead and raced away – to confess, 'Last night, I called you Jamie. Jamie Drew. I'm really sorry.'

Sanna took an apple from each pocket, inspected them for blemishes and then held one out to Alina. 'Deadnaming,' she said. 'That's what it's called.' Then, as Alina opened her mouth, she shook her head. 'Don't,' she said. 'Honestly, Alina. I mean, yes, it's on those ten-of-the-worst-things-you-can-do-to-a-trans-person lists but that's a broad stroke.' She took a bite out of her apple. 'Okay, I'd be miffed if somebody couldn't be bothered or did it deliberately, but it's different with you.'

'Is it?'

'Yes.' Sanna tipped up her head to look at the rushing sky. She gave Alina a sidelong glance. 'Totally. Haven't you gathered yet that this Jamie–Sanna bundle of muddle is actually all your fault?'

'Huh? I don't—'

'You not only gave birth to Fin – you gave birth to Sanna, too.'

'What?' Alina, rubbing her apple on her coat lapel to give it a good shine, nearly dropped it to the ground. 'Er... I'm thinking there's a punchline here?'

'Seriously. Kind of. I realised a lot about me over those few months when you were pregnant,' Sanna said slowly. 'Oh, there was no great epiphany, but at some fundamental level – and if this gets wacky and social-workerish, then sue me, Ally-Bally – I started to face things I hadn't a name for.' She furrowed her brow. 'I knew I wasn't gay. And I wasn't transsexual; that never even occurred to me. But there wasn't anything else to be back then. I just lived with a niggle of something being off, like an occasional ache you can't quite pinpoint. And then one day, you wake up and realise the pain is getting worse, is constant, and you still don't quite know how to put it into words, but you have to do something. Or you won't be you anymore.'

They reached the top of the field and stopped to lean back on the fence, looking out at the half a dozen or so dogs running amok. Sid was right there in the fray.

'In the long run, I did you a favour, then?' Alina tried to match Sanna's levity. 'My moment of madness was always meant to be, so the universe could come to its senses and you could be you.'

'You tell yourself that if it makes you feel better.' Sanna winked. 'I do know that meeting you changed my life,' she added. 'It was the catalyst to everything that's come since.'

'Why now?' Alina asked spontaneously. 'What has made you respond to Fin's tracing of you now, Sanna? Why not two years ago, five? Why not next year?'

Sanna finished her apple before she replied. 'You could probably argue there's all kinds of complicated psychological reasons, but the bottom line is selfish and simple. I wanted – want – to add something good to your lives and I think – I hope – I'm sorted enough in myself to do that now. Finally.'

'I nearly missed you,' Alina confided. 'When Fin told me he'd found you, I knew you'd contact me first, but I was waiting for Sanna Drew. It was only when Kirsten, you know, Fin's wife, said you'd probably changed your whole name, that I went back and checked my emails.'

'I wouldn't have given up that easily,' Sanna said. 'There was always the agency as intermediary. I didn't think about the name... do you know how hard it is choosing your own name?'

'I can guess.' Alina agreed. 'So, go on then, how did you?'

'Sanna means truth – or lily, depending what you google. But I liked the idea of... well, kind of *wearing* the truth about me without it being a statement. Is that wankerish or does it make some sense? And Ellis was my middle name all along.'

'It's nice,' Alina said. 'You suit it.'

'I like it.' Sanna pulled a face. 'The only negative reaction has been from my mother, so no surprises there.' She put on a warbling upper class drawl. '"Darling, why must you carry all your notions to extremes? Jamie is a perfectly good name and if you, er, want to *feminise* it, look at Jamie Lee Curtis. Or what about Janie?"' Sanna shook her head. 'If my name didn't noticeably change, she could pretend to her highfalutin friends nothing else had.'

'What *do* your parents think?' Alina searched her memory. 'Did you ever talk about them back in Trinity? I don't remember.'

'I would hardly even have thought of them. I went to boarding school when I was seven because my dad was a very minor diplomat and got postings in the weirdest out-of-the-way places. My mum still has faded Foreign Office notions of grandeur. Me 'n' Sid are firmly on the "also ran" part of their formal Christmas card list these days. Total nonentities.' Sanna grinned. 'Their loss.'

'Gosh. You're probably the poshest person I've ever met and I didn't know it.' Alina was visualising a skinny little Jamie in short trousers and a cap, heading off to a sort-of Hogwarts prep school. 'Though I do recall my granny saying you spoke very nicely. I didn't know I was your bit of rough.'

'Your granny was surrounded by north-side Dubs when she met me. Any middle-English accent sounded like RP.' Sanna grinned again and turned it into a sigh. 'My folks would have called you my "little Celtic friend", and asked you polite, slightly incredulous questions about "social-services work" and "*your* Salvation Army". As for the half-Bangladeshi bit, they'd have *done you a favour* and rewritten your skin tone as Greek or Portuguese.'

'They wouldn't be the first.' Alina flushed. There were times in her past, pre-Bangladesh, she might have let people think something similar. She moved on. 'Did... do... they know about Fin?'

Sanna shielded her eyes to stare across the field; Sid was

lying in a heap, panting. 'I doubt they'd have wanted to know. A bit too unsavoury. Just like me.'

'You Jamie or you Sanna?'

Sanna swivelled her eyes across to meet Alina's. 'Very perceptive of you, Ally-Bally. And the answer is, both. I'm sure I'll bore you with all the sordid details one day, but the short answer is that we last saw each other for my PhD graduation at Cal Tech.' Then, her eyes twinkled as she pre-empted Alina's next how-to-ask question, 'Jamie got the PhD, but Sanna was hot on his heels.'

'And then she started wearing them?' It was a weak joke, but both of them laughed.

'Come on.' Sanna pointed to Sid. 'Playtime's up for this week.' Then added to Alina, 'I knew you were an ally at heart.'

'Always, Sanna. Just like you were mine.'

'*Am* yours.' Sanna raised her apple core to Alina's and they executed a clumsy high five. 'Power to the misfits. Still reigning after all these years.'

They stopped to eat at a conveniently placed pub called The Yorkshire Pudding.

'Well, we can't not...' Sanna said.

'...with a name like that,' Alina agreed.

Especially since it was happy to let sleeping dogs lie under its tables and served substantial ploughman's lunches.

'Look at us, like the old married couple we might have been.' Sanna gazed around at the neatly paired-off twosomes who filled the other tables. 'Instead, I've got Sid, and you've got...?' She raised her eyebrows.

'I've got Elizabeth,' Alina said. 'My landlady and *so* much more.' Describing her Edinburgh set-up took them through to coffee. 'It seems we're still good at obscure relationships,' she finished up.

'No romances?'

'More brief encounters than anything enduring.' Alina stirred her coffee. 'There was someone for a while in Bangladesh but that was forever ago, more about me falling in love with the country rather than him. Right time, wrong person. He got married to the right girl and had two children.' She hesitated. 'The guy in Edinburgh... well, there never really was a guy in Edinburgh. We worked together, he was married. End of.' *Except it hadn't been.* But Alina kept that to herself.

'Right person, wrong time?' Sanna said gently.

'Something like that. Certainly a bit on the meagre side for a forty-three-year-old.'

'You can't even call it quality over quantity by the sounds of it.' Sanna took Alina's cue to change tone. She lowered her voice. 'And if we're talking about the sex, let's be honest, there wasn't much quality between us, was there? We got the job done is about the best you could say.'

'Like going for a run?' Alina suggested. 'Bit of an effort, feels good to stretch the muscle but the best part is knowing it's done for the day?' She thought Sanna would double over laughing. 'It was totally unconscious, I'm sure, but we always had a treat planned for afterwards.'

'You're so right. Oh, dear.' Sanna took control of herself. 'It wasn't the best introduction to sex, was it? Well, it was my introduction. You had the Damien Blake III experience and I dimly remember thinking I wasn't measuring up.'

'There was nothing to measure up to.' Alina shuddered. 'He was a handsome Yank straight out of the movies, so I thought he'd be good at it. I knew he wouldn't break my heart, so I figured, go for it. But he was totally self-obsessed and as clueless as me. It was, I don't know, just what we did one night because we had an hour to fill.'

'You ended up being a character from one of the Maeve Binchy books you liked so much.' Sanna clearly couldn't decide whether to laugh or commiserate. 'Poor Alina. I wish I could have made you see stars. I did my best, but...'

'From this vantage point, I can't believe you managed so well.' Alina grinned. 'Would it be impolite to ask, well, I don't know how to ask—'

'How I got it up?' Sanna's voice carried, and they both looked around, just in case, but nobody other than Sid stirred. They giggled. 'Sheer willpower, Ally-Bally, sheer fucking willpower. I was a teenage boy, remember, barely eighteen – the child prodigy who was a year ahead. I might have been *questioning*, but whatever hormones were there, they wanted out somehow.'

'You were gentle.' Alina thought back to those encounters, ten of them to beat the odds (she'd kept a record). Always in Jamie's room, always late at night, written into the calendar like brushing their teeth. For a second, Alina was back there, in the almost complete darkness, Jamie spooning her, his hand stroking her stomach gently, then moving further down. The movement was barely noticeable, neither of them speaking, until Alina caught her breath and tensed briefly, and Jamie held her tight. She floated to sleep on soft ripples after that. They never mentioned it, and Alina could almost have dreamed it, except with Sanna opposite her now, she knew she hadn't.

'Thank you for that,' Alina said. 'I never said, but it was as if you knew… as if we were… the same person. Oh, I don't know.'

'It was pure instinct, that's all. I just knew what I'd want if I were you.'

Alina wondered if one or both of them would cry then, but this wasn't about crying over their past selves anymore. She reached across the table and took Sanna's hand, turned it over, back, and let go. Sanna looked puzzled. 'You did have *very* nimble fingers,' Alina said.

Sanna looked back, poker-faced, and slowly raised one eyebrow, a party trick from long ago. 'I still do, Alina. I still do.'

29

Ashley was sitting on Sanna's front doorstep, bouncing a ball up and down, when they got back late that afternoon.

'Uh oh, there's trouble brewing.' Sanna nodded in the little girl's direction. 'This is Ashley's version of running away. She thinks Naisha can't see her.'

As they got out of the car, Alina looked back two houses and there was Naisha herself at the window. She gave a 'what can I do?' shrug, palms raised, and then gestured that she was coming over.

'And Naisha *can't* see her on the step, but she can see if Ashley leaves my garden,' Sanna went on, as she opened the boot to let Sid out. 'It's a great time-out option.' She raised her voice. 'Ashley? Can you come and open the gate so I can let Sid straight into the garden.'

The little girl obediently got up and a yapping Sid bounded at her. 'Oh dear, Sid, Siddy,' she wailed, shoving her tear-stained face into his forgiving fur. 'My mummy's cross with me.'

Naisha arrived at Alina's shoulder in time to hear this and rolled her eyes. 'She's in a right mardy mood, and as stubborn as they come. She heard me and Tanzima arguing and has got the wrong end of the stick,' she explained. 'The kid's been out here the best part of two hours.'

Naisha's sigh was so deep Alina said, 'Shall I talk to her? I'm very good with mardy and stubborn. My last intervention was remonstrating with half a dozen eight-year-olds who had cut off each other's hair.' The exaggeration was to make Naisha smile, and it worked.

'If you can get through to her,' she said, and stayed where she was, hovering as Alina went to crouch beside the girl and the dog. Sanna squeezed round them to open the front door.

Ashley had clearly given in her protest the second she saw reinforcements – mostly canine, Alina thought – coming home. 'My mummy's sad because my auntie is sad,' she confided before Alina even opened her mouth.

'Ah. Do you know why they're sad?'

'My uncle died,' she said. 'I didn't see him since I was a baby so I'm not sad. My auntie wants to go to her home now, but my mum doesn't want her to. She says this is our home.'

'Where does your auntie think is home?' Alina asked.

'Sylhet,' Ashley said carefully. 'I've never been there. I want to stay here.' Ashley jabbed Sid to make her point and the dog licked her lazily. 'But I'll miss my auntie.' Her lips wobbled. 'Will she forget me?'

'Well, I have a niece in Bhola, which is in the same country as Sylhet, but I don't forget her and she doesn't forget me. I can visit her sometimes and when she's bigger she can visit me.' Alina hoped she was saying the right thing; neither Naisha at the gate nor Sanna lurking in the hall rushed to shut her up.

Ashley perked up. 'How old is she? What's her name?'

'Khalya, and she's a bit older than you. Look.' Alina took out her phone and clicked on the gallery. 'That's Khalya, there, with her friends. There's a video… You could make a video to send to your auntie, couldn't you?'

Ashley turned up the sound, listened for a minute and then looked aghast at Alina. 'My mummy will let me make a film but not if I make a noise like that,' she said. 'Why do they make such funny sounds—'

'Ashley!' Naisha rushed forward but Alina waved her away.

'Khalya and her friends are deaf, so they can't hear what they're doing and it makes their voices sound different,' she said. 'You can hear perfectly so your mummy is absolutely right.'

'Okay.' Ashley scrolled through the photos like an old pro, Alina providing a commentary for Sanna, who had moved closer, to look over her shoulder: 'Khalya, Khalya and her friends. That's Mizan. Takdir, the committee, everyone on a picnic by the river, that's me, Mizan's wife and sons...'

When Ashley got bored and decided to play chase with Sid, Naisha put her hand on her heart, mouthed a 'Thank you,' and, Alina noted, nodded to Sanna to produce a well-timed bag of sweets. The little girl went home, holding Naisha's hand and crunching happily.

'Crisis averted.' Sanna led the way into the kitchen. 'You're good with her.'

Alina grinned. 'You'd have talked her round if I wasn't here. I bet you always do.'

'She'd have seen right through me. I couldn't have magicked up a niece. Is... Khalya, is it? Is she a real relation?'

'Poetic licence.' As Alina explained, she decided her Bangladeshi grandfather would be turning in his grave, rightly, outed first to Rory and now to Sanna. 'He was basically a dirty old man, infamous for exercising an old-fashioned droit du seigneur over the women working for him.' Alina grimaced. 'He paid them well, by all accounts, which had the poorest of the poor lining up to work in his house. Until Takdir stopped it.'

'So, Khalya is the product of one of those liaisons?'

'We think so. We won't ever know for sure; we just have Khalya's mother's word and that isn't consistent. But it doesn't matter. She *is* family to me either way.'

Sanna busied herself feeding Sid and Alina made some tea, carrying it through to the sitting room and setting the mugs down where they'd sat the night before. When Sanna came through, she said, 'Can I have a proper look at your photos?'

Alina handed over her phone and Sanna scrutinised the pictures, asking for clarification now and again. She paused at one of Alina smiling down from a rickshaw, her arms around Khalya, then again at one of Mizan, and a group shot at school, zooming in on Alina. When she passed the phone back to Alina, she sat back and took her in from head to toe.

'You look really different,' she commented. 'I didn't expect that.'

'It's all in the packaging, remember?' Alina shook her head. 'I'm still such a foreigner, really. It would be a hell of a lot easier over there sometimes if I *didn't* pass so easily.'

'Whereas I spend my life hoping *to* pass.'

They sat in silence for a few minutes, sipping their drinks, only the click of the boiler and Sid's occasional snore interrupting the peace.

After a while, Sanna asked, 'Are you ever tempted to move over there to live? I can see pros and cons but it must cross your mind?'

'Strange you should say that,' Alina began. 'You see— What?' Alina interrupted herself as her phone began to flash with an incoming WhatsApp call. She angled the screen towards her. 'Speak of the devil. It's Mizan.' The call dropped, only to ring again, almost immediately. Alina swiped to answer but again the call didn't connect. There wasn't a third ring, nor was there a message. 'He'll try again if it's important,' Alina said, tucking the phone into her pocket.

'What time is it there?' Sanna frowned at the clock.

'After midnight,' Alina calculated. 'Early enough for Mizan. He's a night owl – he'd sleep 'til noon if work allowed it. It drives his wife mad.'

'What about you?'

'Does Mizan drive me mad? Yes, and me him. But put us both together and I'd say we make one fine director.'

'I actually meant the sleep routine. You must be busy out there.'

'I go with the flow.' Alina smiled. 'The early hours are

the only time we can have any kind of meeting and not be interrupted fifty times. Mizan isn't above crossing the roofs like stepping stones to get to the balcony outside my room... Don't look like that! The night guard will already have locked the main doors when Mizan has a bright idea, and I'm not wandering from one building to another. We sit on the roof in the moonlight and make our plans for Sonali Homestay. Very civilised.'

'It sounds far more appealing than our bog-standard team meetings,' agreed Sanna. 'Climbing drainpipes or whatever would be a breach of health and safety, for a start.' She set her mug on the floor and wriggled herself into the depths of her armchair. 'That's better. Now tell me some more about this moonlight roof garden, Alina-that-I-don't-know-at-all.'

'Come to think of it, probably every life-changing moment I've had in Bangladesh has been on a roof garden,' was Alina's truthful reply.

30

Dhaka 2004

Her Uncle Takdir was on a mission to acquaint Alina with the country of her father's birth. Two days to rest, overcome jetlag and make herself comfortable in her family home, he said, and then they would make a grand tour of the country.

'I am an old man, my dear. Inshallah, we will have many happy years together, but for how long will I be able to travel with my long-lost great niece? Indulge me. The tea gardens of Sylhet; the Sundarbans UNESCO park; Cox's Bazaar.' Takdir's ambitious itinerary materialised over two hot weeks.

Reading between the lines, she thought he was fitting as much as he could into this first visit, in the event Alina decided it was also her last.

Takdir's car and driver made her feel like the queen consort, given Takdir was a dignitary in his own right; she learned slowly of the clout of even a retired district commissioner. He had a network second to none, and Alina's trip was one of immense privilege. It was the car she appreciated most, though. It might have been a battered Toyota, but it had sufficient air-conditioning to avoid her being a sweaty, grimy puddle dripping into the guest rooms of her uncle's friends and colleagues.

Somewhere on the road to the lush green tea gardens of Srimangal, Alina started to relax. Takdir was easy company, the two of them in the back of the car. She wondered if he mistook her silence when he said, 'I wish I could provide company of your own age,' clearly believing Alina was just being polite when she said she preferred it as they were. Truth was, she had dreaded the entourage that accompanied them around the city, kind as they were. 'You fall between the generations,' he explained, more than once. He and Husna had three children of their own, all older than Alina, and four grandchildren, all younger. Takdir himself was, like Miriam and Patrick, in his early sixties, ten years younger than Alina's grandfather had been. 'Which is much older in Bangladesh than it is in Ireland,' he said, eyes twinkling.

'It's strange to think my mum and dad were younger than I am now when they died,' she told him. It was something she'd thought before: her parents' lives cut short, yet her less than pleasant grandfather had lasted another twenty-six after that – which was also longer than her parents had lived.

'Life is not fair,' Takdir said simply. 'But if we can act to make it fairer, we should do so.'

'Agreed.'

'I hoped you would say so,' Takdir added cryptically as the car swung into the apartment's underground parking. 'Come to the roof terrace later, my dear. There is someone I would like you to meet.'

In Takdir's house, Alina got used to being watched. Her Great Aunt Husna was the main culprit, aided and abetted by the nameless woman Husna called her companion. Neither was secretive about it, and it was less overtly hostile than disconcerting. *What are they expecting me to do?* she thought, because in their watching, there was waiting.

'My wife's lack of English inhibits her severely,' Takdir explained, and Alina accepted the prevarication graciously while thinking that her own lack of Bangla inhibited *her*, but she still managed to make an effort. The two women talked about Alina in front of her – their gestures made it obvious – knowing she didn't understand. Now, they were there at the end of the hall, and Alina, emboldened by her time away, tried a similar tactic, pointing at them and asking Takdir, 'What are they saying about me? Can you tell Great Aunt Husna I'm glad to be back.'

Takdir raised his voice, spoke, and to Alina's surprise, Husna did not disappear into the gloomy back kitchen but spoke at length – then disappeared.

Her uncle cleared his throat. 'My wife is admiring of your fair skin and approving of your healthy appetite. Both are unexpected, she says, in a foreigner. I'll see you later, my dear,' he added.

Foreigner. That was the key, Alina realised as she closed her bedroom door behind her. She felt like an alien; Husna saw her that way. How was the woman to know this strange Irish girl wasn't an imposter, usurper, pretender to Takdir's moderate wealth and powerful good name? Alina had some sympathy with her aunt's suspicions, wrong as they were.

Before sunset, Alina made her way up the stairs to the roof. Her uncle was in his favourite seat under an arch of climbing flowers Alina couldn't name, talking quietly to a small child perched on his knee. He was jiggling the little bundle up and down and pointing to the sky, to the child, back again. They made such a lovely tableau that Alina hung back, not wanting to break the moment, but also racking her brains as to who the child was and whether she'd seen him or her before. She ought to make an effort to distinguish all her family members, she chided herself, though right now that seemed as likely as learning Bangla and getting a job here. When she realised Takdir wasn't alone, that he was talking to someone just out of her view, she made her way across the roof garden to say hello.

To Alina's surprise, it was Husna and her companion. She'd not yet seen her aunt sit with her uncle before, though she presumed they spent some time together. She hesitated a few feet away, wondering if she would be welcome.

'Ah, Alina, come and meet Khalya.' Takdir waved her over.

Alina took the spare seat behind him, smiling at the two women opposite. They didn't exactly smile back but they didn't leave either. 'Hello, Khalya.' She turned her attention to the baby – she could see how small the child was now, maybe only a few months old – and offered her finger to the grasping chubby hands. She was wondering how to ask who the little girl belonged to politely when Takdir said something in Bangla and the younger woman got up and took her from him. Husna added a remark, looked at Alina, and the women carried the baby away.

'That's Khalya's mother with my wife,' Takdir said. 'Your Aunt Husna feels some responsibility to them.' He paused and looked across the rooftops in the direction the sun would go down. There was a murky yellow tinge to the sky, one that no painter would ever choose.

There was some kind of story coming, Alina guessed, *another one*. Had the scene been staged for her benefit? She thought so.

'Mother and baby arrived at our door directly after your grandfather's funeral,' Takdir went on. 'She said that baby Khalya was his youngest child and now he was gone, it was our duty to take the child in. She put the baby in Husna's arms and left.'

Picking up his discomfort, Alina said nothing and just followed his gaze across the non-view beyond them: other apartment blocks and balconies, roofs higher and lower than their own, where other people were living out a similar ritual. From the far corner it was possible to see the still and overgrown pond, where tiny colourful figures waded in to wash or crouched at the edge, doing their dishes; the flash of tin reflected off the sun as it reached a certain point in the sky. There was a hypnotic thump thump beat of a basketball from the Americans' yard underscoring the squeal of brakes, a motorised rickshaw horn, a sudden snatch of conversation. If Alina closed her eyes, she could pick out the individual notes in the soundscape *Before Evening Call to Prayer: Dhaka*.

That and the whine of mosquitoes, she thought, slapping one away from her hand.

The movement seemed to jolt Takdir into speaking again. 'I went after her, of course. She was living in a room with several other women and children, penniless, she said, and with nothing to her name but the baby. She repeated her remark about the baby's father and suggested we pay her money to go away... like my brother had done before his death.' Takdir's voice cracked. 'If we didn't want the baby, we should leave her at the government orphanage.'

'Instead, you took them both in.' Alina joined the dots and her uncle nodded. 'And the story is true?' she asked.

'It is not unlikely,' he said carefully. 'And in any event, my wife has become very attached to both, important because Khalya's mother is not, perhaps, a natural mother.'

'I see.' Alina wanted to reassure Takdir that she'd chosen him as her family, not a man she'd never met and had discounted many years ago. But she had to remind herself they were also talking about Takdir's brother. Before she could find the tactful words, Takdir spoke again.

'*Do* you see?' He smiled at her. 'If Khalya is your grandfather's child then she is related to you, your bloodline. If not, we have still chosen her as part of our family. Her home is here. Little Khalya needs our family. What do you think?'

Good from bad; two waifs and strays taken in, Alina wanted to say, but she didn't. She remembered her great uncle's words that first evening.

'That I don't need to have a Bangla past to have a Bangla future?' Alina said, very slowly.

31

Sunday lunch, here, 2 p.m. You, me, Claire. Rory is cooking: Yorkshire puddings, pigs in blankets, the lot. He invited you; I'm the messenger. E. x

Elizabeth's message popped up when Alina was almost back to Edinburgh. She had left a voicemail for Fin along the lines of 'all good with Sanna, let's talk tomorrow', and was checking to see if Mizan had tried phoning again: he hadn't. But if he'd gone to Dhaka for the weekend to be with his wife and boys – she lived in the city with her parents; they needed care and lived close to a good school, so it suited everyone – he could be anywhere across land or sea.

Alina replied to Elizabeth, with a provocative thumbs-up emoji, then followed it up: *Lovely. What can I bring?* to which the response was, *Nothing but yourself and your news. R knows about S. Shall I tell C? Keeping schtum re D, of course.* Another thumbs up dealt with that and Alina prepared herself to sing for her supper.

'Celebration or consolation?' Elizabeth met her at the top of the stairs, a couple of hours later, and practically dragged Alina into Winston. 'With Sanna. Second dates often make or break. Tell me quick so we can set the tone and direct the talk.'

Alina laughed. 'Very cloak and dagger, but I appreciate the thought. And it's all good. All coming together.'

'Oh, I'm delighted to hear it.' Elizabeth clasped her hands together. Then she looked over her shoulder and lowered her voice. 'And Rory? You're getting there?'

'We're getting somewhere.' Alina hesitated. 'He told me... about his father and... your reason for funding the guesthouse. We were at cross purposes, Elizabeth. He thought I knew.'

'We'd have got round to talking about it sooner or later, lovey. It's not my only reason, but yes, it's one of them. Anyway...' Elizabeth opened Winston's door and added loudly, 'we can't lurk in here or Double-0 will think you're pimping me to jump ship to one of them there fancy London literary agencies.'

'Tell me the lucky agent and I'll write you a personal reference.' Claire's head poked out of the kitchen. 'Hello, Alina. Can you amuse the old lady in Charles for a few minutes? If she's done with amusing herself, that is. I'm going to set the table in Winston. There's so much food we'll never squeeze round the kitchen table.'

'I'll try.' Alina grinned, watching Elizabeth sniff and purport to ignore Claire. 'Hi, Rory,' she called into the kitchen.

'Hello, Alina.' Rory appeared at Claire's shoulder. 'The food's all ready. We can take it through and set the table as we go, if you like.'

The result was a long, light-hearted, harmless-gossipy meal – all the things that the previous mid-week get-together had been lacking, to Alina at any rate. She felt in a better place now, less awkward than she'd ever imagined she'd feel with Rory opposite her, serving her mashed potatoes. Beyond 'Would you like carrots?' and 'Yes, please. I'd like everything,' they didn't make conversation, but there was no visible tension either. And while Connie – currently in Doha – was fondly missed, Morag was just not mentioned.

'I have redeemed myself as hostess,' Elizabeth declared.

'It's the chef you should thank,' Claire reminded her. 'Delicious, Rory.'

'I'm not applying to MasterChef yet,' Rory said. 'If you go through the bins, you might find a few pre-prepared shortcuts.'

'Sensible.' Elizabeth speared the last of the pigs in blankets ('My prerogative on grounds of age'), and turned, eyes alight, to Alina. 'Want to debrief about your visit to Bradford, lovey? You know, while you have a captive audience and our amassed wisdom?'

'Shameless,' Claire stated.

'Concerned, Double-0.'

'Shameless and concerned. Alright, I'll give you that.' Claire turned to Alina. 'Would you like me to make myself useful elsewhere?'

'Er… I could bring dessert?' offered Rory, clearly unsure of the vibe.

Alina grinned. 'It's alright. No such thing as a free lunch and all that… Seriously, I'm not sure what to say. We talked a lot. Remembered a lot. Sanna is lovely, the person she always was. I think Fin's going to like her.'

'Well, there's not much book fodder there.' Elizabeth pretended to be deflated. 'When is he going to meet her? When am I going to meet her?'

'Watch this space.' Sanna had mentioned she might well find good reason to attend a meeting at the Scottish Parliament before the summer term started, combining a visit to Alina and – possibly – meeting Fin and Kirsten. But Alina wanted to run that by Fin first.

'Did it make you feel old?' Claire started to pile up the plates. 'I'm dragging myself to a college reunion next month – I did journalism many moons ago – because it's forty years since we graduated. Forty! I'm ready for everyone to be… what is it you call it, Alina?'

'Dead, disordered or dispossessed?' Alina *and* Elizabeth chorused.

'Yes, exactly that. If we had anything in common now, we'd stay in touch.'

'Maybe you'll be lucky,' Alina said. 'I'd never have

thought we'd get on so easily, given everything back then and the time that's passed. But I suppose if the relationship was important enough or strong enough…' She happened to catch Rory's eye as she spoke and he gave her the tiniest hint of a sad smile. Flustered that he was relating her words to their situation, she took refuge in an obvious excuse. 'Oh – was that my phone? I'm waiting for a call from Bangladesh and thought it vibrated.' She felt in her pocket – only to be caught out in the lie: her phone was in her bag, which was over on the windowsill.

'Some vibration,' said Rory under his breath as he followed her gaze.

Against her judgement she looked at him sharply, but if anything he seemed amused. *Was he laughing at her? Was he teasing her?* 'Sorry. I'd better check,' she said, pushing her chair back abruptly. Of course, the phone hadn't rung, but back at the table Alina went through the rigmarole of checking – to find that Mizan's message had arrived a good half an hour ago. The voicemail was garbled, as if he were stranded in the Bay of Bengal on a run-aground launch (which was not impossible, she thought), but the subsequent text filled the screen loud and clear. The words flashed in front of her, and Alina had to read it twice.

'I can't believe—'

'Alina? What is it?' Elizabeth's concern cut through her making-sense-of-it thoughts. 'Is it bad news?'

Alina glanced up to find all three of them staring at her. Claire had paused her clearing-away efforts and Rory appeared mortified. She held up her phone. 'Message from Mizan. See what he says?' She turned the screen so that the words – in capitals – were visible:

'KHALYA IS KIDNAPPED.'

Alina barely registered the collective intake of breath around the table; she was reckoning her next move. She dialled Mizan, cursing when it went straight to voicemail. 'I'm here now,' she said tersely. 'Phone me back.' She typed a matching text message, then tapped her phone against her chin, wondering what to do next.

There was no point phoning the landline at Sonali Homestay. Even if anyone heard it ringing, it was locked in Mizan's office in the old school building, far away from the dormitories. The only staff with keys were Iqbal, the accountant, who would be sleeping soundly in town with his family, and Farhana, the housemother, who was fluent in sign language, Bangla, Hindi and Swedish – she'd worked for a Scandinavian NGO – but not English. And Alina wasn't confident that her own Bangla was up to this task.

'Huh? Sorry, Elizabeth?'

'Is there somebody else you can call?' Elizabeth was asking. 'What about your great uncle? His finger's on the pulse, isn't it?'

'You're right, but I don't want to bother him if I can help it. He's in Delhi for his annual health check and I said I'd only phone him in an emergency.'

'And this isn't?' Down-to-earth Claire's eyes were unusually wide.

'This is Mizan being infuriating,' Alina said. She couldn't help but notice the looks shared between Elizabeth, Claire and Rory. 'What?'

'You do seem more… er… exasperated with Mizan than worried about Khalya,' Elizabeth said delicately.

'Of course I am. He's an idiot.' Distracted, she tried his number once more, then sighed and put the phone down. 'I'll just have to wait 'til he gets his act together. Sorry to drag you all into this,' she added, looking up. 'Rory, did you say something about dessert? Can I help you with it?' It took a second for Alina to compute the trio watching her as if she were a monster – and another few for her to realise why that might be so.

'Oh, bloody hell,' she said. 'Khalya hasn't really been kidnapped. Mizan would never send a message like that if she had.' Now she felt the foolish one. In the heat of the moment, she'd forgotten none of them knew Mizan. 'Sorry. It was his audacity I was sharing. Um, as you were, folks.'

'Well, if you're sure?' Elizabeth didn't sound convinced.

'You really know this Mizan well enough?' Claire added.

'God, yes. I know him inside out. It's Mizan being dramatic – or maybe there's something lost in translation.' Alina would stake her life on it. 'If Khalya, or anyone else, had really been kidnapped, Mizan would have phoned and phoned and kept phoning. Takdir likewise. And by that time, the current district commissioner, the police superintendent, half the military and representatives from both political parties would be in on it.'

'I feel as if I'm coming in on a film halfway through.' Rory stood up and leaned over to pick up the plates Claire had stacked. 'But Alina knows her stuff, so…' He kept his eyes on the crockery as he said that, Alina noticed. '…it doesn't sound like it would be heartless to bring in the apple pie.'

Alina was back in her own flat – on the understanding she would update Elizabeth as soon as there was any more news – when a contrite yet still excitable Mizan finally phoned back. He'd been on the launch, he said, way out of signal. And then the vessel had run aground, only later to be delayed again by fog in the Barisal area. He had jumped ship at the point and got a motorboat back to Bhola. Alina had no trouble believing any of that; it was an occupational hazard of river travel in Bangladesh. With her prompting, though, he conceded he might have *slightly* overreacted in his message but he wanted to get her attention and he *had* been in the middle of the crisis.

'Mizan?' Knowing he could go on at this rate for some time, Alina interrupted him. 'Just tell me quickly: is Khalya safe?'

'Yes, of course she is safe. She is outside, playing badminton. She doesn't even know she was kidnapped.'

Alina closed her eyes, partly in thanks, partly in disbelief, and flopped back onto her bed, praying for patience. 'Tell me from the start.'

'The start is that her mother said she was kidnapped—'

'And you believed her?'

'No, no, you misunderstand. I mean that it was Khalya's mother who kidnapped her—'

'Her mother?'

'Yes. And then she gave me the ransom demand—'

'Ransom?'

'Alina, you must have patience. If you interrupt every word then—'

'Sorry. Okay, I'm listening.' It was all too surreal. Alina couldn't make head nor tail of Mizan's chaotic storytelling at the best of times.

'Her mother went to the school in Barisal and said Khalya was needed to attend a family funeral and they took the bus to Dhaka. The school was wrong to let her go, and Suni should have known better to allow it until she confirmed with me—'

'Where in Dhaka?' Alina couldn't help herself: Khalya's mother lived in Takdir's house, for goodness' sake. She was glued to Alina's Aunt Husna's side. Mizan did nothing to salve Alina's unease by continuing:

'To Takdir Sir's house. We did not know Khalya was gone from school until Suna arrived yesterday with the other girls. Farhana phoned me in Dhaka immediately. I did my detective work and went to Takdir Sir's house. There was Khalya with her mother. I called my wife to come and collect Khalya while I spoke to her mother alone, and to be ready to return to Bhola all together. This we did, but the travel was disrupted.'

Alina shuffled her pillows to get more comfortable while she digested that. 'It's the marriage thing again, isn't it?' she said finally. 'She's not giving up.'

'I did not expect her to act so quickly after we spoke with her previously,' Mizan admitted. 'It's the same man. A rich man with many lakhs and some land. His wife is dead and his sister cares for his daughters. No sons.'

'So he wants a glorified carer, a servant, and a womb to provide a son and heir?'

'Yes, of course. What else?' In the face of her frustration, Mizan grew equable; it was the way they worked. 'I know a little about who he is. A farmer from Rajoir district. He is an old man, Alina, not a bad man—'

'Too old for Khalya. That's no life for any young girl.'

'She would be looked after, that is the mother's argument. You know already.'

'We look after her – and we look after her mother. Takdir looks after them.' Alina's stomach turned at the thought of an older man, even a kind one, groping Khalya or any of her friends.

'Do not fight me, Alina. I agree with you.'

'The law, in theory, agrees with us. It doesn't make much difference though, does it?'

'Ah, innocent Alina. What matters is money, and money will save Khalya here. This man, he wants more dowry than Khalya's mother can pay. Mr Takdir refuses her a loan. What can she do? She takes Khalya and demands we pay her money to get her back.'

'By that logic we won't get Khalya back. She and the money will go to the husband.'

'What can I say? Khalya's mother is simple.'

Alina had to ask: 'What does Husna have to say?'

'Mrs Husna? Why do you ask that?' Mizan sounded genuinely mystified. 'I don't know. She is in Delhi with Takdir Sir, is she not? I saw no one at their house.'

'It doesn't matter.' Alina felt as if she'd swivelled round too many times on a roundabout. 'So, crisis averted for a second time in, what – two weeks? She's not going to give up. We can talk to the prospective husband but if he's warned off, Khalya will just be hawked to another one. What do we do? What can I do? Offer to marry the old man instead? He's probably my age.'

Mizan gave a bark of laughter. 'You deserve a husband of much higher calibre, and you would frighten the old farmer, anyway.' Then his tone changed. 'We need to talk properly, you, me, Takdir, perhaps Farhana. Like you say, this is a real threat to Khalya's well-being. It's why we have a child protection policy.'

A policy that was strong on theory but less robust in the practicalities of individual situations. Alina sighed. 'As soon as Takdir gets back, let's arrange a Skype call, then a committee meeting. Meanwhile, thinking caps on.'

Alina left a quick voicemail for Takdir, assuring him she was aware of the latest events and that Mizan had it all under control – for now. She checked her watch, decided it wasn't too late at all, and then, true to her word, she ran back next door to fill Elizabeth in. Truth was, a breath of fresh air and a quick debrief really appealed.

'So, the little girl wasn't kidnapped?' Elizabeth greeted her. 'Or she was?'

'No.' Alina considered her words. 'But "taken without permission" probably covers it.' She looked round Charles. 'Has Claire gone? And Rory?'

'You just missed them. Rory's walking Double-0 to the bus stop.'

'Shame. I need to say sorry for adding so much non-drama to a lovely lunch.' Alina passed on the gist of Khalya's situation and the dilemma over keeping her safe. 'It's not fair to keep her in Sonali Homestay, she loves school and she wants to study. And she deserves a life outside – that's the point of the place, making the children independent.' Alina thumped the arm of the chair in frustration. 'So how do we keep her safe in the real world?'

'I wish I knew. Every parent wishes they knew. My mother married me off when I was eighteen,' Elizabeth said, so unexpectedly that it took Alina a second to catch up. 'We were broke. My father had left us; in fact, it came to light after his death he'd had another wife and children in the next town over for years. I was an uneducated adult mouth to feed, but I was neat and quite pretty.'

Alina didn't know what to say, so she didn't say anything.

'Dougie MacLeod worked in an office. He was an accounts clerk, fifteen years older than me,' Elizabeth continued. 'He lodged down the road and my ma had her sights on him from the off. The rest is history. Not like your Khalya, but not unlike her, either.'

'Was it… I mean, did you have a choice?'

'I wasn't forced into anything, lovey, if that's what you mean.' Elizabeth patted her hand. 'It was a great escape for me, too, at the start. I played house in our two rooms, but Dougie was born to be bachelor. He was quite cruel, though I don't think he ever meant to be. cold. Coercive control, they'd call it these days.'

'I had no idea.'

'Of course you didn't,' Elizabeth said cheerfully. 'It's a long time ago. I've put all my demons to rest and anyway, I've had the last laugh. It's made my life, hasn't it? I was sixty-eight when my first book was published, but I wrote a book a year to get through my married life. Even with the awful duds, I've enough novels-in-waiting to see me out. Double-0 nearly wet her sensible Yorkshire knickers when she met me. The "old wee wifey scribbling in secret" had marketability all over it.' More seriously, she added, 'And I've got Rory, Claire, you… I'd say I won, wouldn't you?'

'Second prize.' Alina bit her lip. 'We're the real winners, having you.'

'Och, tosh.' Elizabeth dismissed that. 'See why I would like to come and see your place? Why I positively jumped on the idea when Rory suggested I could fund a guesthouse? I might have been technically an adult when I was married but there was a very frightened teenager in me for years. I don't want your Khalya to go through that.'

'You've put it perfectly,' Alina began, but before the full realisation of what Elizabeth had said could seep into her brain, her phone rang. 'What now?' She sighed, expecting Mizan with a brainwave or Takdir alighting from his Air India flight. It was neither.

'Fin?' Alina said, heart thumping. 'Slow down. What's happened?'

32

Fin and Kirsten's baby – a girl, as promised, but earlier than expected – was delivered long before Alina and Rory veered on to the A74.

That Alina and Rory were going together was a shock in itself. Fin, trying not to panic, phoned Alina and said 'We're at the hospital. They're getting Kirsten ready to have the baby. It's her blood pressure... Can you come, Ali? Please? Mum and Dad are in the Canaries and Kirsten's lot will come, but it's so quiet here...' (He'd said a lot more, but her addled brain had only taken in the headlines), and she'd not been able to settle since, even with Elizabeth's calm presence and, a bit later, Rory's practical one. She was checking out train times immediately after Fin hung up, and was champing at the bit for non-existent twenty-four-hour car-hire companies. She even considered an astronomical taxi fare, knowing Elizabeth would lend her the money in a heartbeat. Fin was asking for her, he needed her. He'd never before asked for her, needed her, like this. She had to live up to it.

Then came Fin's second, slightly less frantic, message: it wasn't life and death. It wasn't ideal either, but the medical staff were optimistic, and even if Alina could beam herself there, Star Trek-style, she'd be pacing the corridors in a parody of long-ago fathers-to-be.

'...so I've said I'll get the first train.' She finished relaying the more positive news to Elizabeth and Rory, mindless of the fact they'd all but listened in to the whole conversation.

'Not a chance,' Rory said. 'What time do you want to leave? I've got Claire's car and its keys.' Rory dangled them at shoulder height. 'We had a couple of drinks, so I said I'd drive it over to hers tomorrow. And,' he pointed out, 'It's only a hundred miles or so to Carlisle.'

'No, you can't do that.' Alina refused automatically. 'Claire might not—'

'Of course she will.' Elizabeth snorted. 'Anyway, I'm already on it.' She held up her phone and tapped in a message. *Keep the car as long as you need it and best wishes to the new family*, was the speedy reply.

'Well, then, I can drive myself.'

'Alina? Let me do this, please,' Rory said quietly. 'It's just a lift to somewhere you need to be on a day when I have nothing to do.'

They held each other's gaze for a moment or two, then Alina nodded. 'Thank you. Thank you very much.'

They left Edinburgh shortly after eight, Alina's overnight bag hastily restuffed, just in case, and still arguing – politely – over whether Rory was driving Alina to Waverley Station or direct to Carlisle.

'No way am I going back in there...' Rory gestured over his shoulder in the vague direction of Edenfield Road. '...and telling my mum I dropped you at the station. I win.'

'Point taken. I'll stop being a drama queen.'

'Maybe you spend too much time with this Mizan of yours,' Rory said. 'It's rubbing off on you.'

Alina looked over at him in surprise, not quite knowing how to take the remark, and he flushed. 'Sorry, that was meant to be funny. It missed by a mile.'

'We're like a seesaw, me and Mizan.' Alina spoke for the sake of saying something. 'He overexaggerates, I bring the common sense. Then when I'm riled up about something, he talks me down.'

'Well, in his absence, let me say that I'm sure things will be alright today.' Rory indicated right and into a stream of cars waiting for the traffic lights to turn green. 'And now I realise even as I speak that it's cold comfort because I know nothing about birth or newborn babies or why this one is coming early... so I'll now shut up and do what I can do and that's being the chauffeur.' His eyes slid over to meet hers. 'What is it with us and babies, Alina? We can't get away from the subject.'

There was no answer to that, so she didn't try. It was shortly after that Fin's message arrived: *She's here. Okay, I think. CU soon x*

'What are we to make of that?' Alina was going for faintly optimistic. 'Six weeks isn't that early, really,' she said hopefully, Fin's night-time voice ringing in her ears. 'Is it?'

They looked blankly at each other.

'It's going to be fine.' Rory repeated. Then he looked over at Alina, again. 'I suppose you could google it?'

'Hmm...' Alina's fingers hovered over her phone before she shook her head. 'Better not. I'm bound to happen on the one percent that frightens the life out of us.'

They didn't speak a great deal for a while. She turned the radio on instead, tuned to Radio 2, and they passed the time randomly commenting on Zoe Ball's choice of music.

Once they'd stopped for petrol and were eating breakfast at a neighbouring Costa, their tongues loosened a little. Alina's text to Fin, telling him she was halfway there and hoping all was well, was returned with a thumbs-up emoji and a pair of praying hands. She assumed this was positive and sent another message, this time to Sanna, giving her the sudden news. Their texts pinged back and forth: *I won't phone*, Sanna's said. *No bloody privacy in a shared office and no signal outside of it. Everything crossed.*

'She's being thrown in the deep end – Sanna, I mean,'

Alina commented. 'A son and the son's baby, all before their first meeting.'

'She's lucky.'

'Yes.'

Rory, putting the remains of his sandwich down, suddenly said, 'Can I ask an awful question?'

'How awful?' Alina smiled faintly. 'It can't be more intrusive than some of the ones I had to ask you.'

'This is pretty bad. And none of my business, actually.'

'Try me.'

Rory screwed his napkin into a ball and dumped it in his empty cup. 'Does Sanna look like a woman?' he said in a rush.

'She *is* a woman.'

'You know what I mean.' Rory looked mortified. 'And yes, it's rude. Yes, I'm just curious. I'm also sorry, I shouldn't have asked. Like I said, none of my business.'

Alina took pity on him. 'You're only putting into words what most people would think,' she said. 'But yes, she does. She looks exactly like the woman she is. I've probably changed as much as she has – no, seriously. Wait.' She picked up her phone and showed him the same photo of her and Khalya that she'd shown Sanna, watching his face.

'That was very much Sanna's reaction, too,' she said, smiling. 'I'm a human chameleon.'

'You definitely haven't aged in the five years since we last met.'

'Neither have you,' Alina agreed.

'I worry about Mum getting older,' he confided. 'I suppose everyone does. It's one of the reasons I decided not to renew my contract in Auckland. Not that she'd thank me.'

'She's amazing,' Alina said. 'Not for her age, but in general. I wish she and my grandmother had got to meet.'

After they'd returned to the car, Rory asked, 'Do you remember your own parents?'

'Tell me to shut up and concentrate on the road if you've had enough.'

'I don't remember them at all.' Alina was looking out of the window. 'Not even a half memory, or a false one. I wasn't even two when they died. Miriam and Patrick *were* my mum and dad. I would have called them that, but I suppose I was afraid it would upset them, you know, writing their daughter and son-in-law out of my life.' She turned to the silent Rory. 'But that's not what you really wanted to ask, was it?'

'You don't have to—'

'I don't mind, I just avoid it because it's still something of a conversation stopper. They were killed, totally randomly, on the seventeenth of February 1978. I was with my grandparents while my mum and dad went for an anniversary at the La Mon Hotel in County Down. There was an IRA bomb. He was killed by the blast, and she died the next day.'

'Fuck. I'm sorry. That's shit.'

'It's okay.' Even his profile looked anguished; Alina wanted to lean over and pat his thigh, but she kept her hand in her lap. 'I mean, it is terrible, truly terrible, like any act of terrorism before or since, but it was my grandparents' tragedy, not mine.'

'I never missed *my* father, really,' Rory said, after a while. 'He was just a stern old man who wheezed a lot. He was retired by the time I was born. I must have been a huge shock. When he died, nothing changed. It was just quieter, and Mum stopped "hurting herself".'

Alina put her hand to her mouth, but Rory was still speaking. 'It's not much of an obituary, is it? I'm sorry I gave you a half-truth during the adoption assessment.'

'An almost-truth,' Alina explained. 'That's what Mizan calls it when there's just a bit of the truth missing – and it changes everything *if* anyone notices.' But her mind was on something else, something Elizabeth had let slip last night. 'She said – Elizabeth, I mean – that you suggested she fund the Sonali Homestay Guesthouse.'

The statement hung there for a few seconds.

'She was looking for something relevant to support. You

needed donors, and it's a very worthy cause. All I did was point out that major funding was way beyond most people, but that Mum could write a cheque and get the building started.'

His clipped tones and obvious discomfort told Alina there was more to it, but she wasn't going to push the point. He'd thought about her, though, over the last five years, as she'd thought about him.

Once they hit the outskirts of Carlisle, Rory redirected the sat-nav. 'I'll drop you at the hospital,' he said. 'I'll hang around for a bit – don't argue, there's plenty I can do – and we can decide later if you want a lift back or are staying over.'

'You're very kind. In lots of ways.' As the turn off for the hospital approached, Alina busied herself collecting her belongings. There was something she wanted to ask, but she hesitated. As Rory followed the signs for a drop-off bay and was pulling up, still she hesitated, not really sure why.

'Okay.' He pulled on the handbrake. 'That's us.'

'Rory?'

'Yes?' He smiled over at her. 'If you've a last-minute awkward question for me,' (*How did he know?* she thought) 'better hurry, as the security guard by the main door has a glint in his eye.'

'Do you ever wonder what would have happened if things had been different before?' Alina said quickly. 'If... if that complaint hadn't been made? Do you think we'd both still have rushed off to work at other sides of the world?'

He looked surprised and then resigned. 'Of course I do,' he said. 'Don't you?' When she slowly nodded, he added, 'Especially since I've come back.'

'It was that last Monday. You know?'

'I know,' he said. He rubbed his chin. 'Look, Alina, hold that thought, okay? Because there's something that you should know. I only learned it afterwards, during the divorce, in fact, and what good would it have done bringing it up then? None.'

Alina rubbed her temples. 'You'll have to spell it out for me. I've had enough of riddles after yesterday.'

'The person who complained,' he said. 'You obviously made the same assumption I did. Turns out we were both wrong.'

'What? Don't be silly. It's on file— Oh!'

The security guard's face loomed over her as he tapped on the glass. Rory put the window down. 'I'm going,' he promised. 'Just dropping my friend off.'

'If you don't, you'll be hemmed in by the hospital transport buses,' the man said cheerfully. 'Arrive every day about this time, they do. That's why I'm here. Just a heads up.'

'Oh, well, thank you.'

The guard put his hand up in a genial wave and wandered back to his post.

'I have to go. You have to go.' Alina released her seatbelt and reached into the back for her overnight bag.

Rory stopped her, with a hand on her arm. 'Leave it. Phone me, and I'll come back.'

Alina nodded. 'It's time we talked about it properly, isn't it?'

'The only thing I do know about *time* is that our timing is always bloody terrible,' Rory said.

33

Edinburgh 2014

People hated social workers. Terrible cases hit the news with demands for better practice and formal inquiries, but sometimes from the inside it was damned if you did, damned if you didn't. In the adoption office, complaints tended to be about waiting lists, delays, miscommunication, rarely about staff – and never about Alina. Until now.

She did not need this. She was due to fly to Bangladesh at the end of the week and her visa and passport were still at the whim of consulate or courier. The lease was up on her flat at the end of the month and house-hunting was soul-destroying. Her grandparents were arriving at the end of the day for a quick visit, and she'd only popped into the office to get her time off in lieu agreed.

Instead, Alina was staring at the team leader, trying to take in what he was telling her.

'A complaint about me? Who from? What about?'

'Well, that's the thing.' With one hand he loosened his tie and with the other, he ran his finger down a printed-off contact sheet that was stapled to an envelope. When his phone rang, he ignored it. 'It's about you alright, you're clearly named. But it's an anonymous letter. As to what…' He knocked down the glasses on his forehead to peer at the notes. '…it's to do with the Holmes/MacLeod assessment.'

Alina's heart sank so deep she was glad she was sitting down. Would she ever be free of that bloody Laura? The woman haunted her. *No, she doesn't*, Alina's conscience told her calmly, you *are resentful and* you *feel guilty*. All she can be accused of is being herself. *Well, bully for her*, Alina thought, *I might just be myself too and bugger off to Bangladesh forever.*

'What did I do?' She held out her hand, determined it wouldn't shake, for the papers. 'Or what *didn't* I do?'

'That's the thing – I have no idea,' the team leader said. 'I was hoping you could throw some light on it.' He opened the envelope, slid out an A4 piece of paper and laid it on his desk, twisting it to face her. 'First there's this.' Alina reached out but he held up his own hand. 'Wait a second, because there's also this.' He took a single contact sheet and placed that down. 'And, finally…' A third contact sheet was added to his neat line-up and he gestured left to right. 'Now, read them in that order.'

Alina shuffled forward in her seat and leaned over the desk, frowning. The letter was neatly printed and not even a paragraph long. It was addressed FAO Mr Adam Daly, Adoption Services Team Leader, dated two days ago, and the header said, Re: Ms Alina Farrell – Conduct. Her eyes flew over the text:

> I wish to raise a formal complaint about the conduct of Ms Farrell in respect of the adoption assessment of Laura Holmes. Over the course of twelve Monday mornings, her behaviour was increasingly unprofessional to the detriment of both parties and the subsequent outcome.

Alina looked up in confusion; she'd expected far worse. Still her heart was hammering. 'Is this it? It doesn't say anything.'

The team leader tapped his desk. 'Read on.'

The second piece of paper was the print-out of an email, dated yesterday:

We have received a copy of a 'formal complaint' sent to your office in respect to Alina Farrell. The allegation is, as you are aware, without substance and we ask that no further action is taken.
Yours, Rory MacLeod & Laura Holmes

Alina rubbed a hand across her nose, took a deep breath and lifted the final page: another anonymous letter, set out the same way, apparently the work of the original sender:

I wish to withdraw my earlier request to raise a complaint in respect of Alina Farrell.

'Who… What…?' Alina's brain was in overdrive but she didn't know what to say.

'…When? Where? How?' The team leader shrugged. 'As I said, not a clue.' His phone rang again before he could say more, and, squinting at the screen, he added, 'I'd better take this. Hang on.'

The call gave Alina breathing space. She read each of the notes again, trying to decipher them like some weird code or clues in an escape room. The immediate conclusion was of Laura stirring up trouble. On the face of it, anonymous notes weren't her thing. She would be – had been – brutally upfront, but Alina could definitely see her penning the first, then adding in a rebuttal and a withdrawal. A game to get her point across. An annoyance for Alina, casting aspersions but leaving her powerless to answer. Oh, yes, after weeks of getting to know Laura, Alina was sure this was payback.

The team leader put his phone down, muttering something that sounded like, 'Bloody idiots,' and turned back to Alina. 'Disgruntled wife, you think? Troublemaking then thinking better of it. Or the husband finds out, gets her to retract.' She was glad their minds were along the same lines. 'Or he set it up in a misguided attempt of support.'

'No,' Alina said quickly. 'I don't think Rory would do that. Not after everything else.'

'I'm inclined to agree,' her team leader said. 'Anyone else you can think of? Oh, it's an NFA, don't worry, I'm just curious.'

Alina was blank. If Rory and Laura had older kids or a loyal family member who thought they'd been treated badly and was indignant on their behalf but 'didn't want to be involved' (it had happened before) then they might have recourse to this. But nobody either Rory or Laura had spoken of sprang to mind, and Alina had met only Rory's mother before the assessment was halted. Anyway, that reference to 'twelve Monday mornings' had to be Laura. Though maybe the team leader was right, and Rory had intervened. Alina peered at the email print-out. Sure enough, it was from his account, not Laura's.

'Well, like I said, no further action,' the team leader said. 'I don't want my best worker under a cloud. But for the record, and to draw a line under this, just reassure me that there's nothing specific you can think of that you did, or as you say, didn't do, that could have led to this?'

Alina looked at him directly. 'I didn't do anything,' she said.

34

Entering the maternity wing didn't bring back a rush of memories to Fin's birth. Alina hadn't expected it to. Her life might be up in the air right now, but back then, she had been certain she was doing the right thing. That hadn't – still hadn't – wavered. And the last birth she'd been in close contact with had been Farhana's, their housemother's sister, which had been an eye-opener. Takdir had offered to send the young woman to the local hospital, but she and Farhana were adamant on an old-school home experience with a midwife in residence. *Absolutely fair enough*, Alina had thought – all for individual choice – until she accompanied the sisters to their village home, when the word 'Dickensian' came to mind. Then again, who was she to judge? The baby was born, he was healthy and so was Farhana's sister. Now, as she checked in at the reception desk and made her way past an empty café area to the stairs, Alina thought back to that day, and was glad Kirsten and her baby seemed to have functional if not pretty mod-cons right here.

She didn't recognise Fin for a few seconds. All she saw was the rear of a young man, slim and sandy-haired, counting money for one of a line of vending machines. Walking slowly in that direction, she watched the figure drop a couple of coins and put out a foot that didn't prevent them rolling under the machine. For a second he stood motionless before giving a token kick to the metal. As he turned slightly, Alina saw who it was.

'Fin. Fin?' She hurried towards him, seeing the light of relief in his eyes as he saw her. *He's never had to deal with a crisis like this before*, she thought, drawing him into a hug. *He's never really been challenged on a personal front; even Sanna is too much on the periphery at present.* Life had jogged along nicely for the kindly and amiable Fin – making him, maybe, a bit complacent in his faith, Alina wondered – and this was his first big test. She sent a fleeting prayer into the ether that he'd pass with flying colours – *or*, she modified a coda, *scrape through like most of us do*.

'She's so tiny, Ali,' he said into her shoulder, then straightened up and looked into her eyes. 'They said she was going to be okay. But she's so tiny. She can't breathe on her own yet. How can she be okay?' His voice cracked.

Alina looked steadily back at him, only hoping she was saying the right thing. 'Fin, listen. If the doctors say she's going to be fine, then she is. They don't say that sort of thing lightly, do they? Not when it's about life and… about life,' she amended.

'Yes. Yes, I'm sure you're right.' He was like a man seizing the right words. 'Of course, you're right. I need to sort myself out.' He gave a short laugh, and his shoulders relaxed a little. 'It's just, I suppose that I've been so calm with Kirsten, you know, reassuring. When her blood pressure rocketed and they said it was a C-section now, or…' He shuddered. 'It's okay now though. It *is* okay. I just needed to give way for a minute.' Fin looked at her hopefully. 'I'm overreacting, aren't I?'

Thank you, God, Alina said silently; he'd be alright. 'No, you're *reacting*, Fin. However you feel is fine.' She looked around. 'Why don't we sit here for a few minutes? Tell me about the baby? And how's Kirsten now? Exhausted, I bet.' She was babbling intentionally as she led him towards a row of orange plastic chairs, and he followed obediently.

'It's something called HELLP syndrome.' Fin shook his head. 'I didn't take it all in. Kirsten did; she asked all the right questions and everything. She was so calm, Ali, whereas me… It's to do with blood pressure and red blood cells. It's quite rare.'

'Like pre-eclampsia?' Alina guessed. Not that she had a clue.

'Yes. I think so. Kirsten had a transfusion and they said she should be okay. The baby too. She might need steroids to help with her lungs but luckily it's just after thirty-four weeks, which makes all the difference.' He shook his head again. 'I've never prayed so hard. Ali, what on earth do people without any faith do when things like this happen?' He looked at her as if he really expected an answer.

'I don't know, Fin. I suppose when push comes to shove, we all find something to believe in,' she said. 'As long as it gets us through. I might even have sent up a few prayers via Miriam and Patrick, and Takdir, too. Well, it can't hurt, can it?'

'Covering all bases?' They shared a smile at that.

'Fin?' Now she had the full story, Alina let a big smile spread slowly over her face, 'You've got a baby. A baby daughter. I can't believe it. Congratulations!'

'I have, haven't I?' Fin's own tentative smile grew broader. 'I can't believe it either. I held her for a minute, after they'd given her to Kirsten. They had everything ready though and whisked her off in an incubator. I didn't know whether to go with her or stay with Kirsten. Ali, I went up to the neo-natal unit – it's just the ordinary one, not the intensive care – with her and then I came back down to Kirsten. Do you think that was the right thing to do?' He started to deflate again. '…I wasn't sure.'

'Well, until you learn how to be in two places at once, Fin, that's what you're going to have to do.' Alina figured a degree of jollying him along wouldn't go amiss. 'Now, do tell me, has this beautiful baby of yours got a name?' There was jollying, and then there was sounding nothing like herself; luckily Fin was too wound up in his new daughter to notice.

'Lisa. We're calling her Lisa Pauline. Lisa because we both like it and Pauline after Kirsten's mum, and for St Paul. What do you think, Ali?'

'Perfect,' she said, enjoying his enthusiasm. 'Lisa is lovely and just uncommon enough.'

'Exactly what we thought.' Fin looked pleased with himself. He jumped up. 'Why are we wasting time down here? We should go and see them.' He caught Alina's eye. 'I'm fine now, Ali. You came at the eleventh hour when I was about to fight the vending machine. But I promise, I just needed a minute.'

'Then let's go.' Alina stood up too. 'Wait – were you trying to get something in particular when I arrived?'

'Idiot. Yes.' Fin hit his fist off his forehead. 'Kirsten's got a craving for something sweet. Her tea and toast didn't hit the spot.'

Alina took her purse out of her handbag. 'I've a pocketful of change. Let's stock up.'

They pushed in coin after coin as if it was an arcade game, gathering three or four packets to slake even the sweetest, hormonal tooth. Alina, estimating that Fin's decision-making skills might well desert him again, suggested they go to Kirsten first; according to the institutional signs, they were way out of visiting hours, which presumably didn't include brand new dads but meant she'd be out on her ear sooner rather than later. Then as they made their way onto the ward, she realised she was empty-handed: no flowers, cards, grapes or beribboned cuddly toys. They must have passed a Lidl or Aldi outlet somewhere along the way, even a service station, which was perhaps half a step up from vending machine Skittles.

She wouldn't have bought anything though; too much like tempting fate. Once she was triply certain everything was okay, she'd rush to the nearest shop and buy her own bodyweight in pink sparkly hearts.

It was all a complete waste of angst because Kirsten, disconcertingly wired up to a drip and some other digital machine, was out for the count.

'Leave her,' Alina whispered to Fin, who was trying to pile up sweets silently on the bedside table. 'She needs all the sleep she can get.' She looked at him as they backed out of the room. 'So do you. How long have you been here?'

Fin ran a hand through his hair. 'Only since last night. Half of me is knackered and the other half couldn't keep still if you held me down. Just as well – her mother and sisters are descending tomorrow.'

'All of them?' Alina blinked; Kirsten's family en masse was equivalent to a large Bangladeshi gathering – with added alcohol.

'Two sisters,' he amended. 'The others can't get off work 'til the weekend. Thank God for small mercies.'

'And Jan and Hugh?'

'On their way back from the Canaries as we speak.' Fin turned to Alina and raised his eyebrow – the thing he and Sanna could do but she couldn't; *isn't that genetic?* ran through her mind. 'If we're *very* lucky, they'll all come over on the same Ryanair flight.'

'You concentrate on Kirsten and the baby and let them sort themselves out,' Alina advised. 'They'll be happy to do so.' Alina blinked; Jan plus Kirsten's mother and three sisters was not for the faint-hearted. 'I will bow out gracefully and return in quieter times.'

'Don't rush off, Ali.' Fin put his hand on her arm. 'I'm sorry for phoning you in a state, and in the middle of the night. It was just—' His fingers tightened.

'I know. And I'm glad you did.' Then, lightly, 'I get first look at baby Lisa, as well,' Alina said.

'Shall we go and see her now?' He ushered her towards another corridor, more stairs. 'By the way, how did you get here so quickly?' he asked. 'It's still early.'

'I got a lift.' Alina pushed down the little bubble of joy

that emerged with her words. 'Rory, Elizabeth's son, is home from New Zealand. He borrowed Claire's – that's Elizabeth's literary agent's – car and drove me.'

'Nice of them,' Fin commented. 'Big favours.'

The high double doors to the special care baby unit were locked. She expected a beeping flurry of activity behind A4 sheets of rules and regulations, which Fin already seemed at home with, but all was eerily quiet and calm.

The nurse who answered the bell smiled her recognition of Fin but was clearly less sure of Alina. 'It's immediate family only,' she began, but Fin, eyes already searching the room for his baby daughter, surprised them both.

'Ali is my second mum,' he said. 'I'm adopted. And she's going to be the baby's godmother.' He turned to her briefly as if his utterance was of no real consequence – on either count. 'Alright with you, Ali?'

'Me? Well... yes, of course,' she managed faintly. 'I'd love to.'

The nurse smiled. 'Go on. I think that constitutes family. Baby Lisa is doing fine.' She led them over. 'Don't be put off by the wires and the ventilator, she'll soon be able to hold her own. She weighs four pounds three ounces, which is huge around here, and she's on a very low dose of corticosteroids. She'll be out of here in a few days.' She checked the monitors and then looked at Alina. 'Say hello to your goddaughter.'

Lisa was scrawny, red and scrunched up, her fists clenched up around her face. She resembled a little old lady in her white bonnet, and one not best pleased at being woken up and dragged from her cosy nest. Alina took a step forward and rested a hand on the side of the incubator. She blinked and tried to think of the right words; she wanted to fall head over heels for her but was more overwhelmed by the fact that she was so tiny. Whatever the nurse said, she didn't quite look ready to be born, and her smudgy features were monkey-like – *never, ever say that aloud*, she thought. Then she looked over at Fin and realised it didn't matter what she said. He was besotted with the baby and wouldn't hear a word.

'Isn't she amazing, Ali? A day ago we hadn't met her, and now, already, I can't imagine her not being here.'

'She's beautiful, Fin. Amazing is the word.' Alina watched the small figure yawn and stretch. They both stood there, staring at her.

After a while, Fin said, 'Back there, sorry, I should have asked properly. But you will be her godmother, won't you? Kind of like you've been to me.' He didn't wait for her to answer, his eyes still on the cot. 'It's scary, Ali. All of it.' Then he did look over at her. 'How on earth did you do this by yourself?'

Alina shook her head. 'I wasn't really alone, Fin. My grandparents were there. Jamie would have been if I'd asked him. And I wasn't looking at the future either – that was for Jan and Hugh.' She thought back. She had cared deeply about Fin, had been overawed by him – the same way he was now – but she hadn't bonded with him. There had been no rush of the all-encompassing maternal love her social worker had cautioned her not to fight. Alina knew they'd all expected her to change her mind, to take Fin home with her, but it had never been an option; Fin already belonged to someone else. 'I didn't have any of this worry either,' she went on. 'You fairly popped out in a few hours. It was easy.' As soon as she'd said it, she wished she'd chosen another word, and she braced herself for Fin asking 'Was it easy to give me away?' which she couldn't answer because he wouldn't understand – how could he, as he looked down at his already-adored daughter?

He didn't take her up on it, though. 'Do you think I could hold her?' he said instead, looking around. 'You, too. Where's the nurse?'

'I'll go and ask her,' Alina said, hurriedly. No need to mention the small matter of her being terrified to hold such a fragile-looking thing – she'd never liked handling puppies or kittens, afraid they would break in two, and the fear was even stronger with baby Lisa.

The nurse was amenable, and went over to sort Fin out after pointing Alina in the direction of the loo. She was only gone a few minutes, and going back into the unit, she smiled at the sight of Fin sitting down, the top of his head bent over. He was quite alone, no hovering nursing staff, and in the crook of one arm he held his baby while his other thumb stroked her cheek. Alina's steps faltered and she caught her breath. It was such a private moment of sheer, focused love. She wasn't sure whether she was being pushed forward or pulled away. Standing there, she felt... she didn't know what she felt.

She had a second of stark, incongruous recollection: listening to *Gabriel's Oboe* with Jamie and hearing him say, 'D'you think that's what heaven sounds like?' And her head spun. This scene in front of her stirred something similar, yearning deeper inside her. It was a recognition of their vulnerability, the terror of responsibility, a desire – *her desire* – to protect them both, her child with his own child...

It had passed her by until now, but there was no question what it was. Twenty-five years after the event, Alina had been steam-rolled by maternal instinct. If she didn't know better, she'd think she was having a panic attack.

A few seconds and the power of it was gone, the spell broken when Fin looked over and saw her. Equally powerfully – and equally short – she was hit by something in his demeanour, something that reminded her of... Jamie? Probably wishful thinking in the circumstances. Jamie had never looked at Fin as Fin was looking at Lisa, and Alina wondered where they'd all be now, if he'd had the opportunity.

35

Dublin 1995

It was their first argument. Or, if Alina were to be honest, the only time Jamie hadn't automatically gone along with what she said. He wasn't a pushover, simply once he'd promised to support her, he wanted what she wanted, or – a very belated doubt crept in – so she'd been letting herself believe.

It was a beautiful day, and they were making the most of it walking in Phoenix Park. Jamie bought Alina an ice-cream wafer from the van and she spilled half of it down the red wool coat that didn't quite close over her bump. She was scrabbling in her pocket for tissues when a young woman with a toddler and a pram stopped and held out a sheaf of baby wipes.

'You'll be wanting shares in these feckin' things,' she said. 'A pack a day we get through I swear to God, and that's just with your man.' She jerked her head at the toddler who was squatting down and eating blades of grass.

Moments like those Alina loved. She wasn't the novelty pregnant student in the university library, or the new mascot who had toppled Sara Smyth in the social studies department. She wasn't the one stifled by her grandparents' matter-of-fact kindness, or their congregation's project to demonstrate faith in action. She wasn't the curiosity on the adoption social-worker's caseload. It was a sunny Saturday and the park was filled with young and expectant families and for a few hours, she and Jamie were no different – even when they started arguing.

'You asked me to be the baby's father, Ally-Bally. And I've done that. I'm doing it. I will continue to do it forever.' Jamie guided her to a bench, where she scrubbed ineffectually at the ice-cream stain, anything to avoid his eye. 'So why are you telling me I can't be at the birth? It's expected.'

'By who?' She went for airy, expecting his acquiescence was a foregone conclusion, and without it she was buying time. 'And anyway, I thought we didn't care what anybody else thinks. We've done fine so far.'

Jamie took one of the wipes from her and concentrated on her coat. 'Fair enough. Sod everyone else, it matters to me, Alina, to *me. I* expect it.'

All Alina knew was that this bit, the giving birth, she had to do alone. If she didn't, then she'd failed after all, and all the careful planning, the subterfuge, was for nothing. 'I'm afraid—'

'Which is why I should be with you.' He said it twice, misunderstanding her, hurt and vulnerability stark on his face.

'*That's* why,' she wanted to say. 'That look right there.' But when she tried to put it into words, what she felt inside didn't translate. 'I'm scared I won't go through with it,' she settled on. She was dissembling and she knew Jamie was sceptical, but it was predestined – she stumbled over the word but hadn't got a better one. This baby already had a carefully chosen birth father and he or she was getting an equally carefully chosen family whose dreams would come true. That was Alina's project. Wrongs would be righted and everything back on track.

There was a hymn that haunted her, she reluctantly told Jamie – another half-truth – as they tilted their faces to the lukewarm sun, Alina trying to get comfortable on the slats of the wooden bench. She could smell fried food in the air and was suddenly ravenous.

'A *hymn?*' Jamie prompted her.

'One of my grandparents' hand-clapping, big-bass

drum-banging favourites that gave me nightmares,' she tried to explain. After breaking the pregnancy news to Miriam and Patrick, Alina had sneaked her grandfather's leather-bound songbook into the bathroom and leafed through the thin pages until she found it: *Are you washed in the blood of the lamb?* That was it. Rather than the gore-fest of murdered farm animals she'd conjured up as a nine-year-old, she saw the symbolism. When Alina had the baby and handed it to its adoptive parents, she would be cleansed. Clean. Free.

He didn't call her insane again, but she could see him thinking it. 'Don't be so... so scathing or... self-righteous,' she said. 'You're an accessory after the fact, aren't you? Or maybe before it.' Alina thought about *that night*. Once Jamie had agreed to Alina's plan, they never discussed whether there was, one hundred percent, a baby to father. Eight weeks later, after what Jamie labelled 'a nought to sixty in ten days fuck-fest', when Alina finally used the pregnancy test, there certainly was, which was all that counted.

'I'm an accessory full stop,' Jamie pointed out. 'Which is why I should be there at the baby's birth. Please.'

It took every ounce of self-control she had to harden her heart. 'No, Jamie, I'm sorry,' she said quietly. 'I love you. I can never thank you enough for this and I don't expect you to understand...' *What a cop-out*, she thought, even as she said it. '...but giving birth is something I have to do on my own.' Alina wouldn't have been surprised if Jamie got up and walked away, but he didn't. Neither did he push her for a real answer. They sat on, side by side, until the sky clouded over and it got chilly.

Alone in her bed that night, Alina admitted the truth to the darkness. She wasn't scared of childbirth or of what people would say – that ship had long sailed – or even that she might bond with the baby and want to keep it. What frightened her was that Jamie would see in them the perfect little misfit family they were already pretending to be. Once seen, that couldn't be unseen, but Alina knew it wasn't their future. Not hers, not Jamie's, not the baby's.

36

Alina crossed the quiet special care baby unit, conscious of the soles of her shoes slapping on the smooth floor. Her hand on Fin's shoulder, she watched the now-sleeping Lisa, her mouth puckered and her little fingers twitching. The white hat covering her head swamped her, making her look more like an elf now than a baby monkey. *Stop it*, Alina told herself, *she's beautiful.* And when she momentarily opened her blue eyes, wide and unfocused, she was.

'I hope she's having pleasant dreams,' Alina whispered.

Fin craned his neck. 'Would you like to hold her?'

Knowing the right answer, she nodded, and they awkwardly swapped places. The baby gave a disgruntled wiggle, but didn't wake, and Alina marvelled – *as everyone always did*, she thought – at how she was too light and little to be a real, live person. Fin pulled over another chair and they sat in silence for a few minutes, Alina gradually relaxing. Fin seemed mesmerised by the baby, or simply exhausted. Maybe he was praying, she thought, watching his mouth muscles move.

Lisa was settled carefully back in her incubator, and the nurse pronounced everything on track. 'Go and get a drink, or some lunch,' she said. 'We'll call you if we need you, but we won't. When Kirsten wakes up, you can wheel her across here. We'll be waiting.'

They walked slowly down the corridor back towards Kirsten's ward.

'Would now be a good time to tell you about Sanna?' Alina asked, wondering when else they'd get the time. Things were going to be pretty full-on for Fin and Kirsten over the next few weeks.

Fin stopped dead and his eyes widened – exactly like his baby daughter's had just done. 'I totally forgot. How could I have forgotten? It was this weekend you went to stay.' Fin looked down the corridor as if Sanna might be waiting in the wings to announce herself and play happy families. 'Let's find a spot to sit down and you can give me a blow-by-blow account. A baby and my other birth parent. Who would have thought it?'

His excitement was infectious, an image of the once-little boy under the Finally Tree. They sat in a row of seats just outside Kirsten's ward. Alina took a deep breath and talked. She was sure she repeated herself as she mixed up her Dublin and Bradford visits and threw in totally unnecessary titbits about Sid the dog and Ashley from next door, but Fin drank it all in. 'It was all good,' she said. 'Both meetings. Awkward at times, but overall there was still a real bond.'

'You really did have something special back then,' Fin said.

'We did. We have.' Alina knew the tears in her eyes were about to fall, but she didn't care. She smiled through them and indicated Fin himself. 'And now, he has a baby of his own.'

'Oh, Ali.' She wasn't sure how long they sat there, arms round each other. Nobody disturbed them, nobody batted an eyelid; Alina supposed a hospital corridor saw everything in the course of a day. Only a middle-aged man in a dog collar, who stopped at the vending machine, glanced their way. Alina saw him obviously wondering whether to speak when his brow creased.

'Fin?' he said. 'Excuse me, but is everything alright?'

Fin looked up. 'Robert. How are you?' His face creased into another grin and he stood up. 'Robert, I've got a daughter.

And, not only that, but Alina here tells me, a whole birth family I haven't yet met. I'm trying to take it all in.'

'Congratulations, Fin! What a way to start the day.' The hospital chaplain – as announced under the smiling photo on his ID – clapped Fin on the back and shook his hand. He gave a friendly nod to Alina, and then asked, 'Mother and baby doing well, I hope?'

'I think so. It was all a bit hairy…' Fin gave a rundown of events, and the chaplain promised to call in to Kirsten and baby Lisa on his rounds of the wards. He went off, pulling a face at his rapidly cooling drink, and it nudged Alina and Fin into action.

'Let's go and tell Kirsten,' Fin said. 'And get back to the baby.' He hesitated. 'Ali, don't think I'm not proud of having you and Sanna as my two birth parents. I just didn't say anything to Robert because I wasn't sure what Sanna would want me to be saying. That's all.'

'I know that,' she replied. 'We've got forever to sort it all out. One thing at a time, eh?'

Several hours later Alina left Fin and a weak but elated Kirsten, who was already in trouble for trying to do too much too soon, settled with Lisa. As agreed, she phoned Rory, who told her he'd be there in twenty minutes. As she thanked him, she was torn: part of her wanted to see him again and follow up the various strands of conversation from the morning, but the other part wanted to sit back and let her mind go blank. Surely she hadn't stopped talking since she arrived at Sanna's on Friday.

I'm exhausted and I haven't even done anything, she thought, waiting outside the main entrance of the hospital. Behind it all was a strong sense of relief and gratitude that everything was working out well, and she sent a swift prayer–message to Miriam and Patrick to look over them all and keep them safe. Then, buggered if she was going to cry again, she sat up and punched out a new message to Sanna: *I've told Fin about our visit and he's so excited.* In another flurry back and forth, she added that she had suggested they all draw breath, that he and Kirsten concentrate on Lisa, and then plan to see Sanna. *You're not going anywhere, are you?* Alina typed.

Then she phoned Mizan. *Please, no more drama there today*, she thought as she dialled.

'Khalya is fine, you worry too much,' he had the nerve to shout down the miles. It sounded as if he were hurtling through a wind tunnel. 'Your Scotland life is turning into as big a Hindi movie as your Bangladesh life.'

'Mizan, I'm going to hang up if you don't get off the motorbike right now,' Alina threatened. The staccato beeps of rickshaw hooters clashing with the more sonorous boom of bus horns as they raced each other along the road to the ghat was a dead giveaway. 'Please tell me you don't have any of the children on the back?' She closed her eyes and tried not visualise two or three of the boys hanging on for dear life, their gleaming eyes and overexcitement egging him on.

There was a pause. The sounds faded to white noise.

'What fool do you think I am?' Mizan's suddenly clear voice protested, making her jump. *Shit*; a puddle of take-away coffee settled around her paper cup and reminded her to buy a travel mug. Alina blotted it with a sheaf of shredded tissues from her pocket and pointedly ignored the question.

'It was just Rihan and Sajid,' he grumbled, as ever unable to dissemble. 'Big boys, you know. We are celebrating. Rihan has won admittance to the deaf school in Dhaka.'

'That's brilliant! Tell him I said congratulations.' It was a huge deal; studying at the special school for the deaf would give Rihan the academic skills he was so ready for. 'Does he have a sponsor?' Alina couldn't remember the application. 'I mean, the fees—'

'Yes, yes, of course.' Mizan sounded impatient. 'I emailed the programme. You would know our planning if your life was not the Bollywood show I said about.'

'If you didn't call me about kidnappings, more like…'

Mizan laughed suddenly. 'My little Alina is a didi, this I cannot believe.' His 'and I can't wait to tell everyone' hovered unspoken over the line.

'I'm not really a grandmother.' Alina sighed at the silence on the end of the phone. She was fighting a losing battle. In Sonali Homestay, and to a certain extent in Takdir's household, and probably Bhola and the whole of Bangladesh, relationships and family lines were more blurred than in her network over here. Mizan had grown up under the adage that it takes a village to raise a child: if his mother was sick, an auntie, a cousin or a sister cared for him – none of them might be blood-related, but why should they be? Alina had once tried to explain the complex legal requirements that existed in Scotland to permit a child to be cared for, say by a grandparent or an aunt, and it had sounded convoluted to her own professional ears. Mizan clearly thought she was mad. For him it mattered not a jot that Fin had adoptive parents: he was her son, so she was Lisa's grandmother – one of many, if necessary. 'I'm going to be her godmother,' she said finally. 'Let me call it that, okay?' She could visualise Mizan's smiling shrug.

'Are you feeling an old lady?'

'I will be if you tell everyone I'm a grandmother.'

'Then it is – godmother, yes? I will say.' Then his tone changed. 'Why do you not come back here? I need you here, Alina. There are many problems.'

'Khalya?'

'Yes, Khalya. But many other things.'

This was more like it. Alina settled back for the tale of woe. Mizan was mercurial: his dramas very high or very low, and boredom made him maudlin. Her trick was to pick through the subtexts. 'You've got…' She checked her watch. '…ten minutes. Go.'

'Hard taskmaster,' he grumbled, then launched into budgets, politics, who had to be bribed, which boy had tried to peer into the girls' room, whether they could keep the once-mute, now chatty-happy twins dumped outside the gates on Alina's watch or whether they should be sent to the government orphanage... All par for the course.

'And Khalya is okay?' she confirmed as he went to hang up. 'Promise?'

'Yes, yes. I say so, no?'

'Two days ago she was apparently kidnapped, remember?' Alina leant back and yawned, another wave of fatigue enveloping her. Damn Mizan and his grandmother remarks; now she felt old and in need of a snooze.

'Today Khalya is fine,' he admitted. 'She is here. Studying her schoolwork. She's mad I kept her from Barisal, but I promised her it's just for this week. Because—'

'Because what?' Alina knew that tone of voice.

'Because next week she'll probably be married.'

He hung up on the punchline, and luckily for him, Alina thought, Rory was inching round the car park in Claire's car. She waved, wondering whether living in Bangladesh would help her gain perspective, keep the drama under the parapets, or whether she'd just end up killing Mizan.

Rory was a very receptive audience, reminiscent of past times at his kitchen table, when he'd asked questions and she'd imparted an apparently endless supply of adoption stories. In the car back to Edinburgh, Alina had got her second wind, reassured that all would be well, and chatted on as naturally as if Rory had been anyone else. She caught him glancing at her once or twice and smiling, nicely, but she pulled herself up.

'I'm babbling, aren't I? Sorry. I'm not usually one for oversharing.' Those Monday mornings reasserted themselves and she added lamely, 'Except with you, it seems. Ironically.'

'Don't apologise,' Rory said. 'It's great to have back the Alina I knew and loved...' His whole body tensed as he realised what he'd said and fleetingly, Alina was grateful his foot hadn't been on the brake. 'Bad choice of words,' he said hastily. 'But you know what I mean.'

'Yeah.' She knew.

For the next dozen or so miles, Alina stared out of the window, watching the road flash by. The silence wasn't uncomfortable – if anything it was charged, as if one or both of them were waiting for something.

'It was Morag,' Rory said suddenly.

'What was?' Alina asked idly, pulling herself back to the here and now. When he didn't immediately reply, she looked over at him, but his gaze was firmly on the road. 'Rory?'

'The complaint. The adoption assessment complaint.'

'Morag? *Our* Morag?' Alina pulled a face in disbelief. *Come on, Alina*, she told herself; what other Morag was he likely to be talking about?

Rory gave a single nod of his head.

'But… How? Why?' Alina had a flashback to the original conversation with her team leader.

'Why do you think?' Rory said grimly. 'Out of some misguided sense of loyalty to Laura and utter indignation on her behalf. She was… *incandescent* that Laura… we, I suppose… didn't pass our test with flying colours and have people queuing up to give us their poor neglected babies.'

'Morag, though. It was such a… a silly thing to do.' There were other more fitting words, but Alina couldn't get her head around it. 'Are you sure?'

'Yup. Oh, Laura egged her on. Played up the devastated, hard-done-by childless woman, misunderstood by the system, the allocated social worker—'

'Me.'

'You,' Rory agreed. 'You, who interrogated us for weeks, liked me more than her, then decided for no good reason to "fail" us. It wasn't fair, she said, and she bet the social worker – you – never gave it a second thought.'

Alina made a choking noise and Rory glanced at her

sympathetically. 'I know. But she had Morag eating out of her hand. The thing was that Laura, true to type, did all that, got bored and moved on – much like she did everything, our marriage and wanting children included – but Morag didn't.'

'I was sure it was Laura playing games.' Alina shook her head. 'That it was personal because she didn't like what I was doing. I hadn't even met Morag.'

'It *was* Laura playing games. Morag bore the brunt. She didn't tell Laura what she'd done but she was bursting with something – you know Morag – and expected praise when Laura got it out of her. Laura thought it was tacky, and Morag is probably still trying to make up for it. I wrote the email refuting the allegation and, to be fair to Laura, she agreed and made Morag retract the allegation. Maybe I should have contacted you, let you know, but there didn't seem any point. Maybe I was wrong.' He lapsed into silence.

Would it have changed anything if she'd known? Alina wondered. No, it wouldn't. It was sad more than silly. Poor Morag. It did explain why the woman had such a down on her though – it wasn't just that she was foreign. Alina could only imagine what Morag had felt when she learned that she was Elizabeth's new tenant.

'Does Elizabeth know?' she asked.

'No. Nobody else. Like I said, what would be the point? You didn't get into any trouble, did you?' he added.

'It was all too vague.' Alina gave a short laugh. 'My team leader just asked me to confirm that I'd done nothing that could come back and bite me – or more likely, the agency.'

'Well, you didn't.'

'I know.'

As they approached the ring road for Edinburgh and then the Morningside turn off, Alina and Rory lapsed into silence, but Alina couldn't throw off that niggling feeling that something had shifted in their relationship. It was almost as if they'd gone back to their pre-panel selves, which was good – it had to be good – but it threw up a whole host of new complications. That was if Rory even felt the same way. Friends? She didn't know.

'I'll see you to your door,' Rory said as they finally found a parking space what seemed like a mile away. He took her bag and they made their way along Edenfield Road and through the gate of number 36. The devil got into Alina as Morag's coach house confronted them, and she gave a merry wave – just in case Morag was on the look-out. Rory stifled a bark of laughter as they rounded the corner to Alina's flat.

On the doorstep he handed her the overnight bag.

'Thank you,' Alina said. 'For the lift, the company, for telling me… everything.'

'You're welcome. Any time.'

They looked at each other uncertainly. It was definitely a hug rather than handshake moment, Alina thought. *Oh, what the hell…*

She and her bag grasped him in an awkward hug. Rory's arms tightened around her, and there they stood, for far longer than was warranted.

'I'd better go,' he said into her hair.

'You better had.'

Alina's heart was hammering suddenly, and instead of pulling apart the hug turned into a kiss, short as it was sweet.

'I'll see you later. Bye, Alina.' Rory gave her one last squeeze and turned back to Elizabeth's.

'Bye,' she echoed, standing watching, letting a teenage-like trickle of warmth – *Alina fancies Rory, Alina fancies Rory* – slowly spread through her.

37

The next morning, Alina jumped out of bed, invigorated. She phoned Fin, spoke to Kirsten, and discovered all was well. Baby Lisa was still in the special-care baby unit, but both of them had spent most of the day and night with her, and she was sleeping peacefully – 'unaware of the family onslaught about to be let loose on her,' Fin added, with only a hint of trepidation.

'Maybe you should take a leaf out of her book and rest while you've the chance,' Alina suggested cheerfully.

'Are you joking?' he said. 'I won't get near my daughter once we're all out of here. I'm making the most of the quiet time with her.'

Hanging up, reassured, Alina set to and cleaned the flat from top to bottom. In her bedroom, with a bright 'Aha!', she came upon a memory stick of Fin's baby photos. It felt like karma. Alina zipped a file and emailed them to Sanna, firing off a quick text at the same time to warn Sanna what she'd done. *Cool*, came back. *Oh and Scottish Parliament meeting is on – okay to visit?*

Alina typed an affirmative, hesitating before sending it. She and Sanna had met first on neutral ground, then at Sanna's home, and now Sanna was coming to Alina's. Three significant steps out of four: all that would be left was for

Sanna and Fin to meet. *Could – should – a twenty-five-year gap close so quickly?* Alina wondered. *It's good, all good,* she told herself, *and even if it isn't, there's no going back.* Hurriedly, she sent the message, and moved to take out her anxiety on the bed linen, hauling the jumble of sheets from the machine and out to the washing line. It was usually a job she hated, the damp, tangled mess irritating her, but today it was a distraction.

Battling the wind, she pegged it out on the washing line and stood back, hands on her hips. There was much, she reflected, to be said for taking a thin cotton covering down to the water and beating the hell out of it with a bar of Lux soap before leaving it on the roof to dry. Smiling now, she pictured the girls at one end of the pond getting the washing impossibly white and the boys at the other gutting and cleaning the fish they'd just caught. In summer, they jumped into the dense water afterwards, to cool off and clean themselves down, lunghis acting as swim shorts and towels both. The little girls copied them, their miniature salwar kameezes doing the same job of modesty, but the older ones, Khalya among them, had to look on wistfully, deemed too grown up to join in.

Alina, lost in the security of Bhola, was still staring at the billowing cotton sails when her phone rang. She reached into the pocket of her oversized cardigan: Takdir.

Safe home from Delhi, he was playing golf in Dhaka before taking the overnight boat to Bhola – if the storms in the Bay of Bengal passed over. Dhaka was hot, humid and smog-filled – nothing new there – and the start of the monsoon not far off. As ever, he sounded delighted to hear her voice, and apologised for his lack of contact over the previous few days.

'I managed to complete some charity business while I was there,' he said. 'A possible partnership. I'll write up the details and email them to you and Mizan.' He paused, then went on, 'My health check also took a little longer than expected – but before you worry unnecessarily, I am an old man with an enlarged prostate gland. I've had some tests, just to be sure, but everything else is tickety-boo, as you might say.'

'I've never said tickety-boo in my life. I don't know anyone who has!' The faint alarm bells that threatened to jingle in Alina's mind receded as Takdir laughed and suggested they move on to more pressing matters.

'Khalya,' Alina said immediately. 'Mizan's filled you in, I know, but Khalya's mother is hell-bent on marriage. She's a piece of work…' Remembering who she was talking to, she pulled back. Whatever the woman had done, she was very close to Husna, and did nothing without Husna's say-so – the natural progression of that thought was inconceivable. 'I think Mizan handled it very well and Khalya's safe. But it's not the end, is it? It's just the start.'

'Alina, my dear, stop there.' Takdir's voice was soothing. He was well aware of the nonsense (his amused word) of Khalya's mother, and he intended to have a sharp word with her. Maybe he hadn't been forthright enough on other occasions. 'I will ask my wife to be stern with her, too,' he promised. Your Aunt Husna was with me in Delhi, and I am confident she wasn't party to this action. Inshallah, we'll all be back at Sonali Homestay tomorrow and we will regroup then.'

By mid-afternoon, Alina's early energy was spent, leaving her about to crash. Stretching out on her bed, she tried to invoke her Bhola self and nap, but her Edinburgh half was having none of it. She congratulated herself on having banished Rory from the forefront of her mind all day, and now gave herself permission to dwell on what had happened on her doorstep yesterday. There was no angst, just a fizzy warmth that said everything between them was alright. It was the most immense leap from where she'd spent the last five days – scratch that, the last five years – but for no good reason they'd moved on. And she'd lay bets he felt the same way. The kiss, well: that either drew a line under the past or it made a promise for the future. Which, she didn't know.

There was no need to be wary of calling in on Elizabeth

now, Alina decided, and Elizabeth would want to know all about Fin, so she hauled herself up, made herself presentable and a few minutes later was knocking on Elizabeth's door.

There was no answer. Alina fumbled with her key, opened the door and called up the stairs, but the house had that unmistakably empty air. No Elizabeth. No Rory. She was deflated as she wandered back. No Connie either. And Morag... well. She'd cook, Alina decided, brightening up. She'd cook and she'd share.

Her European dishes were passable, but she could do a decent biryani from scratch – impressing people who hadn't had the real thing. Invention over authenticity. The food in Sonali Homestay was rice and vegetable-based, with goat meat or hilsa fish when market prices allowed. Since neither were readily available on Morningside Road, lamb would shine.

Alina rooted around in her cupboards, and figured she could put chickpeas, potatoes and cauliflower to good use, and mix a dough to make flatbreads, too. She'd feed half to Elizabeth and Rory – and Connie, if she were home – and freeze the rest. She amused herself imagining taking a tray of cauliflower bhajis over to Morag; even better, she'd get Rory to take them. *You're a wicked, wicked woman*, she told herself, grinning. Poor Morag.

When she'd chopped, fried and simmered to her heart's content, Alina cast an eye at the clock – hoping Takdir was safe on the boat to Bhola, and wondering if Sanna was looking at the pictures of Fin – and started on the bread. Kneading the dough with far more vigour than required, Alina vent her adrenaline in the old-fashioned way. She pushed and pulled and split the mixture into sections. Then, flinging flour around with unusual abandon, she flattened each piece and shaped it into a thin circle with her fingers and the heel of her hand. It was instinctive, mundane, and as such, settling. When she stopped, she stood back and blinked. On autopilot, she'd made enough rounds to feed the five thousand, or the residents of Sonali Homestay, at least. With the panache of a food blogger, she arranged and rearranged the evidence into a semblance of arty disorder and photographed it all. The children loved seeing pictures of her domestic life in Scotland, exclaiming at everything as if it was from an alien land, which it was for them.

She sent the pictures and then a text to Elizabeth: *Called but you were out. I'm making a Bangla feast. Alright to put some in your kitchen?* The speedy reply was, *I insist! I'm at A Thing with 007. I'm pretending to be gaga and playing Candy Crush under the table. Can you phone in a bomb threat? E. x*

Armed with an array of pots and dishes, Alina picked her way carefully to Elizabeth's. Morag was just entering the gate.

'Meals on Wheels?' she said, with a flicker of a smile that suggested she'd made a joke.

'Bangladeshi food. I've made far too much.' Alina was finding it hard not to blurt out, *I know what you did.* Instead, she said, 'You're welcome to some, but I didn't think you liked' – she bit back *foreign* – 'spicy food.'

'No. Thank you. Well, goodbye.' Morag thrust her key into the lock on her door and took herself and her shopping bag in, locking the door behind her with ruthless efficiency.

'Bye,' Alina muttered, in the process of having to put her baggage down on the stoop to root for door keys. *Shite.* Before she could do so, the door opened a narrow sliver, and one of Rory's eyes appeared. Alina suppressed a squeal.

'Has she gone?' he asked, and when Alina nodded, he opened the door and invited her in. 'Mum sent a warning text. In case I was in the bath, she said, and got a fright. Though you'd have been more likely to get a fright...' Rory reddened slightly. 'That came out wrong.'

'It's fine. I know what you mean. Can you give me a hand with these?'

Together they carried the food to the kitchen and found places to put it.

'Try something,' Alina urged. 'There's enough for the street.'

'It's good.' Rory munched on a cauliflower bhaji and took a spoonful of the biryani. 'Delicious.'

'That needs longer to cook, really. It will be nicer tomorrow.' Alina hesitated. 'I'm sure you're busy, so—'

'Stay,' Rory said quickly.

'Alright,' she replied even quicker.

Rory opened the fridge and took out a bottle of prosecco. 'I bought you this,' he said, holding it up. 'To celebrate the baby and, well, to make up for all those endless cups of coffee and chocolate biscuits that were all I could offer you. Do you... Shall we...?'

'Yes, please,' Alina said. 'Prosecco's a Charles drink. I'm sure Elizabeth wouldn't mind.'

'She'll be dead jealous. I don't think she's enjoying her evening.'

In Charles, sitting at either end of the large sofa, Rory and Alina raised their glasses. 'Cheers,' he said. 'To new babies, and... er... old friends.'

'New beginnings,' Alina supplied. 'Cheers.' She sipped the prosecco, enjoying the bubbles on her tongue and what she still thought of as grown-up taste.

They just looked at each other for a couple of minutes, awkwardness still hovering. *Maybe this was a mistake*, Alina thought uneasily. Maybe they couldn't be friends, or whatever they were, not yet. The kiss... that was just emotion of the moment, the shock of birth and of betrayal. Maybe drinking prosecco together was too intimate. *Maybe, maybe, maybe*, she mocked herself.

'Fin asked me to be godmother,' she said suddenly. 'Did I tell you that? He called me his sort-of mum, and then I had a mad moment when I found my dormant maternal streak.' She cursed the tears she could feel filling her eyes. *What a thing to tell Rory, of all people.*

'Oh, Alina.' Rory put his glass down, got up and crouched in front of her. 'That's a lovely thing. Isn't it?'

'Yes. But it's not fair on you.' She pursed her lips together. To her surprise, he laughed.

'You've got the wrong impression of me, you know,' he

said. 'I'm not a blubbering barren wreck. I like my life. Most of the time I don't think about children. *And*, I'm godfather to two.' He shook his head. 'They're absolute horrors. I'm clearly not doing my job.'

'Oh.'

'Cards on the table?' He was still in front of her, hands either side of her knees; Alina nodded. 'Yes, I still would like children. No, you didn't ruin my chances during the adoption assessment. Yes, it would have been wrong to have them with Laura. No, there hasn't been anyone else I've imagined having them with...' Alina waited for him to say it, and he did. '...other than you.'

38

Edinburgh 2014

There was no question that Rory and Laura's adoption assessment brought a new light to Alina's Monday mornings.

No. She might as well say it as it was, she admitted, as she drove round the bypass heading to their estate. Seeing Rory was the draw, the thing that got her up half an hour early to do her hair, choose her clothes, and have an extra cup of coffee while going over her notes – forcing herself to focus on this as *work*.

Laura wasn't at these Monday meetings. Her individual sessions were wrapped up in two hours – Laura's decision – but Rory's had grown legs. He had a lot of questions, she justified it; it was standard practice, good practice not to leave any unanswered. That it was with Rory's tacit collusion, and accompanied by a rationale and follow-up notes to support each session, was pointless: Alina knew by now that the assessment would never get to panel.

Each week, Alina and Rory sat either side of the kitchen table, a bundle of documents between them, and they talked. There was no impropriety, nothing Laura or the department, or indeed, an official inspector, could find in evidence. Only if professional misconduct of the thoughts could be recorded was there an issue. Alina mused on the philosophical: was something wrong if she thought about it but never acted on it?

This morning, she was a bit earlier than usual arriving. Traffic was light – one of those strange Monday holidays parts of Edinburgh had throughout September. Which meant— Oh.

She thought for a second she'd conjured Laura up. As Alina drew into the estate, she saw two cars still parked on the drive and accordingly she bumped onto the pavement in front of the house. As if it was choreographed – was she being watched? – the front door opened and Laura stepped out in head-to-toe Lycra, a headband pushing her hair back. Alina gathered her things together slowly, fleetingly considering faking a phone call, but if Laura had something to say, she'd simply wait in silence, her eyes fixed on the person keeping her waiting. It was a deliberate ploy, honed. 'It demonstrates who's in control,' Laura had said, forthcoming about boundaries and discipline. The coldness – Laura called it neutrality – of it unnerved Alina, and she wondered what effect it would have on a small child. Laura had made it clear that she modified her behaviour for nobody whether they were six, sixteen or sixty. To be fair, she expected nobody to change for her, either. 'Consistency,' she'd said. 'Aren't you all about consistency?'

'Good morning, Alina,' she said, as the two came face to face on the path. 'This is getting silly, isn't it?' She didn't pause. 'You trekking out here week after week. My husband is getting too fond of these little interviews with you. I don't know what *issues* he still has that he needs to share with you rather than me, and I know you won't tell me, so I've told him we need to move on.' She looked at her watch while Alina was trying to get some words out. 'I need to go. Back me up, please, and we can *all* meet, once more, next Monday.'

'Whatever you say, Laura,' Alina muttered to the air as Laura hopped into her Mazda. Encounters with the woman always left her feeling inadequate, but this time guilt entered the mix. She knew Laura was right.

'Hello?' she called, pushing the open front door. 'Rory?'

'Come in.' He appeared at the other end of the hall, wiping his hands on a towel. 'I heard,' he added. 'And what I didn't hear I can surmise. Laura's called time. We're beyond the period she's allotted to this assessment, and she needs a result.'

Alina walked slowly to the kitchen, put down her bag on the counter, and began to unbutton her jacket. 'It seems so.' She looked up then, but his back was towards her as he filled the kettle. 'She does have a point, Rory.'

'That we're – you and me, I mean – getting into a rut?' He clicked the switch on and turned round. '*Mother hens over the tea cosy*, apparently.'

'Not exactly.' Alina wanted to laugh at Laura's image, but again she was just a bit too near the mark. 'The assessment itself, I mean. I've met you both more than the recommended minimum. I've looked at your bank statements and checked the house for baby-proofing. We've covered all we can, and I should have taken up references and met your families by now. Instead, I've only met your mother.' She swallowed. 'I admit I've probably been dragging my heels a bit recently—' She suddenly wasn't sure which direction to go in, but Rory beat her to it.

'It's alright, Alina.' He motioned her to sit down, while he methodically opened cupboards, spooned coffee into a cafetiere and filled it with water. He put it on the table and they both looked at the swirling, murky grains. 'We're all of us aware you're not going to approve us for adoption.' Alina didn't contradict him. 'We've all been playing a game. I don't exactly know what yours or Laura's is, but mine, well, I'm not proud of myself.'

'That's nonsense,' Alina protested, sure of herself on that point if nothing else. 'You are the one person, I mean, if it was just you... That is, Laura...'

He shook his head. 'You're trying not to say that Laura is the problem. Well, she is. Alina, Laura doesn't want a baby, she just doesn't want to fail in her latest five-year plan. More so, she bloody doesn't want to fail an assessment, but if she's going to, she'll quit while she's ahead.'

'And make a new plan.' Alina smiled faintly. Of course

he was right. Why wouldn't he be? He'd been married to the woman for six years. Laura was practical and productive: instead of kitting out a bedroom and choosing schools, she would start a charity for childless couples or write a book about her experiences.

'So, this is it, then,' Alina said. 'It's all very simple, after all.'

'No. No, it's not.' Rory surprised her by banging his – thankfully empty – mug on the table and glaring at her. 'You can write whatever you like in your report, but I've learned a lot about myself, Alina, and I'm not proud. Laura has been *herself* all the way through this, but I haven't. I've been stringing you – and her – along because I'm the one that's not suitable. I want to have a kid, I'd love a whole host of them, but I can't do it with Laura. We don't love each other enough to withstand the realignment and the shock to the system.'

'Rory, I—'

'No, Alina, it's okay.' He sounded defeated. 'I knew it before we started but I told myself it might work out, you know, "make us stronger" or whatever they say. Bollocks. I'd call off the assessment even if you didn't. I've cheated you, Alina.'

'Me?' Alina was taken aback. 'Don't be silly. That's what these assessments are for. How can you be sure until you've gone through it all? You haven't cheated, I'm just sorry.' She stopped because she didn't know exactly what she was sorry for.

'Are you? Well, so you should be.' He held up his hand, 'I'm joking. Sort of. If it wasn't for you, for these Mondays, I, well, I wouldn't have known I was with the wrong woman.' Then he glared again. 'How crap do you think I feel when my wife is beside me, we're faking an adoption assessment, and all I can think about is you?'

There was no excuse in the world good enough for not taking him up on that remark, except for the sudden bang and clatter of the window cleaner, propping up his ladders and asking for water to fill his bucket. By the time he left, Laura had returned, and Alina drove back to the office, shocked.

Rory had shocked her. Shocked himself, she thought. But, eleventh hour or not, he'd been honest, which was more than Alina had.

39

'The idea of being friends seems a bit tame now, doesn't it?' Rory said eventually. 'I don't know whether to lunge towards you or away from you.'

'Life was much easier when I asked the questions and you answered them,' Alina agreed.

He stretched his legs, then sat beside her on the sofa, the gap closer this time. 'Where do we go now?'

'You could try kissing me properly,' Alina suggested, heart beating fast. 'An inside, in-private kiss, rather than a chaste doorstep one.'

Rory's face was torn. 'God, I want to, Alina. I really want to. As much as I ever did before. More. But—'

'But.' That bloody little word always popped up. She uncurled her legs. 'But what if it's all a fantasy? But what if it's better in our heads than in reality?' He nodded slightly.

'But what if it's not? Better to know, surely?' Slowly, Alina moved towards Rory until their thighs were all but touching and she could feel his body heat. 'Right,' she said, 'Count to three, then – go.'

It made them both laugh, and in doing so broke the tension. They leaned in towards each other for a kiss that was short enough, sweet, and held the promise of much more. It was the first time they'd ever properly touched each other, and Alina felt a buzz of electricity course through her. Rory must have felt it too because he stroked her hair and said, 'I think we'll be alright.'

And in *that* kiss, the next one, every last vestige of five years rolled away. It felt as if a thick dark line had been not only crossed but rubbed out, and they were back where they should have been on that final Monday morning.

What seemed like hours later, Alina wriggled to release her numb leg and said, 'I should go home. But I don't want to move.'

'Then don't.' Rory kissed her hand and untangled himself, leaving Alina snuggling further into the sofa cushions and smiling to herself.

'I'd better. Your mum will be home soon and this... us... I haven't the energy to explain it all tonight.'

'Good point. And I'm too old to have my mum catch me in a compromising position on the family sofa.'

'She'd just raise her eyebrows and say, "Well, as a romantic novelist, I wouldn't do it like that, but if it works for you..." That would be cold water enough.' Alina stifled a yawn, but Rory noticed anyway.

'That's my cue to walk you home,' he said. 'Come on.'

We're on and off stage left like a French farce crossed Alina's mind as they stood, again, at her front door. 'Do you have to go?' she said, surprised at her own forwardness, even more surprised at how natural it felt to ask.

The invitation hung unspoken.

'I would very much like to stay.' Rory looked at her evenly. 'Very soon.'

'Very sensible.' Alina pulled a face, but she knew he was right.

'I can't leave with "sensible" hanging over me,' he objected. 'If I wasn't forty years old and sensibly aware of being in a posh street on a cold night, I'd be pushing you up against your windowsill and being ungentlemanly.' He held her at arm's length and added, 'I fully intend on doing those things, but somewhere more comfortable, out of the Neighbourhood Watch range.'

Alina smiled. 'This suggestion isn't necessarily connected, but why don't you have dinner here? Tomorrow, the next day?'

'That sounds like a very good idea. In the meantime, I'll tell you what.' Rory patted his pocket. 'I'll text you until you fall asleep.'

He did exactly that. They were awake, on and off, most of the night.

Takdir's phone call came when Alina was deciding whether to get up and seize the day or find an old airline eye mask, blot out the light and get a couple hours of proper sleep.

'Alina, my dear,' Takdir said. 'I may have been too complacent. We may have the makings of a problem.'

Alina's stomach lurched and that shiver of unease ran through her again. She stiffened. 'There is something wrong, I knew it.'

'Alina, Alina. Be calm.' Takdir's tone was soothing over the miles.

She took a deep breath and told him she was fine. 'Just worried.'

'Maybe I spoke with haste; I have spent too much time speaking with Mizan,' Takdir tempered. 'It is a situation, an uncomfortable one, with which we would appreciate your help.'

'Khalya's marriage? Or—'

'It is mostly Khalya. Her mother is determined to pursue this man she has found for marriage. He is a good man, a kind man, I believe, and rich, but Khalya is too young for him.'

He was repeating Mizan's philosophy. Alina rubbed her eyes. 'She won't listen, even to you?'

Takdir sighed. 'Alina, you understand my very difficult position here. I'm afraid that my wife is, well, more invested than I would like her to be. It requires delicacy and diplomacy.' Her uncle had those in spades, Alina thought. If he couldn't pour oil on these troubled waters, then who could? But putting Husna in the mix made it insupportable. 'I have been asking myself,' Takdir went on, 'is it my right or responsibility to forbid this marriage? I cannot condone it, but I would rather we solved the problem and set a precedent without my ordering of directives.'

'Do you think that's possible?'

The silence was heavy. 'It means we should try,' Takdir said finally. 'This situation is important. It is bigger than Khalya, you understand. A test case, isn't it? We need to stand firm and united. Other NGOs are waiting for us to act.'

'I see.' Alina took a long breath in and blew it out of her nose. There was a question she had to ask even if she dreaded the answer. 'You said it was *mostly* Khalya. What else? It's your health, isn't it? Please tell me the truth.'

'You're right, of course,' he said gently. 'I wasn't dishonest yesterday, my dear, just not in possession of all the facts.'

'Which are?' Alina's voice was a whisper.

'My MRI scan results require further investigation. I feel fine, that I promise you, but it would be foolhardy not to take this warning seriously.'

'What do you want me to do?' Alina asked simply.

'To come back to us.'

She knew he was going to say that but the fact that he'd asked was significant; Takdir had never asked anything more of her since he had introduced her to Sonali Homestay and his dreams there.

'Just for a short time, two weeks, I thought. And at my expense – no, Alina, this is my request, not the charity's.'

'I'll check out flights.' Alina counted rapidly. 'The weekend? My passport is fine, I can get a visa on arrival.'

'It is possible? Your life in Scotland will not be disrupted?'

Alina stifled a laugh. Fin had a premature baby; Rory had professed, if not undying love, *something*; Sanna was centre stage; and Elizabeth… would Elizabeth want to come with her? she wondered. Short notice, but she might. Alina was walking out on all of them. She felt the turmoil of indecision.

They all needed her. What was she supposed to do? Then an image of Miriam swung into her mind, saying, 'Do they all need you right now, Alina, or is it you that needs them?'

'Alina?' Her great uncle prompted her.

'Everyone here won't miss me for a couple of weeks.' She crossed her fingers.

'One more thing, my dear. Your friend, our donor Mrs Elizabeth, we wondered would she bring forward her visit? We here are ready to lay the foundations of her generous gift. If she is.'

'I'll ask her. I'll do it now.'

'I am thankful, Alina, my dear. As Mizan will be. Together, all will be well. Inshallah.'

Inshallah. Alina echoed it long after Takdir had terminated the call and she was making another one. 'Elizabeth? Are you home and are you decent?' she asked as the phone was answered. 'Good. And is Rory there? Good.' Alina did a mental check. 'I suppose it's too much to hope that Claire... excellent. I'm coming over. We need a huddle of Winston proportions.'

'Will Elizabeth want to go?' Alina said aloud as she had a quick shower and got herself together. 'Come on. There'll be no holding her back.'

An hour later, armed with a homemade checklist and a lot of enthusiasm, Elizabeth commandeered Claire as her assistant and closeted them in Winston. Alina and Rory were banished to Charles for the foreseeable, and Alina was graciously told she could book their flights.

'It's all very exciting,' Alina heard Elizabeth say. 'Don't you think so, Double-0?'

Claire's reply as she closed the door, was, 'You are creating havoc with our schedules and I'm doing you a favour here. You owe me. I'm only doing it to help Alina out.'

Alina grinned, concentrating on dates and times. Flights were frighteningly easy to book with a mobile phone and a credit card. 'Done,' she said, as Rory entered the room carrying coffee. 'Sunday via Doha. Details being printed out in the other room as we speak.'

'I feel totally superfluous,' Rory said. 'But you've made my mother's day. She's like a child with a surprise trip to Disneyland.'

'I hope she likes it.' Suddenly, their long-planned, almost mythical pilgrimage of a trip was happening. 'I wasn't actually expecting Takdir to ask me to go back,' Alina confessed to Rory. 'And you know that thing about you and me and timing...'

'Ah. You're anxious about loving me and leaving me?' He sat down beside her.

'Something like that.'

'Can I come?' was Rory's surprise response.

'Would you want to? Really?'

'Why not? I'm not tied to New Zealand, Alina. I only went there because it was the furthest place that could offer me a contract at the time. That contract is up. There's plenty of work if I want it. There and here.' He paused. 'I don't mean this time – who would dare steal my mother's thunder? And I'd probably turn into one of middle-aged tossers wearing a sarong-thing—'

'Lunghi.'

'Wearing a lunghi and white-mansplaining to the locals.' He shuddered. 'God forbid.'

When Alina stopped laughing, she said, 'You will still be here when I come back?'

'I promise. You will *come* back?'

'I promise.' Alina looked down at her list, but there really was very little to do. Thank goodness for Miriam and Patrick and their money that meant she could go off on a whim, however practical the reason, like this. She sent up a little thank you, feeling Miriam's 'It's all part of God's plan' echoing back.

'Tell me about it,' Rory said. 'Your place. There was never time on those Monday mornings for everything we had to tell each other.'

40

Bhola 2004

'There's one more place I want to show you,' Takdir said as Alina's third week in the country was drawing to a close. She was playing peek-a-boo Khalya on the roof terrace. 'It will be a different kind of journey, without the car or recourse to DC residences.' He rested one hand gently and briefly on Alina's shoulder. 'I think that, like me, you might find it's your favourite of all.'

'I'm intrigued.' Alina meant it. She was slowly carving out a very tentative Bangladesh-sized niche for herself, and she liked it. But right now, something else was concerning her. 'Uncle Takdir? Come here to Khalya.'

With an enquiring gaze, he came and perched opposite the baby and took the little hand she held out. 'What is it? Is she sick?'

'Not sick, no, but watch.' Alina moved her hand, her uncle's hand and a bright pink water bottle she happened to have handy. Khalya's eyes followed them all. When the pink bottle was hidden, her face puckered up. 'She sees everything, right?'

'Yes.'

'But now listen.' Alina clapped, stomped, sang la-la-la loudly, all without moving. She did the same by each ear, out of Khalya's line of sight. The baby didn't respond at all.

'What are you saying?' Takdir asked but Alina could see he was ahead of her.

'I don't think she can hear. I think Khalya has some kind of deafness.'

'I'll arrange to have it checked,' Takdir said. 'Immediately. You and I will travel tomorrow evening, but my wife will remain here with the child and her mother. Your Aunt Husna will see to it.'

They left the following evening, taking an overnight launch from Sadhar ghat, the quayside as frenetic as the airport on Alina's arrival. The darkness added to the chaos. Only the huge and rusted ferries, lit up as if for an old-fashioned dance, offered any light, and hawkers, traders and passengers scurried in their shadows like a colony of ants. Her uncle had paid for a VIP cabin for Alina, though one glance at the narrow bed and moth-eaten blanket, the rat trap in one corner and the enthusiastic mosquitoes and she wished she was taking her chances in third class on the open lower deck. But testament, she thought, to how far she'd come, she laid her clean towel over the bed, pulled a travel mosquito net around her like a body bag, and dozed to the sound of the ship's horn.

Eight hours later, they were in port on the island of Bhola. 'Don't be misled,' Takdir said. 'There are at least one million residents, more.' His house, a two-storey concrete building painted pale blue, was large, set alone amid fields and trees, out-houses scattered like poor relations.

'This is our family home place,' he told her. 'It was from here my brothers and I made our lives, and from here your father left for London. My children grew up here, their children visit, but now there is nobody to stay here all the time.'

It was a shame, thought Alina, because this was a place of calm, of safety. Years of family life had warmed it somehow. 'If there is one place in Bangladesh I feel at home, it's here,' she admitted to Takdir, a day and night after their arrival. She was nervous of saying it, as if there was ingratitude in singling out this place from all the others he'd shared with her, but his face lit up.

'I am glad to hear that, my dear.' His eyes twinkled. 'Because I have a vision.'

Together they made their way to the top of the house, on to the roof, where the view was of green, or trees, of – a novelty in such a crowded country – nothing else.

'Over there.' Takdir pointed. 'There, I wish to build a memorial to your parents, to Helen and to Nozmul. To celebrate their lives and to build other lives up.'

For a second, leaning on the balcony, Alina imagined a mausoleum, a concrete monstrosity, an engraved monument with all the charm of a cyclone shelter. But as Takdir talked on, she was ashamed of how she underestimated her uncle.

'A living memorial,' he said. 'I want to build a home for children who are abandoned, unwanted, for no reason other than minor infirmity. I want to educate them, teach them a trade, make something of their lives. The money is in a trust dedicated to your parents; we will create a charity.' Takdir turned to Alina then, took her hands and said, 'I would very much like your blessing and your input.'

Alina was captivated. The romance of it, the image of a happy, fun-filled home, the promise that her parents would live on in these children. Of course she wanted to be part of it. Then realisation hit. 'Who's going to do all this?' she asked.

'I am. You are. And a third person, my young volunteer. We three will lay the foundation and the project will grow. Come.' Takdir led Alina away from the view and downstairs to the main entrance. 'Meet Mizan.'

The boy she was introduced to seemed shy in her company, though he probably thought the same about her. Alina wondered if he were embarrassed by his English, but with her negligible, literally laughable Bangla, they had to push on. Before long, Alina realised with Mizan that she had the makings of a friendship last experienced with Jamie. With Takdir as interpreter, they discussed dreams, made plans, drew diagrams of the future. They would take in deaf children, they decided. They couldn't help every child, but deafness was a huge problem affecting millions. They'd start learning sign language right away.

And they laughed. They laughed a lot. By the time Alina's trip came to an end, they had the seeds of their home sown. But what to call it?

Mizan said one day, 'It would be like receiving gold, getting a home here.'

It was true, they all agreed, and out of a thought, Alina asked, 'What's the Bangla word for gold?'

'Sonali,' Takdir and Mizan said together.

And so, Sonali Homestay was born.

41

'Sanna. Come in.' Alina held the door wide, but Sanna seemed rooted to the spot.

'You look frazzled,' she said. 'Are you sure this is a good time? You don't have to entertain me along with finding the safe place you left your passport, packing your bags and emptying your fridge.'

Alina grinned and held up three fingers. 'One, the passport is always in my travel bag; two, that single travel bag is ready and waiting; three, I've already eaten all the leftovers – hers is the main door you came past.' If she looked less than equable, that was probably the stream of texts from Elizabeth, all beginning: *Do you think I need...* and having been up since dawn cooking a dinner for Rory that said, 'relaxed with effort'.

'That's very impressive.' Sanna crossed the threshold.

'That's practise.'

In the kitchen, Sanna sat down while Alina pottered about making tea and cutting sandwiches for an impromptu lunch. Sanna was unaccountably quiet, and Alina knew she was overcompensating. She talked about Fin and baby Lisa – almost at an acceptable weight to go home – and asked about the meeting with the Scottish Parliament ('Forgotten already,' Sanna said. 'Next question.') and how Naisha and Ashley were doing. She was just, slightly desperately, going to ask after Sid's health and well-being when Sanna put her hand out and touched Alina on the arm.

'There's something I want to show you.' She reached into her bag and took out a plastic folder. 'I need a second opinion.'

'Oh? More memorabilia from 1994?'

'Not exactly.' Sanna hesitated. 'Have a look.'

'Alright.' Alina frowned slightly. Now *her* nerves were on edge.

She opened the flap on the wallet and pulled out two photographs and glanced at them: scanned and enlarged. Slightly pixellated photographs of Fin. *Is this it?* 'Great,' she said, sounding pleased. 'You opened my email, then.' As Sanna didn't say anything, she added, 'It was a good idea to print them off.'

'Look again.' Sanna spoke evenly, but there was a glint in her eyes that suggested she'd proved some kind of point. 'More carefully.'

Obediently, Alina placed the pictures side by side and stared at them, willing herself to see whatever it was that appeared blindingly obvious to Sanna. They seemed like perfectly ordinary baby photos. Dated, of course, one black and white, one in colour. The baby was in a black, sleek-looking buggy in one picture and in the other, an old-fashioned Silver Cross pram—

'Oh.' It was little more than a whisper because Alina had seen a ghost.

The click of the second hand was the only proof that time hadn't stopped. A few more seconds stretched, like elastic, the worst parody of that gameshow moment when the results are left hanging.

Sanna's voice rang out loud and the band of tension snapped. 'Am I just seeing what I want to see and putting it in your head?'

Alina shook her head slowly. 'The camera doesn't lie,' she said, although they both knew it could. But on an old Polaroid that nobody would ever have thought to Photoshop? She held the photos up in front of her. Fin was certainly in the image on the right, but now she looked closely, it wasn't him on the left. That was Jamie at the same age, not alike enough to be Fin's twin, but sufficiently similar to be mistaken for him. One clutching a knitted sheep, the other with a plastic ball, one in sunshine, one in shadow, the children sat with legs slightly bent, and splayed for balance, their chubby knees exposed, and in each, the left eyebrow quizzically raised as if to say, 'Another photo? Really?'

'There's a likeness, for sure,' Alina said. Look how she'd assumed, she thought.

'Yes, but a proper likeness? Or is it that all babies kind of look the same, especially when you want them to be. The thing is, it struck me unconsciously when I opened your file. I went off and found that.' Sanna nodded at her baby-self and sat back. 'Then I started overanalysing.'

'But you don't look anything like each other now.' Alina ran her hand through her hair and frowned. Her eyes searched Sanna's face with the intensity of a crime scene investigator, but there was no epiphany.

'My, Grandma, what big eyes you have.' Sanna shrugged off the scrutiny. 'You said it to me before. Fin's grown up to look like your dad with your mum's colouring… which is more or less the same as mine. I bet if I asked my folks,' she said, an aside, 'they'd find a colour pic of me, too. They were the original keep-up-with-the-Joneses.'

'But even as a child…' Alina tried to recall those early years; her meetings with Fin in the Botanic Gardens, them hiding under the Finally Tree. Fin had just looked like himself. Or had she never let herself question his looks. It had been Miriam, or maybe Jan, who had pointed out the likeness to Alina's father and she'd taken it and ran, never looking back.

Sanna was saying as much now.

'…And he'll have all his adoptive parents' mannerisms, I bet. Alina, we see what we want to see most of the time – what we *expect* to see. You did it there,' she pointed out. 'Besides, you had no idea what I looked like as a kid. And let's face it, at eighteen, I was nondescript to say the least.' Sanna grinned as Alina opened her mouth. 'Don't contradict me. It was the way I liked it.'

Alina changed tack. 'Eye colour, I thought that might be a clue. I looked it up once, but you and,' she swallowed, 'Damien, have blue eyes. Only mine are brown. The chances of brown and blue-eyed parents having a blue-eyed baby are something like twelve percent anyway and it's no help here.'

'I suppose DNA is the only surefire way of knowing. But...'

'But, indeed. And that's up to Fin.'

'You know – and don't hate me for this – I'm not sure I ever believed I was biologically Fin's father.' Sanna frowned around the kitchen. 'I assumed it was Damien and I was the happy cover-up. Until I saw these photos. I got a shock, Alina. I wasn't expecting *evidence* – however circumstantial. Actually,' she admitted, 'I was... scared. Then I kept remembering something you said when you told me you were pregnant. Not the first day at Clerys' clock, sometime after that. Early on, though.'

'I said many things. Probably a lot of them were nonsense.' Alina looked at her. 'What was it?'

'You said you were terrified, not horrified. Remember? Well, that's about how I feel now. It's also how I felt when Fin found me, and it's how I felt when I stood you up in Dublin, and then when we did meet again.'

'Me too.' Of course she remembered saying that, Alina thought, remembered being in the college canteen buying a ham salad roll before they went and sat at one end of a refectory table and Jamie had asked her how she was feeling.

Alina tried to analyse her feelings, but after that first visual shock, she settled on a sense of anti-climax. *What do you want?* she muttered to herself as she brushed her teeth, *dancing girls and a mariachi band?* No, just proof, her conscience said. As far as the world was concerned – as far as

Alina was concerned, surely – Jamie had been Fin's father all along and the afternoon's events were nothing but a phantom denouement. The interesting thing was, she realised, like Sanna, she was convinced she'd been pregnant with Damien's baby before she and Jamie slept together.

Except that it appeared she hadn't.

Could she have miscarried in that first couple of weeks? She'd always had an erratic cycle, prone to spotting and pain that came and went; she still did, in fact. Or was it a common phantom, brought on by the stress of it all? The odds were, well, even, surely. She had deliberately fudged the dates at her early ante-natal appointments and nobody had pushed her to be more accurate. *And*, she turned over, and brought her knees up to her chest, *did it matter?* If these photos were proof, she'd got what she wanted, what she'd – they'd – planned all along.

'I don't know what to think,' Alina said eventually. 'All I can think of is that whatever happens it's still an absolute minefield trying to decide how and when to tell Fin.'

How different Lisa's birth might have been in a parallel universe, Alina thought: Alina and Jamie, a couple celebrating their twenty-fifth wedding anniversary, reminiscing over their son's unlikely birth, and looking to their first grandchild. There was no regret in the thought; Alina couldn't imagine such cosy domesticity with Jamie and had never harboured such fantasies, and she expected he had felt the same way.

'I'd really like to talk to Fin,' Sanna said suddenly. 'Do you think he'd be up for it? Fairly soon, I mean. Not to rush him.'

'I'd say he'd be delighted.' Alina thought it through. There were probably agency guidelines and advice leaflets, even regulations, but Fin was an adult, a self-possessed one. 'He's on such a high with Lisa and he's really excited about me talking about you. Why don't I ask him? If it's a "not yet", no harm done.' She looked at Sanna. 'Are *you* sure?'

Sanna physically squared her shoulders as if she was gathering all her reserves of courage. 'I'm never going to fetch up in the hospital waving palm leaves and shouting Hosanna, here's your father,' she said, 'so really there'll never be a better ice-breaker, will there? Better you pave the way than a cold call.'

Alina nodded. She was nervous as she dialled. She was aware of going all round the houses before Fin said patiently, 'What did you really phone for, Ali? There's only so many baby updates.'

She said, 'There's somebody here with me that you might like to speak to—'

'Sanna,' he jumped in immediately. 'It's Sanna, isn't it. She's there with you? She wants to talk to me?'

Alina could hear the excitement in his voice, so 'Yes,' was all she said, and she gave a quick thumbs up to Sanna, who looked as if she was mentally hopping from one foot to the other. Then back to Fin, 'Shall I put her on?'

There was a pause. Then Fin said, 'Yes, please, Ali.'

Alina handed over her phone, gave Sanna a quick peck on the cheek, and quietly left the kitchen. All she heard was Sanna's soft, 'Hello, Fin?' before she closed the door behind her and left the two of them in private, taking their own first steps in bridging a twenty-five-year gap.

42

A giant step taken, Sanna recounted the brief call word for word with a big smile on her face. They'd talk again, she said, maybe a couple of times, before they'd arrange to meet up. They'd go back to the tracing agency, too, and see what recommendations they had. For Alina, and she guessed Sanna, too, the weight of Fin's biological parentage hung heavy again. It was all very well for their united front to present Fin with his chosen birth father, and to rely on Fin's understanding, but it wasn't cut and dried. Ever. Slightly guiltily, Alina grasped the concept of happy-for-now; she would shelve the issue (again) until she returned from Bangladesh, and in the meantime, she had an all-important evening with Rory to savour. *Or get through*, her pessimistic side reared its ugly head. 'It's just dinner,' she told herself in the hall mirror, but it wasn't *just* anything. That was like telling Sanna and Fin that they'd *just* had a phone call.

Ages. She had ages. The food was already waiting, and all Alina had to do was get herself ready. She forced herself to relax, have a shower and wash her hair, choose her dress, unable to stop half-laughing at herself for such prettification for a date. It wasn't really a date. Yes, it was. She was going out – staying in, rather – with a man she liked and who liked her. It was definitely a date. But try as she might, Alina couldn't imagine how it would play out. Fast or slow? What was suitable for two people who had known each other five years on the one hand, not much more than five days on the other?

Alina worked herself into a bag of nerves, inclined to fabricate a migraine and put off the evening until after her trip, except she wanted to see Rory more than she didn't want to see him. That she knew. Beyond that she couldn't decide what she wanted. Rory, it seemed, had no such qualms.

When the bell gave two staccato bursts a little while later, Alina opened the front door, smiling, standing back to let him pass, but he didn't. He reached for her, straightaway, taking her in his arms and kissing her with a thoroughness that took her aback. It didn't take Alina long to get into the spirit of it. Her dithering inhibitions magically disappeared. She leaned over his shoulder to push the front door into place and felt her body mould into his.

'Not too full-on?' He moved his head back slightly to look into her eyes.

'Well, I don't usually greet the postman like this, but—'

They kissed again, dissolving it into a tight hug.

'Come in properly.' Alina took his hand, then hesitated over which room to lead him towards. She took refuge in good manners, cursing herself as she did so. 'Would you like a drink?'

'No.'

'No?'

Rory grinned at her. 'Alina, if I have to look at you politely over the top of another cup of coffee, I will burst. I spent months waiting for that bloody kettle to boil, knowing just how it felt.'

'And I was going to offer you a nice glass of elderflower cordial,' she said primly.

'Lovely,' Rory said. 'Where's the bedroom?'

She'd expected fast and furious coupling, but it wasn't like that at all. The bedroom was in darkness – some seductress, she was – but the floor-to-ceiling curtains were open and the three-quarters full moon shone in, its shape casting a circle in the centre of the duvet.

'Christ.' That stopped Rory in his tracks. 'It's like a stage set complete with spotlight.'

It was a bit. Alina smirked; she'd never noticed before. Then the cloudy Scottish sky came to their rescue, muting the moonlight and its spell. His kiss was gentler this time, lingering and soft, as he expertly – or luckily – pulled on the zip of her dress. Alina wasn't sure how she felt about it. It gave her space to think, for trepidation to take over from instinctive passion she'd felt a few minutes before. *What if—*

'What's wrong?' Rory was on to her in a second.

'Nothing.' She tightened her grip on him. 'Really. Nothing.' She meant it; that he'd noticed her sudden tension was reassuring. It was time to be frank. 'I'm a bit of a control freak, Rory, that's all. I hide it usually, but sometimes – well, there just aren't any places to hide.' She didn't add how out of practise she was.

'Oh, Alina, there are always places to hide until you're ready to come out.' He surprised her by tucking her hair behind her ears and planting a kiss on her forehead. Then he stood her to one side while he pulled back the duvet on the bed. 'Take off your dress and get in,' he said. 'We'll hide under the covers.' He gestured at himself. 'I should probably lead you gently up to a full frontal anyway.'

'You're just a boy-toy,' Alina said, doing as he suggested. 'I know your date of birth, remember, and it's three years behind mine.'

'Hardly cougar territory. Now, come on. I'm shy.'

She scrambled in beside him, and lay there trembling: nerves, cold, anticipation; she wasn't sure. There was a conversation that they had to have first, probably should have had before it got to this. She stifled a hysterical giggle. How irresponsible could a woman in her forties be?

'There's that thing we'd better talk about first, isn't there?' Rory took the words out of her mouth.

But Alina wasn't irresponsible. She had been expecting this, and she knew her answer, she'd always known it. She shook her head slowly. 'There's nothing to talk about, Rory,' she said. 'I knew back then that if you and I... not that I ever thought... well, I want what you want.' Silence.

'Are you *sure* you're sure about that?' Rory looked serious. 'I wouldn't dare suggest you might be led by your hormones, but your experience in the hospital... and I believe new babies make women – and men, mea culpa – broody...' He frowned. 'Oh. It seems that actually is what I'm suggesting.'

'In the very unlikely possibility that new life is even possible in this peri-menopausal temple of my body, then yes,' she replied. 'I'm sure.' But it was Alina's time to look serious. 'And I'm not exaggerating, you know, about the depleted hormones. Are you sure you can live with what *that* means?'

He nodded, too. Then grinned. 'Don't I know a great adoption social worker who has a whole orphanage...' ('Homestay,' she murmured automatically) '...to boot— Hey, I'm joking.'

She'd think of it all later, playing the scene over and over in her mind like a teenager in the throes of first infatuation, wondering if it was the honesty, the reverse psychology or the humour, which had worked the best. Most likely, Rory simply knew her better than she'd thought; months of talking to him, about him, must have given away a lot about her too. They both knew what they wanted, and in a few words, they realised they both wanted the same things.

Whatever, the warm stuffiness of the cocoon around them, their bodies against each other, hands, lips, tongues exploring, took away enough of her inhibitions for her to push against him until, groaning – 'That's pleasure,' he opened his eyes to say – he was inside her, and she savoured the feeling of her muscles tight around him, turned on by his lack of control.

'Wow,' Rory said finally. They fought their way out of the crumpled covers, cuddled up, Alina no longer caring about her nakedness.

'Good?'

'Very good. Although…' Back to rational thought, his tone was laced with concern. '…it wasn't so good for you, was it? Sorry, Alina.' She would swear he was blushing. 'I tried to hold out but, well, you…'

She propped herself up on one elbow and traced a finger down his chest. 'Okay. No, I didn't have a scream-inducing, earth-shattering multiple orgasm. I don't think I ever have. I'm not good at the first times of anything and…'

'…and you're a control freak,' Rory added. 'I get it. And now you're going to. We need to equalise this relationship.'

'What—'

She gasped, as without warning he slid down the bed and wriggled to put his hands under her buttocks. 'Sometimes, Alina,' he said, eyes travelling from her hips up to her face, 'You just need to take the plunge.'

'Well, you've done that alright,' she muttered, gasping again as his mouth disappeared between her legs with a sudden firmness that left no time for embarrassment or uncertainty. Physical pleasure overcame her in a way she hadn't realised it could, and she gave in to it, pushing upwards. For a second, the absurdity, the indignity of their positions made her giggle; *wanton woman and it's great*, was the last coherent thought she had.

'Dear God,' she breathed – when her breath was normal enough to allow it. 'Where did you learn to do that?'

43

Within a week of their arrival in Bhola, Elizabeth had taken up residence on the rooftop terrace of Sonali Homestay's children's hostel and was holding court as if born to it.

'You'd think we were just nipping down to London for the weekend,' she'd said more than once on the journey, her tone somewhere between awe and disapproval. She repeated it liberally on board the flight to Doha, where Connie, also mustered at the last moment, had wangled a shift on the main leg of their journey, and it evolved into something of a party.

She was, Elizabeth said, from an age when overseas travel garnered romance and mystique, and even the home-grown sort demanded nigh on a year's worth of planning. It shouldn't be this easy.

'Wait 'til you get there,' Alina promised her, to which the reply was a spirited, 'Bring. It. On.'

Now, she was relaying all this to Takdir – who had clearly been enthralled (*or should that be 'stupefied'?* Alina wondered) with Elizabeth the second he set eyes on her – as they sat side by side enjoying the balmy late afternoon. Alina was feeling more like a chaperone every passing moment.

'Oh, yes.' Elizabeth nodded, surveying her surroundings in satisfaction. 'Every November, Doug, my husband as was, used to write to Mrs Bloss and book the front room at her guesthouse in Blackpool; the first two weeks of August, rain or shine. And it was mostly rain.'

Alina looked up from the accounts she was pretending to study, and squinted into the setting sun that obscured the older woman's face. She had no idea how much Takdir was following, but she found these titbits of history intriguing.

'Yes. Worst fortnight of my life for twenty-odd years,' Elizabeth went on cheerfully. 'I do believe I finally fell for Rory just to get out of going. Mrs Bloss didn't allow children, you see. Or anything involving noise, pleasure or fun.'

'Then why...' Knowing Takdir was far too tactful or too bewildered to enquire, Alina couldn't help herself.

'...Did we go? We went because Mrs Bloss and Doug got on famously. Nothing untoward, just a miserable pair united in austerity.' Elizabeth held up her glass. 'Cheers,' she toasted, as if unadorned Coca Cola was her drink of choice.

Moving over to the white-painted railing, Alina looked down at the smaller children playing on their lopsided and proudly home-manufactured swings and slide – there was nothing invented that couldn't be recreated in the carpentry shed, and disability was never an excuse not to play. Below her, Ahsan plucked Rahim out of his wheelchair, slung him over his shoulder and had him up the steps and piggy-backing down the slide before she could decide whether to yell caution. Not that it would have done any good; Rahim was screeching in pure joy and Ahsan couldn't hear anyway.

Alina sighed and tucked a stray strand of hair behind her eyes. One of the girls had oiled and plaited it that morning, and the residue stuck to her hand. Elizabeth was in her element. She'd sailed through the arduous task of getting a visa on arrival, stoically survived the onslaught of Dhaka, adored the seaplane that Alina told her was a treat for both of them, rather than a concession, and pronounced Sonali Homestay 'magical'. Which Alina fully agreed with, and Mizan preened on hearing; external validation was nice once in a while.

So Elizabeth was on great form, but Alina... She knew

she was out of sorts – off colour, Miriam would have said, resolute that anyone could have growing pains at any stage of life. Bangladesh, even Sonali Homestay, just wasn't fixing it for Alina in the way it usually did. Oh, sure, she was glad to be back, loved every quirky bit of it, but she couldn't muster the quiet thrill that usually filled her first days in her second home. She was tired. She was worried about Khalya, about Takdir's health, and about her decision – or lack of – to move here permanently. It was all to be expected, she rationalised. She usually came back here softly, easing herself in gently. This time she'd been thrown in, a mission to accomplish in two weeks and counting. And that was after the rollercoaster that Scotland had been this time.

Most of all, Alina missed Rory. She admitted privately that she was slightly put-out she might be *missing out* with Sanna and Fin, but mostly she was missing Rory. Their night together had merged into the next day, Saturday, and a second night, before Rory reluctantly crept back to Elizabeth's flat, fearful of her reporting him missing-in-action. This time, unlike the last, Alina had let herself fall head over heels for him. Mills & Boon, coming-of-age first love, a coup de foudre: none of them did justice to her starry-eyed passion. It thrilled her and frightened her in equal measure. *What if it all goes wrong; what if it all goes right?* Two little voices fought for her attention. The saving grace was that Rory felt the same. She'd have seen it in his eyes even if he hadn't admitted it.

'I've written you a letter,' he said in a snatched moment at the airport. Claire and Elizabeth had gone on ahead, leaving Rory and Alina searching for a totally unnecessary luggage trolley. He took it from his pocket and tucked it into the side of her overnight bag. 'Don't read it yet. In fact, read it the day you leave to come back. That's important. Trust me?' She'd left it where he put it, resisting the urge to cheat, but it was burning a hole.

Alina watched Mizan emerge from his office, a square block of a room off what used to be their only permanent building and was now the clinic – that meant it housed the locked medicine box – and treatment room, and her spirits lifted slightly. They'd come a long way, Alina and Mizan and Sonali Homestay, all of it down to Takdir's savings in the name of her parents, and his faith in what they could achieve. Because, she reasoned, when they'd started out, she and Mizan had been good-intentioned, enthusiastic and far too wrapped up in the vision, each other and the romantic game of it all. Totally clueless, to be fair.

As if he could sense her scrutiny, Mizan looked up, and waved. 'Have you made tea?' he called.

'I can,' she shouted back. 'Ten minutes. Bring biscuits.'

He replied with the sideways head jerk that always meant, *good, okay, why not*, and continued across the courtyard. Alina grinned as she watched him deftly oust three of the older boys from the watchman's hut beside the main gate and shepherd them, with fervent sign language, towards the homework room. If ever the phrase 'eyes in the back of his head' applied to anyone, it was Mizan. The spark between them might have long settled into a warm glow, but it was none the worse for that, and she did love him.

Alina leaned down and rubbed a nipping ankle; the sign it was verging on mosquito hour. Once the sun fell, it fell – no long-lingering twilight here – and the dusk-borne bugs were the vicious ones. Behind her, she heard the scraping of chairs on the concrete as Elizabeth and Takdir disappeared inside. Alina reached over to take down the flag, then thought better of it. The children took it in turns to do it, and they loved fighting over their sneaky view into life on the upper floor – somewhere kept for guests and usually out of bounds – where, if anyone was staying, a sweet or a cookie was a good bet. Sure enough, Ahsan reappeared, genie-like, and gave a garbled shout; seconds later he was beside her, holding out a packet of plain biscuits – 'From Sir,' he signed – before deftly catching the green and red flag, folding the material and storing it on its shelf. Alina gave him a couple of boiled sweets and winced for his poor teeth as he shoved them in his mouth and crunched them hard.

In the tiny kitchen, her thoughts flittered. She twisted the tap but the water was still off. Luckily there was enough of the already-filtered stuff in bottles in the fridge, so she filled the tin kettle and set it on the gas ring. Would Rory like it here? she wondered suddenly. It was a far cry from New Zealand. Would Sanna? She wasn't sure the country would be kind to Sanna. Fin liked it. He'd visited once, and she didn't doubt he'd meant it that day when he said he'd come back with Kirsten and the baby. The girls, especially, would love that.

Alina glanced at her watch. Here, she was six hours ahead of the UK, which meant that somewhere back in Carlisle, Sanna and Fin were shortly about to spend an afternoon together for the very first time. *Let it go well*, she wished for the hundredth time. *Let them find common ground. Don't let either of them get cold feet.* Ultimately, things had moved as fast for them as they had for Alina and Sanna. All this was part of her current ennui, she realised; she was never usually as preoccupied with the other half of her life.

She was interrupted by a shout from the curtained doorway to the set of rooms. 'Alina? I'm here. Bring my tea.'

Grinning, she stuck her head out of the kitchen and uttered a demure, 'Yes, Mizan. Of course,' and winked at a surprised-looking Elizabeth who appeared from her bedroom. They both watched Mizan leaning on the doorframe to undo his sandals. When he looked up, his eyes widened in horror, which turned to embarrassment.

'Apa, Elizabeth,' he said. 'I forgot you were here. It's a joke, that's all. Always I shout for tea, always she brings it, yes, Alina? As if I am the authoritarian husband...'

'Oh, don't mind me. I'm so old I've seen and heard everything,' Elizabeth said.

'But...'

'It's alright, Mizan.' Alina took pity on him. 'She knows you're teasing. Come and have tea, both of you.'

They sat down in the wooden armchairs in the small room while Alina hitched her orna over her left shoulder and went back into the kitchen to bring the tray. Coming back, her head swam slightly; an instinctive response to seeing Elizabeth comfortable in an easy chair, chatting to a visitor, the only difference being she'd swapped Charles for this tiled ante-room on the third floor. Alina hesitated and Mizan jumped up and took the tea things from her, setting them on the rickety glass-topped side table that comprised the only other furniture in the room.

'Are you alright, Alina?' Elizabeth frowned.

'I'm fine.' Alina sank down into the third chair. 'Just a bit dizzy. It's gone now.' She paused for a second, but she really was fine. 'Jetlag has a lot to answer for.'

'Jetlag does not usually upset you,' Mizan objected. 'I'm already thinking you are not yourself this visit, Alina. Maybe you are sick. Do you have diarrhoea?'

'I never get an upset stomach here, you know that. It's my Bangla DNA.' She leaned forward to take her sweetened, milky tea, and dunked a high-energy biscuit in it. An overly sweet experience, but it proved her appetite was intact.

'Then maybe you have anaemia.' Mizan didn't like to be thwarted and he'd always been an enthusiastic hypochondriac, by proxy if necessary. He turned to Elizabeth. 'It is very common in women of child-bearing age,' he confided.

'And who are wives and pregnant.' Alina clarified. 'And as I'm definitely neither,' she drew out the word slightly, warning Mizan against smart-Aleck 'you were my first wife, really' innuendo, 'I can also promise you I'm not anaemic. I'm tired,' she tempered. 'And I'm worried about Khalya. And Takdir.'

'Khalya will be home from school tomorrow, and we have made a programme to meet her mother.' Mizan slurped at his tea. 'This is what I've come to confirm with you. Not,' he glanced at Elizabeth, 'to demand tea. We will see her at Takdir Sir's house. You will talk to her, Alina.'

It was the last thing she wanted to do but he was right. It was Khalya, it was Alina's job, and it needed, at this stage, to be woman to woman; not, she thought, that any of those were likely to endear her to Khalya's stubborn mother. She nodded.

'The day after...' Mizan turned to Elizabeth. '...our kind donor will dig the first sod for our guesthouse, and unveil the plaque that says "Elizabeth House", yes? A fine finale to your visit.'

'A fine finale to *this* visit,' Elizabeth corrected him happily as she accepted another biscuit. 'I was thinking, I could become an ambassador for you. All the best charities have them, you know.'

Alina giggled. 'We're hardly Save The Children, Elizabeth. Not even Sreepur Village. We're a tiny organisation that celebrates when we hit forty grand in the reserves. But I appreciate the sentiment and... let's say the directors will keep it in mind.'

'I think it is an amazing idea,' announced Mizan.

Elizabeth's smile was nothing if not regal.

44

Later, after they had all eaten and everyone else had disappeared directly off to bed, Sonali Homestay was in silence. Alina and Elizabeth surveyed the shadows from the third-floor roof.

'This is the time of day I like best here.' Alina leant on the wall. 'Looking out over everything, knowing that a day's work is well done.' Her voice was low; it wasn't a random observation. 'In Edinburgh, it's the opposite. It's waking up to a whole fresh start.' She wondered, as she often had, how one whole person could be made from dichotomous halves.

Elizabeth was looking away into the darkness, past the roofs and the tree-tops, to the inky sky; there was no yellowy haze of smog here, just the deepness of night. 'You fit in so well here,' she said after a long pause. 'I hadn't realised. I hadn't understood that this place is as much a part of you as home is – as Scotland, I mean.'

Alina waited; Fin aside, Elizabeth was the first person she knew well who was party to both her faces, that lifetime of incongruence. Yes, she'd met Takdir in the UK, but he'd been little more than a stranger back then, and Connie was periodically present for Alina's transition, but neither was sufficient to tell her whether she was two people or one.

'I thought coming here with you would be like going on

holiday, a case of us-and-them. Whereas it's me, and them, and you're one of them.' Elizabeth's pause plainly asked if she was making sense. 'But... *they* aren't actually very different anyway. It's circumstantial.'

'You fit in so easily, Elizabeth,' Alina told her sincerely. 'It took me so much longer to find my feet, but here you are rocking it!'

'Rocking it – I do like that.' Elizabeth looked as if she was filing that away to use again. (She was sending daily updates to Claire, who got an intern to tweet for her. Every morning, at breakfast, she'd taken out her phone, saying, 'Must check what I've said on Twitter.' Alina had asked why she didn't just write the posts herself, but according to Elizabeth it was too much of a 'faff'.) 'Ah, but lovey,' she went on, 'Remember, I have far less at stake than you had.'

'It's my colouring that blends me in,' Alina pushed for more. She looked down and smoothed her palms over the – slightly tight – blue cotton of her salwar kameez. The girls in the tailoring room spent her six-month absences sewing Alina new outfits, with ever more intricate embroidery. Sometimes, they had reams of donated material and the whole school wore the same pattern; Alina liked that best. She must get them to retake her measurements, she noted; this one definitely skimped on the shoulders, but then they would have hurried to be finished for her sudden return.

'It's more than that,' Elizabeth said, finally. 'It's the way you move, the way you are. I remember being in a play once, oh, years ago. I was a wee thing at school, and I was Queen Elizabeth, or Mary Tudor, maybe, I forget... anyway, it doesn't matter, I didn't have to do anything but stand there. But I do remember the drama teacher telling me it was the hardest part to play because being regal couldn't be taught, it was ingrained. It just *was*. That's what I see in you, Alina. It's more than you learning to be here, it's a part of you.' She stopped with a giggly *hmm*. 'Oh what do I know. I'm just a foolish old woman who makes things up for a living.'

Alina smiled. 'I want to believe you, Elizabeth. I'm going to, in fact.' She repeated what she thought she'd said to Sanna. 'I've always suffered with a sort-of imposter syndrome here, wondering if I'm just playing at being Bangladeshi.'

'No.' Elizabeth sounded certain. 'It's one of what we writers might like to call the many colours of you.' *Another tweetable phrase*, Alina's lips twitched. It was Elizabeth's turn to consider her clothes, also a salwar kameez, hastily and proudly produced by Asma, the teacher, after Elizabeth spent her first morning swamped by a startling kaftan-type summer dress, even more startlingly borrowed from Claire Bond. 'I could live here,' she said. 'Take up residence as mammi – isn't that what the children call me? And be ever revered for my age.'

'Being chastely courted by dadu? Aka Great Uncle Takdir?'

'That too.'

'Do you think he's well?' Alina voiced her worry. 'Has he said anything to you during your cosy little chats?'

'Mostly he listens to me, as if he can't believe I'm real,' Elizabeth said, and despite herself, Alina stifled a grin: Mizan had once treated her the same way. 'I do know he's old, Alina, like I am. We have ailments. I think he'd say if he were really sick, though I'm a good distraction. You and Mizan, though. There's a history there, of course there is. Is it something I should know about? Something on the pros list for staying here?'

'No,' said Alina, firmly. 'I won't say we haven't had our moments, but they were in the early days, ancient history. Once Mizan got married, that was that. We're friends, colleagues. We're close, but we are not lovers.' Alina laughed at the odd mix of relief and disappointment on Elizabeth's face. 'Mizan has a lovely wife who has so far provided two sons. Her family are well connected, and she is dutiful and modest. She also absolutely rules the roost while letting Mizan think he's in charge. She's the perfect Bengali wife. What we had, he and I, was a… a summer of love, a mutual infatuation, a coming of age.' Let it up now, Alina, she said to herself, before you start talking complete bollocks. 'He says she knows all about him and me, but I haven't delved into what *all* actually means. His wife is a good bit younger than Mizan and he's younger than me, so I'm probably seen as an old lady. Especially now he's insisting on calling me didi – grandmother,' she explained.

'I'd like to see a little real-life romance.' Elizabeth sighed. 'Do you know, I'm wondering if Rory is seeing someone,' she confided. 'It's just a few little things... I'm sure Morag will be on the case. But I hope it works for him and I hope she's an improvement on Laura.'

How Alina managed to keep a straight face she'd never know. And from Elizabeth's next words, she knew she'd failed.

'What?' Elizabeth's eyes narrowed. 'You know something, missy. Out with it.'

Alina found she was bursting to tell someone about Rory. They talked into the night, sitting under the ceiling fan when it was working, moving back onto the roof, searching for a puff of breeze when the electricity failed. Elizabeth was a rapt audience, as Alina confessed to the five-year-old non-affair that had put herself and Rory on their current path. She enjoyed watching Elizabeth's jaw drop – literally.

'I had no idea. How could I have no idea?' she said. 'How very vexing! Still, it makes me feel better about the fast-track approach you've hurtled into, the two of you. Better it's a climactic slow-burn than a mid-life crisis any day. Don't look at me like that,' she side-swept.

'I'm agreeing with you,' Alina protested.

'If you say so, lovey.' Elizabeth stretched her arms out in front of her, flexing her damaged wrist in careful circles. 'It seems like you've plenty to be thinking about,' she added. 'Enjoy the options, Alina. Don't agonise over them.'

'But it is agonising, Elizabeth. Here, I have Takdir, Khalya, Mizan – all this...' she gestured to the compound. 'There, I have you, Rory, Fin, Sanna. How can I pick one over the other?'

'Don't.' Elizabeth shrugged. 'First, they are not mutually exclusive. Er... hello?' She pointed to herself. 'I'm here, aren't I? Second, Takdir encouraged you to think about settling here because he thought you were all alone and lonely in Scotland. I've put him right on that.' Elizabeth nodded complacently. 'So carry on as you are for a bit longer. Things change. See how it all pans out. Oh, lovey, you do tend to overthink the teeniest things.'

'You're the last in a long line to tell me that,' Alina agreed. 'And I love my life as it is now. Maybe I don't need to change it... yet.'

'On which note I shall say goodnight.' Elizabeth got up. 'I bet you're itching to phone my son.'

Alina watched her step around the dying mosquito coil and move slowly towards the screened door. Pressing on the handle, she turned back, Columbo-like. 'And Alina?'

'Yes, Elizabeth?'

'One more thing...'

'Yes?'

'Rory aside, you already know I was miserable for nigh on all my married life. Never a day went by when I didn't feel inadequate or think "if only". It took me forty years to find my way – and now look at everything I have. For heaven's sake, I've even found my own version of a soulmate in Claire Bond. And I'll have "Elizabeth House" here. Who would have believed it?' Elizabeth smiled and shook her head, as if *she* wouldn't have. 'Alina, there will always be a "but". *But*, you know what you have to do?'

Alina, mesmerised, shook her head.

'What you have to do is tell that "but" to fuck right off. Goodnight, lovey.'

'Goodnight, Elizabeth. Thank you.' There was a smile in Alina's words that she figured outweighed the tears in her eyes.

Alina stayed where she was, motionless. She didn't try to phone Rory. She was content to let Elizabeth's words sink in, picturing, too, his letter just waiting to be read. It was a declaration, she knew it. She was happier than ever when a text from Sanna beeped, saying, *No cold feet this time! Stop worrying, doll-face*, followed by Fin's, *I never expected to find such joy in both my birth parents*. Alina might even have admitted to feeling a little teary-eyed.

If the plastic chair had been more comfortable, she'd be inclined to doze right there, and take herself inside only for respectability's sake when the muezzin called salat al-fajr at dawn. The silence was unusual. Inside the fans whirled and groaned, and when they stopped for a power cut, the silence took on the moisture of the air and was heavy, almost loud; outside, the main road that ran alongside the compound roared with a constant stream of motor rickshaws, motorbikes and buses, their horns squealing as they raced to overtake each other. Apparently, the middle of the night offered some reprieve. How could it be that she'd never taken time to sit out like this before? But the temperature was a novelty, of course; Alina was used to cold, blanket-covered nights and hot afternoons. Her memories of long, warm nights went back to the travelling she and Mizan had done together, huddled on the deck of the rocket ferry when *Titanic* was all the rage and there was a steady stream of newlyweds infiltrating first class to take up a Leonardo and Kate position at the helm. Or on another roof, another time long before, in a rundown guesthouse at Cox's Bazaar. Fifteen years ago. Alina felt a twinge of nostalgia.

There was a scrabbling behind her, somewhere in the walls, and idly Alina wondered if rats could get this high. She doubted they'd bother: what self-respecting rodent would need to, when all the cooking was done on the floor in a largely outdoor kitchen? Then she tensed. The noise was too loud, and too human. Alina got up and went to the small side gate that blocked off the top of the narrow, dangerous and 'emergency' stone steps that huddled against the rear of the original building next door. A monkey, or an idiot, could clamber from one roof to the next but was thwarted by the locked gate.

'Mizan, you idiot,' Alina said softly through the wood and metal. 'I know it's you. What's wrong with the normal way in? And during normal daylight hours?'

'Where is the fun in that? We need more fun in life, Alina.' He appeared to be breathless. 'Let me in. I'm too old for fun. I need to lay down.'

'I'll need to get the key. Wait.'

'Why do you not keep the keys on your belt, or in your purse like other people?' he grumbled.

'Because I'm not a gaoler. You'll have to wait. Or go back the way you came.'

'Hurry up before I die.'

Listen to them; they *were* like an old married couple, Alina thought as she went to the kitchen to collect the keys from the tin box in which everyone knew she hid them – no wonder Elizabeth had commented. No doubt she'd discussed it with her new best friend, the far more circumspect Takdir.

'Your friend, Mrs Elizabeth, is very nice, but she does go to bed late for an old lady.' Once through the gate, Mizan collapsed into a chair and downed in one the bottle of water Alina had had the foresight to tuck under her arm.

'You must have been lurking out there for ages,' Alina said. 'Good. I hope you heard plenty to make it worthwhile.'

'What are you thinking? I am not a spy. And… the Scottish accent is so strange to me.'

'Serves you right. What didn't you hear that can't wait 'til tomorrow?'

Mizan looked at her, the teasing on hold. 'Everything,' he said. 'We have had no time to speak. I miss you. I want to know why you are not your usual self.'

'You know why. Khalya. Takdir.' Alina had her reasons in order and she'd see what she could get away with.

'She is not the only reason. He is not the only reason. I am waiting, Alina.' When she didn't immediately reply, he went on, 'It is this man, the electrician, Rory. Mrs Elizabeth's son...'

So he *had* been listening; she was impressed by his dissembling. Mizan responded to her raised eyebrow by nodding complacently. 'I knew it. So, this is what I think. This man, Rory, is the returned father of your son and he wants you to marry him and have more babies, but you are unsure and have come back to me, your first husband except in legalities, for advice.' Mizan glowered. 'I hate him already.'

Alina put her hand to her mouth; it was all she could do not to laugh out loud. It sounded so plausible, yet he was so, so wrong. She glanced quickly at her watch. She'd been joking about staying up until she heard the muezzin, but it was going to take that long to come clean, and that was without taking him up on the *first husband* comment.

'Right, Mizan,' she said. 'Listen and listen good.'

45

Khalya was beside herself at seeing Alina again and complained that they hadn't brought her home from school sooner. None of them had wanted her term interrupted unnecessarily, so she arrived back as planned, home in preparation for the month of Ramadan. She tumbled out of the auto-rickshaw and the grip of Suna, the interpreter and chaperone, losing one flip flop, and having to hold her orna over her head while running the length of the drive to throw herself at Alina, who hugged her tight. She was like an exuberant seven-year-old and Alina's immediate thought was: how could anyone think this little girl was grown up enough to be married? Khalya's first sentence brought it home, though.

'Have you spoken to my mother?' She stepped back, looking between Alina and Mizan, who had also emerged to greet her. 'I will not get married until I am twenty. It is illegal in the law to force me.' Her signing was deliberate, slower than usual for emphasis, and with finality, and in the words were the spirit of an emerging young woman. 'I want to stay at school. And I don't want to marry an old man. I want to marry one who is young and handsome.'

Well, that was fair enough. And very clear. 'We're going to visit your mother this morning.' Alina signed rapidly. 'She can't force you, Khalya, but she might not change her mind easily. You know that.'

'I love my mother, but Sonali Homestay is my home. You, apa, are my family. Mama is worried I will not find a husband because I am deaf and so she will have no one to care for us when she is old. This is silly because she has Takdir Sir, and I will have a husband and my job as a teacher. Will you tell her this? You might have to give her money.'

Alina swapped a glance with Mizan; Khalya was nobody's fool, and she was far more clued up than Alina had given her credit for. When had the little girl got so grown up? Surely six months ago she was still playing hopscotch and swimming in the pond. Still, time passed, and this could only be good, couldn't it? Alina gave herself a swift talking to; their aim was to raise girls to take care of themselves and this was what Khalya was doing.

The girl's next signs floored her though. 'I love you, apa, and do not be sad, but I do not want to live with you in Scotland...' Alina's glance flew to Mizan, her eyes semaphoring, '*What?*' He looked studiously over her head. 'When I am grown up I will visit you, but I would be lonely without my sister-friends. I like you living here with us. Will you tell that, too?'

Alina gathered herself. 'I'll try my best,' she told the girl. 'Now, I've got someone here I'd like you to meet.' She pointed up to the third floor and explained Elizabeth. 'Will you look after her for the morning while we're gone?'

She waited until Khalya had trotted happily up the stairs, gathering her 'sister-friends' along the way, before she turned to Mizan. 'Would you care to explain that?' she asked icily.

Not really, said Mizan's body language. 'You make me afraid when you use your Queen of England voice,' he protested.

'If I were the Queen of England I'd send you to the bloody Tower.' She didn't care that the reference would be lost on him. 'You told her mother I was coming over to take her back to the UK, didn't you? Mizan, didn't you?' There was only one prize greater than a rich husband, in Khalya's mother's world, and that was a sponsored passage to Europe or the States.

'She stole away the child, Alina. I had to think to put out the heat of the crisis. And I did not tell her that,' he added. 'She said it to me, an ultimatum: UK or marriage. I said we would ask you... Then it became a problem.' He hesitated in such a way that Alina got an immediate inkling of the way this was going.

'Okay,' she said. 'Sorry I shouted.' But *honestly*. 'Was it Husna?' She had to be blunt.

Mizan nodded. 'Mrs Husna is always spokesman. When I say I will ask you, she says to Khalya's mother, "You hear, bandhu-be, she will take your daughter to live in Scotland. Or if not, it will be marriage here."' He kicked some sandy gravel back towards the play area. 'The mother looked as if she was not sure, but Mrs Husna looked at me in a – gloating?' He did a good impersonation, and Alina grinned despite herself. 'Yes, gloating way. It was a trick on me and I saw too late.' He looked at her hang-dog. 'I failed us.'

'Don't lay it on too thick,' she warned him. 'But it wasn't your fault. I'm just not sure what Husna thinks she's getting out of this.' *Take her away or we marry her off* was the message, loud and clear.

'It was difficult to tell Takdir Sir. This is why I waited until his return. He looks in pain and says he will talk to Mrs Husna. Then we decide it is best if you come.' He grinned then, shyly, shades of the younger Mizan. 'And here you come, and we fix the problem together as always we do.'

'Right,' said Alina. 'We need to revise our game plan.'

'I feel as if I'm going into battle,' she said later, as they sat in the back of an auto-rickshaw, grabbing the straps as the tiny metal cage swerved through the crowded streets, horns blaring.

'You are our secret weapon.' Mizan grinned. 'Khalya's mother will face any of us; with me and Takdir, she goes as deaf as her daughter. With you, authoritative woman, she is entranced. I think Mrs Husna put in the seed and then she pushed hard this marriage for when you were gone. Too late she sees Mrs Husna meddling with a different idea and bringing you back. Nor did they realise Khalya herself would meet them like an adult.'

'Neither did I,' Alina admitted. 'I thought I was rushing in to protect my favourite little girl and instead I'm negotiating on behalf of a savvy young woman.'

'This is good, Alina, no?'

'Yes, yes of course it is.' But still she sighed.

A few minutes later, as they turned down a quieter side road and drew up outside Takdir's house, Alina reflected on Khalya's farewell as they'd left Sonali Homestay: 'Apa,' she'd signed, 'be kind to her. She is an old village lady.'

Wise words – although it weighed heavy on Alina that Khalya's mother was her own age, or thereabouts. The woman had had a family once, a husband who died young, and several older children, half-siblings to Khalya, who had long been assimilated into their father's extended family. Khalya's mother, whose maternal claim was secondary – the law called fatherless children orphans – had found work in Takdir's home, ultimately laying claim to that hazy illegitimate connection, tearing out all previous roots. If she saw Khalya as her – their – pension, then who, fundamentally, could blame her?

They congregated in the back sitting room, two and two, either side of the table as if shaping up for a game of chess: Alina and Mizan versus Takdir's wife and Khalya's mother. There appeared a plate of biscuits, a bowl of fruit and four glasses of water between them, served by two young girls clearly under the tutelage of Khalya's mother; her eyes directed them. It might have been any polite meeting, anywhere, to discuss the arrangement of a marriage, Alina and Mizan had been in similar situations, in loco parentis, several times. Waiting in a silence designed to encourage the servers to do their best, Alina wondered, as she often had, about the relationship between Takdir's wife and Khalya's mother. Once, it must have been mistress and servant; now it was of long-time companions, confidants.

She thought back to that initial visit to Bangladesh, her first stay in Takdir's Dhaka home, and as a member of the family. Khalya's mother was in the shadows, rarely more than a few feet away from Husna, who had never become Alina's great aunt beyond a loose title. The woman remained polite, distant and suspicious, as did her maid. Alina had never been sure if she, as the foreigner, her estranged father's legacy, was the problem, or whether it was her indirect connection to the man who had deflowered the stubborn maid who had refused to be bought off and had become indispensable to the mistress. Takdir maintained his wife was shy, ashamed of her rudimentary English, but Alina had gleaned, over the years, that Takdir had chosen to contact her against his wife's wishes, brought her to his home with only her grudging goodwill. No doubt they speculated about her as she had them. Once she'd hung around long enough to show she wasn't a do-gooder or a gold-digger, things had eased, and Alina had learned to let it go; the undercurrents of the family, of the relationships and of her place within it were far too deep-set to be unearthed. In that they were no different to thousands of other extended, displaced families.

It had been in the back of Alina's mind they would be fighting uphill to get Khalya's mother to talk, yet when they'd meandered through the stilted small talk, conducted in an organic mix of English, Bangla and sign, of how everyone, and particularly, Khalya, was doing, it was like opening a dam. Alina felt her defences crumbling, and she let them, wondering to what extent they'd been needed anyway.

Yes, of course, she wanted her daughter married, Khalya's mother attacked it head on. What good mother wouldn't, especially when the child was handicapped and the mother getting old, her own husband dead. Why wouldn't a mother wish this, when a good, rich man, an educated man, had come forward with a generous dowry? A man who had a large family, all ready to welcome Khalya – and, when the time came and she could no longer work, her mother, too… Alina tried to interpret the look in Takdir's wife's eyes when her aid said that, but Khalya's mother beat her to it… A man well known to her good friend and employer here… *Ah*, thought Alina… Please, Khalya's mother said, looking earnestly between Alina and Mizan, and to Takdir's wife for approval, why would they, good people who had known and loved Khalya since she was born, try to prevent this opportunity?

She sat back and gulped down her glass of water in one go, wiping the back of her hand with her mouth, and flicking her eyes to Takdir's wife once more. She relaxed, visibly. She'd obviously said her piece, had been coached well; she'd done her bit. Except – where was any mention of Khalya leaving the country?

It was clear to Alina that Husna certainly was calling the shots here. If Khalya were to be married, it was to this particular man. Why? 'What do you think, Ama?' Alina turned to her.

'I want security for my friend and her daughter, the only family she has,' was the measured reply.

'Does she not have that here with you?' Mizan asked. 'This is her home; it has been for many years. *You* are her family, no?'

'Which is why I want to ensure her daughter has the best introductions. You have done this with her education and training. We are thinking of the next stage of Khalya's life. She does not have to be married,' she added pointedly.

Ah, thought Alina. 'And is that why I'm here now, Ama?' Alina asked gently. 'Do *you* want me to take Khalya to live in Scotland rather than have her married here?'

Husna inclined her head. 'It would be a great privilege for Khalya, and it would be a great honour for you.' She fixed a gimlet eye on Alina. 'Your opportunity to give back to our family, as any good Bengali girl wishes to do.'

And there it was: payback time. Khalya was a pawn in Husna's determination to see Alina do her duty. *Boy, would she and Morag get on like a house on fire*, flew through Alina's mind. But there was something more... Years of complex interventions under her belt had sharpened Alina's instinct, and she dug just a little bit more.

'Would you like this, too?' she asked Khalya's mother directly. And the response was all she needed to know: the woman's mouth said yes, but her eyes, darting towards Husna's then immediately lowered, told the truth.

'Of course she would miss her daughter,' Husna said sharply. 'But she will stay with me, and I will look after her. She will not be left alone.'

The words confirmed, for Alina, the true issue. With Khalya away, Husna would have an ever more needy and grateful constant tied to her; *Husna* would not be left alone.

'Oh no, don't worry, that wouldn't happen at all.' Alina gave a brilliant smile. 'I can certainly arrange to take Khalya with me but there are complexities and incompatibilities in Scottish and Bangladeshi law,' she went on glibly. 'As I understand it – and remember I'm a social worker not a lawyer, but we'll ask Takdir Sir to confirm – the process would take eighteen months to two years and under Scottish law, Khalya's mother, her next of kin, would have to accompany her until she comes of age at eighteen. I couldn't become her guardian unless her mother relinquishes parental responsibility, for which there are no grounds.' *And no desire*, she added mentally.

All of them – Mizan included – looked at Alina open-mouthed. She waited, watching Husna, in particular, compute what this meant. Then she went in for the kill. 'So I would suggest marriage here is the best idea. On that, we agree with everything you've said, don't we, Mizan?' Alina bit her lip; he looked so surprised. She wanted to wink at him but instead touched her bare toes almost imperceptibly against his. 'We want a good marriage for Khalya. She wants it herself. We're all in agreement.' There was a confused silence. 'Yes?' Slight nods all round. They hadn't been expecting this, clearly.

Alina continued, 'And in three and a half years that can happen. Three years is nothing! When Khalya is seventeen,' *or twenty, or never*, 'all of this can be hers. *Legally.* She wants what you want, we want what she wants... and I imagine an honest and good man – a friend of yours, Ama, isn't he?' Alina chanced, 'Will want a bride who is legally an adult. During those three years, we will continue to take financial responsibility for Khalya, and I, personally, will ask you, Ama, to ensure her mother always has a home with you.'

Making their way back down the lane to hail the rickshaw driver who would, invariably, be smoking under the trees while he waited for business, Mizan was jubilant and Alina dissatisfied that they had, for now, won.

'How did you know what Mrs Husna was thinking?' he asked. 'And where did you learn such information on the immigration laws? Alina, you are a genius.'

'I'm trained to interview people,' Alina replied. 'Though most of it was luck, as well as watching the two of them and knowing their relationship. As for the law...' She bypassed the worst of the rubble-strewn pavement and stepped over a tiny black goat laid out in the sunshine. 'Mizan, I am not proud of this, but I made it all up. Once I realised it was all about Husna not wanting to be abandoned, I figured the UK thing was a red herring so it didn't matter.' Did it, though? Did the means justify the end? She had just lied to her great aunt, and she'd have to come clean to Takdir. But with a bit of genuine straight talking in the middle, she *had* bought time for Khalya. Alina still had reservations about the fabled age of seventeen, but it gave them time to play with.

Mizan simply looked at her in admiration. 'Like I say, you

are a genius. Now it is very clear why Takdir Sir requested you to come back.'

'What I am interested in,' she went on, ignoring him. '...is this paragon of a man, whoever he is – they weren't forthcoming on a name, were they? – who is so keen to marry our underage little girl. It's obviously an arrangement with Husna, and in their circles, he's bound to have some social or political sway... in which case, why doesn't he care she's barely fourteen and why hasn't Takdir stepped in?'

'I expect he doesn't know. People lie about their daughters' ages all the time, Alina.' Mizan shook his head. 'When my parents were arranging my marriage, I met a sixteen-year-old and a thirty-year-old both presented to me as "maybe nineteen".' Mizan stood at the edge of the road and whistled. 'Eh, bhai?' They watched three rickshaw drivers cycle towards them, arguing over the fare. 'But, Alina, I guess this is the answer. Mrs Takdir should not be underestimated. She has her own network and her own contacts, but hers is a lonely life. Her privilege means her children have taken a Western route to life, but her husband is a traditional Bangladeshi man with his separate life. Like you say, she is engineering not to have a sad and lonely old age.'

'*Would* Khalya's mother leave her?'

'The traditional maternal desire for a daughter's security is ingrained, Alina. Takdir can provide that, *you* could provide that, but... neither of you can be the ultimate prize, the good husband. So, yes, she might, and it's a risk Mrs Husna cannot take.'

'It feels as if we've just delayed the evil moment.' Alina climbed into the rickshaw and tucked her orna carefully round her back. 'I suppose it's a fact of life. Mind you,' Alina turned to Mizan and nudged him. 'If whoever-he-is can't have Khalya, I'm quite tempted to put myself forward.'

'No, Alina, no. Not even in jest. You cannot break my heart two times in two days.' Mizan pretended anguish. 'Shall we go to a restaurant and you can tell me more about the man who is taking you from me?' He wrinkled his nose and shuffled slightly. 'Okay, okay.' Mizan put his hands up. 'This Rory. I have many questions.'

'Then that makes two of us.' Alina was too hot, too jostled and too busy trying not to slide off the tilted bench seat to argue. 'I don't feel like lunch. Let's get some frusca and sweets and have a picnic with the children. A half-holiday. Why not?'

'Fine.' Mizan leant forward and shouted instructions to the driver, who obediently swayed round the corner and mounted the pavement before stopping inches from a school bus. He jumped down, and looked back at Alina, fanning herself with her hand. He reached up and touched it briefly, catching her fingers. 'I will always be here for you, Alina, as your Bangla husband,' he said. 'We understand each other. But I have my life, and you – you must make the life you want to have.'

46

When Alina woke in the early hours the muezzin was ringing out. *Wonderful*, Alina thought groggily, the only time she heard the call to prayer was when the fan died. No wonder she was so hot and sticky.

Wrapping her orna over her shoulders, Alina reached up and unlocked the door to the roof, propping it open with a plastic chair to encourage the air – any breeze, even a hairdryer-warm one – to flow through. The concrete under her feet was cool-ish as yet, and she leaned on the railings watching Sonali Homestay come alive; the slap of sandals as someone crossed the courtyard; a wail from the girls' dormitory below her and a corresponding shout from Farhana; a rickshaw bell at the front gate. Behind her, she heard curtains drawing back and a window opening; Elizabeth was up. Alina leaned on her hands and took in a deep breath, gazing up to the blue sky as she blew it out slowly. *Please, God...* she mouthed, leaving it to the cosmos where Miriam and Patrick surely roamed – united, in their own beliefs, with their daughter and son-in-law – to fill in the blanks she couldn't yet articulate. Then she relaxed her shoulders. This was one day, their last day – they were booked onto the late afternoon launch to Dhaka – that called for serious compartmentalisation. 'Do what you do best, girl,' Alina muttered to herself. Then she turned to greet Elizabeth.

'I feel that my soul has been refreshed.' Elizabeth wiped her eyes. 'I don't mind admitting, lovey, that deep down I was in a bit of a rut. Now…' She wiped her eyes again. 'How lucky I am. How lucky you are.' She was sitting behind a trestle table in the meeting room, half obscured by a pile of embroidered bed linen and tablecloths – gifts from the girls in the tailoring room. But Elizabeth wasn't talking to Alina, but to Rory, blessed with a near-perfect Skype link – Elizabeth was clearly charmed, Alina thought – involving him in her party. Beside her were a pile of drawings created by the art class – she'd been competition judge – and the remains of a box of sweets and a clutch of donated toothbrushes – Mizan hadn't seen the irony – she'd handed out as prizes. Takdir, sitting close, had taken on the role of her interpreter, and left no doubt that Elizabeth was now honorary mammi to fifty lively children.

Earlier in the day, they had tramped the land where work on the new guesthouse was scheduled to start directly after Ramadan. With her junior fanbase behind her, Elizabeth was presented with scissors to cut a white ribbon hung between two wooden posts, and with a shovel, shined up specially by the boys, and instructed where to dig the first hole. Then, the icing on the cake: she had been escorted back to the meeting room, where she unveiled a plaque – to be erected when there was some semblance of a building to erect it on – naming the new venture Elizabeth House. She'd already promised to return for its opening.

Now, retreating to lean against the wall in the background, Alina, listening to the children (hearing loss no handicap), belting out verses of *We Shall Overcome* – in English, Bangla and sign language – finally found her absent equilibrium in Rory's letter:

Alina,

I love you. I loved you then and I love you now. This time my declaration is loud and clear: no miscommunication, no wondering, no more years of wishing. I want to marry you. I want us to live together. I want us to find our way. I ran from you once, but now I want to run with you, wherever you want to go.

It's a lot of wants. But I think, I hope, you have the same ones.

All my love, Rory

Without needing to think very much at all, Alina tapped a message into her phone and didn't hesitate before pressing 'send'.

Now to tell Takdir. Well, sort of.

She found him – where else? – on the roof terrace, enjoying the peace and quiet. Alina knew her anxiety showed on her face when he held out a hand and said, 'Come and sit for a moment. Breathe.'

'Can I tell you a story, Uncle Takdir?' she said after a moment.

'Please.' He sat back and fixed his eye on Alina rather than the tree tops.

'When I was at primary school,' she spoke slowly, 'we had a carnival float one summer and one of the teachers dressed me up as, well, an "Indian girl" she called it. But my grandparents had a Salvation Army float and I wanted to be on that one too. I spent the day running over from one to the other, doing a quick change from my salwar kameez into my junior soldier's uniform, and vice versa.'

'Go on, my dear,' Takdir said when Alina paused.

'I remember the teacher asking me about it later, and I said I'd felt like two halves of one person that day. And she said, "Won't it be exciting when you grow up, finding out which one you'll turn out to be?"' Alina sighed. 'I know it was well-meant, but it did me such a disservice.'

'You grew up believing you had to be one or the other?'

'It's only now I'm learning it's not that clear cut. That it's okay to be both things, maybe many things.'

'Ah.' Takdir nodded. 'You're telling me you are not ready to change your six-months-on, six-months-off rotation, not yet anyway.'

'That's it,' she admitted. 'It's just not—'

'Stop there, my dear. I understand. I understand completely. Perhaps I pushed you in wanting you to know you will always have a home here. This is yours.' He waved a steady hand over the boundary. 'You *are* this. But as your dear friend, and now mine, Mrs Elizabeth explained to me,' he quoted carefully, '"if it isn't broken, don't fix it". We'll keep the offer open and always on the committee agenda.'

Takdir alternately apologised for asking her back so soon, to confront his wife in a way he could not do, and thanked her for doing so. 'And for bringing Mrs Elizabeth,' he added quietly. 'She has enlivened me. My fears of old age, of ill health – of which I have just learned there are, thankfully, none – are gone again. I had what Mrs Elizabeth called "a wobble" and I did exactly as she would have done and called my family to me.'

Alina could hear Elizabeth's voice and mentally thanked her for it. 'It's a fallacy that we can't choose our families, isn't it?' she said thoughtfully. 'You have. I have. I've seen it more and more in all the work I've done.'

'We can choose our families for sure; we just can't choose who they will turn out to be,' Takdir said. Then he added, looking puzzled, 'Alina, what are Pop Tarts?'

'Pop Tarts?' she'd repeated, equally baffled. 'They're like biscuit, cake things with a sweet filling. You toast them. I think. Er... why, Uncle Takdir?'

His face cleared as if that made perfect sense. 'I see. Mrs Elizabeth told me she had recently damaged her wrist when she climbed on a chair to fetch the Pop Tarts she had secreted in a tall cupboard. I was concerned for her welfare,' he explained, 'and did not have the opportunity to ask what Pop Tarts were.'

Neither did he get the opportunity to ask Alina why his words were so hilarious, because they were called down and chivvied out into the courtyard for the final send-off – Alina still smirking at the mileage she would get out of teasing Elizabeth on that one. Around them, as many children as could plead their case and then physically fit in the big tractor-trailer crammed themselves in – Khalya grinning up from the footwell of the cab, between Alina and Elizabeth's knees – and the losers resignedly formed a ragged guard of honour towards the gates.

At the ghat on the riverbank there was another final farewell. 'There's no society wedding on earth could match this— Whoops!' was Elizabeth's verdict, as she hugged everyone in sight, and then looked back, waving regally as she was led by Takdir, a decorous hand on forearm, up the rickety gang plank to the launch.

On deck, sharing a makeshift supper of leftover rice and boiled eggs, she said it again. 'My soul has been refreshed. Cheers.' She held up her glass of lukewarm coke.

'Then we will see you again soon, *inshallah*,' Takdir said. 'I look forward to that.'

Alina wondered if Elizabeth was aware that for Takdir, this was tantamount to an expression of the highest affection, that another man, another time, would have kissed her. It seemed that Elizabeth did understand, because she – the only adult female who would have dared such an action – leaned forward and patted his knee. 'Indeed, ye will. If ahm no' deid first,' she said.

'That's Elizabeth's version of *inshallah*.' Alina translated for him, then she winked at Elizabeth. 'Maybe, between us, we can finally get my uncle, here, to Scotland.' *And your son to Bangladesh*, she added silently, finally realising that the catastrophic bang she had always expected when her two worlds collided was merely a pleasant jolt.

'*You* are returning? As planned?' Mizan asked Alina, as they walked along deck. The boat trundled through the silent water, its searchlight sweeping a route ahead of it, occasionally picking up a single-person rowing boat, seemingly indifferent to the swell that threw it off course.

'I'll be here, for sure, the first week in September,' she promised. For how long, and with whom, remained to be seen, but that was a decision for another day.

Mizan nodded, hesitated as if about to say something, then clearly changed his mind. 'There is change in the air, good change,' is what he did say. 'You feel it, too, don't you? Your glow is back, my Alina.'

Surprising herself, and him, Alina drew Mizan into the shadows of the deserted upper deck, where she kissed him properly, a real goodbye. Then she stepped back out into the light, took out her phone and looked at the words she'd sent in reply to Rory's letter. She read them again, a simple, unambiguous, *Please, Rory, I want it all x*

This time, for the first time, there was not a single 'but' on her mind.

ACKNOWLEDGEMENTS

So many people have been part of this novel's journey, and if I haven't said it fervently enough - thank you, all.

The Almost Truth is fiction now but remains rooted in two very real lives; they say I've done them justice...with a twist! I hope so.